I'll Take You There

Joyce Carol Oates has been a recipient of the National Book Award, PEN/Malamud Award for short fiction and was an Oprah Book Club Selection with *We Were The Mulvaneys*. Her recent novels include *Blonde* and *Middle Age: A Romance*. She is a member of the American Academy of Arts and Letters and is the Roger S Berlind Distinguished Professor at Princeton University.

Also by Joyce Carol Oates

NOVELS

With Shuddering Fall (1964) • A Garden of Earthly Delights (1967) • Expensive People (1968) • them (1969) • Wonderland (1971) • Do With Me What You Will (1973) • The Assassins (1975) • Childwold (1976) • Son of the Morning (1978) • Unholy Loves (1979) • Bellefleur (1980) • Angel of Light (1981) • A Bloodsmoor Romance (1982) • Mysteries of Winterthurn (1984) • Solstice (1985) • Marya: A Life (1986) • You Must Remember This (1987) • American Appetites (1989) • Because It Is Bitter, and Because It Is My Heart (1990) • Black Water (1992) • Foxfire: Confessions of a Girl Gang (1993) • What I Lived For (1994) • Zombie (1995) • We Were the Mulvaneys (1996) • Man Crazy (1997) • My Heart Laid Bare (1998) • Broke Heart Blues (1999) • Blonde (2000) • Middle Age: A Romance (2001)

"ROSAMOND SMITH" NOVELS

Lives of the Twins (1987) • Soul / Mate (1989) • Nemesis (1990) • Snake Eyes (1992) • You Can't Catch Me (1995) • Double Delight (1997) • Starr Bright Will Be With You Soon (1999) • The Barrens (2001)

SHORT STORY COLLECTIONS

By the North Gate (1963) • Upon the Sweeping Flood and Other Stories (1966) • The Wheel of Love (1970) • Marriages and Infidelities (1972) • The Goddess and Other Women (1974) • The Poisoned Kiss (1975) • Crossing the Border (1976) • Night-Side (1977) • A Sentimental Education (1980) • Last Days (1984) • Raven's Wing (1986) • The Assignation (1988) • Heat and Other Stories (1991) • Where Is Here? (1992) • Where Are You Going, Where Have You Been?: Selected Early Stories (1993) • Haunted: Tales of the Grotesque (1994) • Will You Always Love Me? (1996) • The Collector of Hearts: New Tales of the Grotesque (1998) • Faithless: Tales of Transgression (2001)

NOVELLAS

The Triumph of the Spider Monkey (1976) • I Lock My Door Upon Myself (1990) • The Rise of Life on Earth (1991) • First Love: A Gothic Tale (1996)

POETRY

Anonymous Sins (1969) • Love and Its Derangements (1970) • Angel Fire (1973) • The Fabulous Beasts (1975) • Women Whose Lives Are Food, Men Whose Lives Are Money (1978) • Invisible Woman: New and Selected Poems, 1970–1982 (1982) • The Time Traveler (1989) • Tenderness (1996)

PLAYS

Miracle Play (1974) • Three Plays (1980) • Twelve Plays (1991) • I Stand Before You Naked (1991) • In Darkest America (Tone Clusters and The Eclipse) (1991) • The Perfectionist and Other Plays (1995) • New Plays (1998)

ESSAYS

The Edge of Impossibility: Tragic Forms in Literature (1972) • New Heaven, New Earth: The Visionary Experience in Literature (1974) • Contraries (1981) • The Profane Art: Essays and Reviews (1983) • On Boxing (1987) • (Woman) Writer: Occasions and Opportunities (1988) • George Bellows: American Artist (1995) • Where I've Been, and Where I'm Going: Essays, Reviews, and Prose (1999)

FOR CHILDREN

Come Meet Muffin! (1998)

YOUNG ADULT

Big Mouth & Ugly Girl (2002)

I'll Take You There

A NOVEL

JOYCE CAROL OATES

FOURTH ESTATE · London

First published in Great Britain in 2003 by
Fourth Estate
A Division of HarperCollins*Publishers*
77–85 Fulham Palace Road
London W6 8JB
www.4thestate.com

Copyright © The Ontario Review 2002

3 5 7 9 10 8 6 4

Quotations from Spinoza's *Ethics* are taken from the translation by
W. H. White and A. H. Stirling.
Quotations from Nietzsche are taken from translation by
Walter Kaufmann.

Excerpts from this novel have appeared in different forms in *Fiction*, 1997;
Conjunctions, 1997; and *TriQuarterly*, 1998.

A catalogue record of this book is available from the British Library.

ISBN 0-00-714644-2

Book design by Claire Vaccaro
Printed in Great Britain by
Clays Ltd, St Ives plc

To Gloria Vanderbilt

Contents

A *picture* held us captive. And we could not get outside it, for it lay in our language and language seemed to repeat it to us inexorably.

LUDWIG WITTGENSTEIN, *Philosophical Investigations*

I.

THE PENITENT

1

Every substance is necessarily infinite.

Spinoza, *Ethics*

In those days in the early Sixties we were not women yet but girls. This was, without irony, perceived as our advantage.

I am thinking of the house on a prominent hill of a hilly and wind-ravaged university campus in upstate New York in which I lived for five wretched months when I was nineteen years old, unraveling among strangers like one of my cheap orlon sweaters. I am thinking of how in this house there were forbidden areas and forbidden acts pertaining to these areas. Some had to do with the *sacred rituals* of Kappa Gamma Pi (these very words a sacred utterance, once you were initiated into their meaning) and some had to do with the sorority's British-born house-mother, Mrs. Agnes Thayer.

They would claim that I destroyed Mrs. Thayer. *Pushed her over the edge* which makes me think of an actual cliff, a precipice, and Mrs. Thayer falling by some ghostly action of my flailing arms. Yet others would claim that Mrs. Thayer destroyed me.

The Kappa Gamma Pi house! The address was 91 University Place, Syracuse, New York. It was a massive cube of three floors in that long-ago architectural style known as neo-Classic; made of heavy dusky-pink-pewter limestone like ancient treasure hauled from the depths of the sea. Oh, if you could see it! If you could see it with my eyes. The looming ivy-covered facade and in the perpetual Syracuse wind the individual ivy leaves shivering and rippling like thoughts. Insatiable questions. *Why? why? why?* The lofty portico and four tall graceful white columns of the kind called Doric, smooth and featureless as telephone poles. The house was located at the far, northern end of University Place, a quarter-mile from Erie Hall, the granite administration building that was the oldest building on the university campus. University Place itself was a wide boulevard with parkland as a median, slowly dying yet still elegant elms. Walking from the Kappa house to the university campus on the worst winter mornings was like climbing the side of a mountain, the incline was so steep in places, sidewalks icy and treacherous so you were better off trudging across the brittle grass of lawns instead. Returning, mostly downhill, was less of a physical effort but could be treacherous, too. A half-block from the northern end of University Place the earth shifted as if in a cruel whim and there was a final steep hill to be climbed, an upward-jutting spit of land, at the top of which was the stately Kappa house with, above its portico, these mysterious symbols—

Κ Γ Π

The Kappa Gamma Pi house, unlike most of the local fraternity and sorority houses, had a history. It was, in fact, "historic": it hadn't been constructed for the mere utilitarian purpose of being a Greek residence, but had once been a millionaire's home, a mansion, built in 1841 (as a plaque proudly noted) by a prominent Syracuse clockworks manufacturer and deeded to the newborn local chapter of the national sorority Kappa Gamma Pi at the death of an elderly-widow alumna in 1938. *Her name sacred in our memories* as Kappa alums would solemnly instruct us but her name has vanished from my memory, it's only the house I recall.

Before I was initiated into Kappa Gamma Pi in the second semester of my freshman year at the university, I would often walk far out of my way to pass the house from below; I was a pledge by this time, yet not a "sister"; I drifted lovesick and yearning gazing up at the somber, ivy-covered facade, at the tall white columns in my imagination so many more than four columns, five, six, ten columns! The floating letters ΚΓΠ filled me with wonder, awe. For I did not yet know what they meant. *Will I be a Kappa?* I thought. *I—I!—will be a Kappa.* It didn't seem possible, yet it had to be possible, for how otherwise would I continue? I was possessed by the wayward passion of one to whom passion is unknown; denied, and thwarted; if falling in love had been a game, the object of the game would have been, to me, to resist; as in chess, you might sacrifice pawns in the service of your queen; your queen was your truest self, your virgin-self, inviolable; never would you give away your queen! And so I was one whose immune system had become defenseless before the assault of a virulent micro-organism invader. My eyes, misted with emotion, purposefully failed to take in the patina of grime on the limestone walls and on the columns, or the just perceptibly rotting, mossy slates of the roof, which, iridescent when wet, in rare, blinding sunshine, were so beautiful. Nor did I see the rust-tinctured network like veins or fossil trails imprinted in the limestone by English ivy that was dying in places, had been dying for years, and was withering away. There were more than twenty Greek houses on or near University Place, and Kappa Gamma Pi was neither the largest nor the most attractive. You could argue that it was the most dour, possibly even the ugliest of the houses, but, to me, such qualities suggested aristocratic hauteur, authority. To live in such a mansion and to be an initiate, a sister of Kappa Gamma Pi, would be, I knew, to be transformed.

I wondered if, at initiation, I would be given a secret Kappa name.

I didn't believe in fairy tales or in those ridiculous romances beginning *Once upon a time.* A fairy tale of a kind had prevailed at my birth and during my infancy but it had been a cruel, crude fairy tale in which the newborn baby isn't blessed but cursed. Yet I believed in Kappa Gamma Pi without question. I believed that such transformations were not only possible, but common. I believed that such transformations were not only possible, but inevitable. Not I, not I exactly, but another girl with my name and face, a girl *initiate*—an *active*—would one day soon live in that house; with tremulous pride she would wear the Kappa pin, gleaming ebony with gold letters and a tiny gold chain above her left breast, where all the privileged sorority girls wore their sacred pins, in the proverbial region of the heart.

The Way In. Climbing to the house on wedges of stone that looked aged, ancient. Stone that had begun to crack, crumble; stone worn smooth by many feet, over many years. If the steps were icy or there was a wind (in all but the stale, stagnant air of summer, there was always a wind) you might take hold of the old, ornate, not entirely steady wrought iron railing. This hill, above the city-owned sidewalk, was so steep that there couldn't have been a lawn in the conventional sense, no grass to be mowed, only a craggy outcropping of granite, in the interstices of which grew dwarf shrubs and hardy ferns of the dark, bitter-green variety and *Rosa rugosa* in bright splotches of color; such a formidable fronting on the street was characteristic of most of the properties at the northern end of University Place, and may have assured the outsider's sense of their dignity, inaccessibility, and high worth. From the top of the steps (I'd counted them many times: eighteen) you might pause breathless to look back, to contemplate the view behind you, which was startling as a scene in an old woodcut: there was gothic dark-granite Erie Hall floating atop its hill, a higher hill than the Kappa hill, its bell gleaming (in memory, at least) in a perpetual fading yet golden-sepia, hauntingly beautiful light.

So often, the Syracuse sky was overcast and glowering, as if with withheld secrets, passions. Clouds were never two-dimensional like painted scenery but massed, massive, bulging, tumescent, pocked and pitted and creviced and boiling, rarely white, rarely of a single hue, but infinitely varied shades of gray, dark-gray, powder-gray, bruise-gray, iron-gray, purple-gray, shot with a mysteriously advancing, and abruptly fading, sunlight. Rain was falling, or had recently fallen leaving everything slick, wet, shining, washed-clean; sullen, punished-looking; or gleaming with optimism, hope. Unless it was snow imminent—"Oh God, smell it? Like iron filings. That's *snow*."

The large, stately front door of the Kappa house was made of oak with an iron knocker; there was a doorbell that, when rung, emitted delicate, melodic chimes deep in the interior of the house. This "feminine" doorbell contrasted with the heavy masculine architecture and may have suggested something of the atmosphere within that was sly, subversive. The downstairs public rooms (as they were grandly called) were impressively formal, dark, high-ceilinged and gloomy even with their filigree gold-gilt French wallpaper; the heavy old furniture was "Victorian antiques." *A legacy* the local chapter of the Kappa alums assured us solemnly *of priceless things, irreplaceable. Take care!* We were made to feel like overgrown blundering children in a sacred space.

Yet it was sacred, I suppose. In its way. In its time. Who could resist the tasteful glitter of crystal chandeliers, dust-encrusted by day perhaps but, by night, iridescent and sparkling; the lavish carpets—"heirloom Oriental antiques"—vividly colored, jewel-like in certain areas if, in other, more trodden areas, worn thin as much-used woollen blankets. In several downstairs rooms there were imposing marble fireplaces like altars (rarely used, as it turned out, since they smoked badly); everywhere were filigree-framed mirrors with singed-looking glass that enhanced the plainest face if you tiptoed to stare into them, like Alice approaching the Looking-Glass World; these mirrors seemed to double, even treble, the proportions of the somber rooms as in a dream of fanatic clarity that leaves the dreamer exhausted and strangely demoralized, as if emptied of personality. Confused by these mirrors in my first visits to the house (during second-semester sorority rush week) I staggered away from the Kappas with a misleading sense of the house's grandeur, as if I'd been in a cathedral.

In a corner of the stately living room, near an oil portrait of the house's first owner, was a Steinway grand piano of dark, dully gleaming mahogany, with stained ivory keys, several of which stuck; it was a beautiful piano, but somehow melancholy, exuding a dark, rich odor, that quickened my heart to know the piano's secrets, to be able to *play*. Unfortunately the Kappa housemother had declared the piano off-limits even to those two or three skilled pianists among the Kappas, except for a single hour following dinner and Sunday afternoon between the arbitrary hours of 4:30 P.M. and 6:00 P.M. when the more aggressive Kappas banged out old favorites like "Chopsticks" and "Begin the Beguine."

Several times when I found myself alone in the living room, I dared to sit at the Steinway grand and fitted my shy fingers to the keys; gently I depressed the keys, calling up a faint, quavering, undersea sound deep inside the piano. (The piano was always kept closed, lid shut like a coffin.) I knew very little of pianos; I'd tried to play in imitation of a friend who took lessons, when I was twelve; I'd grown up with my grandparents who were farm people, German immigrants, with no time for music, still less classical music. Yet the fact of the piano in the Kappa living room was a consolation. As if in some way it were a sign of home. Even if I couldn't play it, and would not have been allowed to play it in any case. *Still the piano exists. As the world-in-itself*—I'd begun, in my sophomore year, to study Immanuel Kant—*exists, unattached to us.* The physical solidity seemed to argue for a reality beyond my own; more valuable than the fleeting, always unsatisfying moment through which I, a sophomore, a lonely girl amid a clamor of "sisters," was passing. For what was my mood except reluctance to return upstairs to the crowded smoky third-floor room to which I'd been assigned because my roommate, who chain-smoked Chesterfields and lived in a giddy clutter of clothes, nail polish (and nail polish remover that smelled virulent as a chemical defoliant), tubes of greasy lipstick, makeup in jars, and mimeographed course outlines from her education courses, would be there, and other Kappas would be lounging in the doorway or sprawled across my bed, exhaling smoke with the luxurious abandon of girls away from adult scrutiny, tapping ashes in the vague direction of a communal ashtray with a plastic hula girl at its center. Reluctant to return upstairs because to my dismay I was finding myself as isolated as I'd been before I had become a sister—an "active"—of Kappa Gamma Pi with no recourse except to conclude *You! It's your own fault. You, always dissatisfied.*

This was my curse. I would bear it through my life. As if a wicked troll had baptized me, in infancy, as my mother wasted away to Death, unknowing; a flick of the troll's fingers, poisonous water splashed onto my forehead. *I baptize thee in the name of ceaseless yearning, ceaseless seeking and ceaseless dissatisfaction. Amen!*

Once when I'd sat at the piano too long, lost in a reverie, depressing keys with both hands in near-inaudible chords that reverberated like ghost music heard at a distance, the harsh overhead lights of the living room were suddenly switched on (it was a late afternoon in November, dark as midnight outside) and there stood our housemother Mrs. Thayer staring at me from beneath the dramatic arch of the doorway. She had a regal figure and a powdered face that glowed pinkly moist and meaty as a canned ham; her expression was one of hauteur tinged with disbelief. "*You!* Is it—Mary Alice? What are *you* doing here? Have I not explained—and explained—that our piano is to be kept shut? Otherwise it will be clogged with dust, it will go out of tune, an expensive and irreplaceable musical instrument, an antique, a Sternway, an irreplaceable Sternway, for goodness's sake, you gurls! Have you no *memory?* Have you no *mind?* Have to be told, told, told! Again, again, again!" As if a spring had been tripped in her brain, Mrs. Thayer began to scold; this was her preferred way of scolding, in a bright, crisp, corrosive British accent. Like gas jets her close-set blue eyes flashed; she drew her tightly girdled, fattish little figure to its full height of perhaps five feet three inches, and regarded me for a long devastating moment. This was the look, the Brit glare, for which our housemother was famous. Girls belonging to rival sororities knew of Kappa's Mrs. Thayer; boys dating Kappas came away with accounts of her, shaking their heads in reluctant admiration. I cringed before the woman's contempt like a guilty child, my face burning, stammering, "Mrs. Thayer, I'm s-sorry. I actually wasn't—" Mrs. Thayer interrupted impatiently, loftily, for this too was a pet annoyance of hers, the way in which *American gurls* will apologize yet in the same breath try to deny that for which they are apologizing— "No excuses, please! I have heard, heard, heard these excuses all, already!" Airily Mrs. Thayer laughed to show she wasn't angry, of course; such trifles couldn't make *her* angry; she who'd survived what she spoke of proudly as the London Blitz. Except of course she was bemused, amused—"Oh, you American gurls." It was a dramatic gesture of Mrs. Thayer's to switch off the light to leave me in a gloomy darkness alleviated only by the hall light, to turn adroitly on her heel and stride away.

· · ·

My first glimpse of Agnes Thayer was at an open house during sorority rush the previous February. Not a member of Kappa Gamma Pi herself, Mrs. Thayer wasn't involved in the ritual of "rushing"; but she was an impressive presence among the Kappas, overseeing the pouring of tea with a look of benign, smiling confidence. I'd never met anyone who spoke like Mrs. Thayer, with so distinctly British an accent, thrilling to my ears. "Mrs. Thayer, our housemother, is British, you know. She's from London." So it was several times explained to me. When I advanced to the head of the line, taking a cup of tea in a slightly shaky hand, taking a small gold-rimmed plate with cookies on it, I smiled nervously at this woman of youthful middle age who smiled serenely toward me. I murmured, "Thank you," as others were doing, and Mrs. Thayer murmured in reply, her blue gaze passing through me as it's said those infinitesimal sub-atomic particles called neutrinos pass through solid matter continuously, "My dear, you are welcome."

My dear! No one had ever spoken to me, even in jest, in such a way.

Once I became a Kappa initiate, and moved into the Kappa residence, I became one of Mrs. Thayer's girl-subjects. Mrs. Thayer was our "house-mother": our adult-in-authority. Mrs. Thayer's dominion was supreme.

Like royalty, or what I might have guessed of royalty, Mrs. Thayer could not be approached casually. A ritual of a kind had to be observed, before one could speak with Mrs. Thayer in private. (But what would one speak about with Mrs. Thayer, in private? I could not imagine.) Her quarters, a small suite of rooms on the ground floor of the Kappa house, were otherwise taboo.

The suite opened out onto an inner parlor, a library, and ran parallel to the large dining room, to the rear of the house; this parlor, though a public room, was tinctured to some degree by Mrs. Thayer's proximity. Sometimes Mrs. Thayer's door was open, sometimes ajar; most of the time, snugly closed. If the door was open and you stepped into the library, you were immediately aware of Mrs. Thayer's inner quarters; you were immediately alert to the possibility of her presence. I recall standing in the parlor staring at the open door with a vague fixed smile and hearing, though not listening to, murmurous voices within, and even laughter; Mrs. Thayer was talking with one of the senior girls, a favorite. *What are they talking about? Laughing about?* When at last the girl appeared, and Mrs. Thayer behind her, they glanced toward me indifferently; Mrs. Thayer may have called over, in her brisk, brusque way that meant no reply was expected, "Ah, Mary Alice! How are *you*."

I had not the audacity to tell Mrs. Thayer that my name was not "Mary Alice"; nor did it sound anything like "Mary Alice"; I knew Mrs. Thayer would be offended.

The parlor was much smaller than the rather grand living room, papered in ebony and gilt in ingenious two-inch-square replicas of the Kappa pin, which gave to the interior a dizzying perspective such as one might experience swirling down a drain. Its fourth wall was floor-to-ceiling bookshelves crammed with aged, respectable books including sets of leather-bound classics, the *Complete Works of William Shakespeare,* the *Complete Works of Sir Walter Scott,* the *Complete Works of Edward Gibbon* among others, which had the embalmed look of books unopened for decades. On the fiercely patterned walls were dozens of framed photographs of Kappa officers and members dating from 1933 when the local chapter of the sorority was first established on the university campus, consisting of only eleven determined-looking girls. (How does a sorority "begin"? I could not guess. Parmenides' famous question *Why is there something, and not rather nothing?* did not seem to me, in this context, more profound.) Everywhere in the room were brass-and-mahogany trophies, plaques, medals, congratulatory certificates in gilt lettering dating back to the mid-Thirties; mementos of long-ago formal dances, teas, one or two softball teams, picnics, and ceremonial occasions at which Kappas received awards from other, elder Kappas at national assemblies. So fleetingly did the proposition cross my mind, it wasn't a true revelation—*These are all what's called white: to be among them, I too must be white.*

Prominent in this room was a large glass-topped piece of furniture—the proctor's desk. On this, affixed by an actual chain, was the official "sign in/sign out" ledger of the residence. Every evening at 8:00 P.M. the Kappa house, like all university residences, was locked; the rear door was not only locked but bolted; the designated proctor for the evening would sit at this desk; her task would be to answer incoming telephone calls, buzzing girls in their rooms (for individual telephones were forbidden), and above all making certain that girls did not slip out the front door without signing the ledger. "Under my roof curfew will be strictly enforced," Mrs. Thayer gravely warned. This meant 11:00 P.M. weeknights, 12:00 A.M. Fridays, 1:00 A.M. Saturdays, and 10:00 P.M. Sundays, university regulations that applied solely to undergraduate women. (No curfews at all were imposed upon men, who might be absent from their residence for days without being reported to authorities.) Since the parlor was adjacent to Mrs. Thayer's quarters, loud talk, laughter, and "carrying on" of any kind were forbidden. On selected tables were arranged Kappa yearbooks and other publications adorned with the Kappa insignia, and on a coffee table newspapers and magazines were arranged in a fan-like spread, mainly back issues of Mrs. Thayer's *Harper's & Queen, Punch, Manchester Guardian,* and other British publications she received in the mail. The very paper, thin as tissue, exuded an air of the elite. It had to be conceded by anyone acquainted with Mrs. Agnes Thayer that anything British in origin was of a higher quality than its American equivalent. No doubt the Kappa alums who had hired her, impressed with her accent and bearing, had this in mind. Yet virtually no one apart from me so much as glanced into, let alone read, these publications, apart from glossy *Harper's & Queen,* which was occasionally leafed through and tossed back down. None of these publications was to be removed from the parlor, nor were they to be left in a "disordered" state. Even the daily Syracuse newspaper, which a few girls glanced into, had to be replaced on the table pristine in appearance, each page in alignment with the others, and in the exact arrangement which Mrs. Thayer favored.

Eagerly I read the British publications, exotic as no other printed matter of my acquaintance. I was from a remote wedge of rural upstate, western New York. I scrutinized the *Guardian,* especially its arts and culture sections, I tried to decipher the obscure codified cartoons in *Punch.* It was amazing to me that the English language into which I'd been born was yet a foreign language, and its truest culture a foreign culture. In *Harper's & Queen* I contemplated photographs of "home county estates"—enormous manor houses such as Jane Austen and Charlotte Brontë had written of, acres of radiantly green grass, enormous beds of daffodils, iris, and tulips rippling in the wind; elegantly if absurdly costumed men and women on horseback, "riding to hounds." (Hunting foxes? Such small, beautiful creatures? These were not photographed.) I contemplated stiffly posed photographs of the Queen and the Royal Family adorned in heraldic regalia and looking like ordinary, rather plain people at a costume party. Something twisted in my heart: I felt suddenly that I despised such pomp and pretension, I was an American to my fingertips and did not believe in inherited privilege. Yet I was careful to replace the British publications exactly as Mrs. Thayer had positioned them.

The parlor, the proctor's desk, the nearness of Mrs. Thayer's private quarters—this was a space soon fraught with anxiety for me. To envision it now, years later, is to feel my temples ache with the dizzying pressure of the Kappa insignia-wallpaper. As a sophomore I was required to do proctor duty every ten or twelve days, and I was so intimidated by my elder "sisters" that when they boldly left the house, laughing and waving at me, or blowing kisses, or ignoring me altogether as they ignored the official ledger book, I didn't dare call after them, let alone run outside after them; nor did I report them to our housemother as I was required to do. *Under my roof curfew will be strictly enforced* Mrs. Thayer warned repeatedly, yet out of cowardice and a yearning to be liked, I could not bring myself to enforce it. The first night of proctor duty, which set precedent for months to follow, a half-dozen girls blithely ignored the ledger book, and, yet more defiantly, trailed in after 11:00 P.M. curfew, delivered giggling and swaying-drunk to the door by their dates; to disguise the situation, I turned out the parlor lights so that Mrs. Thayer would have no suspicion, and assume that everyone was safely inside for the night; in fact I crouched on the foyer steps by the front door trying desperately to read, in weak light, fifty pages of Spinoza's *Ethics* for my European philosophy class the next morning. Again and again reading without comprehension *By cause of itself, I understand that, whose nature cannot be conceived unless existing*. I had no idea what to do: suppose some of my Kappa sisters stayed out all night? Suppose something "happened" to them? I understood that I would be partly to blame; I would have accepted this blame; in a way I was more guilty than the absent girls for I'd failed to report them to Mrs. Thayer, endangering her authority as well. But the girls returned. At 1:15 A.M., at 1:40 A.M., at 2:05 A.M., and the last at 2:20 A.M., none of them ringing the doorbell (which would have wakened Mrs. Thayer immediately) but stealthily rapping on the leaded-glass panel beside the door, for they seemed to know that I would be waiting for them, uncomplaining and compliant as a handmaid. The last girl to return was a glamorous, popular senior named Mercy (for Mercedes), a sorority officer whom I'd admired for her brash good looks, infectious laughter and "personality." Mercy was delivered on shaky legs to the door by a football player Deke to whom she was "pinned"; this hefty blond boy squinted at me like a dazed, good-natured ox as I opened the door quietly—"Thass a goo' girl." Mercy's blond hair was disheveled and her elaborate makeup smeared; she looked as if she'd hurriedly thrown on her clothes in the dark, or had been thrown hurriedly into her clothes by another; she reeked of per-fume, beer, and vomit. As she shakily ascended the stairs she tripped and giggled, "Damn!" and I caught her, for I'd come up close behind her, and dared to touch her hot, humid body; she drew away from my cold fin-gers with a look of dazed dignity and said in a slurred, contemptuous voice, "*You?*—who in hell're *you?* Takey'r goddam handsoff *me!*"

And did it begin then, the unraveling.

Or had it begun months and even years before and at this late, exhausted hour the clarity of it: the absurdity: waking to discover yourself in this place among strangers indifferent and impervious to you who wished only to adore them, in desperation clutching a textbook of ethics set forth in seventeenth-century theorems and propositions like geometry. And trying not to cry. For you are not a child. Nineteen years old, an adult. Yet so hurt! heartbroken! fated to recall the sting of that rude drunken rebuff for a lifetime.

❧

SISTERS! Always I'd yearned for sisters of my own.

From first grade contemplating with undisguised envy and won-derment the large farm families of most of my classmates. For even when sisters quarreled—and sisters were always quarreling!—the fact remained they were sisters. The fact remained: they lived together, ate meals together, shared rooms, often beds. They wore one another's clothing. Mittens, scarves, and boots freely mingled. They shared facial features, ways of moving their eyes and heads, ways of gesturing. They shared a last name. And I had no sister, and would never have a sister. Except in my memory, which others derided, I had no mother. I was pitied as a freak, without a mother. My brothers were much older than I and took no interest in me except sometimes to tease and taunt, as big dogs might play with small dogs, injuring them occasionally but without rancor or intention; my father who was "in construction" was often absent from home for weeks, even months—it wasn't clear where he went, or wasn't clear to me. My brothers and I lived with my father's parents on their twelve-acre dairy farm near Strykersville, in Niagara County, New York, thirty miles northeast of Buffalo and three miles south of Lake Ontario.

The Snow Belt as it's called.

A childhood of snow. Blank amnesiac patches of snow. Beside the window of my small room beneath the eaves, a cave-like opening in snow formed by the drooping limbs of a juniper tree; after the fiercest snowstorms, there was yet this sheltered space outside the window, I could look out and see, beyond, a blinding expanse of white like a frozen sea transforming the familiar terrain of our farm.

My mother died when I was eighteen months old. I would be told *Your mother has gone away*. In time, I would be told that my mother had wanted a daughter so badly she'd "kept trying" after three sons—and two miscarriages—and at last had had a baby at the age of forty-one, and never recovered. This would be told to me with an air of disapproval, reproach. For in those years, forty-one was a repugnant and even obscene age for a mother. It seemed fitting then that my mother had not been able to give birth "normally" but had had a caesarian that failed to heal; her milk-laden breasts developed cysts like tiny pebbles; the gossamer-thin web of nerves that constituted her mysterious and unknowable self grew tight, tighter, tighter until one day it broke and could never be mended; the way a spider's delicate web, once broken, can never be mended. When I was eight, having annoyed my grandmother in some childish way, she told me in a bitter yet gloating voice that my mother had died of something *eating her up: cancer.* My grandmother gestured clumsily, shamefacedly, at her own big, sunken bosom, saying, "They had to cut off her . . ." She fell silent. I was speechless with horror. Her breasts? My mother I loved so much, and missed so badly, her breasts had been . . . cut off?

I ran from the house and hid in a field. It was not winter then: I hid in a cornfield. I ignored them calling for me. I hated them all, I would never forgive them.

After that day my grandmother seemed to have forgotten what she'd told me. Or behaved as if she'd forgotten. Yet it was tacitly assumed that I knew this shameful secret about my mother, and must take responsibility for knowing. Sometimes I'd overhear my grandmother speaking to relatives or neighbors, careless of whether I might be within earshot, in her dour, dogged voice, "He blames her, you know—the little one. For Ida dying." Even as a small child I understood the fatal juxtaposition of that *he* (my father) and that *her* (the "little one" who was myself).

Yes but I remember her. I am the only one who remembers.

"Ida"—the name was magical to me. In whispers, in the dark. Beneath bedcovers. Forehead pressed to a windowpane coated with frost. "Ida." What a strange, beautiful name: I could not say it often enough: it was easy to confuse "Ida" with "I"—the sharp simple sound I learned to make with my mouth and tongue when I meant myself.

In the interests of truth, with the rapacity of an invading army, my brothers belittled my childish claim of remembering my mother. "*You!* You were too little, only a baby when she died. *We* knew her." They hated me for having been born; having been born, I caused our mother's death; yet they could see I was just a little girl; I wasn't a worthy enemy. They argued it was only in snapshots of my mother that I "knew" her, not in my own true memory; confusing the sallow-faced mature woman with the younger, much prettier woman of the snapshots in the family album, dark hair bobbed in the sexy-boyish style of the Twenties, hands on her hips, knuckles inward. A brash smile flying to the camera like a bird flying toward a window. I did not wish to consider that this striking young woman was not, precisely speaking, my mother. But these early snapshots were the ones I adored. Others, taken in the Thirties, my mother with my brother Dietrich who was eleven years my senior, my mother with my brother Fritz who was ten years my senior, my mother with my brother Hendrick who was seven years my senior—these engaged me far less, though they were nearer in time to my own birth. For I couldn't bear to see my mother with babies not myself. Young children in her lap, clambering about her legs. She was beginning to look tired, drawn, her smile had become forced, in the later snapshots. Her chic bobbed hair was gone, now flyaway hair, or skinned back severely from her face and knotted at the nape of her neck. Her body had thickened, grown shapeless. After my birth, my mother's health was so poor that no snapshots of her with me were ever taken. No snapshots of the little one at all. Yet I claimed to remember my mother and held firm in my obstinacy against all detractors. My German grandparents who were old, old, old all my life like trolls peering at me in pity and reproach. It was clear that they hadn't liked my mother yet they liked me less for killing her and for making their only son deeply unhappy. Muttering together in that language I could not comprehend, and had no wish to comprehend, would never study in college, though sometimes they spoke in heavily accented English for me to overhear—"That one! Where does she get her ideas!" Inwardly I answered, "Not from *you*. None of *you*."

Rarely did my father speak of such personal matters to anyone. He was hurt, sullen, angry, and baffled. He was a big man, well over six feet, weighing perhaps two hundred twenty pounds. His footsteps made the house vibrate. A deep inhalation of his breath could suck most of the oxygen out of a room's air. My mother's death was a livid wound in his flesh. He would not have wished it healed, though it maddened him. He would seem to forget my name; never would he call me by name; "you" would have to do; "you" was as much as I could hope for; "you" was much more desirous than "I" for "I" was uttered only by me, and "you" might be uttered, if only in a slurred, negligent voice, by my father. "You!—didn't see you in here." Or, "You?—not in bed?" My eagerness to be with my father, even if he collided with me in a darkened hallway, or stepped on my feet entering a room, was not matched by a corresponding eagerness on his part to be with me. It was not just (I believed) that I had killed my mother but, without my mother, a woman, to mediate between him and me, there was no way for him to comprehend me. A girl? A little girl? And those eyes! He was wary of me as one might be wary of a puppy that might leap against legs and dribble saliva onto hands and whine piteously when abandoned. If my father discovered himself alone in my presence his startled eyes would shift a few inches above my head as if seeking out—who? (Our vanished Ida?) My father smoked Camels, lighting them with kitchen matches scraped noisily against the iron stove; I can see still, always in my mind's eye I will see the sudden leaping bluish flame that turned at once transparent orange, the mysterious and indefinable color of fire. At such times my father was obliged to squint against the smoke he himself exhaled; it was a curious ceremony, hurtful, yet profound, the way my father squinted, coughed, sometimes coughed at some length, as a result of this smoke. (My youngest brother would claim he'd never smoked, never wanted to light a single cigarette, having heard my father "cough his lungs out" every morning he'd been at home, but I had only a vague memory of such protracted coughing; my relationship to my father's cigarettes, like my relationship to my father, was hopeful, never critical.) If I dared to squint or cough myself or wave weakly against the drifting smoke, my father would say at once, flatly, "You don't like smoke, better go somewhere else." It was not a command, still less a threat: it was a statement of fact.

Don't like smoke, go somewhere else.

This remark I would pretend not to hear. Children are so resourcefully deaf, blind. We smile in the face of hostility, that hostility will turn into love. I was fascinated by my father's left hand that had been injured in what he called a work accident; the knuckles were grotesquely bunched as if they'd been squeezed together in a vise, and most of the nails were ridged and discolored; the smallest finger had been amputated to the first joint, and it was this hand he used to smoke with, bringing it repeatedly to his mouth.

I imagined this hand touching me. Caressing my small head.

My mother I knew didn't I? But not this man. Father.

He never kissed me. Never touched me (even with the disfigured hand) if he could avoid it. My brothers he might punch—lightly, yet hard enough to make them wince—on their biceps, in greeting or in farewell. ("O.K., kid. See ya.") For always our father was *going away.* His car was backing out of the driveway, more swiftly and purposefully than it had turned in. Cinders flew behind its spinning wheels, in rainy weather the windshield wipers were already on. It came to seem only logical—I mean to a child's primitive, wishful way of thinking—that my father would have to return to the farm in Strykersville if he wanted

to leave it. The zest in leaving it depended upon the reluctance in returning, didn't it? You could not have the one without the other, could
you? It was something of a joke, the degree to which my father hated
farm life. The dairy cows. Since the age of six he'd been made to milk
their long rubbery udders. Not a task for a boy. Well, yes: it was a task
for a farm boy. But my father didn't want to be a farm boy. Those slip-
pery teats, tits. And the smell of the cow manure, so much stronger
when fresh and liquidy, than it was after it had settled, solidified. My
father had infuriated his father by hurting the cows, yanking the udders,
causing these large placid beasts to bawl and kick; some of this would be
preserved in family legend, for even families deprived of warm, happy
times, mythic significance, cherish some legends, however threadbare.
"Hurting the cows" as my father had done would be a way of indicating,
decades later, that my father was "independent in his mind." For at the
young age of seventeen he left the farm to work at Lackawanna Steel, a
notorious mill that paid high wages for that time and place but was
known to be dangerous, especially for unskilled workers. He'd driven a
truck. He'd joined unions. He'd made money gambling and he'd spent
money and he'd married a city girl who knew not a word of German.
He had something of a reputation among men of his generation in the
Strykersville area. He was a "fighter"—"a tough son of a bitch"—he
"took no shit from anybody." By the time I was in high school my father
was older, ravaged; he had "problems" of some ambiguous kind, no
doubt associated with drinking and its consequences—tavern fights, ve-
hicular accidents, arrests, brief stays in county jails. Hospitalizations in
cities too far for any of us to visit. In a drawer I collected each of the
postcards my father sent us: from California, a cartoon of loggers saw-
ing down redwoods subtly shaped like women; a card from Anchorage,
Alaska, depicting cartoon salmon leaping into a fishing boat; cards from
British Columbia, Manitoba, Saskatoon, Saskatchewan. (From Saska-

toon my father sent six one-hundred-dollar bills in Canadian currency which my brother Dietrich took to a bank in Buffalo where, it turned out, they were worth 10 percent more than American dollars.) Yet there were times when my father called home after 11:00 P.M., collect. My grandmother whose heart was a dry root vegetable hardy as a turnip burst into tears when she spoke with my father at such times: he was her only son. My grandfather would snarl over the phone in elderly impotent fury *Ja? What? What tricks of yours?* If my brothers were home they would speak with my father one by one; Dietrich spoke for the longest time, in the most somber voice; Fritz was slow and inarticulate; Hendrick, the youngest, murmured in a dazed boyish way *Geez Dad, you are? Gal-ves-ton? On the Gulf of Mexico? No kidding!* Anxiously I would wait beside Hendrick for my turn to speak with my father but often it happened that my father "ran out of coins"—"was cut off by the operator"—before I could take the receiver.

I was saving up surprises for my father, though. Straight A's in school, shiny red stars after my name (which included his name) on the class bulletin board, even my picture now and then in the Strykersville weekly newspaper. He couldn't help but be impressed and proud of his daughter. Could he?

I'd become shrewd speaking of him. Never asked questions about him of my grandmother. A clumsy question could set the old woman clutching at her hair that was like wire filings, half-sobbing, grimacing and muttering in German—prayers or curses, who knew? Among the oldest snapshots in my grandmother's keeping was my father as a young man, dark, brawny, good-looking with thick tufted hair and a roguish smile, by degrees this young man aged into a sullen, slack-faced stranger with a perpetual two- or three-day growth of beard. The man who was *my father*. The red-veined eyes, the nose swollen as if stung by a bee. Teeth discolored like stained ivory. He gave off an odor associated in my mind with threat, dread, yet a kind of swaggering glamor—to-bacco, whisky, stale sweat, agitation. My father spoke little to any of us but worked words in his mouth as if chewing a wad of tobacco he badly wanted to spit out, yet did not. Sometimes I caught him staring at me by lamplight, drinking a pungent, colorless liquid from a glass, smoking one of his Camels. The veil of smoke shielding his gaze. *That's her, is it? The one to blame.* There must have come a time in my father's life when he forgot what I was to be blamed for, but so ingrained was the habit of blaming *the little one,* so much was it part of my father's character as racial bigotry or left-handedness might be in others, he could not have wished to change. Just as Dietrich the eldest son was always his favorite son, no matter what.

I tried to imagine my father and my mother as lovers. How did a man and a woman *love?* What had brought them together, why had they married? Their lives were vanished from me almost with no trace like fossil remnants worn smooth and bleached in the sun. It made me feel faint to realize how I could have entered the world only through a conjunction of these strangers' bodies; no other pathway was possible; the great question that underlies all philosophical inquiry applied to the mystery of my conception and birth. *Why is there something, and not rather nothing?*

"How easy, never to have been born."

I spoke aloud in the wonder of it. In a mirror I saw, where my diminutive face might have been, a hazy glow like phosphorescence.

During my last two years of high school my father was away most of the time in the Midwest and I had a recurring nightmare of a cinder block prison wall and a stench of stopped-up drains, but probably this was my overwrought imagination, I didn't dare inquire of my grandparents or my brothers what it might mean. And there was a time my father was in a "drying out" hospital in Erie, Pennsylvania. Unexpectedly, he turned up for my high school graduation, my valedictory speech which was tremulous at the outset but gathered strength as I continued, my eyes misting over so that I was spared seeing individual faces in the audience, including my father's. He was there in a white shirt and pressed jacket to witness my receiving several awards and being named as the sole graduate of Strykersville High School that year to receive a New York State regents scholarship for college. My father, returned to me at last!—jaws stubbled and eyes gleaming bloodshot, his broad smile showing missing teeth like a jack-o'-lantern. His formerly thick, tangled dark hair had receded unevenly, exposing a dented-looking dome of a head; his jowls sagged, a collar of flesh. Yet his eyes shone fierce with pride. He'd been drinking (that was hardly a secret) but he wasn't drunk. As others observed us, staring in wonderment, my classmates in their caps and gowns and their decent, sober parents, my father strode up to hug me after the graduation ceremony, this man who hadn't touched me in years, and then only inadvertently, saying boastfully, "Helluva speech you gave, eh? I always knew you had it in you. Like *her,* you are. Smart as a whip. But you can do something with it. Don't let no fuckers out there sell you short."

A reporter for the Strykersville paper took several flash photos of us, without asking. In the one that would appear in the paper my father was scowling, his right hand lifted toward the camera as if to block the view; I stood just beyond his arm, smiling uncertainly, my face overexposed in the camera's flash so that I looked like an ink drawing by Matisse.

Three days later, my father was gone.

Gone again from Strykersville, and the old farm. And would not return, this time.

He'd told my grandmother he was headed west—"Some place you can breathe." His work was construction of a kind involving heavy earth-moving equipment, and dynamite. He never wrote, or in any case I never heard he'd written. (After her death years later, I would discover among my grandmother's things two carelessly scrawled postcards, one sent from Colorado and the other from Utah, addressed to the family, undated by my father but postmarked at about this time.) And I was in my freshman residence at the university when, one evening in October, my brother Dietrich telephoned to inform me in a curt, dazed voice that "word had come" that our father was dead. He'd died, evidently, in a "work-related accident" involving one or two other men as well, in Utah. There would never be a death certificate mailed to us and if there'd been a body, or the remains of a body, it had been buried in Utah—"In the Uinta Mountains." Dietrich's voice was stunned yet embarrassed; there was no warmth in it, for me; no effort to console me, or even to acknowledge that there was extraordinary news here, only rather the kind of news, considering our father, we might have expected. Neither Dietrich nor I had heard of the Uinta Mountains. I looked the area up on a map, it was in northeastern Utah; not a single place but several, it seemed, scattered over hundreds of square, unpopulated miles.

And so—I yearned for sisters: I reasoned that I'd had the others: mother, father, brothers, grandparents. *If Ida had left me a sister. Two sisters! I would be happy forever, I think.*

❧

I N THE KAPPA GAMMA PI HOUSE where I had gone to live in search of sisterhood there were numerous acts that were "forbidden." Under the predator vigilance of Mrs. Agnes Thayer, these forbidden acts exerted a certain attraction.

It was forbidden, for instance, for any girl to slip into the kitchen when "help" was on the premises. A middle-aged female cook, several busboys (of whom one was a rare Negro undergraduate), occasional delivery men. It was forbidden to enter the dining room after the sonorous gong had sounded for the second time and Mrs. Thayer had taken her seat at the head of the head table, regal and watchful. Nothing less than "ladylike"—"gracious"—"well-bred" behavior was required of Kappa girls at all times in the public rooms. It was taboo to appear in the dining room in slacks or jeans for evening meals; on Sunday, a full-course, heavy dinner was served at 1 P.M., and for this "good" dresses and high heels were required, though many of the girls, especially the more popular girls, would have only just staggered from bed at the sound of the first gong, throwing on dresses with little or no underwear beneath, dragging a brush through matted hair and smearing on lipstick, shoving bare feet into high-heeled shoes and rushing downstairs with unwashed faces, reddened eyes, heads throbbing with hangover headaches—yet these canny girls managed to be seated at the favored table, farthest from Mrs. Thayer, while luckless girls like me invariably wound up at the head table where impeccable manners and stilted and stiff conversation were required. There, it was forbidden to lift your fork before Mrs. Thayer lifted hers, and it was much frowned upon, though not openly forbidden, to continue to eat beyond the point at which Mrs. Thayer crossed her fork and knife primly on her plate, for the busboy to clear. It was forbidden to speak of disturbing, scandalous, controversial, or "needlessly negative" subjects at mealtimes, at least in Mrs. Thayer's hearing; it was forbidden to address the busboys in any casual, let alone flirtatious manner—"The very worst of bad breeding," as Mrs. Thayer described, with a shudder, such behavior known to occur at other, less rigorously maintained sorority houses on campus. Except for emergencies, it was forbidden to rise from your seat at any time before

Mrs. Thayer, who lingered over coffee and dessert, rose from hers. It was forbidden to rush from the dining room when the meal finally ended though by that time you might have so gnawed at your lower lip as to have drawn blood. It was forbidden to weep, or to scream.

"Mary Alice, what is that"—Mrs. Thayer paused, with bemused perplexity, provoking others at the table to turn to me, to scrutinize my blushing face—"curious *facial expression* of yours?" Mrs. Thayer laughed easily. Her wide smile suggested only good humor, not fury at my seeming indifference to her conversation. "You are all frowns and creases like one whose head is being squeezed by a vise."

My Kappa sisters giggled appreciatively, as much at Mrs. Thayer's continued muddling of my name as by her wit.

Mine was not the sole name Mrs. Thayer muddled. New girls, sophomores, were somehow not quite real to her and must prove themselves, in some manner not known to us, and not to be revealed by our older sisters.

(Was I meant to apologize for my rudeness at the table? I lingered behind hoping to catch Mrs. Thayer's eye, and judge by her expression whether an apology was wished, or would only exacerbate her annoyance, but Mrs. Thayer did not so much as glance at me, as she left the dining room.)

Of course, it was forbidden to enter Mrs. Thayer's private quarters at any time, for any reason, unless Mrs. Thayer invited you inside. (As she did occasionally with her favored girls—ironically, these were girls who didn't especially like her.) It was forbidden to peer into Mrs. Thayer's private quarters from either the front entrance in the parlor, or the rear, near the side door. Even if the doors were invitingly open, and the Negro cleaning woman vacuuming inside.

It was forbidden to touch, still less examine or sniff Mrs. Thayer's "special dietary foods" in the pantry refrigerator or cupboard. These were often bulky, wrapped in aluminum foil, taped with adhesive. It was suspected that there might be a code in the fussy crisscrossings of the adhesive, or shrewd Mrs. Thayer had affixed a hair or thread in such a way that would signal intrusion if it were missing. The smells of these mysterious foods varied considerably, ranging from briny-sour to cinnamony-sweet.

Of course it was taboo to examine Mrs. Thayer's mail. As much of an affront as touching her person. You were not to have an early peek at her English publications, you were not to hold to the light her airmail letters from England in their tissue-thin blue envelopes adorned with exotic stamps. (Mrs. Thayer was known to have been a *war bride* whose American officer-husband had brought her back to the United States to live after the end of World War II, and who, after his eventual death, had decided pluckily to stay on in the States because she could support herself here; but clearly her heart was attached to England. Her sole correspondent was a sister who lived in Leeds and whose handwriting was elegantly spidery, as I imagined a ghost's handwriting might be, with three dramatic strokes of the pen beneath the letters USA.) However, if it happened that Mrs. Thayer was close by, in her sitting room for instance, you were allowed to bring her mail in a forthright fashion, holding it in such a way to indicate that you hadn't examined it except to ascertain that it was hers; knocking quietly on her door with the back of your hand (as Mrs. Thayer had demonstrated was the way in which ladies knocked on doors), even if the door was open and you could see her inside. "Yes, dear?" Mrs. Thayer would say, peering over her reading glasses, and you would say, "Mrs. Thayer, may I bring you your mail" and Mrs. Thayer would say, with an air of being pleasantly surprised, like a child offered candy, "Why, is the mail here already? Thank you, dear." Having delivered the mail to Mrs. Thayer's plump beringed fingers you were not to linger in her cozily cluttered sitting room with its myriad glints and glistens of old silver, china, gilt-threaded fabrics and reproductions of English landscapes and framed photographs of presumed family members; yet it was bad manners to back away too quickly as if eager to escape. Precisely how you should behave at this delicate social moment was a matter of the elder woman's discretion, whether out of housemotherly duty or personal whim or a surge of genuine emotion she might wish you to remain, or whether in fact she had other things on her mind and wished you gone; yet it was bad manners to stare at her inscrutably pinkly smiling face in an effort to decipher her thoughts, still more was it unacceptable to blush, stammer and stare at your feet like "an American farm gurl."

Why did I persist in volunteering to bring Mrs. Thayer her mail? She could have gotten it for herself. I didn't think of myself as a particularly shy girl; I hadn't been shy in high school, in Strykersville; my diminutive, sloe-eyed appearance suggested shyness, but I knew that this was deceptive and often traded upon it. Yet under our housemother's icy blue gaze I became tongue-tied and clumsy. I felt my face prickle with heat. Still I was drawn to the woman as one might be drawn to the most exacting of judges. Perhaps it was her mail that fascinated me, as well. The British postal stamps with their look of being "historic"; the exotic promise of the blue-tissue airmail letter; the British publications in their tight-rolled tubes, not yet opened. *Documents from another world. Let me be their bearer!* More urgently I felt an obligation to be "good"—or to be so perceived by Mrs. Thayer and by others. I was too poor and plain not to be "good"; my sorority sisters with indulgent, well-to-do parents, and numerous boyfriends, could be as careless as they wished without a thought of being "good." I didn't want to think that I was desperately lonely in the company of more than forty aggressively well-adjusted, outgoing girls; perversely hungry for the company of a woman of Mrs. Thayer's approximate age, somewhere in her forties and stolidly maternal. However Agnes Thayer coolly declined to play that role beneath the Kappa Gamma Pi roof.

Once, having given Mrs. Thayer her mail, having received her bright, indifferent thank-you, I hovered in the vicinity of her doorway waiting to be summoned inside, or dismissed with an airy smile, and there came one of my older Kappa sisters rushing toward us red-faced, tearful, and panting. Before the girl could speak Mrs. Thayer said with a sharp intake of breath, "Wini*fred!* I can hear you *breathing*." Freddie, as the girl was called, a pretty, fox-faced girl with fluorescent-pink lips, stammered that she'd been "accosted" in the park, she was sure it was the same man who'd been reported harassing other girls in the neighborhood, he'd brushed against her and said "nasty, filthy things" to her; and Mrs. Thayer quickly interrupted, backing away with a look of repugnance, "My dear, that is *no excuse* for such a public demeanor, such a heated, head-on approach, such a display of *yourself*. You needn't advertise your encounter for all the world to see, need you?"

Yet Mrs. Thayer invited Freddie inside her sitting room, and shut the door; they would report the incident to university security, for such incidents, however vulgar and demeaning, were required to be reported. I was summarily dismissed and crept away with a tinge of regret, I hadn't been the one to rush to Mrs. Thayer in distress, I hadn't been the one invited inside, and the door shut quietly behind me.

Here was a surprise, I belatedly learned: for all her authority over the Kappa residence, Agnes Thayer was not a Kappa. She would have been forbidden to attend meetings of the sorority, should she have wished to attend; she would have been banned from the ritual meeting room, should she have wished to step inside it. She knew nothing of the "sacred sisterhood"—the letters Kappa Gamma Pi held no secret, luminous meaning for her. Mrs. Thayer's responsibility had solely to do with the social behavior of the girls in the residence; she was account-able to the university's Dean of Women and to the local Kappa Gamma Pi association that paid her salary. When I revealed my surprise at this fact, saying naively, "Mrs. Thayer isn't one of *us?*" my Kappa sisters laughed at me saying, "God, who'd want that ugly old Brit-bitch snoop-ing on us any more than she does? Use your head."

꒰

I *HEREBY CONSECRATE MYSELF heart, soul, and intellect to the ideals of Kappa Gamma Pi and the promise of sacred sisterhood. United in our bond, so long as I shall live. None of the aforesaid secrets will I reveal. This bond I shall never forsake. I pledge my heart.*

In the basement of the imposing old house at 91 University Place was a consecrated space: the ritual meeting room.

Each sorority and fraternity surely had its consecrated space, proba-bly in the basement of their houses, but it was the ritual meeting room of the Kappa Gamma Pi house that seemed to me so very special.

In 1938, this room had been sanctified for Kappa ritual by national Kappa officers, and meetings of the sorority involving "ritual" could take place only here, according to the bylaws "under strictly confidential and private circumstances." A locked door, absolute secrecy, and no out-siders anywhere near.

Even for Kappas it was forbidden to enter the ritual meeting room except at such times as the room was officially opened by the door-keeper. Only this elected officer and the president and vice-president of the chapter had keys to the room which was kept locked at all times; Mrs. Thayer, of course, had no key. *This is a room, a space, no ordinary individuals can enter.* It was strikingly decorated in Kappa ebony-and-gold wallpaper; its low, soundproofed ceiling was a somber slate blue. At the front of the rectangular room was an altar on a raised platform; the altar was draped in cream-colored silk embossed with ΚΓΠ in gold. Many-pronged silver candelabra were placed on the altar. At the tops of three of the walls were small square windows covered in opaque gauze (to prevent anyone from looking in) like bandages over empty eye sockets. The ritual meeting room spanned the length of the cavernous living room overhead, but not all of the space was used. Folding chairs were set in rows at the front; the rear of the space was used for storage. And it didn't seem very clean or tidy at the rear. The aura of romance ended at about the halfway point. During ritual ceremonies (pledging, initiation) which were sacred events in the Kappa calendar, the meeting room was softly lit by thirty-six candles; at other times, for business meetings, it was lit by practical overhead lights that cast shadows beneath our eyes and chins, and made the most glamorous Kappas look haggard.

You did not simply walk into the meeting room: you had to be, following the bylaws, "granted entrance." This meant lining up in silence on the basement stairs outside the room, seniors first, then juniors, and underclasswomen; at the shut door you gave the ritual Kappa knock (rap, pause, two quick raps and a pause, a final rap); when the door-keeper opened the door you gave her the ritual handshake (crossed hands, twined fingers squeezed in a code replicating the knock) which I would invariably fumble out of nervousness and embarrassment at such intimacy with a girl I scarcely knew; you then whispered in the door-keeper's ear the password (a Greek phrase of which I was never certain and always murmured softly: it sounded like *Hie-ros minosa* or *minoosa*); the doorkeeper then granted you entrance, quietly you slipped into the room and took your place amid the rows of seated girls.

My initiation ceremony passed in a haze of anxiety and light-headedness tinged with nausea. Like most of the pledges I hadn't been allowed to sleep for forty-eight hours; I'd had to fast, and follow Hell Week instructions scrupulously. Though I was the most obedient and craven of pledges, dreading a last-minute dismissal, the initiates seemed to see in my very complicity the seeds of rebellion, even treason; they were hard on me, and I acquiesced in every particular. Physical hazing in fraternities and sororities was supposed to have been banned from campus since deaths and disfigurements and serious injuries had occurred not many years before; my Kappa sisters did not lay hands on us, except to steady us, and "walk" us blindfolded along mysterious corridors and up and down flights of stairs. Inside the meeting room, however, our blindfolds were removed. *Why am I here? What is this place? These strangers? Who are they to me, who am I to them?* I blinked like a nocturnal animal blinded by light. I tasted panic, nausea. I was frightened of becoming hysterical. Bursting into laughter, rushing to the door, slapping and kicking at anyone who tried to stop me. I knew myself in the presence of individuals capricious and arbitrary in their cruelty as the ancient Greek gods. I'd meant to make my family proud of me, initiated into a national sorority. But my mother and father were dead. I began to cry softly, helplessly. *No no no this is a mistake. This is a lie this ridiculous ritual you yourself are a lie.* The president and another officer were solemnly intoning Greek words at the altar and burning parchment paper on which had been written secret words "too sacred to be uttered aloud except at this time and in this place" in a silver bowl, amid rose petals; someone tugged at my arm, I glanced up partly blinded and allowed myself to be led on trembling legs to the altar to make my "final vow."

I was both fully conscious of my surroundings, yet unconscious as an infant. I seemed to be floating against the acoustic-tile ceiling. I saw that my face was streaked with tears and my forehead and nose greasy. I understood that my mother who was Ida was one of the gowned officers, a beautiful senior at whose glowing face I scarcely dared to look; I was aware of sanity slipping from me like ice melting beneath my feet; my father too was grinning at me gap-toothed, with an air of angry satisfaction *Don't let no fuckers out there sell you short* and I vowed I would not, my hand pressed against my pounding heart as I vowed my life as the ceremony concluded and I stood with my dazed sister pledges weeping like newborn infants in the realization *I am a Kappa Gamma Pi for life.*

And then I fainted. Softly limp as a bundle of laundry, onto the chilly and not-very-clean concrete floor.

*In the mind there is no absolute or free will,
but the mind is determined to this or that volition by a cause, which is also determined by
another cause, and this again by another, and
so on ad infinitum.*

SPINOZA, *Ethics*

*How happy I am here, I love my Kappa sisters and my new life as a sorority
girl, I am breathless so busy every minute almost!* so I wrote to girlfriends
from high school who'd gone to other colleges or to a few selected girl
cousins *This is certainly a change from my old life, I'm a KAPPA GAMMA PI
sometimes I have to pinch myself or give myself a little stab with my pin.*

There was no one to whom I might tell an obvious fact: Kappa
Gamma Pi was too expensive for me.

I was a scholarship student, I had virtually no "spending money" as
it's called. Of course I knew this before pledging yet somehow had ignored the fact like a diver who suspects that the water into which she
wants to dive is freezing, and lethal, yet she dives into it just the same.
As if behaving in the manner of X without acknowledging your perver-
sity will have the magical effect of bending X to Y, which you can
endure.

Often in my freshman year, before pledging the sorority, I had to
work ten hours a week to supplement my scholarship; for I'd been overwhelmed by unexpected fees, expenses, the cost of hardcover text-
books and of living even a meager, modest life wearing discount-store
apparel brought from home; in the autumn of my sophomore year

when I'd moved into the Kappa residence, I had to work a minimum of twenty hours a week. These were long afternoons in the registrar's office typing and evenings and Saturdays in the university library stacks shelving books, in probable violation of university regulations into which I didn't dare inquire; I would have applied to Mrs. Thayer for kitchen work in our house but there was a Kappa bylaw forbidding Kappas from working in any sorority houses on campus and I saw the wisdom of this, I suppose. *We are being taught elegant manners. What a lady I am being turned into (you would laugh at me maybe!) I am happy happy HAPPY.* And now in my sophomore year I was in terror of losing my ability to reason, I was in terror of losing my scholarship for poor grades, I was in terror of being dropped from the university and made to return home to my grandparents' farm on that desolate rural wedge of land in Niagara County. (My brothers had long since departed the farmhouse, though they lived in the area.) *Never enough time for so many activities once you're a sorority girl and Kappas are among the most competitive I've discovered. So BREATHLESS!* The fact of time, the swift and irremediable passage of time, was making me desperate; sometimes I was aware of my heart racing, in actual fact I was often breathless; climbing a flight of stairs or one of the campus's notorious hills left me breathless, as if I'd ascended a great height; these were not stairs and hills I was climbing, but mountains; mountains made of glass down whose sides I was sliding, helplessly; never enough time! never enough time! even if I rationed my sleep to four or five hours a night there was never enough time! Though I worked twenty hours a week, my paychecks were painfully small; at the outset, I believed there must be some mistake, and with tears brimming in my eyes I'd gone to make inquiries. Ninety cents an hour? Ninety cents an hour? Can that be right? Federal and state taxes. Social Security deductions. One of the women librarians said frowning it's the same for everyone if you have no dependents. She meant well; she meant to be kindly, if a little curt; I glanced at her lined, stoic face and suppressed a shudder. Still I could not give up my jobs, poorly paying as they were. Alone of my sorority sisters I was obliged—literally—to count pennies. I counted them in neat piles of ten; I would have been ashamed to have been seen (by my sisters) for I would have embarrassed them. They'd taken me on, I supposed, out of charity. They looked upon me as one might look upon a poor relation. *This is the Kappa house!* I wrote on the backs of postcard-sized reproductions of the house to send to my friends and cousins, even to my brothers and grandparents. *Even larger than it appears from the front. So many rooms.* In the cloud-massed sky beyond the jutting roof I made an *X* to indicate the approximate location of my room on the third floor; though in fact my room was at the very back of the house, a cubbyhole not much larger than the room I'd been assigned in my freshman residence. Except, at the Kappa house, I had to share the room with another girl.

Except, at the Kappa house, the room was costing me much more.

The price of happiness. Such happiness you crave.

When the first bill for dues came to me from Kappa Gamma Pi, I was puzzled by "social fees" and other surcharges in addition to the monthly dues. Then to my horror I began to accumulate fines: because of my jobs, I had to miss business meetings, committee meetings, a "required" mixer with Kappa's brother fraternity Phi Omega. These were fines of $21 in October, $28 in November. I pleaded with the Kappa treasurer to excuse me: I had to work, had no choice but to work, what could I do? The girl, a junior with a pixie cut and wide-set imperturbable eyes, smiled with her mouth and suggested that I cut back on my academic courses and reschedule my work hours so that I'd have more time for the sorority—"Kappa Gamma Pi is your first obligation, don't forget."

Late that night in the basement study room of the house (to which

I'd become habituated to retreating, not wanting to quarrel with my gregarious roommate, Deedee, unable to endure the pounding repetitive beat of calypso music from the room next door, or the shrieks and cries of laughter generally through the upstairs) sometime after 3:00 A.M. drifting into a deranged sleep as my vise-clenched head sank slowly to the paperback *Ethics* whose pages swam in my vision as if undersea. *Happy!* the voice of Spinoza taunted. *The happiness you deserve.*

My grandmother spoke English with a heavy German accent that seemed to mock the very language, as the tics and grimaces of her raddled face mocked her smiles. " 'Made your bed, now lay in it'—that's what they say, *ja?*" She laughed, though without mirth. She was a guardian of the most banal and self-evident truths; one of those old, sour, but unfailingly energetic fairies in Grimms' tales who oversee disaster out of personal spite; her response to the assiduously argued, painstakingly structured metaphysical system of Baruch Spinoza, that martyr for truth excommunicated from the Jewish community in Holland, in 1656, would have been to take his collected works and fling them into her wood-burning stove—"There!"

I did not call her from Syracuse, ever. I did not call her to beg her forgiveness. I did not call her to say *I am in despair, I am lost to myself, what can I do?*

The study of philosophy is the study of the human mind. Though philosophers claim they are studying "reality"—"the world"—"the universe"—"God." Yet to study the human mind up close, to probe into one's own mind, one's own motives, is to be baffled utterly.

My first year at Syracuse, I'd been indifferent to the campus presence

of the Greeks, as they pretentiously called themselves. I was immersed
in my studies—and in my part-time jobs—and in the vast, intimidating
adventure of books, books, books. Never in Strykersville had I imagined
a true library: a library like the university library in whose stacks I might
wander mesmerized for years. The brightest of students in my high
school, yet I saw myself at Syracuse as alone and beleaguered and fight-
ing for my life; I loved the excitement of it, even the anxiety; I was in a
perpetual state of agitation; I returned from the library staggering with
books; if one of my professors assigned X, I would read, and reread, not
only X, but commentary on X; I was writing, parable-like little prose
poems; I had little interest in other girls in my residence, and often
skipped meals; I had not the slightest interest in joining a sorority, in the
time-squandering activities called "rush"—"pledge week"—"initiation."
Yet even in my indifference I wasn't unaware (I would have to confess!)
of the sobering fact that the majority of freshman girls, including girls I
admired and would have wished to consider friends, the most attractive,
the most popular, in many cases the most intelligent, scholarship students like myself, had pledged sororities. These girls would seem to have
been plucked by supernatural intervention out of the university residences and would be living, beginning the following fall, in sorority
houses; leaving prospects for companionship, let alone friendship, severely diminished. For who would remain in the dreary undergraduate
dorms for "independents" as we were flatteringly called?—the left-
behind, the losers. Outcasts at life's feast, in a memorable Joycean
phrase. In my pride I was hurt; I understood that I would be banished
from a glamorous world in which in fact I took no interest; that I would
be banished was a spur to my desire. And perhaps out of the corner of
my eye I'd been uneasily aware of the cruel and discriminatory Greek
world, synonymous with University Place, those absurdly elegant man-
sions (with dormitories extending at the rears) boasting cryptic Greek

letters on their facades which were meant to tease and tantalize and rebuff the uninitiated. I'd walked past the Kappa Gamma Pi house on its
craggy hill, I'd stared at the ivy-covered facade, the stately Doric
columns, the slate-covered high-pitched roof, and turned away shaken.
In my rural background there'd been nothing like this. In Strykersville, a
country town of about 10,000 people, nothing like this. A world of ex-
plicit and outrageously unapologetic preferences and discriminations indicated by the word *cut*. For *to cut* was the privilege of the Greeks, and *to
be cut* was the fate of the unworthy. This was intolerable, this was un-
American, you wanted to laugh in derision. *Cut from the Deke list, cut from
the TriDelt list, cut to ribbons, cut your throat, what a loser.* Every year after
fall rush there were incidents of attempted suicide among the rejects.

Which only underscored, as some said, the Greek truism: survival of
the fittest.

Oh, the Greeks were contemptible, their self-aggrandizement comical, but who could laugh?

Then somehow it happened, remarkable at the time, wholly unexpected and flattering, that a girl in my residence hall began to seek me
out. Her name was Dawn; I'd scarcely noticed her in one of my lecture
classes; in my fever of concentration upon my work, I scarcely noticed
others my own age; my attention was fixed upon professors, whom I admired and feared as minor deities. But there was Dawn entering my life
as one might open a door and step inside, uninvited. She was a striking
young woman; not pretty, nor even attractive, but glamorous like a film
star of the Thirties with a perfect moon face, sleepy hooded eyes, heavily
lipsticked lips, and a perpetual cigarette burning in her fingers; smiling
at me, squinting through a veil of smoke; one of those compelling young
females of whom there were several in my high school, prematurely
adult and sexually alluring however young. Her hair was bleached
and teased; she wore tight sweaters and painted her fingernails. Her

fur-trimmed black cloth coat, her handsome leather boots and other items of apparel suggested that her family was well-to-do, and indulged her. Dawn whose very name came quickly to captivate me: DAWN I'd find myself writing in my notebook or in the margin of a textbook or tracing with my fingernails in the gritty film of ice on the window of my room. DAWN DAWN. She playfully chided me for studying too hard—"You'll have a nervous breakdown! Really. It can happen." At the same time, she was childlike in her appeal for help in writing papers. "If you could just glance through it? Just to tell me is it good enough to hand in." Of course, I would end up doing much more, for I enjoyed such challenges; by sixth grade I was helping friends of mine with their schoolwork, as much for the pleasure of solving another's problems as for helping a friend in distress. When Dawn received high grades on these assignments, she was elated and grateful, and invited me to meet her friends, freshman Kappa pledges who were girls like herself, not-intellectual, not-brainy, but brimming with energy, clever and funny and good-looking in a way to make boys stare after them on the street. *But why am I with these strangers? Not my type!* Yet there I was. Flattered. Dawn insisted upon "restyling" my hair. Dawn insisted upon lending me clothes, though she was a size eight, and I was several sizes smaller. She invited me to visit the "beautiful, elite" sorority she'd just pledged, Kappa Gamma Pi—"What a terrific bunch of girls! I love them." And soon after this visit, Dawn and the other pledges encouraged me to sign up for the spring semester rush. And I did. I knew that I couldn't afford to live anywhere except in university housing, and that the lowest priced housing, yet I signed up for "rush," and suddenly became another person fixated upon a group of strangers, a sorority of which I knew little except it had a name, it had a campus reputation—for what? "Social life, activities." (That these were things in which I had no interest seemed not

to occur to me; if I'd investigated, I would have discovered other sororities far more suited for my situation: a sorority of arts majors, a sorority
of scholarship girls, a sorority for girls with limited finances who helped
defray the cost of room and board by sharing work-duties in their residence. But I didn't investigate.) Where Dawn had pledged, there also I
would pledge, or nowhere. The very Kappa house, the intimidating neo-
Classic mansion at the far end of University Place, loomed large in my
imagination like an image in a Technicolor film. I believed I'd seen it before; years ago; not in Strykersville of course where there were no man-
sions, but—where? In Buffalo? Its lofty portico, the interior illuminated
by chandeliers and candlelight, furnished with polished and glittering
things, enormous white peonies in tall urns; the Kappa girls smiling like
Hollywood starlets and bursting with "personality" and all of them remembering my name. And there was the British housemother Mrs.
Thayer with her exotic accent, her brisk impeccable manners, those
eyes blue as the ice rimming Lake Ontario well into April. In the giddiness of my delusion it seemed to me that Mrs. Thayer was the very
mother of the house, and I liked it that she wasn't American, she spoke
with no accent I knew, and would be a harsh, exacting judge. Not for
this woman the fate of the merely mortal.

It was a shock to me that I was invited back to the Kappa house in
the second week of rush; an even greater shock, that I was invited back
in the third week. Was it possible that I was surviving the rush? (I had
dropped out of or had been cut from other sororities without taking
much notice.) I cared only for Kappa Gamma Pi.

In secret, I could not comprehend why anyone, let alone so sophisti-
cated and glamorous a group of girls as the Kappas, would want me to
join them. I knew that, if they knew me as I truly was, they wouldn't
like me at all. Yet it became my obsession to convince them, a challenge

like achieving high grades, a perfect or near-perfect academic record. The less worthy I believed I was of being a Kappa, the more ardent my desire to be a Kappa. Now in the ice-crust of my window I scratched ΚΓΠ. On a Kappa questionnaire passed over to perspective pledges I'd lied freely, desperately. It was believed by some of my relatives that the family was partly Jewish: that my father's grandparents were German Jews who'd changed their name to a German-sounding name when they'd moved from a village in western Germany to Antwerp, Belgium; before the outbreak of World War I, my father's mother, the daughter of this couple, and her German-born husband emigrated to America, to settle as dairy farmers in the volatile climate of upstate New York; the family's vague, not-much-practiced religion was Lutheran; my mother, Ida, may have been a truer Lutheran, for she was buried in the church cemetery in Strykersville. (You could not ask my grandparents personal questions. Asked about Europe, her own parents, my grandmother would grimace in contempt. "Why you want to know, that old dead time?" and make a spitting gesture.) Yet on the questionnaire I unhesitatingly indicated *Episcopalian*. My father's employment?—*independent contractor*. My life goal?—*to help in the betterment of mankind*. I told myself that this was not lying; it was my Kappa self speaking. I had noticed how in conversations with Kappas I'd overcome my natural inclination toward skepticism to emerge as open, uncomplicated, easygoing, warm, with a dimpled smile and high ringing girlish laughter. My Kappa self did not brood, was never melancholy. If she wrote parable-like prose poems in the style of Franz Kafka, she showed no one among the Kappas. She had clear skin, shining eyes, a glossy pageboy, and lipsticked lips. She was no one I knew personally but an inspired composite of a dozen Kappa girls, including Dawn, whom I greatly admired. The more poised Kappas had a way of hugging and kissing you on the cheek—"Loveya, sweetie!" when saying good-bye, and while I was never able to emulate this extravagant display of feeling, there were times when I came close.

Whoever awaited me back in my book-strewn room in my freshman residence was increasingly a stranger, and a boring stranger at that. I had yet to discover Nietzsche's cruel aphorism *To seduce their neighbor into thinking well of them, and then to believe in this opinion of their neighbor: who has greater skill in this than a woman?* Yet such efforts of seduction were all I had to shore up against the terrible loneliness of my life. Or so I believed.

When at last on the evening of the official end of spring rush when the sealed Kappa "bid" was ceremoniously delivered to my room, by Dawn and several other pledges, I stared at these beaming strangers and burst into tears.

My Kappa self.

❧

How proud Ida would have been of her daughter! Becoming a Kappa was but the first of many achievements, I promised.

Not that I was worth your death. But your giving birth to me?

Away at Syracuse where I rarely thought of home, I thought of my mother often. In the late night, I felt that my loneliness drew me to hers: aren't the dead lonely? My brothers would have laughed at me, pointing out that I was remembering, not a living woman, but old snapshots. Yet at such times I felt my mother's nearness; if I glanced up from my desk, to see an indistinct face reflected in the windowpane beside my lamp, I could imagine that the face was hers. There were exciting half-conscious dreams in which I returned to Strykersville. Or these were vivid memories. In the cemetery behind the Lutheran church where she was buried. In life, I had not visited this grave many times. If my father had visited it, he went alone and never spoke of it. Yet in my memory I could smell freshly mown grass and feel the stubble beneath my feet. Beyond the church's squat steeple and dully gleaming cross the northern sky was darkening over Lake Ontario. The Strykersville Lutheran church had been founded in 1873, built of crude fieldstone and stucco. The cemetery was only a meadow behind the church, of small rocky hills and ridges that in rainy weather filled with water; in winter, angry-looking dunes of snow covered half the graves' markers. The earliest markers, dating back to the 1870's, were worn thin as playing cards and tilted in the earth; these were closest to the church; more recent graves like my mother's were farther away, fanning up a partly cleared hill. It swept over me that no one really expects the future, no one truly believes it can happen. All that is, is now. The modest gray-granite marker engraved with my mother's name, birth, and death dates, was at the far end of a row; close by was an uncultivated field; how *of the earth* is death, which Spinoza never acknowledged; none of the philosophers spoke of smells, damp earthy leaf-rot mingled with woodsmoke (in the distance, a farmer was burning stumps: the worst smoke-stink you can imagine). I drew my fingers across the rough stone. Freezing stone. *I'm a Kappa, I'm so happy, Mother! Sometimes I think my heart will burst.*

My mother hadn't been a frequent churchgoer. She and my father had been married in a civil ceremony in Buffalo. The family legend was, the minister of this country church had allowed my mother's body burial in the cemetery with the understanding that my father would now attend church, and bring his family. How eagerly the minister must have anticipated new members to his congregation, a father and four children, and maybe the father's parents, too? Of course, nothing had come of it.

For Ida's sake I was uneasy that her body lay in sanctified ground through a lie. Otherwise, I smiled to think of it.

❧

IT WAS AN ERA when such words as *sex, sexual* were never uttered even by those who routinely engaged in sexual practices. *Sexy* was a word that might be murmured in an undertone, with a sly movement of the eyes, a knowing smile.

Mrs. Thayer, whose delicate task it was as housemother to allude to certain things without ever naming them, like most mothers of the day, spoke of *ladylike behavior at all times, standards of decorum,* and maintaining *a reputation beyond reproach.* She used such expressions as *male visitor* and *male person* as if speaking of a distasteful and untrustworthy species. You would not have believed that Agnes Thayer had ever been married, despite the conspicuous rings she wore on her left hand; you would not have believed that this woman had been married to any *male person.* Mrs. Thayer lectured us at mealtimes and at formal house-meetings (not Kappa ritual meetings) held on Sunday evenings in the parlor. "Our house rules regarding male persons are simple. They are set by the Dean of Women and they are not to be violated under any circumstances." It was forbidden to allow any *male person* (other than an approved workman) to ascend to the upper floors of the house; it was forbidden, in fact, to allow any *male person* to sit on the first few steps of the sweeping staircase to the second floor, or to enter the basement stairway for any purpose whatsoever. Of course it was forbidden to hide, or to attempt to hide, any *male person* on the premises before or after the house was officially locked for the night; it was forbidden to "carry on" in any manner unbecoming to a lady with any *male person* in any of the public rooms or elsewhere technically under Mrs. Thayer's jurisdiction. In the public rooms of the Kappa house, where *male persons* were admitted as guests, the rule was classic in its simplicity: "*All feet* on the floor, gurls, *at all times.*"

Mrs. Thayer's arch, overbearing accent made her speech irresistible to mimic. In this way, her speech pervaded every room of the thirty-bedroom house.

You thought of sex continuously. Even if, like me, you had few sexual feelings, and no desire to translate those feelings into relationships with *male persons*. Sex was a tide, vast and virulent and unspeakable. A tide that could wash over any girl at any time, and destroy us. *Male persons* were primed to discharge this tide, in hot little spurts: *semen*. (Yet *semen* was never named.) *Male persons* were the natural predators of *girls*.

"What Thayer's scared of, like all the housemothers," it was remarked slightingly of our vigilant housemother, "is one of us getting knocked up. She figures she'd be blamed, and fired."

Forbidden for undergraduate girls to ascend to the upper floors of male residences or to slip from their public rooms at any time. *Forbidden for undergraduate girls* to visit the rooms or apartments of men living off-campus, and so not under the jurisdiction of any university authority. Especially it was crucial for girls to avoid being alone with one or more *male persons* at fraternity parties where unfortunate incidents were rumored to occur, occasionally. When a girl drank too much, and became careless. Got passed around upstairs, from "date" to "date." But there were no male equivalents of housemothers like Mrs. Thayer at fraternities, only house managers or advisors, and when Kappa girls went to fraternity parties on campus or at Cornell as they did every week-end, they did as they pleased. Or as their dates pleased. *C'mon! You'll like this guy, he's a great guy, you can't be working all the time!* I made up my face like the other faces, I brushed my snarled hair till it shone. I was given a pink taffeta dress to wear, a skirt to mid-calf and a big bow tied at my back to make the waist fit. I was given sparkly earrings. Smiling and blinking like a nocturnal animal prodded out into the sunshine. In the fraternity house the din was deafening. The young men, en masse, were *tall.* Laughter, music. Beer. Paper cups, beer. The sacrament was beer. In the rest room reserved for LADIES (a poster in smeary red paint taped to the outside of the door) there was a giant blue box of Kotex promi-nently in view. Some wag had put, in each of the toilets, goldfish. Were you supposed to laugh? Flush the beautiful golden little fish down down the toilet, and laugh? I lacked an appropriate sense of humor, I lacked an appreciation of beer. And mouths tasting of beer. Was I expected to dance in this din, in a crush of grinning strangers, in a grinding em-brace? Expected to kiss a stranger? Some boy who didn't know me, had forgotten my name? What was the purpose of drinking to get drunk? My Kappa sister Chris, vomiting off the back steps onto garbage cans marked ΦΩ. *Chris, come on. Chris, please.* I was begging but she refused to listen. Back to the party! I was trying to explain to Dawn, Jill, Donna, Trudi, who were impatient with me, eyes hotly shining, skin heated, arms slung around their grinning dates' necks. *She'll be fine, Chris can take care of herself, she's been at these parties before.* I provoked em-barrassment and disgust among those Kappas sober enough to notice how I left drunken Eddy my "date" walking out of the music-blare run-ning across the snowy spiky-grassed park in ridiculous high heels, my borrowed pink taffeta dress swishing like ice against my stockinged legs, breathless, cursing, tears leaking out of my eyes though God damn I wasn't crying, why cry? *My feelings can't be hurt where I have none.*

Next day around noon, Trudi looking coarse-faced and homely without makeup brought the black cloth coat I'd left on the crammed coat-
rack at the fraternity house, tossed it onto my bed with a look of pity
and contempt. "Here. You forgot something."

What happened to Chris?
Hey if she doesn't remember, so what?
Whose business? Yours?
No memory, nothing to forgive.
Her date took precautions, probably. He isn't a complete asshole.
Was it just him?

Returning from the library along University Place, just before
11:00 P.M. Crossing the snowy park. I was carrying books in my arms as
you might cradle a baby. One of them was eight hundred pages, a history
of European philosophy. I was walking swiftly, my breath steaming in the
freezing air. I'd been working in the library stacks and was almost late
for curfew. My mind was empty of all thoughts except the urgent need
to get up the steep hill to the Kappa house, to get inside before
11:00 P.M. For Mrs. Thayer would not be sympathetic, Mrs. Thayer
would not even listen to my stammered excuse. *You American gurls!*
Suddenly I heard whispering—"Missy? Mis-sy?" The figure appeared
from behind a tree as a child might, out of a hiding place. In the dim
light of a street lamp on University Place I saw his face: a stranger's: fattish jowls, clean-shaven jaws, thin wormy mouth stretched in a leering
grin, black-rimmed glasses like a schoolteacher's, that magnified his eyes
like minnows. *He's letting me see his face. Wants me to see his face.* "Mis-sy," he
was saying, the tip of his tongue protruding between his lips, "—gonna

hurt your titties runnin'! Take care." He might have been any age between thirty-five and fifty. There was a singsong mock-solicitude to his
rather high-pitched voice. I knew him at once as the man who'd accosted Freddie and other girls; but I was not one of these girls; I was a
Strykersville girl; without hesitation I threw my heavy books at him, directly at his face, knocking his glasses off. He cried out in surprise and
pain. No girl or woman this crude bastard had ever approached had behaved like this, he wasn't prepared, his fantasies hadn't prepared him for
me. I was screaming at him, short yipping breathless cries like a dog.

Watching him then limp across the park, along a side street, out of
my vision. Like liquid fire adrenaline coursed through my veins. I was
thrilled, I was buoyant. This incident, I would have liked to tell my
father.

In the snow lay the black-rimmed glasses. I picked them up with my
gloved hand and had an impulse to snap them in two, in rage. But I
didn't. I slipped them into my coat pocket instead.

No one had heard my short breathless little screams. They'd faded
immediately, like my steaming breath.

What if he'd hurt me? There was the glint of madness in his eyes.
Saliva at the corners of his wormy mouth.

When I entered the brightly lit Kappa house a few minutes later, my
heart still pounding, I was two or three minutes late but the proctor on
duty, smoking a cigarette, waved me indifferently inside. She took no notice of my flushed, excited face. My dark, dilated eyes. I did not rush to
Mrs. Thayer's door, which was closed at this time of night; I did not bring
her the gift of my female distress after all. The library books were damp
with snow but otherwise undamaged. I knew I was a very lucky girl.

My feelings can't be hurt where I have none.

· · ·

What I would do: I'd picked up the glasses with gloved hands and I would never touch the glasses without wearing gloves; I would mail them to Syracuse police headquarters with a terse typed note. *These belong to a sex offender. He is yours.*

Thunderous hooves! Shrieks of laughter. Soap-splattered mirrors in the third-floor communal bathroom. The smell of cigarette smoke everywhere and cigarette butts strewn like confetti. Empty Tab and Coke cans kicked along the corridor, down to the stairway landing, for Geraldine the Negro maid to clean up; Geraldine with no expression on her dark creased face, wordless, dropping trash into her plastic bag. (Passing Geraldine and her bulky vacuum cleaner in the corridor, I lowered my eyes, I was ashamed of my skin. In the Kappa Gamma Pi house that autumn of my sophomore year I knew for the first time what it was to be ashamed of my skin. But Geraldine took no more notice of me than any white-girl Kappa deserved.) *Bitch* they were incensed *Why doesn't she mind her own God-damn business.* Mrs. Thayer had dared to scold certain senior girls. *Conduct unbecoming ladies and in public rooms!* There was Lulu who played repeatedly at a high volume "The Song from *Moulin Rouge*" to celebrate *See look?* lifting her left hand where a tiny diamond ring flashed like a naughty wink *Engaged before I'm twenty-one.* Where a younger girl was crying, there several seniors circled her *C'mon, sweetie! Get real.* When I approached, one of them cursed me, shoved me aside and away and I retreated in shock never knowing *Why?* I could not tell myself the old story *Once upon a time* because the time was now; the story was now; I'd believed I was causing the story to take place, but in fact the story was taking place around me, as a tide rises, brackish and muddy and filthy with debris. My Kappa sisters were fascinating to me as giant, brightly feathered predator birds would be fascinating to a small songbird hiding in the brush. Or trying to hide in the brush.

In my *Ethics* text I underlined *The endeavor to understand is the first and only basis of virtue.*

Yet it began to happen: the *Guardian, Harper's & Queen, Punch* and other British publications were left in disarray on the parlor table, sometimes on the very floor. Smoldering cigarettes left behind to foul the parlor air seeping beneath the door into Mrs. Thayer's private quarters. The laughter of anonymous *male persons* in the front foyer as the door was slammed, hard enough to make every crystal chandelier in the house shiver. Hyena laughter on the stairs after curfew. Heavy pounding footfalls in the second-floor corridor above Mrs. Thayer's bedroom. On the mahogany banister so fiercely polished by the silent Geraldine, dried threads of—was it human vomit? Mrs. Thayer called, "Gurls! *Gurls!*" One of her elaborately wrapped food packages was missing from the pantry cupboard. Simply gone. Where? None of the kitchen help could explain. At mealtimes Mrs. Thayer's icy blue eyes were alert, shrewd, darting from face to face. Only the younger Kappas smiled; we wouldn't have known we'd had any choice. "It is very quiet in here. The quiet of *guilty consciences,*" Mrs. Thayer observed. With trembling fingers, at the conclusion of the meal, Mrs. Thayer rang the little silver bell. Summoning the bulky troupe of us into the parlor, except those senior girls who'd defiantly slipped away. "Who has been doing these things?" Mrs. Thayer calmly inquired. "Who has been so—unmannerly? So *crude?*" You knew Mrs. Thayer wanted to say *so American!* It might have been the magazines of which she spoke—again scattered about the parlor, shocking to see. And the crossword puzzle page of the local newspaper, on the floor. There was an embarrassed silence. A restless silence. In my nervousness I began to count heads but gave up at beyond twenty-five. Mercy and Trudi exchanged simpering-guilty glances, Bon-Bon and Chris clenched their jaws trying not to laugh aloud. Dawn licked her glossy lips frowning into space. Freddie surreptitiously scratched her left underarm. Deedee suppressed a yawn, or a belch. Daintily the mantel clock chimed the quarter hour. A reminder: Kappas are first and foremost *young ladies.* But upstairs a phonograph was play-ing rock and roll. Low-down dirty, thumping white-boy black-blues. From where I was seated on the carpet, I could see beneath the sofa upon which Mrs. Thayer sat stiffly girdled and erect; I saw what ap-peared to be a sanitary napkin. I was transfixed by the sight. Thinking *But it can't have been used, it isn't blood-stained is it?* Mrs. Thayer restated her question. But who could remember her question? Ice-eyes darting from face to face but these were innocent big-American-girl faces closed to her. She turned to me, a few feet from her, who was staring at her plump little feet in calfskin shoes; I'd been seeing that Mrs. Thayer's ankles were oddly thick, perhaps swollen. "You"—Mrs. Thayer said sud-denly, waking me from my trance—"do *you* know? I command you to speak." I was so startled, I must have reacted in a way to stir amusement in the other girls; my eyes blinked guiltily of their own accord. A wild desolation touched my heart. I did not want Mrs. Thayer to discover the sanitary napkin, I did not want her to be publicly shocked and humili-ated, I did not want the poor woman's trembling to become more visi-ble, how the Kappa girls would giggle, mocking the Brit-bitch behind her back. Without thinking I said, "I—I must have done it, Mrs. Thayer."

There was a shocked pause. Even the mantel clock seemed to cease its minute ticking.

Was it the magazines we were discussing?—I was pointing at them, and pages of the Syracuse paper scattered on the carpet. My voice cracked, nasal and frightened. "I'm the only one who reads your magazines, Mrs. Thayer. I do the crossword puzzle." This was false, I had never "done" a crossword puzzle in my life; never would I waste my intelligence on a mere game. "So I—must have done this." There was another pause, an awkward blank silence. My Kappa sisters did not move yet there was a sense of collective movement away from me; a single indrawn breath. Mrs. Thayer, wholly unprepared for this confession, stared at me, a slow heated flush rising in her face. Almost faltering, she asked, " 'Must have'—or in fact 'did'—?" but her sarcasm lacked force, authority. I was smiling blankly. I heard myself say in a stammer, "I—I did, Mrs. Thayer. I promise it won't happen again." I was shivering suddenly, it must have been the onset of flu. I recalled that the man-in-the-park, my would-be assailant, had seen my face as clearly as I'd seen his. My mistake had been, I hadn't run to Mrs. Thayer in tears. Now my bowels churned hotly. What little I'd managed to consume at dinner, was clenching itself in spasms of revenge. Perhaps Mrs. Thayer knew that I was not even lying purposefully, to any point. Of the Kappas, I was the only girl who wore the same clothes day after day. A rumpled charcoal-gray wool skirt with a waistband so loose, the skirt twisted around, side to front, back to front, without my noticing. A long-sleeved white cotton blouse, much laundered and insufficiently ironed, with pert button-down collar in the style of the day. And an oversized navy blue orlon V-neck sweater, from the Strykersville Sears outlet, going at the elbows. My socks were mismatched but both were white wool. My hair lifted in uncombable clots of frizz, like iron filings stirred by a passing magnet. Whoever I was, seated amid the Kappas, nervously pleating her already creased skirt, I represented a valiant if somewhat smudged variant of the collegiate ideal. Mrs. Thayer, who'd been staring gloomily at me, decided, suddenly, out of spite perhaps, to believe me; she sighed, and struck at the sofa with a vexed little fist. "Oh very well, then! *You* are careless like all the rest. You gurls! I tell you and tell you." With an airy gesture of her hand Mrs. Thayer dismissed the other girls, only just in time before the boldest drifted away. I remained behind, contrite, biting my lip, busily tidying up the parlor. In disgust Mrs. Thayer said, "I would have expected better behavior from *you, you* of all these—'Kappas.'" The word *Kappa* was pronounced as a mild obscenity. I waited for Mrs. Thayer to ask about the other infractions of her rule, the theft of her food for instance, but she said nothing, stalked out of the parlor and slammed the door. By this time no one remained in the parlor except me.

With a folded newspaper I managed to nudge the sanitary napkin out from beneath the sofa. In fact, it had been used: wizened and clotted with dark, caked blood at its center, dazzling gauzy white elsewhere. A Kotex. If Mrs. Thayer had been spared, so had Geraldine. I wrapped the thing in newspaper to throw into the trash. I'd returned the magazines to their original fan-shaped order. Hearing my Kappa sisters overhead, their heavy insolent feet. I'd been reading in a book of ancient mythology of the Harpies, storm-spirits that carried souls to Hades. Their whispers, murmurs, mocking laughter sifting downward, on my head.

Underlining in my philosophy text *We endeavor to affirm everything concerning ourselves and concerning the beloved object which we imagine will affect us or the object with joy, and, on the contrary, we endeavor to deny everything that will affect either us or ourselves with sorrow.*

So it began to happen that God touched me in unspeakable ways. At first I ignored it, ignored Him. (In whom I did not believe; I was too cerebral for God-games.) A few times, I'd been taken to the Lutheran church in Strykersville. Sleety rain pelting against the windows. The minister with his raw hopeful voice and winking eyeglasses. I was seated between my brother Dietrich and my grandmother. There must have been some reason. A relative's death? A funeral? The muddy cemetery, the forlorn little marker. A ticklish sensation that grew tight, tighter like wires stringing my body together so I wanted suddenly to laugh, I was nineteen years old and living amid strangers in a millionaire's mansion atop a hill. *How happy I am, I've escaped you. And lucky. So much more lucky than I deserve.*

Yet I could not sleep. I had more or less abandoned my room to Deedee and her friends, returning to it only to change my clothes. When the basement study room emptied out, after midnight usually, I tried to sleep there; on the battered old leather couch smelling of cigarette smoke and laced with burns. In the Kappa house I yearned for the aloneness of my previous life; as, in that previous life, I had yearned for the sisterhood of the Kappas. I was writing a paper titled "Free Will and Determinism in Spinoza" but it was a paper meant to penetrate the actual truth. For each page of my paper, each paragraph, each sentence, I was afflicted by others of equal authority swarming into my head like hornets. In my notes for this paper, there were strips of paper marked A, B, C, etc.; others marked 1, 2, 3, etc. There were vertical scribblings in blue ballpoint, horizontal scribblings in green ballpoint. Some of this was smudged. In an ecstasy of sudden clarity I wrote *Spinoza made of his madness, art.* I did not believe that my professor would admire this insight so I attributed it to an invented scholar. I could not sleep, yet to my dismay I could not maintain a reliable wakefulness at other times. My eyes open, I felt myself begin to flicker like a candle in a draft. Going out, out. And good riddance. My German-Jew grandmother scolded, shaking a flour-whitened forefinger. Why does flour, grainy and powdery, on human flesh, so appall? My mother, Ida, stood in a doorway staring at me, a hand lifted in greeting, or in farewell. Where her smiling mouth had been there was now a blood-blotch. They were concerned for my health, my sanity; though they did not give that name to it—*sanity*. A decent girl did not speak of *sexual,* and a decent girl did not speak of *sanity.* I became worried that the soiled sanitary napkin might be traced back to me because I'd been the one to wrap it in newspaper and throw it into the trash. There was the fatal closeness of *sanitary, sanity.* I caused a gang of Kappas to laugh raucously by suggesting how the two might be linked. Oh, I was funny! *Crazy sense of humor, that one.* I'd been taken by surprise when four of my sisters came by, one Sunday morning, to rap on my door and ask if I'd like to join them?—they were wearing their good coats, they were wearing hats and gloves; if they'd been out late the night before, their faces were relatively fresh, their eyes sparkly as good Christian eyes. They were going to St. John's, the Episcopalian church, wasn't I Episcopalian, wouldn't I like to join them? I was deeply ashamed, I stammered explaining I would go with them another time, they went away clattering in their high heels denouncing me. My brothers laughed at me, my distress. To them, I'd always been a liar; if you'd asked would they have wanted me born, they would have said in a single voice *No!* If I needed a Kotex I might steal one from another girl's toiletries for I could not afford to buy Kotex, I hated the look of the very box, the prim medicinal smell. In fact, my menstrual periods had become irregular and would gradually cease. (I feared I might be pregnant: no one would believe I'd never "done it" with a guy.) My brothers would stare at me in greater disgust. Before dawn, I crept upstairs to take a shower in the third-floor bathroom. Where in the past I'd never taken more than two or three showers a week, now I took a shower every morning. And sometimes at night. For the blood-smell was unmistakable, even if I didn't bleed. It was the blood-smell that had attracted the man-in-the-park to me. (I hadn't mailed his glasses to the Syracuse police after all, I'd thrown them away in the trash.) In the shower, I touched my breasts lightly with just my fingertips. You're taught to knead your breasts to search for lumps. *The first symptoms are like tiny pebbles. Then they expand.* I wondered if they sliced your breasts from you, off the chest wall, in a smooth scraping maneuver; or if the breasts were hacked off, in pieces. Raw chicken breasts, the sticky skin still attached.

"You!—what the hell are you doing here?"

I stammered what sounded like *Nothing* and fled.

Behind the day-old bakery on Mohawk Street a few blocks from the university. Off-campus, another world. I walked with my head lowered in shame, my face burning. It wasn't the first time I'd prowled behind the bakery but it was the first time I'd been caught. If I couldn't eat with my Kappa sisters, I'd discovered other ways of eating, or at least of locating food. (For sometimes I was unable to eat the purloined food, too. Teeming with invisible bacteria, the germs of hepatitis and death.) Unsold poppy seed rolls, broken cookies, smashed pies, rock-hard loaves of bread and coffee cake, stuffed loosely into garbage bags.

Should be ashamed of yourself!

Why? It's delicious.

Beyond the university in the reverse direction was Auburn Hills, a residential neighborhood of large, handsome houses on tree-lined streets, where sometimes on Sunday mornings I would prowl the alleys between Auburn Avenue and Palmer Street, making my way sniffing like a hungry dog; for in this well-to-do neighborhood, no one parked on the street or brought garbage or trash to the curb; there were garages to the rear of houses, opening onto unpaved alleys; it was caterers' cartons that caught my eye in the trash, the aftermath of Saturday night parties, leftover canapes, caviar jars where always some caviar remained, even deviled eggs, or parts of eggs, bread sticks, even, once, a sizable portion of an angel's food wedding cake. Sometimes I devoured these foods where I stood, hardly troubling to glance around to see that no one watched; sometimes I stuffed them into my duffel bag to carry away and eat in private; sometimes, stricken with remorse, or a fear of food poisoning, or a wish to punish myself further, I threw everything away. I saw no contradiction between my ideal self and my animal self. As Spinoza said *We yearn to persist in our being.*

In terror that tiny cysts were forming in my breasts I dared not touch myself. In terror that I would fall asleep in one of my classes or faint and fall out of my desk, embarrassing myself in front of a professor I adored, I cruelly pinched the insides of my arms or stabbed myself with my pen. On my pale forearms were smears of blue ballpoint ink like broken arteries. *In any philosophical system of genius* the professor pronounced *there co-exist contradictions.* A hand was raised like a puppet's jerked on a string. I was not one to speak in large classes, this could not be me. Not my voice ringing anxiously amid the banked tiers of old-fashioned desks. *Yet if X is not wholly non-Y, how can it be X? Or is it something else? Which we agree to call X?* In our cavernous lecture hall on the top floor of the ancient Hall of Languages. The professor mimed applause at the question but said it might best be addressed later in the course, in the study of Hegel. My eyes began to cross with fatigue. There came in quick cartoon flashes the humiliation, but it was comical, of having been chased from the rear of the day-old bakery, the apparition of a startled-looking young black man with whom I nearly collided; but I'd had no incriminating evidence on my person, I'd dropped the rolls, the breads, the smashed cherry pie in order to flee. At the Kappa house, I dragged

myself to the table. My vacant place at the head table. There, the humiliation, less comical, of a sinewy piece of roast beef quivering at the end
of my fork, tumbling to the floor to escape like a living thing. Mrs.
Thayer spoke briskly, her Brit accent brittle with sarcasm. The other
girls looked upon me with pity; or did not look upon me at all. Perhaps
I had mistaken them as predator birds. Mrs. Thayer summoned me into
her sitting room. The glare of her impatient gas-blue eyes. I could not
keep straight what I'd overheard: Mrs. Thayer had had no children, or
Mrs. Thayer had had children and they'd died in the terrible London
bombing? *What is wrong with you, Janice? Do you behave like that to annoy? To
annoy me? No, you are Mary Alice, aren't you! How can you be so slovenly?
Where is your pride? Your manners? If you are sick why don't you report to the infirmary? They are paid there to treat the sick—aren't they? Sickness is not a
housemother's responsibility thank you! A housemother has responsibility and
drudgery enough thank you! A housemother already earns her small pittance
thank you!* Discovered sleeping downstairs in the study room in my
cheap cloth coat, barefoot. My legs were sickly pale yet bristled with
fine curly brown hairs. The Kappas were indignant, legs require shaving,
like underarms, but this was a girl who feared razors and would have to
borrow (yet how could you *borrow?*) a razor blade. Upstairs, two floors
of more than forty girls. Their sinewy muscular legs shaved smooth,
skin glaring. Their armored breasts. Deodorant, hair spray, mascara, silver eye shadow. Radios, phonographs, the calypso, Ricky Nelson's
"Travelin' Man," the slamming of doors and the flushing of toilets.
Chain-smoking. More not-quite-emptied Tab and Coke cans kicked
along the corridor. Kat, Tammy, Trudi, Sandi leaning in the doorway
frowning. Without makeup they were the same girl almost. Without
makeup their young faces were pale, lumpy, puffy. Without mascara,
their eyes were naked. What did they want from me? Help with their
term papers? I stole bars of soap, but only the most worn-down bars of

soap, to wash myself clean. A soapy lather, to wash my hair. I missed meetings and so must be punished: fined: $12, $15, $18. I could not pay for I had no money, unless I stole money, but where could I steal money, pride prevented me where it didn't prevent my stealing food so long as it was garbage, not food. In the infirmary on the far side of the windswept campus when at last a nurse called my name I'd changed my mind, walked out. I couldn't miss my work at the registrar's office (though I was twenty minutes late). There they asked me in that kindly way you can't trust, was something wrong with me? This flu? Asian flu, so-called? I smiled the Kappa smile. I bared my teeth like a cheerleader. I raised my hand to ask the professor a question but when he frowned at me, clearly not wanting me to speak, my throat closed up. The trembling was under control now, it had gone inside. I shampooed my hair digging my nails into my scalp and brushed it with such ferocity it shone and crackled with electricity. And my eyes, people said were so like my father's eyes, all black: all pupil. The clever girls avoided the head table, there were seven of us seated at the head table, Mrs. Thayer refused to glance at me. When she ate, moisture glistened in her eyes. *In fact the Brit-bitch is a hog. Watch her eat sometimes.* At midterm I'd become popular, as usual. Girls came to see me smiling and pleading. It was strange: I could not complete my own work, yet I was able to glance quickly through others' work and see what was required. Errors leapt to my eye. As punishment for missing meetings, I was assigned proctor duty. Ringing the gong at five minutes before curfew. Ushering the last of the "dates" out the door. Heifer-sized boys, football players of Upsilon Beta, Lambda Alpha Chi. Their faces were covered in smeared lipstick as if they'd been devouring raw meat. They beer-belched in my face, without apology. Intestinal gases floated in their wake. It was the proctor's duty to bolt the front door, switch out the lights, clean the ashtrays, tidy up the disheveled living room where passionate Kappas and their dates of the evening had been "saying good night" sometimes for as long as two hours. (Crusted clumps of tissue wedged between cushions, wads of still-damp gum imprinted with teethmarks on the undersides of tables.) Mrs. Thayer was depending upon me as she could not depend upon the others. Mrs. Thayer had her own bottle of wine, a bitter-smelling red wine we were not supposed to know about. (The Negro house boy, flirty and sexy and of the creamy hue of Harry Belafonte, pals with certain Kappas, reported this startling fact.) I'd been showering in the third-floor bathroom, desperate to wash away the stink of cigarette smoke; the girls stared and spoke of me openly. *What's with her? She sick? Oh ignore her, she's nuts. Just wants attention, ignore her.* At curfew they returned glassy-eyed and swaying and their clothes haphazardly buttoned. Sometimes they couldn't make it to a bathroom and vomited on the stairs. Chris who'd been puking every day of her life (as her roommate complained) had dropped out of school, her shame-faced parents came to drive her away. Upstairs, the Kappa faces were pale and coarse as uncooked dough. No eyebrows, no lashes, hair twisted onto pink foam-rubber curlers. A smoke haze prevailed. Geraldine was doubled over coughing. I was in awe of the Kappa breasts worn like armor. All the breasts were D-cups jacked up in satin bras, hoisted and (sometimes) padded. Even the pixie-girls' breasts were D-cups. Breasts preceded girls into rooms. Breasts preceded the girls who bore them with shivery female pride and restrained haste, descending the spiral stairs to their staring dates. Their smooth-shaved calves shining like pewter. Underarms doused with deodorant and liberally dabbed with talcum powder. You would not recognize Kappa girls upstairs but downstairs and on campus, at fraternity parties and in taverns they emanated the Kappa look—glamorous, sexy, determined. Exuding "personality" like a lighthouse beacon flashing light. Their rooms were whirlwinds of disorder, pigsties out of which they emerged radiant and avid for romance, like the phoenix out of his flaming nest. Their lives were worn on the outside of their skin like another item of apparel. Their lives in the presence of *male persons* were fanatically prepared performances, sustained for hours at a stretch. They were such fierce actresses, they might not have known they were acting at all. They were fighting for their lives. Their goal was to become engaged before graduation. They would be married before the age of twenty-two, they would be mothers before the age of twenty-three. Some of them would be divorced before the age of thirty. I adored them. I feared them, and I loathed them, and I adored them. I did not imagine that I knew them. They spoke in code; even their shrieks of laughter were in code. The smoke curling from the sides of their mouths like exhaust from a car's tailpipe. Marble-hard sharpness of their eyes. The Kappa smile beaming *Hi! How are ya! Loveya!* Like tossing coins at beggars. As if they were worthy of such blessings. As if they were, not Kappa Gamma Pi's, a sorority of the second rank, but Chi Omegas, TriDelts, Pi Phi's, sororities of the first rank. As if they were not mainly elementary ed. majors, struggling for C's, but proudly on the dean's list. As if they weren't party girls with dubious reputations but popular Hellenic council officers, class officers, homecoming queens; as if they were respected, admired, emulated, not pursued as girls who drank, and *put out*.

I knew none of this, how could I know. Scarcely did I know what the ugly term *put out* meant.

My date Eddy sneering *Think you're hot shit, eh? You're a Kappa you put out.*

I wept when I lost my Kappa pin. My beautiful ebony-and-gilt Kappa pin. My Kappa pin that had cost me $75. My Kappa pin I could not afford. My Kappa pin with my initials engraved on it. My Kappa pin lost in the library stacks where I'd been shelving books, pushing a creaking cart for miles of poorly lit corridors as in a nightmare of comic repetition. It might have fallen off as my fingertips half-consciously caressed my A-cup breasts in terror of what they might discover. I wept for the loss of the pin; I could not replace it; my Kappa sisters were angry with me; *no one ever loses her pin.* And Mrs. Thayer staring, frowning. A sagging of her powdered jowls. She took note in silence of my reddened fingers, a scaly rash across the backs of my hands from washing them too often in the winter, in the harsh soap available in university lavatories. Deedee gave me her Jergen's lotion to rub on them but the perfumy liquid made the rash worse. *Maybe I have leprosy* I joked. *There's leprosy in my family.* Deedee's look of alarm was a warning yet my mouth continued. *My mother died of it.* In classes I took to wearing my coat and kept my scaly hands inside the sleeves. *For Descartes the universe is essentially irrational while for Spinoza the universe is essentially rational and it is the nature of the human mind to know.* And looked up to see several of my Kappa sisters in the doorway smiling at me, having forgiven me? Sweetly pleading: could I help them with their term papers? These were confused, incoherent papers interlarded with pristine passages copied from "sources" without footnote attribution. Some I would remedy piecemeal, others I would rewrite completely. It was a bonus for my Kappa sisters, as Dawn had discovered the previous year, that I could type so well. I could "think with my fingers" the girls marveled. But something happened overnight, I could not think with my fingers after all, nor even type with my fingers; I could not think with my brain; my thoughts lurched, skidded, leapt and were derailed; I couldn't concentrate; even speech became a feat, with my deadened tongue. Ideas slid away like melting snow. *Please forgive me, I can't. I haven't been able to sleep. I'm behind in my work too. I'm so afraid sometimes . . .* And there was Dawn staring coldly at me, twisting her fluorescent mouth, cursing *God damn why else d'you think you're here? Your good looks?* Stomping away in her grimy white wool socks.

Night following night the calypso music penetrating the walls. Mechanical-moronic downbeat reverberating through the floorboards. The girls sang along with the mildly pornographic lyrics, swinging their hips and breasts as they'd seen in the movies. Like spikes in the brain these words I could not escape when curfew locked me inside the Kappa house at the northern end of University Place.

> *Hey c'mon Kitch let's go to bed*
> *I gotta small comb to scratch ya head——*

> *Hey c'mon Kitch let's go to bed*
> *I gotta small comb to scratch ya head——*

In such unspeakable ways, God touched me.

3

In the end, Agnes Thayer and I left Kappa Gamma Pi within a few days of each other, in February 1963.

In the end *the end* comes swiftly!

Our housemother had received a call from the Dean of Men alerting her to the "reckless behavior" and "disregard for their own safety" of certain of the girls under her charge, at the Winter Weekend fraternity parties at Cornell; the exact identities of the girls were not known, except they were Kappas from Syracuse—"Girls with a certain reputation." Mrs. Thayer promptly summoned the most likely candidates into her sitting room, each in turn, and spoke sternly to them; and may have thought that the issue was resolved for the girls were subdued, sullen and quiet, and made no serious attempt to defend themselves. ("How the hell did I know what to say?" Mercy said. "I was so wasted all weekend, I didn't remember a thing.") It was reported through the house that Kat, a red-haired senior with a reputation for quick tantrums and crying jags, began to cry as Mrs. Thayer scolded; Mrs. Thayer took pity on her, for Kat was a very pretty, sweet-seeming girl when she made the effort;

she allowed Mrs. Thayer to take her hand, and squeeze it, and gently admonish her, "My dear, our little talk today may *save you!* You may look back upon this hour, many years from now, as a mother, or indeed a grandmother, and—" Mrs. Thayer's icy eyes suddenly brimmed with tears. "Remember Agnes Thayer kindly!" And Kat whispered, her eyelids quivering, "Ohhhh, Mrs. Thayer. I promise *I will*."

Next day Kat and her roommates took delicious revenge upon Mrs. Thayer by creeping into the parlor and tossing magazines and newspapers onto the floor; when the mail was delivered, they snatched up Mrs. Thayer's mail, including one of the airmail letters, and mutilated it, leaving the evidence on the carpet outside Mrs. Thayer's door. Other girls observed, but no one tried to stop them. If I'd been present maybe I would have . . . said something? Pleaded with them? Or would I have laughed nervously and giddily with the others? "This Brit-bitch needs to get the message," Kat said thrillingly, "—she is *not one of us*." And another time, less forcibly now, Mrs. Thayer rang her little silver bell at dinner, trembling with indignation and her eyes bluely bright with fear. Had she been drinking?—a flush in her already ruddy cheeks, a just-perceptible slurring of her words. Yet how brave the woman's tight-girdled posture, there on the sofa: "Gurls, gurls! What is this—anarchy! I demand an explanation." And there was silence; an air of resentment, verging upon mutiny; a few of the bolder girls exchanged droll glances, smirking; some girls were openly smoking, or noisily chewing gum; a number of girls hadn't obeyed Mrs. Thayer's summons at all; Kat had gone out drinking with her Deke boyfriend, and her roommates were playing rock music upstairs. Mrs. Thayer looked pleadingly at those girls she imagined were allies: kewpie-doll Lulu who was one of her favorites, big blinking innocent eyes and a mouth Mrs. Thayer could not have guessed was riotously foul, often at Mrs. Thayer's expense. But Lulu, unaccountably, was staring blankly past Mrs. Thayer's head. Again, as if on cue, as in a movie in which mere repetition is an element of comedy, the mantel clock chimed. At the back of the house the busboys laughed a little too loudly. And girls' giggles—someone must have been in the kitchen with them, a taboo zone at this hour. I hoped that Mrs. Thayer wouldn't notice me. I'd come reluctantly into the parlor, sensing disaster; I had not been feeling very well, though I'd smeared bright crimson grease onto my mouth, Deedee's lipstick, at Deedee's suggestion; I'd even allowed Deedee to smear silver-green eye shadow on my eyelids; it was being urged upon my roommate that she "do something" about me, for I was looking, my Kappa sisters thought, in their blunt, helpful way, "like shit." I was wearing my coat, however; though it was forbidden, Mrs. Thayer seemed not to have noticed; but I was very cold even indoors, and susceptible to fits of shivering; and I did not want to provoke my Kappa sisters into more disgust with me than they already felt, exposing my flat sweater front where no Kappa pin glittered. In her agitation Mrs. Thayer locked eyes with me and I understood that I had no choice. I raised my hand and said in a soft, penitent voice, "Mrs. Thayer, I—I did it." Mrs. Thayer stared at me incredulously. "*You?* You did not." Her response was unhesitating. But I persisted, softly, "I did, Mrs. Thayer. I'm truly sorry." Perplexed, Mrs. Thayer said, "But—why?" To this reasonable question I could think of no reasonable reply. I was aware of my Kappa sisters murmuring to one another; my mind was functioning slowly, in large windmill arcs. Hadn't I already confessed, a few weeks before? Why was it so unexpected that I would confess again? I heard myself say, "I—I guess I don't know why, Mrs. Thayer. An urge came over me." "An urge! To destroy mail? My mail? It's a federal offense in this country, I believe, to destroy another's mail." Mrs. Thayer was trying to speak with a vengeful air; Mrs. Thayer was trying to convince herself that I was indeed the criminal; on all sides the Kappas were regarding me with dread, embarrassment, the behavior of Kat and her roommates was widely known; it could make no sense, that I was confessing; Lulu, boldly lighting up a cigarette, her diamond engagement ring flashing, glanced at me disapproving, as if she'd never seen such a pathetic specimen in her life. *Who the hell are you? Why are you here? What are you doing among sane people?* Feeling the need to seem more convincing, I began to cry; I was unpracticed in crying, for I'd always resisted my brothers' efforts to make me cry; to make me into a girl; a weeping girl, and inferior to boys; yet I cried now sincerely, and felt my face contort like an infant's. A girl passed me a slightly used Kleenex without looking at me. At the back of the house, an eruption of laughter and a sound of breaking plates. Yet Mrs. Thayer did not seem to hear. She was staring at me, a plump hand pressed against her bosom. She wore, most days, boxy woollen suits with frilly blouses beneath. Today there was a faint stain on her white silk blouse. "Well, then. Gurls—the remainder of you, seeing that *you are innocent,*" Mrs. Thayer puffed out her cheeks, possibly trying for sarcasm but lacking the confidence, "—are *dismissed.*" And within seconds the pack of them was gone, thundering up the stairs, laughing.

There remained the stoutish woman breathing audibly, brooding upon me as I sat, penitent and stubborn, on the carpet a few feet away. At last she said, exasperated, "Elise—no, Alicia?—if you are telling the truth, and not simply protecting another girl or girls, you will have to cease this—unnatural behavior. At once! Or I will notify the Dean of Women! And if you are not telling the truth—if you are lying to me, at this moment, I—I will have to notify the Dean of Women." I was staring at Mrs. Thayer's swollen ankles. I could not bring myself to contradict her, to point out that my name was neither "Elise" nor "Alicia" nor was it a name that resembled these names. I could only repeat, quietly, "But I am telling the truth, Mrs. Thayer—what would be my motive in lying?"

The question was an appeal; yet not an appeal Mrs. Thayer could have answered. It was a question put to the Void.

Mrs. Thayer was trying to push herself up from the sofa, leaning on the armrest; her breath came short, her fleshy face was raddled and drawn with fatigue. I sprang up quickly to help her. Her weight on my arm was warm and livid. Once Mrs. Thayer had regained her feet, however, she pushed from me; her eyes shone with indignation. Turning to leave, fluttering her beringed hands, making a snorting sound of bemused disgust—"You may tidy up in here, you strange, perverse gurl. I accept your apology. But if ever you repeat such behavior, I shall notify the Dean of Women, I shall demand your expulsion from this house."

I murmured in her wake, "Yes, Mrs. Thayer."

Following that hour, neither my Kappa sisters nor Mrs. Thayer ever trusted me again.

For how could I explain to Mrs. Thayer *Better to think that there is only one responsible, and not many. Better to think that the universe is rational and you might come to know a tiny portion of its truth, however false that truth.*

Next morning I wakened in the winter dark before dawn. I was out of the prison-house before 7:00 A.M. The kitchen help was arriving but would not take notice of me. Nor would I speak to anyone. I'd avoided the upstairs of the house in order to avoid my sisters' averted eyes. I understood that my roommate, who'd lent me her makeup, who'd offered to put up my hair in rollers, had been shamed by my behavior. *And she says she has leprosy! I want another roommate. I hate her.* I'd lain on the tattered couch in the basement study room planning the remainder of my life. Or did the remainder of my life come spinning past me like a comet trailing flame. I was panicked to have lost Ida: when I tried to recall my mother, I could see only the dog-eared snapshots. I did not see a living woman, I saw the black-and-white two-dimensional snapshots my grandmother had begrudgingly allowed me to examine as a little girl. *No sticky fingers!* my grandmother had cautioned me. Yet the snapshots collected loose in the album often stuck together.

At the registrar's office in Erie Hall I was told I'd come too early. "But can't I work *now?* Isn't my work ready for me *now?*" The urgency in my voice might have alarmed the administrative assistant, a youthful middle-aged woman who'd taken an interest in me as a scholarship student, and who'd always seemed fond of me; the bond between us had been broken like a cobweb, for I'd come to work in the morning and not in the afternoon, and there was no place for me. And my hair was uncombed, my eyes unnaturally dilated, and the lids were inflamed and smeared with greasy silver-green eye shadow. Where I went next, in the sub-freezing air, as a glaring opalescent sky gradually lightened overhead, I wouldn't clearly remember. To Auburn Heights, possibly. Where a German shepherd barked excitedly at me as I stood hesitantly at the mouth of the alley lined with trash cans. A gritty snow-crust lay over everything, like hardened plastic. I did not believe I was hungry, yet I knew I should eat; yet the dog barked, barked; he was Cerberus barking me away, I had no choice but to retreat. My breath came in steaming pants and ice rivulets hardened beneath my eyes where tears ran down my cheeks. Around my head, tied like a scarf, I wore a soiled gray woollen muffler; it was of good quality, I'd found it in a carton of curbside trash on Genesee Street a few blocks from the sorority. As I walked, hiking across snowy stretches of the hilly campus, my lips moved silently. *Don't hate me! All I wanted was for both of you to be proud of me.* Not only my mother's face was fading from my memory, my father's face was fading, too. He'd been dead more than a year. Strength is required to retain the faces of the dead and my strength which I'd always taken for granted, a frantic nervous strength like a rat rushing through a maze, was draining from me. I'd written to my grandmother asking her to send me one or two snapshots of my father, but my grandmother never replied. My father's body had never been recovered; no death certificate had been sent to Strykersville, that I knew of; when one of my sorority sisters asked, as if suddenly suspicious, maybe Deedee had primed her, where my father lived, I'd said he'd gone to Smithereens. She'd asked *What?* as if she hadn't heard right and I said *He's gone to Smithereens, it's a town in the Rocky Mountains. Maybe someday your father will go there, too.*

In European Philosophy there was a girl hunched in her coat, seated in an outermost row beneath tall glaring windows. Where other students took dutiful notes, the girl stared avidly at the professor lecturing in a calm, droning voice on the problem of God's existence. Plato and Aristotle, St. Augustine, Francis Bacon and Spinoza, Voltaire, Kant and German Idealism . . . The girl's skin was luridly pale and her dark, sunken eyes unnaturally alert. She'd shoved both her fists deep into her coat pockets. She searched for a pen, the pen flew from her fingers and rolled along the worn, varnished floor. *Oh, ignore her. She's nuts. She's pathetic. Takes it all so seriously. Just wants attention.* Other students glanced at the girl warily. No one was seated near her. The lecture room was a place of abstract thought and bodiless speculation; it was not an appropriate place to bring a body, still less a body quivering with emotion. Near the end of the class when the professor invited questions, you could see his crafty eyes avoiding the girl seated beneath the window, a trembling hand raised. These were academic questions, please! No emotion, please! In a nasal, urgent, quavering but stubborn voice the girl asked what sounded like *If there is God in a book why are there so many books? Why would He manifest Himself in so many?* There was a respectful silence. The professor frowned as if he were seriously considering this question and not calculating how many more minutes before the bell rang to end the class. The girl laughed nervously. Wiped at her eyes. No one wished to look at her. Instead of addressing the class in his customary manner, while answering an individual's question, the professor stood silent regarding the girl with somber eyes; at last he said he'd speak with her after class. You could see how he'd slipped the class list out of his manila folder to glance rapidly through it; he meant to ascertain the girl's name, for in the discomfort of the moment he'd forgotten her name. One of his most brilliant, vexing undergraduates, whose papers were three times as long as papers written by her classmates, invariably A's, and—he'd forgotten her name? *Not on the list. Not on any list. Not registered at the university. Not registered in the Universe.* Class ended, at last. Relief! The sickly pale girl remained seated, no she was managing to stand, in the aisle beneath a tall glaring window like a deranged eye of God smiling uncertainly to herself; a girl in an overcoat, so you wouldn't see her small girl-breasts lacking a Kappa pin to redeem their smallness; a girl rumored to *put out;* yet hardly knowing what *put out* must be, except something very ugly. An action involving, afterward, stiff crusted wads of tissue. The professor was waiting at the front of the room to speak quietly with her, his worried eyes drifting on and about her, but the girl failed to come forward; she moved her lips, silently, and she smiled; she was a quarrelsome girl, and too damned smart for her own good; everyone in her family, plus farm neighbors, relatives said this of her *Too damned smart for her own good;* the professor, placing his papers in his briefcase, snapping the briefcase shut, was pretending now not to notice the girl at the edge of his vision; possibly, in the exigency of the moment, for another student was coming forward to speak with him, he'd actually ceased to be aware of her.

Biting my lip to keep from shouting my name. But suddenly I didn't know my name.

Dunes of windswept snow. The dying elms barren of leaves now in continual contorted motion, their upper branches especially, in the wind. In overcoats and hooded jackets we hurried. We were young: herded by our elders like cattle. The weakest of us would stagger and fall and be forgotten. At dusk the parkland median of University Place continued to emit a dull glowering magical snow-light while the sky, massed as usual with clouds, identical clouds I'd seen the previous day, was heavy as a ceiling about to collapse. *Fraternity row*. The professor would never have understood. (Or would he have understood?) Even at this time of defeat and disintegration I felt the old thrill of romance, helpless romance, seeing the large houses, and lights in every window, from a distance. And the Kappa house at the far, northern end with its stately ghost-white Doric columns illuminated by a floodlight, its high-pitched roof like an illustration in a child's storybook, the promise of warmth within. Even now.

Though I had passed many times by the spot where the man with the black-rimmed glasses had approached me with a juvenile taunt of titties, the man had never reappeared. His pale ghost lingered, at a distance. I looked for him, the abrupt surprise of him, his poky little tongue and steaming breath, I was both fearful and hopeful of seeing him, as one takes a perverse comfort in repetition, an affirmation of identity at least; but the fierce, cold weather had banked his ardor; my unfeminine behavior had discouraged his sentimental notion of *girl*. I'd been thinking of him as near-blind and groping without his glasses but of course he'd gotten new glasses long ago.

Will you have sugar? Cream? Dreaming with open, dry eyes I smiled until my mouth ached pouring tea into heirloom Wedgwood cups reserved for such special occasions; I was but one of several tea- and coffee-pourers; with my scaly nail-bitten fingers I handed out small silver teaspoons and small linen napkins monogrammed ΚΓΠ. The public rooms of the Kappa house were transformed: tall urns of white flowers, roses, carnations, gardenias, even tulips; at the Steinway piano, an older Kappa alum named Marilynne was playing stormy Liszt alternating with Broadway show tunes. It was the annual WELCOME BACK KAPPAS! reception. The guests were alums, some of whom had driven or flown long distances, as well as a number of selected university women designated as *honorary Kappas* for the evening; there were only a few of these, for few women were on the university faculty; predominant among them was the Dean of Women, a friend of Agnes Thayer's, or at least an ally in the ceaseless struggle to maintain standards of ladylike behavior in the face of determined assaults by *male persons*. The Dean of Women was a heavy-set individual with slabs of chin, pancake cheeks and merry, suspicious eyes; she wore a heather-colored tweed suit with a jacket that barely contained her sloping shelf of a bosom. The Dean of Women was the threat Mrs. Thayer and other residence housemothers wielded, for the Dean of Women had the power to expel female students from the university "for cause." Rumors were rife of her harsh judgments, which were cloaked in smiles, and a concern for "proper procedure." When the Dean of Women came through the line, given tea, cream and sugar, it seemed to me that she fixed her gaze upon me with a knowing little twitch of her mouth. *Are we acquainted, my dear? Yes?* Before the reception, I'd quickly showered upstairs, for my body exuded an odor of something damp, like toadstools; I had not had time to wash my thick, snarled hair, but it was partly damp, or perhaps I was perspiring, tendrils stuck to my forehead like deranged commas. Of course I'd had to remove my coat: my Kappa sisters were heartily tired of that ugly coat: I was wearing a "good" wool dress someone had lent me, and around my neck to disguise my thinness and the absence of my Kappa pin the woollen muffler which in the bustle of the reception and the flickering candlelight might have been mistaken for an elegant silk-woollen scarf.

So many women! So many names! Faces! And most of these Kappas. Many of the alums were young, stylish, good-looking women who'd graduated from the university within the past ten years; others were well into their thirties, and others were well into middle age but all were bonded: the Kappa pin, ebony and gilt, with the tiny gold chain, proudly worn above their left breasts like a jeweled nipple. How inadequate I felt: a freak among normal females. Some of the women had maintained youthful, even voluptuous figures but many had grown plump, stout, fattish, fat. My older Kappa sisters, skilled at such receptions, moved among the women smiling happily and shaking hands vigorously. *The purpose of our annual alumni tea: to forge strong links between alums and actives, to renew our bond of sisterhood, and TO HAVE A TERRIFIC TIME!* We younger Kappas were not to be trusted to mingle with the well-to-do alums; the most charming, good-looking Kappas had been assigned to these women, whose names were sacrosanct in the Syracuse chapter for their generous donations in past years. There was Mrs. K___ whose husband was chairman of the board of G___; there was Mrs. T___ whose husband was an investment banker with ___ Trust; there was Mrs. B___ whose husband owned T___ Realtors; there, seated on a settee in a corner of the festive living room, a half-dozen beaming young Kappas paying court to her, was the legendary Mrs. D__ whose daughter had been a Kappa Class of '45 who'd died shortly after graduation and so in honor of the girl Mrs. D__ had established a million-dollar legacy for the Syracuse chapter of Kappa Gamma Pi. It was understood that Mrs. D__ would remember the chapter in her will, but Mrs. D__ would not be the only alum, and we'd been warned not to "underestimate" any of the older women no matter how ordinary they might appear to the untrained eye. None of these scruples were my concern at the present, for sophomores exclusively were serving; we'd been drilled at length in "proper behavior" by our social director Judi as well as the ubiquitous Mrs. Thayer, who had also supervised an exhausting five-hour bout of silver polishing by our overworked housekeeper Geraldine, the day before.

Remember, we were grimly warned, you are a Kappa. At all times.

We were instructed to move about gracefully with heavy silver trays bearing Wedgwood plates of petit fours, hot buttered scones and other delicate pastries; uncertain of ourselves as waitresses, we smiled without pause. Especially, I smiled. I would not think of my terrifying near-breakdown in philosophy class but of exalted, abstract philosophical queries. *If there is God are we in God? If there is God how can we not be in God? Yet in God now? Here, in the Kappa house at 91 University Place? In the belly of the beast?* Distinguished elders from Plato to Spinoza, from Aristotle to Nietzsche would have paled at these shrieks of female laughter like ripping silk. The humming buzzing confusion of William James's universe would be drowned out by these raised ecstatic Kappa voices. The air was porous and intoxicating with perfume, powder, hair spray. We lived in a robust era of American military vigilance abroad, the ceaseless scrutiny of "atheistic communism" that would soon erupt in a cataclysmic war with a remote Far East nation allegedly

Communist-threatened, about which no one in this gathering knew the most elementary facts; it was a heady macho era, and yet an era of voluptuous female figures and bouffant hairstyles teased and tormented and lacquered to the sheen of hornets' nests, like those heraldic heads on ancient scrolls and on the walls of ancient tombs. Little wonder that dainty pastries and cups of sweetened tea and coffee were being consumed with appetite on all sides. To reproduce the species, one must be fertile; to be fertile, one must eat. Only I, at the center of my attenuated universe, had no appetite. It was Spinoza who seemed to wish to believe *Things could have been produced by God in no other manner and in no other order than they have been produced.* I saw in a flash that I might revolutionize all of philosophy by daring to ask *Why do you wish to believe what you claim to believe?* Breathing open-mouthed, dazed by my sudden brilliance, I foresaw that such an inquiry would meet with hostility from (male) philosophers; and all philosophers were (male); though never once in all of classic philosophy is a penis acknowledged, let alone the concept *penis.* My inquiry would meet with hostility because it presupposed that there were purely contingent factors in life having little, or nothing, to do with philosophical speculation, only to do with the haphazard motions of individuals desperately seeking to survive. Only survive! I doubted that I would have Spinoza's stubborn integrity: offered a "decent" winter coat in place of my old, shamefully worn coat, would I have declined, as Spinoza famously declined such an offer? My hand shook, offering a Wedgwood teacup to DEBBI JACKSON '49 TROY NY.

DEBBI JACKSON raised her voice to be heard over the din asking me in girlish complicity did I just love living in the Kappa house, what a great weird old house it is, fond memories of "saying good night" for hours in the living room, how'd I like being a Kappa active, and my smile deepened, I raised my voice to say Yes, I liked my life here very much, I was very happy here except, and DEBBI JACKSON leaned forward inquiring Yes, what? and I heard myself murmur that I wasn't certain that I belonged in Kappa Gamma Pi, I thought it was "maybe morally wrong of me." DEBBI JACKSON and a sister alum smiled at me perplexed asking Why? Whyever? and I stammered, "Because I'm— I have—I think I have—Jewish blood."

There. It was said.

Yet DEBBI JACKSON and JOAN "FAX" FAXLANGER '52 continued to smile, somewhat perplexed. There were but two modes of social-Kappa expression: the happy smile and the look of vague perplexity. DEBBI, or JOAN, asked me what I'd said, can hardly hear yourself think in here, and I said, louder than I meant, "—Jew, I think. I am Jewish. I think." Now a cascade of words tumbled from my lips like soapy-dirty water from a broken, overflowing clothes washer: I explained to these older, adult Kappa sisters that I had reason to believe that I might be *one-quarter Jewish;* I had reason to believe that my father's parents were German Jews who'd craftily changed their name to disguise their background, and to throw off their pursuers, and—"Kappa Gamma Pi blackballs Jews on the first ballot, don't we?" DEBBI JACKSON and JOAN "FAX" FAXLANGER stared at me as if I'd shouted obscenities into their attractive powdered faces; blushing, they shook their heads in a tactful pretense of deafness, refused to meet my eye or even each other's eyes in their haste to escape; teetering in their pointy-toed high-heeled pumps they bore cups, plates, linen napkins to another part of the crowded room as if indeed they hadn't heard my outburst, and the bizarre exchange had never occurred. A vigilant senior fiercely waved me back to my duty as a tea-pourer at the head table.

There, I was badly needed. Even with my clumsy skills, pasteboard face and distraught manner. Even perspiring beneath the arms of the "good" wool dress not my own, not adorned with the Kappa pin. For new guests were arriving, a flood of more Kappa alums, more faces, smiles, name tags. As the reception progressed, alums were becoming conspicuously stouter, ruddier-faced, with jutting breasts and water-melon hips, piercing brass voices and blinding jewelry; some wore fash-ionable suits adorned with fur trim like living, captive creatures. The din of their voices and laughter rose to a fever pitch, yet continued to rise. I saw Mrs. Thayer covertly observing me from her position of honor at the table, as she was observing all the younger Kappas; she must have been deceived by my neon smile, and my mimicry of "proper behavior"; I had programmed myself like a windup doll, with only a sin-gle (unheard, unreported) outburst to my discredit; it was a principle of the Spinozan universe that all was predetermined; predestined; no swerve of chance or free will was possible, or perhaps desirable. If I kept my thoughts in order, like a beekeeper delivering bees to the hive, I could perform brilliantly, I would not be stung to death. And yet: the *tick-tick-ticking* somewhere inside my ear canals. My shaky hands, with not-entirely-clean fingernails. The rashes on my knuckles some whis-pered was a symptom of leprosy. The bedraggled gray muffler dangling about my neck like a useless noose; why? I refused to consider that morning's philosophy class, I cringed in shame wondering at my behav-ior; for it had not been "proper" behavior; it had not been "sane"—"san-itary"—behavior. Through my lifetime, I would recall the look of alarm, pity, dismay in the professor's eyes; his realization that he had a mad girl in his tutelage, which was the last thing he wanted; he was a professor of words, and not human beings; he'd collided with his own briefcase in his haste to leave the lecture hall. And yet I adored him. Or I wished to believe I adored him. Frontally, the man had a stolid, noble head given further dignity by a neatly trimmed pewter beard; in profile, the man had a chin that melted away, and the beard was a pasted-on wisp you could see through.

Were Plato's eternal forms transparent, or solid? No commentator in more than twenty centuries had taken up this query.

I was distracted by the happy din of female voices. I saw with alarm that the crystal chandeliers, sheer Venetian glass, quivered. My arms ached (pleasantly, normally) as I continued to lift the surprisingly heavy teapot to pour, pour, pour. To pour Earl Grey tea (Mrs. Thayer's choice) without dribbling it, as Mrs. Thayer had sternly cautioned, onto the "heirloom" Irish linen tablecloth so rarely unfurled from storage in the mahogany sideboard. I was having to *introduce* alums to actives; actives to alums; no one especially sought me out for this honor, which happened more or less by chance; yet, like an understudy in a play, called upon suddenly to perform, I found myself performing, to a degree. The proper motions of the hands, the proper words to be uttered in the proper tone, "polite but not obsequious, gurls!" Mrs. Thayer had tirelessly rehearsed us in the "nearly forgotten art" of introductions. Never did one say carelessly, like most Americans, *I'd like you to meet __ ;* instead one said *May I present __ ?* Always, a gentleman is presented *to* a lady; a younger woman *to* an elder woman. (The very same principle that determined who preceded whom through a doorway.) Each of us murmured numerous times *May I present __ ?* and *May I present __ ?* Of course, Mrs. Thayer's clipped Brit accent was beyond our powers of emulation, like the flash of her wonderful blue eyes. We spoke only American English, a degraded, bastardized dialect; many of us had flat, nasal, upstate New York accents, hideous to Mrs. Thayer's refined ear as fingernails scraped on a blackboard. The poor woman had winced innumerable times hearing my speech and making everyone (including me) laugh, by saying she supposed we gurls didn't speak so barbarically on purpose.

This past week there'd been sly hints in Mrs. Thayer's hearing that one day "soon" the chapter would vote her an "honorary Kappa." This great honor visited upon a few, but only a few, of sorority housemothers on campus: the girls in their charge would thank them for being wonderful by voting them "honorary members" of their respective sororities. Of course, this was not going to happen at Kappa Gamma Pi. The rumor had been cruelly started by Kat and her friends to raise Mrs. Thayer's expectations and to inflate her sense of herself.

That Brit-bitch. She's gonna get what she deserves.

Unsuspecting how every undergraduate Kappa, with the helpless exception of one, despised her, Mrs. Thayer had dressed splendidly for the reception in her electric-blue nubby woollen suit that fitted her tight as sausage casing at the hips, the most desperately frilly of her silk blouses, a pearl stickpin, pearl earrings and that brave enamelled smile. Did the woman sense that, despite the rumor that she would "soon" be an honorary Kappa, time was rapidly running out for her? Tick-tick-ticking like the mantel clock? Blindly I smiled in her direction and saw her eyes go opaque in a pretense of unseeing. In a corner of the room, bearing replenished plates of pastries, DEBBI JACKSON and JOAN "FAX" FAXLANGER and an older, plumper alum sister regarded me broodingly. This was not a Kappa expression: brooding. I saw their sticky lips move, I saw their offended eyes.

Jew? Who?

Jew? *Here?*

Where?

Her?

I shivered, sweating under my arms. An aphorism of Nietzsche's I had thought exaggerated and melodramatic now coursed through my brain like an electric current. *Not their love, but the impotence of their love keeps today's Christians from—burning us at the stake.* Yet I continued undaunted to pour Earl Grey tea skillfully into an infinity of delicate china cups. If my philosophy professor, doubting my sanity, could see me now! Had the glacier-tormented New York State landscape shifted, and the entire female half of the population begun to funnel through this room, in an unbroken line past this table, I would have continued to pour, pour. I had decided that life is probably mostly a matter of memorized words in sequence; words, gestures, smiles and handshakes, in a certain sequence; life is not as the great philosophers taught in their loneliness, not a matter of essences pared back to theorems, propositions, syllogisms and conclusions, but instead a matter of mouthing the correct word-formulae in the correct setting. Maybe it wasn't so serious, after all: life? Maybe it wasn't worth dying for.

Traded your life for a daughter. Am I that daughter?

There came Mrs. Thayer like a listing ship. The older the Kappa sisters, the more genuinely they seemed to like Mrs. Thayer. The younger were less demonstrative. These were the women who paid Mrs. Thayer's salary. These were the women upon whose whimsical goodwill her employment depended. As the reception swelled, Mrs. Thayer had been observed greedily drinking tea laced with sugar and cream, and devouring pastries with unseemly avidity; strands of crumbs gathered like beads on her bosom. Though she mingled with the guests, taking care to appear to recall old, beloved faces, her true attention was on the food and drink; her eyes glistened. Here was a woman who loved sweets, that was Mrs. Thayer's secret. One of her secrets. She was a greedy, anxious woman, tightly girdled to constrain and deny her greed. And a secret drinker, it was more and more openly rumored. *Smell Thayer's breath! Thinks she can hide it chewing mints.*

More pointedly now Mrs. Thayer was moving in my direction. Under the pretext of carrying a tray into the kitchen I turned from her, collided with a large warm body and nearly dropped the tray, rallied quickly, though losing a cup that tumbled to the floor; a senior Kappa deftly snatched the tray from my weakening hands, with a hard smile; I moved off, reasoning that my Kappa duty was over for the day. I would slip away upstairs. I would hide in the third-floor bathroom. I would shower frantically to remove all smells from my body, I would shave my body with a borrowed razor, I would slash my carotid artery neatly and without sentiment, I would shampoo my shameful hair. I would stuff tiny wads of tissue into my ears and read, for the third or fourth time, David Hume's *Enquiry Concerning Human Understanding* with the conviction that it would change my life. But at the foot of the stairs there stood our vigilant chapter president who wheeled me about by the elbow and marched me into the deafening hive of the living room where an alum was playing a simplified rendition of "Rhapsody in Blue." I was led to meet several smiling alums defined by "a love of poetry"—or was it "a love of pottery"—and I shook hands with them, a giddy smiling little group uncertain of our subject until pert five-foot D-cup blond-bouffant TONI ELLIS '52 PLATTSBURG NY inquired of me how did I like living in the sorority house, isn't it a great old house, so much tradition, ever seen the ghost?—and I wasn't sure I'd heard correctly so I smiled and nodded. Other questions were pitched to me, for some confused minutes we spoke of the "Kappa ghost" (of which possibly I'd heard but had discounted immediately for there was no place in my fiercely rational imagination for such nonsense) who was believed to be the millionaire's elderly widow who'd once lived in the house and had died in 1938, and somehow I heard myself say that with my background I could not believe in superstition, I was biting my thumbnail confessing that I did not believe I belonged in Kappa Gamma Pi, a Christian sorority, I was an imposter in this gathering; and these older Kappa sisters laughed thrilled as if I'd said something witty, it might have been my face, people wished to believe that I was being witty and not something else. TONI ELLIS asked, Why? Whyever did I think I was an imposter? and I said, "I'm not a Christian and Kappa Gamma Pi is for just

Christian girls—no Jews—but no Negroes either—isn't it?" I faltered, the women stared so blankly at me. "But—of course—a Negro girl might be Christian, but—that wouldn't be sufficient cause for her to be pledged a Kappa—I guess?" By this time I was pleading to be understood, it little mattered what I'd said or had tried to say. LUCI ANNE REEVES '59 AMHERST NY was so startled, she'd spilled milky tea on the bosomy front of her dusty-rose cashmere suit.

We were an island of consternation amid a sea of innocently festive voices and laughter. I could not think of an apology. For in truth I didn't feel apologetic but defiant. I was defiant! I'd been wiping my eyes with the back of my hand and had smeared silvery green eye shadow onto my cheeks. I turned and left the Kappa alums gaping in my wake, my heart was pounding as it had when I'd been chased out of the alley behind the day-old bakery, or barked away by the German shepherd protecting his master's turf. I stumbled in high heels, I panted through my mouth like a broken, defeated boxer whose legs unaccountably have kept him erect through an infinity of rounds, I foresaw that I would shortly be expelled from Kappa Gamma Pi—within the week, in fact—my scandalized sisters would call an emergency meeting in the ritual room downstairs, one by one they would stand and denounce me in tremulous, valiant voices, they would cast their ballots, unprecedented in the chapter's rocky history a sophomore Kappa would be *de-activated*.

This I foresaw clearly. Almost, I could hear the Kappa whispers rising to a din of loathing. *She was never one of us! Lied to get pledged, and lacks even the decency to sustain the lie.* I foresaw that I would be de-activated not because I was part Jewish (if in fact I was "part Jewish") but because the Kappas, masters of deceit, would not want a clumsily deceitful girl in their sorority. They would not want a girl whose mother was not only deceased but disfigured. They would not want a farm girl from Strykersville, New York, a girl who had somehow managed to receive a scholarship and whose grade-point average was A and yet who had failed to help as many of her Kappa sisters academically as she might have done if she hadn't had a breakdown. They would not want so selfish a girl. They would not want a girl with a leper's rash. A girl $322 in debt to the sorority (dues, fees, fines) and only barely able to pay the monthly bill for room and board. A girl with clothing from Sears, and an A-cup bosom. Yet in my distraught state I seemed to know (for always, however agitated, debased, distraught I have been, I've been shrewd enough to calculate how to turn my predicament to my advantage) that, formally *de-activated* by Kappa Gamma Pi, I would be eligible to re-enter an undergraduate women's residence; the Dean of Women might take pity on me, and make arrangements. I would move into one of the modest residence halls, fit for financially disadvantaged scholarship students; at the far end of the campus from the fraternity and sorority houses; I would be happy; if not happy, I would be free of deceit, which is perhaps the same thing.

Then, this happened.

I could not escape upstairs to an *Enquiry Concerning Human Understanding* for my way was blocked by a bevy of Kappa sisters on the stairs, I found myself in the parlor blindly pushing open the door to Mrs. Thayer's private quarters as if, in the midst of this confusion, our Brit housemother was there beckoning me inside. *Come in, dear! You can hide with me.* Quickly I shut the door. I had not been seen—had I? This action of mine was so reckless, so unprecedented in my prescribed behavior, I could not believe at first that *I was where I was,* in taboo territory. I may have smiled, as a child smiles in treacherous circumstances. Deeply I breathed in Mrs. Thayer's unique scent: that odor of lavender, hair spray, underarm deodorant, and something yeasty-sweet like bakery. I was very excited. I was having difficulty breathing. I understood that never in his lifetime had the saintly Spinoza behaved so rashly; so without

reason; so without concern for consequences. And yet: this reckless behavior of mine was predetermined, as the conclusion of a syllogism is
predetermined given its terms. *All of human life is tautological, an organic
syllogism.* This astonishing insight, like others I'd had since philosophy
class that morning, flashed through my mind like an electric current,
and was gone.

Like an enthralled child I was gazing about Mrs. Thayer's sitting
room, as she called it. Disappointingly small it seemed, in the woman's
absence. And not so attractive: fussily oppressive, with a fecundity of
"feminine" objects. There, the rose-velvet settee (upon which I'd never
been invited to sit, like Freddie, Lulu, Kat, and others); there, a pair of
plushed, faded Queen Anne chairs; Wedgwood figurines, embroidered
pillows, a lacquered Chinese screen leaning against a wall, reproductions of Constable landscapes misty, or fading, in the half-light. Eagerly I
examined what I took to be photographs of Mrs. Thayer's family, on a
bureau. These were photographs of an era that preceded my mother's,
in stark black and white and with a look of the grave about them; sad
hopeful doomed individuals of a bygone world. Was there something
distinctly English—"Brit"—about these people? I could not see it. Most
were fair-skinned, ordinary-looking; two or three specimens were
dark-haired, dark-complected, reminding me uneasily of myself.
("Jewish blood"?) I examined a photograph (dated 1919) in which a
child of about six (Agnes Thayer?) stood stiffly posed outdoors between
a plump, rumpled woman and a rail-thin man with drooping whiskers
and shoulders (Mrs. Thayer's parents?). Long dead now. And little Agnes
herself prematurely adult-looking in layers of dour clothing, frowning
worriedly at the camera. Another, more lively snapshot showed Agnes
as a girl of about sixteen, not a girl one would call pretty (at least in
America, in the Sixties), but good-looking; with a busty figure, hands
on her solid hips, regarding the camera at a cocky angle. *Here I am, look*

at me. This is my season to bloom. A girl in a rakish costume, long flared skirt, bolero jacket, a man's cap on her head, a girl who thought well of herself or wished to be so perceived. And yet: this girl had not realized she was posing before a dingy, crumbling brick wall, in the background laundry on a line. Puddles on the ground shone as if after a spring shower. How many decades ago those puddles had evaporated! I'd picked up the framed photograph to stare and my vision blurred with moisture. *We might have been friends. My older sister.* Even more intriguing was a pastel-colored wedding photograph framed in mother-of-pearl of Agnes Thayer as a bride, a mature bride in her thirties, wearing an oddly shiny white satin suit with boxy shoulders and a pert little hat and veil; close beside her, standing with an arm around her waist, was a tall spindly-limbed boyish man in a dark suit plain as an undertaker's, white carnation in his lapel like a protruding bone. This was Mr. Thayer, the "American army officer" to whom Mrs. Thayer so often alluded, with an air of self-importance——he'd been younger than Agnes! He had a narrow horsey face, thinning hair, prominent ears, and a tucked-in charming smile. A boy who may have stammered at times but who was sweet, "witty." What could these two have possibly had in common? Generally it was believed among the contemptuous Kappas that our housemother had had no children. So this couple was fated not to have children? Yet they didn't know, in the photograph. I felt a tinge of melancholy, regarding the photograph. Agnes Thayer and her young husband had loved each other, enough to be married; even if their love wore out, or was revealed as delusion, yet it had been love at the time of this photograph; and this love had ended with his death. And now it was years later and the smiling bride was a widow, a housemother in an American sorority the majority of whose members hated her, and were gleefully conspiring to get her fired. *If only you'd known, Agnes! Never to come to America.*

Carefully I replaced the photographs on the bureau. On the very spaces, defined by outlines of faint dust, they'd been resting. I intended now to leave this risky place, yet—I pushed open the door to Mrs. Thayer's bedroom instead. Perhaps I reasoned I might escape by the rear, where no one was likely to see me except the kitchen help. Here, the talcumy lavender smell was more concentrated, underlaid by a more powerful odor of stale food, sweetness. What a small, cramped room this was! The size of my room back in Strykersville. It was dominated by a high double bed with a vibrant blue satin quilt and a mirrored bureau and more framed photographs, several of Mr. Thayer in a more mature, jowly mode. The man was nearly bald and wore rimless glasses and his smile for the camera was strained. *Leave me be, can't you? I'm perfectly content, dead.* I knew that I should leave this place, I was trembling with the audacity of what I did; yet, so strangely, I switched on a light, opened the closet door, inhaled a briny-sweet fragrance of perfume and sachet. I marveled at Mrs. Thayer's clothes on their wire hangers, how familiar each of them was, familiar to me as my own. And she had few clothes, crowded into the narrow closet; yet she'd costumed herself for us with such flair, such bravery, with an assortment of scarves and other "accessories." I touched the sleeve of a beige jersey dress with a pleated bodice, lifted it to my face. A dread, thrilling sensation ran through me as if Mrs. Thayer herself had lifted her hand to touch me. I pleaded *Why did you never like me? Why did you repel me? Wasn't I the one who read* Punch? *Did you never see how I adored you? Had you always seen through me, an imposter?*

Next, I rummaged through bureau drawers. Stockings, undergarments, a flesh-colored latex corset that squirmed at my touch as if alive. The scent of lavender was suffocating. In a bottom drawer I discovered a cache of airmail letters: fascinating to one so naive, to see how the small sheet of tissue-thin blue paper opened out into a rectangle, as in a child's game. The spidery hand of the sister in Leeds, the fading blue ink. *Dearest Agnes* I squinted to read, lifting the letter to the light. *You will want to*—I couldn't decipher the maddeningly small, cramped words—*as of last month*—another indecipherable phrase—*her final days were serene after the Hell of years & will it please you never once did she speak of you?* These words penetrated my heart, quickly I refolded the letter as if it were precious, and hid it away in the drawer. I was trembling badly now but could not seem to stop what I was doing. *You American gurl!* I yanked open a cupboard drawer and an empty bottle rolled—Gordon's Gin. I saw a colorfully decorated tin marked FORTNAM & MASON: I pried off the lid to discover a half-dozen wrapped toffees. Also in the cupboard was a wedge of chocolate nut fudge wrapped in aluminum foil. I broke off a piece of this fudge and tasted it and the concentration of sugar made my mouth ache. Though I would have said of myself, now I was grown up, I'd lost my taste for sweet things, yet I broke off another piece of the stale fudge, and another. My mouth watered with saliva like rushing churning ants. I opened another cupboard—here was Mrs. Thayer's cache of gin, wine, bourbon. There were a half-dozen bottles, most of them about half-full. I recalled, with the force of an old, bittersweet dream, my lonely father sitting at the kitchen table late into the night, in my grandparents' farmhouse; every room was darkened, except this room; he was still youngish, though with thinning hair and downturned eyes and the disfigured hand; unshaven, in an undershirt and soiled work trousers; elbows on the faded oilcloth, a bottle of whisky and a glass beside him; a Camel burning in his stained fingers; the overhead light casting crevice-like shadows downward onto his brooding yet somehow peaceful face. I saw that *Where he is, no one can follow.* And there was a kind of peace, too, in this realization. For there was no point in trying to follow my father—or my mother—to wherever they'd gone. A child stood in a darkened doorway in a flannel nightgown, barefoot. Watching, yearning. A childhood of yearning. And thinking now, in Agnes Thayer's bedroom smelling of lavender and gin, what solace must be in drink, drunkenness, utter secrecy, solitude. I had never understood that alcoholism is a condition of the soul: a hiding place, a shelter beneath evergreen boughs heavy with snow. You crawled inside, and no one could follow.

"You!—what are you doing here? How dare you?"

I turned in terror to see Mrs. Thayer in the doorway behind me, staring with widened incredulous eyes. She too had escaped the Kappa festivities. She'd entered her suite from the rear. For a long moment I was paralyzed; a wave of horror passed over me, like filthy water; yet I felt too a kind of relief; for now it was over between us, or nearly. Mrs. Thayer strode to the cupboard and shoved in the drawers with such force that the bottles clattered together. In her bulging eyes I saw fury. Loathing and fear. "Bloody beastly *gurl! Sick disgusting gurl!* Out of my room, out! Out!" Yet when I moved to ease past her, Mrs. Thayer struck at me; grabbed at me; clung to both my arms, beginning to cry. I could smell the fumes of her labored breath. Her powdered face was streaked with tears, rivulets like acid in the caked powder. I tried to speak, but my throat had shut tight. I was helpless as a child trapped in terror; in desperation trying to escape by crawling across Mrs. Thayer's bed but the older woman seized me in her arms that, though fattish and flaccid, were surprisingly strong, and she held me fast, sobbing angrily, "—of all the gurls! These demon gurls! Only you I could trust! In this hellish place only you! And now! How could you! Betray me! You are a pawn, a pawn in their bloody game! Run, run for your life!" Mrs. Thayer's voice rose in hysteria, her words were senseless for even as she cried for me to run for my life she was clutching me against her, we were two swimmers drowning together; her arms so tight around me, I was in terror of suffocating. Sobbing, cursing, so terribly strong for a woman of her age, I struggled against her crazed and yet unable to break her grip, in that instant I felt the madness rush out of me like dirty water and into Mrs. Thayer. I could not have named her: only she was *she,* the female, smelling of talcum, sweet wine, sweaty desperation, this person clutching at me. Uncontrollably she wept, knocking her head against my head, suddenly I was too weak to struggle, I ceased to resist. My face was contorted like an infant's though I could not cry, I had no tears left, I was a child, penitent, a child who has been punished, my heart broken. Beyond the bed as in a nightmare scenario faces had gathered aghast and avid in the doorway—my Kappa sisters. At first there were only a few, then more faces crowded in, and yet more. Astonished glittering eyes, bouffant heads bobbing like cobras' heads. Moist parted scandalized lipsticked lips. Behind these, yet more pushed forward eager to see. Kappas! Their thrilled sibilant voices lifted like the winds that blow across our glacier-tortured hills. *What is it? What has happened? What are those two doing? Who is that girl—the Jew?*

II.

THE NEGRO-LOVER

I will analyze the actions and
appetites of men as if it were a question of
lines, of planes, and of solids.

1   Spinoza

The danger of falling in love, in winter.

2

. . . a voice of logic, reason, conviction; a voice of irony, cajoling; a
seductive voice; an arrogant voice; a young impetuous voice; a voice of
occasional hesitation, uncertainty; a voice that provoked, annoyed, be-
set like the bared teeth of an attack dog; a shrewd voice; a *Now just listen
to me, I'm the one to tell you* voice; a voice of humility; a voice of (mock)
humility; a voice sharp and cruel as a knifeblade; a voice like warm but-
ter; a low throaty trombone voice; a voice of hurt; a voice of sorrow; a
voice of pain; a voice of yearning; a voice of rage; a voice sinewy and sly
as a glimpsed glittering snake; a voice I would have wished for myself if
I'd been born *male,* and not *female;* a voice I did wish for myself though
born not *male* but *female;* a voice that so seeped into my consciousness
that it began to emerge in the late winter of my second year at the university in my most vivid, ravaging and exhausting dreams.

3

Deceptive from the start: he lived in the most ordinary of places. Very quickly I saw, I'd tracked him to his lair. A second-floor rear apartment in a squat three-story lard-colored stucco apartment building at 1183 Chambers Street, Syracuse. In this "mixed" neighborhood beyond the showy complex of university hospital buildings; in the harsh shadow of new, cheaply stylish high-rise buildings and multi-level parking garages; a sublunary region of small storefront businesses, shamefaced wood frame houses partitioned into rooms for university students, many dark-skinned and foreign. *There can be no beauty here, therefore no hurt and no hope.*

Chambers Street was one of the most cruelly steep hills in the vicinity of the university; cars parked with their wheels turned shrewdly inward to the curb; the pavement was cracked and potholed and littered; a number of the curbside elms, blighted by Dutch elm disease, had been chainsawed into oblivion, only their stumps remained. Yet Chambers Street was a place of fascination and romance. Yet Chambers Street had entered my imagination. Imprinted in my brain like an ink stain on something white, moist, boneless as a mollusc was the facade of the stucco building at 1183 Chambers: I understood that it was not beautiful, nor did it possess even the diminished melancholy of those dream-like city buildings painted by Edward Hopper; it was a purely functional setting, a place of mere expediency; the sign beside the front entrance never changed, as if to confirm its futility—APTS FOR RENT INQUIRE WITHIN. My sharp eye took note of a row of badly stained and battered metal garbage cans at the curb; a shingled roof that looked as if it must leak; a fractured concrete walk leading to the front entrance, but also forking around the side of the building to the rear, and to a flight of outdoor steps that led to the second floor of the building; a stairway of raw planks with a makeshift roof. Up those stairs he sometimes climbed.

I told myself *I am only just passing through this neighborhood, I have a true destination.*

In those months I walked everywhere, I was restless, a prowler. Never did I walk on University Place, though. I'd been cured of the Kappas. I'd been cured of my Kappa-yearnings forever. My walking, wayward and seemingly improvised, took me often to the eastern edge of the sprawling campus, though my residence hall was in another direction. Sometimes I passed 1183 Chambers twice: there might be a plausible reason for twice. Sometimes I passed 1183 Chambers three times, for which there could be no plausible reason. And so I walked swiftly, guiltily. Eyes averted from the object of my interest. I had no way of knowing if he was home unless light shone through his windows, and I had no way of knowing if light shone through his windows unless I went around to the rear of the building, at twilight or after dark; though solitary walking by young women in this part of Syracuse was discouraged. (Once, a patrol car slowed at the curb, its occupants stared at me without expression as quickly I continued to walk glancing toward them with a small frightened smile *I am a good girl, I am a university student, don't arrest me!*) To linger in the vicinity of 1183 Chambers was tricky, for he might be on his way home and might recognize me; if he recognized me, I might not know since, given his secrecy and arrogance, he would not have allowed me to know that he'd recognized me; and so I would not know if in his eyes I'd been exposed, or if, in fact, he'd taken not the slightest notice of me, and so I remained innocent. Sometimes, seeing a man approaching on the sidewalk, I panicked and fled into the trash-littered alley; sometimes this was the very alley beside 1183 Chambers, and I was forced to pass close by the outdoor wooden stairs; so suddenly tempted to climb those stairs, or to sit on the lower stairs as if I belonged there. Usually he entered the building from the front, to get his mail I supposed, for there were rows of battered metal mailboxes just inside the foyer, with names inked onto adhesive tape to identify them; but if luck ran against me, as I could not assume it would not, for possibly I deserved luck to run against me, behaving as I was, he might decide to enter the building from the rear, for the stairway was for the convenience of tenants like himself who lived on the upper floors of the building at the rear; he was a tenant like any other, most of them dark-skinned and foreign with smiles that seemed uniformly flashing-white and eyeballs of unnatural glistening whiteness; if these young men saw me, sometimes they paused to stare as if they hoped I might know them; they hoped that there was some reason for me to be where I was, and that this reason might extend to them; what they'd been told of American college girls intrigued them, perhaps, though surely I didn't fit any likely description of an American college girl. Behind his building, if no one was around, and if I dared, I lifted my eyes to the windows I had reason to believe were his, the windows of apartment 2D; I'd learned that his was apartment 2D by examining the mailboxes in the foyer where, on a grubby strip of adhesive tape on the box for 2D, V. MATHEIUS had been inked. It intrigued me, his blinds were so often drawn to the windowsills. Sometimes I saw a shadow

passing behind a blind, the fleeting silhouette of a man; yet so indis-
tinctly, I knew that I was gazing at the idea of *V. Matheius* and not at the
man himself; I thought of Plato's allegory of the cave, and of how
mankind is deluded by shadows; mankind is infatuated by shadows; and
yet, what solace is there, otherwise? *And his not knowing that I am here,
that I exist. For I am invisible to him.*

My naked face, raw female yearning.

4

. . . that voice.

In my Ethics class. In a large lecture room on the topmost floor of an ancient and revered building, the Hall of Languages. It was not the classroom in which the sickly girl in the soiled coat, smeared eyeshadow and bitten lips made such a fool of herself some weeks before, it was another, larger room; it was a place of hope. At the conclusion of his lecture on Plato, the professor made a show of inviting questions, perhaps truly he wanted questions, hoped for questions, intelligent and provocative questions, to alleviate the unnatural stillness of the lecture hall; perhaps, on his raised platform, behind the podium, as an avatar of long-vanished Plato, he was lonely. Questions from undergraduates interested him far less than questions from the several graduate students who were taking, or auditing, the course, for these were fellow professionals; clearly he was enlivened when one or another of these volunteered to speak.

"Yes, Mr. __" the professor would say, with an expectant smile, pronouncing a name that sounded like "math"—"mathes." The young man who'd raised his hand sat at the back of the hall, out of my range of vision; when he spoke, as he did nearly every class period, I noted how students around me turned, to frown; with disapproval, and yet with admiration; with curiosity, interest, and resentment. "—how Plato can promote the strategy of the 'noble lie'—as if any lie can be anything other than ignoble—" And the professor tried to smile, to argue in defense of Plato: "The *Republic* is best understood as a myth, a dialogue about justice," and he at the back of the hall objected, " 'Justice'? How can there be 'justice' in a totalitarian state?" Like a musical instrument, a horn of subtle modulations, clarinet, trombone, the voice was both respectful and insolent; the voice was searching, and earnest, and yet (almost you could hear this) quavering with indignation. Where the professor argued, "—myth, allegory, parable—" the younger voice argued, "—nightmare fascist state—slave-state—" The professor frowned, not liking it that he was in danger of losing the allegiance of the class to an interloper thirty years younger than he, "That's a common fallacy, Mr. ___. To interpret Plato literally. When clearly the entire dialogue is a metaphor, a—" By this time few in the class were listening to the professor, we were listening avidly to *him*.

The curious proportions of that lecture hall: imprinted in my memory like any space in which our lives have been altered. There were fifteen rows of seats in steeply rising tiers that curved far to each side in the shape of a crescent, so that the room was much wider than it was deep. The ceiling was extremely high, and water-stained; fluorescent tubing hummed and quivered overhead like racing thoughts. Beside the professor's podium was a ten-foot leaded-glass window that yielded a pale wintry glare. On a badly scuffed hardwood platform the professor sometimes paced, lecturing on Plato, Aristotle, Thomas Aquinas, Descartes, Spinoza, Leibnitz, Locke; he was in his early sixties, perhaps; his manner congenial, but authoritative; his near-bald head like an eggshell, his mouth like something that has been mashed; his eyes watery but shrewd, alert, deep-set beneath knurly grizzled-gray eyebrows.

An attractive man, I thought, for his age; though I did not wish to judge the appearances of those of my elders whom I revered. For what were appearances, as the Greek philosophers taught, but illusory, deceiving? Who but the very young, and fools, put their faith in "appearances"? Nor did I want to be reminded of my father, by contemplating a man who was my father's age, or a little older; my father who'd disappeared into the West as if following the passage of the sun, beyond the western range of mountains and into oblivion.

As if I could compare them! I thought with a smile. This learned man and my poor uneducated alcoholic and embittered father.

One morning following the professor's lecture on philosophic ideal-ism there was a protracted exchange between the professor and an ar-ticulate if rather dogged young man who sat at the back of the room; I felt a collective wave of dislike directed toward the young man, from my fellow students; but I simply listened in fascination, excitement and apprehension; thinking *Who is that, what kind of person is that? Like no one of us.* Behind me a male voice muttered sullenly, "Oh for Christ's sake shut up," and another what sounded like "N'ggg shut yo mouth," and both laughed unkindly. By this time the professor was speaking defen-sively and at length; he would punish the entire class by keeping us be-yond the end of the hour. I thought *We should not have such power over one another.* When finally the class dispersed I was slow to rise to my feet, and to stumble into the aisle; still I had not allowed myself to look at the back of the room; I did not yet understand that I was in love; I'd fallen in love with a man I did not know; with a man's mere voice; and that love is a kind of illness; not a radiant idea as I'd imagined but a physical condition, like grief.

That night in February 1963, the night his voice first entered my sleep.

5

You! You are capable of any thing. My brother Hendrick once told me.

Any thing. How strange these words: *any thing* and not *anything*. As if that of which I was capable was a thing, a palpable thing, and not an action.

It was at my grandfather's funeral that Hendrick told me this. Yet my brother had no idea what I was capable of, nor did anyone in my family. They distrusted me; around me there glimmered a dark, mysterious aura; I carried both the fact and the possibility of doom. *He blames her. We all do. For Ida's death.* I escaped from them, yet I bore their condemnation. Perhaps I accepted it. I was so lonely! Yet I thought *Loneliness is my due. It's only just.*

I was nineteen years five months old when I fell in love for the first time. This seemed to me a profound, advanced age; never can we anticipate being older than we are, or wiser; if we're exhausted, it's impossible to anticipate being strong; as, in the grip of a dream, we rarely understand that we're dreaming, and will escape by the simplest of methods, opening our eyes. At nineteen, to my disgust, I continued to look much younger. I would be mistaken for a high school student through my undergraduate years. Even in my winter boots (not chic

leather of a kind worn by my better-dressed classmates but clumsy rub-
berized boots from Sears, wonderfully practical for deep snows and tor-
rential spring rains) I stood about five feet three inches. I never weighed
myself but, at the time of my "crisis," when I departed the Kappa
Gamma Pi house, I was put on a scale by a nurse in the university infirmary, and my weight noted as ninety-six pounds. "Have you stopped
eating? Do you vomit up your food? This isn't your normal weight, is
it?" the woman asked disapprovingly. I told her I didn't know what my
"normal" weight was; I wasn't interested in my "normal" weight; I had
other things on my mind, matters of pressing significance. *The meaning
of life. The possibility of truth. The analysis of consciousness as if it were a question of lines, of planes, and of solids.* I did not wish to consider that I was a
body, and that I was in some way responsible for this body. (And what in
fact *is* a body? Descartes had hypothesized that a mysterious and unknowable substance constituted mind, and an entirely other mysterious
and unknowable substance constituted body.) In the infirmary I was
forced to look at myself as an act of penance. I avoided the sunken eyes
in the face, but looked frankly at the rest of myself: the papery-thin
tallow-colored skin stretched tight upon slender bones, breasts the size
of Dixie cups and hard as unripe pears, nipples the size of wizened peas
and nothing at all like the warm roseate aureole of those girls' breasts I
presumed to be "normal"; the heavy, full breasts of other girls which
looked as if already they held liquid, sweet milky precious liquid, the
very elixir of life. I remembered how in junior high I saw older girls in
the locker room laughingly peeling off their outer clothes, yanking
sweaters over their heads in a single quick gesture that exposed their
torsos even as their heads and faces were obscured; you could see that
these girls were sisters; these girls were "female"; standing defiant or
proud or indifferent in their burgeoning bodies while I turned away in
embarrassment; not that I felt inadequate or inferior in my spindly

body, but of another species altogether. I stood outside their category entirely, a marginal sub-species, *girl*.

When I was growing up, there were relatives who, at a distance, felt sorry for me. *Feeling sorry* was their permanent attitude toward me. The women would admonish *If you'd smile more often, not frown.* (What then? I'd be loved, as I wasn't loved for myself?) Such remarks cut me to the quick, though I showed not a ripple. *But I am smiling, smiling constantly. Laughing in your faces!*

I wanted none of their pity, sympathy, or solicitude. They felt sorry for me because they took a certain pleasure in feeling sorry for one so deprived, so disfigured; because I had no mother, alone of the girls of my generation in Strykersville I had no mother; sometimes it seemed to my horror that my mother had actually died before I was born, not after; if such a fairy tale could be, it would apply to me as the cruellest of curses: *The Girl Whose Mother Died Before She Was Born.*

No: I remembered Ida. I did remember Ida. More than just the snapshots. I did.

My three older brothers. I was intimidated by them, and I feared them, and my secret may have been that I adored them, at a distance. Always I looked up to them: literally! Up at their handsome faces. Up at their unreadable eyes. They fascinated me even as I dreaded them. "You? What do you know? *We* know." They were custodians of memories; Dietrich had been twelve when our mother died, Fritz had been eleven, Hendrick eight; I'd been a baby, and helpless.

By the time I went away to college, both Dietrich and Fritz were married, and had become fathers; they'd inherited our grandparents' farm, and were specializing, like many small farmers in Niagara County, in pears, apples, and peaches; Hendrick was more of a loner like myself, though never easy with me, resentful of me, my high school success, my college scholarship, for he'd gone to a vocational school in

Olean to study electrical engineering, and he'd had to pay his own way. Now he boasted of a good job with a division of General Motors in Lackawanna. I most keenly remembered my brothers when they were growing up: their crude, derisive talk of girls and women, which invariably involved jokes; as if girls and women were jokes; from my brothers I learned that *the male* is all eyes; his sexuality is fueled through the eyes; he assesses through the eyes; judges swiftly and without mercy through the eyes. Sometimes, laughing coarsely, speaking of a girl or a woman of their acquaintance, my brothers would rub their crotches gleefully. You could see that the male's eyes and his penis are connected, perhaps identical; except the one is hidden from view.

I understood that even when a man is alone, his sympathies are with other men, and with maleness. He doesn't feel himself alone as a woman might. His swift, unerring judgments are forged in boyhood and are a collective judgment. He has the power to see with others' eyes, not just his own.

I did not expect mercy from those eyes. By the age of thirteen I'd been trained to shrink from their pitiless gaze.

I understood that my body was not a body to be loved; and so I was not a girl to be loved. Had not my own father shrunk from me, with a look of faint revulsion? When I was thirteen, overnight it seemed to happen that brown tufts of hair fine as cornsilk sprouted in my armpits and in tight curls at my groin; my slender but hard-muscled legs, disproportionately long for my torso, were covered in a feathery down which, through high school and while living with the Kappas, I'd scorned to shave off, as other girls made such a fuss of doing. When I sweated, my smell was sharp and rank; there was something secret about it, and satisfying; I liked it that I could turn into a foxy little creature, with a creature-smell. After I left Strykersville and learned what it was to be alone, no family to define me, amid thousands of strangers who knew neither my name nor my face, let alone where I lived, whose daughter or granddaughter I was, I came to think of my body as invisible; a body to hide inside clothing; a body that was a continuous shrinking from being *seen, defined;* a body my brothers and other men could not jeer at, for they could not see it; a body from which, I believed, the great dead male philosophers whom I revered would not turn in disgust. A body in the service of Mind.

Impulsively I cut off my hair when I was eighteen. The summer following high school graduation and my valedictory speech; the week after my father, only just returned home after years of absence, had departed again abruptly with a vague promise of "keeping in touch." My hair was thick and wiry and inclined to snarl; it had become an animal-hair, a kind of pelt; a drab-dark brown enlivened here and there by streaks of lighter brown or dark red; heavy and inert it pressed against my back; heavy and inert it pressed against my soul; when I tried to comb it, my eyes filled with tears of annoyed pain; when I ran a brush through it, the brush sprang out of my hand and clattered to the floor. On the street, men looked at my hair; boys looked at my hair; women and girls looked at my hair; I was vain about my hair, at the same time I was deeply ashamed of my hair, and one hot-humid summer day I took my grandmother's sewing shears, the big shears used for cutting thick fabrics like felt, and I ran off to my room and began cutting; slowly at first and then with mounting glee, almost a kind of gloating, *click! click!* just missing my ears, and with each greedy *click!* of the shears I felt lighter, freer. And with each greedy *click!* I laughed aloud as a rebellious child might laugh. I threw away the clipped-off strands of hair like trash. I had no sentiment, I vowed I would never be so burdened again.

As it happened, I had to attend my grandfather's funeral in a few days. He'd been driving a tractor in hot sunshine and had keeled over with a heart attack; he'd died almost immediately; it was shock more than grief the family felt; he and my grandmother had been emotionally estranged for some time, though of course they'd continued to live together and even to share a bed; my grandmother's reaction to me, to my jagged cut hair, at such a public time, when others would see us, and comment upon us, was *Isn't that just like you.*

The funeral was held at the Lutheran church. My grandparents, particularly my grandmother, had begun attending services there; she was a stoic with an unsentimental vision of life, and no doubt death, and yet she wanted to "be" a Christian, like her neighbors; like most Americans; in addition to being a Christian, you had to "be" some denomination, and the Lutheran church was the most logical choice, for those of German descent. And there was the fact that her daughter-in-law Ida was buried in the churchyard, as a kind of pledge that the rest of us would find our ways back there, too. I was made to wear black; a lumpy black nylon dress borrowed from an aunt; it was several sizes too large for me, which suited me; a sullen-faced brat who might have been thirteen, not eighteen; frightened of what had happened to my grandfather, and not wanting to think about it; not wanting to think about death, dying; not wanting to think about the burial in a grave site close by Ida's, in the cemetery that was only just a field, a place suited for tall grass and weeds. My female relatives stared at me appalled. *Oh how could you! Your hair.* The aunt who'd lent me the dress said *At least let me trim it for you?* I turned coldly away. I wasn't about to defend myself. My brothers looked at me and shrugged. This only confirmed their suspicions of me: I was weird, I was a freak, I would only get worse when I went away to college. Until leaving the cemetery my brother Hendrick nudged me saying in an undertone, almost admiringly *You!—you are capable of any thing. Now you really are ugly, that must make you feel just great, right?*

6

VERNOR MATHEIUS.

How many times in a trance that winter writing VERNOR MATH-
EIUS VERNOR MATHEIUS on sheets of notebook paper, in midnight-
blue ink. VERNOR MATHEIUS traced with a fingernail in my flesh, the
soft inside of a forearm, the palm of a hand. VERNOR MATHEIUS the
mere sound of the syllables, like a melody distantly heard, immediately
memorized if not understood. VERNOR MATHEIUS VERNOR
MATHEIUS spoken in an interior voice in the presence of others, even
as I was smiling, nodding, speaking quite normally with others who
could have had no idea how distracted I was, how indifferent to them
and even to myself. VERNOR MATHEIUS: what a strange, wonderful
name! a beautiful name! a name like no other! VERNOR MATHEIUS
like one of those riddle-names in a fairy tale, you had to guess the name,
or what it might mean, to save your life; to become the fair young
princess, his bride.

I hadn't the courage to ask others in our Ethics class about him. The
articulate and argumentative graduate student at the back of the room.
He was clearly a "personality"—everyone knew him, or was aware of

him. I dreaded strangers reporting my interest to him. They'd smile in my direction *See that girl? She's been asking about you.*

Now when our professor spoke his name—"Mr. Matheius?"—I heard the name perfectly. I could not comprehend how I'd ever mis-heard.

I looked up the name in a university directory, and so noted the Chambers Street address. *Never would I be so reckless as to visit that address* I told myself.

7

It was a morning in March when I first dared speak to Vernor Matheius. Unbidden, unwelcome, yet unable to resist, I entered a stranger's life.

You are capable of any thing. This was now a prophecy, an encouragement, and not an insult.

By this time I'd visited Chambers Street not once but several times. I'd passed the house, I'd lingered in the alley, I'd ventured into the foyer to examine the mailboxes, I'd contemplated his windows at the rear of the building, I was without shame as I was without hope. For it didn't seem to me at that time that I would ever actually make contact with Vernor Matheius; it was enough simply to contemplate him, at a distance.

Yet I'd moved my seat in the lecture hall. Now I sat nearer the back, in such a position where I could turn my head unobtrusively and look at him, or in his direction; when he spoke, many in the class turned to look at him, and I was one of these; I didn't believe I was calling attention to myself; I was no lovesick high school girl.

That morning climbing three flights of stairs and entering the cavernous lecture room breathless and hopeful; several minutes before the professor arrived, and class would begin; I seemed to be stepping into a roiling, treacherous space; a space of vertiginous unease, like a room in a fun house that's tilted, or spinning upside down; for what if *he* was already there, and might glance casually at me, the lenses of his glasses winking like sparks of flame? (For so they winked in my imagination.) Most mornings, Vernor Matheius wasn't in the room so early. I timed my arrival to precede his so that I could take my new, strategic seat at the end of a row on the center aisle; the experience of the class had become for me, virtually overnight, an emotional and no longer an intellectual one. I felt the way I'd felt as a girl about to dive off the high board at the YWCA in Strykersville; I wanted to dive, I intended to dive, I was thrilled at the prospect of diving, yet frightened as well; as I strode to the end of the board, readying my arms and head, bending my knees, I would hear a malicious little voice *Don't! You'll regret it.* But on the high board, you couldn't turn back.

There were perhaps forty students in Ethics, concentrated in the front rows and scattered elsewhere. Vernor Matheius sat by himself in the last row, beneath a wall clock. It may have been accidental that he sat beneath the clock. It was not a position one would wish, who liked to check the time. One of those old-fashioned institutional clocks with plain black numerals and black hour and minute hands, a moving red second hand, against a blank moon face. As a child I'd gazed at such clocks on the walls of classrooms. The inexorable forward-movement of time. My heartbeat. All the heartbeats in the room. Linked by mortality. And now seeing Vernor Matheius, I was seeing also the clock.

Vernor Matheius's face. Covertly and slantwise I contemplated that face. To me it was beautiful as something carved out of mahogany; though it may have been, to another's cruder eye, ugly. It was not a comforting face. It was a face crinkled and even mutilated by thinking. Thinking as a physical, muscular act. Thinking as an act of passion. It was a face that, though technically young, the face of a man in his early thirties, had never been youthful. A mask-face. A flattish nose and wide, deep nostrils that looked like holes bored into flesh. A head that seemed too large for his narrow, somewhat sloping shoulders. Eyes hidden behind scholarly glasses except when abruptly he removed the glasses to rub the bridge of his nose with the thumb and forefinger of his right hand. My heart contracted, seeing Vernor Matheius without his glasses. His face so suddenly naked, exposed.

Negro. "Negro." A word, a term, that had come to fascinate me, too.

Vernor Matheius's features were "Negroid" features, and Vernor Matheius was, if you were compelled to categorize the man in blunt racial, or racist, terms, "Negro." For his skin was the color of damp earth; sometimes it was dull, and without lustre; at other times it was rich and smooth with something smoldering inside; a coppery-maroon; skin I imagined would be hot to the touch. (Unlike my pale winter-chapped skin that felt cold to me, the tips of my fingers often icy.) Vernor Matheius's hair was a Negro's hair, unmistakably: dark, somewhat oily, woolly-springy, trimmed close to his head that looked to me wonderfully hard and resolute, a work of art.

Because I had come to him through his voice, his language, his obvious intelligence, Vernor Matheius's race was not his predominant characteristic to me. I supposed that, if I'd seen him in the Hall of Languages previously, or on campus or in the city, my eye would have glided over him and my brain would have categorized him as *Negro;* but now the fact of his race (if "race" is a fact) was no more remarkable to me than other of his qualities. On the contrary, these qualities were remarkable because they were Vernor Matheius's. I may even have thought, with the primitive logic of one so deeply and so newly in love that her powers of reason have weakened, that Vernor Matheius had chosen his qualities. In which case, they were remarkable and valuable not in themselves, but because he had chosen them.

In philosophy, you're trained to distinguish between what's essential and what's accidental; in our personalities, it's believed that there are essential qualities and accidental qualities; yet so powerful a presence was Vernor Matheius, unique in my experience, it didn't seem that there could be anything accidental about him, as there is about most people. (My own life seemed to me a haphazard sequence of accidents.) I would not have isolated *Negro-ness* from any other of his qualities. True, it was a fact of his being, the first thing that struck the eye, but it wasn't a defining or definitive fact.

Any more than I was a *white girl,* a *Caucasian.* What did that mean?

If Vernor Matheius was Negro, and there was nothing accidental in his personality, then somehow he'd chosen Negro-ness. As I had not chosen my skin, or anything in my life.

I believed this! For already I idolized the man, who was all that I could never be, nor even imagine.

Vernor Matheius and the professor were having one of their spirited exchanges. You could see that the professor was flattered by this brilliant young man's attention; at the same time, the professor was wary of being outpaced, like a middle-aged man playing tennis with a man forty years his junior. They were discussing "idealism"; which, in philosophical terms, differs considerably from ordinary usage; "idealism" vs. "realism"; the subtly argued idealism of Immanuel Kant in contrast to the less subtly argued realism of Plato. The professor pronounced X, and Vernor Matheius at once rebutted with Y; not impudently, though almost so; with a lightness of touch that discomforted the older man, and provoked a ripple of laughter in the room. The professor visibly recoiled; he realized his blunder; his authority had been challenged, if only in play; he'd surrendered that authority, if only for a moment; he had to reclaim his authority, or lose the respect of the class; or so it might have seemed to him, in his quivering vanity. He was a flush-faced man with a skin that appeared loosened, as if he'd lost weight too quickly; his graying-brown hair parted on the left side of his head and brushed damply over his skull. In the philosophy department, which was one of the strongest departments in the liberal arts college, this professor was perhaps the most highly regarded; he had an advanced degree from the University of Edinburgh, his books were published by distinguished university presses, he reviewed for the *Times Literary Supplement*. (An English publication to which Mrs. Thayer hadn't subscribed.) Even his undergraduate courses were frequently audited by graduate students. Yet he felt the sting of Vernor Matheius's irreverent wit, and spoke coldly and curtly to him—"Mr. Matheius! Your sophistry ceases to amuse." So the indulgent father at last chides the favored son, revealing that, maybe, the favored son isn't so favored after all.

I saw the hurt and humiliation in Vernor Matheius's face. I saw him shut up his face as he might've clenched a fist. In a quick, rough gesture he shoved his glasses against the bridge of his nose, slouched in his seat, shoved out his lower lip. Which was a fat, fleshy lip. His skin was so dark, so without light or lustre, you couldn't imagine it darkening with a rush of hot blood. There was a moment's pained silence before Vernor Matheius politely muttered, "Sorry, sir."

The rest of the class looked on, thrilled and vindicated.

Even I, infatuated with Vernor Matheius, felt that mean little thrill.

Thinking *He has been wounded to the heart. He, too!*

It was as if, an intimate witness, I'd had a hand in that wounding.

After class, I found myself standing in the aisle beside Vernor Matheius's row of seats as, tall and lanky and slope-shouldered, whistling a faint, just subtly derisive tune, Vernor Matheius was making his way into the aisle. He didn't see me. He wouldn't have seen me. He seemed oblivi-

ous to, indifferent to, every undergraduate student in the room. I
wanted to—what?—offer words of sympathy and commiseration. Even
as I knew (of course I knew) that Vernor Matheius didn't want words of
sympathy and commiseration; not from anyone, and certainly not from
me. There was a roaring in my ears. The hardwood floor tilted. Of
course I didn't dare utter his name—"Vernor." I had no right to that
name, I shouldn't have known that name. For a moment, staring at him,
I couldn't speak at all. The man's physical presence confused me; his
height; he was at least a head taller than I, towering over me; a powerful
throbbing heat lifted from him, as if he were sweating inside his clothes;
his skin dark and smoldering with blood; close up, his skin was darker
and coarser than I'd imagined. Behind the smudged lenses of his wire-
rimmed glasses his eyes were damp and glaring. He wore a white shirt
and even a necktie, both rumpled, not-clean; with an air of sullen dignity he was shrugging into the bulky sheepskin jacket and with rapid
deft motions winding the crimson wool scarf around his neck; as if, in
his fury, he would have liked to strangle himself; his fingers remarkably
long, his hands rather narrow, the palms curiously pinkish-pale as if they
might be soft, even tender to the touch. I saw that he wanted only to escape the lecture hall, the last thing he wanted was to speak with anyone
who had witnessed his public humiliation, yet I followed beside him as
he pushed into the aisle, I stammered words meant to console; to my astonishment I saw my hand reach out timidly to touch his—*his* hand; but
at the last second I dared touch only the soiled cuff of his jacket; if I'd
touched his skin he might have flung my hand off in sheer nervous reaction; and all the while I was smiling, trying to smile, a fixed ghastly grin,
in longing and terror seeking the very source of terror for solace, pro-
tection. *I can love you, I am the one who can love you. Who am I except the one
whose sole identity is that she can love you?*

Vernor Matheius was staring at me. It was as if he'd heard, not my shy halting insipid speech, my well-intentioned words in imitation of such gestures of commiseration made to me by women or girls who'd hoped to console me for whatever hurts, deprivations, but my desperate thoughts. *I, I can love you!* He had seen, not felt, the brush of my fingers against his sleeve; how near I'd come to touching him. Sharply he said, "Yes? What?"—still staring at me, as if I'd accosted him; yet at the same time he was turning on his heel to escape; rudely giving me no time to answer, had I had an answer; he bounded up the steps to the rear exit, and was gone.

Yet: I have done it, touched you. And now you know me.

That morning, unlike most mornings, I did not follow Vernor Matheius out of the building and across the snowy quadrangle; I did not follow him at all; in confusion, a kind of delirium, I descended the stairs to the first floor of the Hall of Languages; the corridors, the stairs were crowded at this hour, just before eleven o'clock; I took refuge in anonymity. *Now you will know me, the connection has been made.* I could not believe my recklessness, my daring. I could not believe I had done such a thing, and not only dreamt it. Around me on the stairs were students from the class, familiar faces though we didn't know one another's names; with childish zest we spoke of the humiliation of the formidable "Mr. Matheius"; even I who adored him spoke in this way, smiling, greedy, not wanting the subject to be dropped; a hatchet-faced boy who was a senior in pre-law said, grinning, " 'Math-e-ius'—who's he think he is, anyway?" and another boy said vehemently, "It's weird a Ne-gro caring so much about—that kind of stuff." I did not object, I listened intently, it may even have been that I seemed to concur. For whom we love helplessly we love, too, to betray: any connection is thrilling.

Even to hear brilliant Vernor Matheius called "Ne-gro" so carelessly, crudely—to hear his name spoken at all—thrilling.

I found myself in the basement of the Hall of Languages where there were additional classrooms, cramped and ill-lit and melancholy rooms; low-ceilinged corridors and a sharp smell, in winter, of wet wool, rubber boots, a perpetual haze of cigarette smoke. In a remote corner of the basement there was a women's lavatory; often I used this lavatory, for it was always empty; a sickly odor of drains and disinfectant wafted from it. Here was a space that seemed older than the aging building that loomed above it, lodged deep in earth with only a small window to emit a wan, spent light. I remember this dismal place as distinctly as any place of those years and wonder if perhaps, in those dreams of mine that rake my soul and leave me, in the morning, exhausted yet curiously revived as if *I have harrowed Hell, that region of the grindingly mundane, and survived,* I dream of it often. For it was a place in which to hide; a place in which to weep; a place of inexplicable shame and melancholy; a place in which to use the antiquated toilet, and pull a chain flush that reluctantly and somberly released water from a rust-stained overhead tank into a yet more stained bowl; a place in which to check worriedly if, finally, my period had "happened"—as rarely it did, for I was twenty pounds underweight and experienced brief though painful periods no more than two or three times a year. *For I was not truly female in certain crucial ways and both anguished and gloated in this fact.* In the water-speckled mirror above a row of sinks I was struck by my face—was I smiling? I'd behaved with Vernor Matheius as I had never behaved in my life; approached a man I didn't know, and dared to touch him; almost, I'd touched the back of his hand, his skin; I'd forced him to look at me; to see me; I'd spoken directly to him; I'd offered him words of sympathy ("He didn't mean it, he spoke without thinking, he admires you very much, anyway there's nothing wrong really with being a Sophist—Protagoras was a Sophist and really so was Socrates") that were genuine, heartfelt if breathless; I'd acted without premeditation, not so much as an instant's premeditation, as one might rush forward to save another from harm.

Almost it seemed to me, and would seem increasingly to me with the passage of time, that Vernor Matheius had somehow drawn me to him, physically; I'd had no real power to resist.

In such involuntary acts, there is innocence.

"But now you must leave it at that. You must not pursue him."

These words were uttered in my voice. I was staring at the floating pale oval of a face in the mirror and so happy!—the face on this side of the glass, my living face, ached with happiness. I was feverish, I touched my fingertips to my lips, I kissed my fingertips that had touched the soiled sleeve of Vernor Matheius's jacket. Never again would I sleep. I might have died on the spot, I was so happy. Deep in the interior of the subterranean mirror with its discolored surface splotched from the sink, its lead backing corroding the glass like leprosy: how many generations, how many decades of girls since the building had been constructed a hundred years before, had gazed into such depths as I did, stark yearning eyes, female eyes, our reflections tangled together as in the marshy bottom of a pond, or a common grave.

Yet I smiled, smiled—I *was* happy.

8

"Not following me, girl, are you?"

The voice, his voice—not irritable but brash and teasing, as unexpectedly, to my embarrassment, Vernor Matheius halted on the sidewalk; turned abruptly to me, so I hadn't time to sidle away; I'd
imagined myself invisible following him at a discreet distance, sometimes walking close beside others as if I were in their company; I had
not seen him so much as glance over his shoulder as he'd strode along
whistling; in this way I had followed him from the university library
across the quadrangle and down a steep hill to College Place, from
College Place to Allen Street, a business district of fast-food restaurants, bookshops, supplies stores, from Allen Street out to University
Avenue and along University Avenue to the area of the medical center;
of course I was in no hurry to overtake Vernor Matheius and when he
slowed his pace, I slowed mine; he must have noticed me somehow; or
sensed the intensity of my concentration upon him; my gaze so fixed
upon him; and now he'd stopped at a curb, turned to me and laughingly
called out, "Not following me, girl, are you?—eh?" This was meant to
be playful; a flirtatious joke; yet the joke (of course) was that he wasn't
joking, he knew very well I'd been following him, yet he could not

absolutely know, he could not be one hundred percent certain (for we both knew Hume's indisputable argument regarding causality); yet there was the probability that I'd been following him; yet I could not acknowledge that I was, for—what a shameful admission! And what could Vernor Matheius have said in reply? So I had to protest as I did, my face burning as if it had been slapped, "Oh, oh no—I'm just—walking this way."

"And what way is that, exactly?"

Rapidly I invented a plausible destination: the University Health Services office which was about a block away. I had to return a form, I said.

Vernor Matheius, towering above me, sucked at his mouth in a show of mock disappointment. "Just a coincidence, eh?"

"A—coincidence."

"Just 'atoms and the void,' eh?"

Democritus was a philosopher of ancient Greece who was famous for a single axiom—*In reality there is nothing but atoms and the void.* I wasn't sure if he'd been a Sophist; he was one of those who, at the very start of philosophic inquiry, had handily reduced the mysteries of existence to shreds. For that was the way of philosophy: to reduce existence to pitiful shreds, or to inflate it to gigantic, smothering proportions. Either way, existence became unrecognizable.

I laughed uneasily, and did not disagree. Somehow we were walking together on University Avenue; we crossed a wide windy expanse of pavement as a yellow DON'T WALK! sign flashed.

I was overwhelmed and confused by Vernor Matheius's nearness. Hearing his voice, the voice, the voice that had so entered my consciousness, his voice like a roaring in my ears. His height, his quizzical bemused skeptical eyes, his habit of grinning to bare uneven yellow predatory teeth with a prominent gap between the two front teeth.

Slyly thinking *Don't imagine I can't see through you, girl: your skin is transparent.*

It would be a matter for me to contemplate afterward: how rapidly, how irrevocably I'd stepped out of invisibility into visibility once Vernor Matheius had sighted me. How, one moment, I had been lost in my concentration upon him; I'd been anonymous, unseen; the next moment, I was forced to speak, to act, to *be;* forced to quickly improvise and invent, as in a game of rapid motions and counter-motions, like badminton (at which, as a high school girl, I'd won county tournaments). My very way of carrying my body, my facial expressions, the movement of my eyes, my hands, my legs; the way in which I walked, needing to keep stride with the man's loping gait; the way in which I displayed my "self"—all were a surprise to me, a revelation. As if a blinding spotlight were suddenly shining on me, and I had no choice but to perform.

Yes you see through me, you know me. This must all have happened before.

Since the morning of the professor's insult, Vernor Matheius had ceased attending the class. Suddenly, irrevocably—he was gone. At the back of the hall was the row in which he'd sat, there was the desk in which for weeks he'd sat, beneath the clock; but now he was gone, and would not (I seemed to know, with resignation) be back; though I glanced over my shoulder repeatedly during class as if with a nervous tic, needing to check the time; for the hour between ten and eleven was interminable now, and empty of meaning. How dull, disappointing European Ethics was without Vernor Matheius to enliven it!—I wasn't the only person who felt the loss. Even those students who'd disliked Vernor Matheius intensely regretted his absence. And most of all the professor who seemed to me sad, elderly, reading from his lecture notes, adjusting his glasses and clearing his throat; in the harsh glare from the leaded-glass window his creased, windburned-looking face exposed; like me glancing frequently toward the empty desk beneath the clock. I glared at him, doodling in my notebook. *Now you see what you've done, you ridiculous old man. Out of vanity.*

I had no choice, I had to comment on his absence from the class, it would have been unnatural for me not to; and Vernor Matheius shrugged indifferently, and said, "I wasn't enrolled, just auditing. Not much in it for me, frankly." So I said, hesitantly, "It's very—quiet now, without you," and Vernor Matheius said, "Good. I was intrusive, I think," and quickly I said, "Oh, no—not at all," and he persisted, "Yes, wasn't I? Come on: I always talk too much," and I said, almost vehemently, "No. You made the class come alive." At this, Vernor Matheius made a curious sucking sound with his teeth, as if sucking spit through his teeth, a comical-mocking sound I'd never heard before but interpreted as an expression of extreme doubt, and grinning sidelong at me he said, "So now it's dead without me, eh?" and I found myself backed into a corner by the logic of his argument, forced to say, "Yes."

Vernor Matheius was not walking me to the University Health Services but the office happened to be in the direction in which (by chance and coincidence) we were walking. So it happened that we walked together; people on the street, glancing at us, might have imagined us as a couple; an interracial couple, of whom there were a few at the university; not many, for there were not many non-Caucasian students, but a few. I was carrying a duffel bag, and was in horror it would bump against Vernor Matheius's side; yet I didn't want to switch it to my other arm, for that would remove the buffer between us; and he might misunderstand; or understand too well. We weren't talking now; Vernor Matheius had resumed his whistling. I had sometimes noticed how, striding across campus, making his way through slower-moving groups of students that seemed to part, like molecules, for his swifter passage, he often whistled; frowning and smiling to himself, lost in thought; yet his eyes moving continuously, restlessly—you could see that nothing eluded him. How tall the man was, six feet three or four; how lean, like a knifeblade; his handsome head disproportionately large for his shoulders and body, as if the rest of him had failed to keep pace with his intelligence. There was a slight lurching hunch to his left shoulder as if he had an old injury, and carried himself guarded against pain; yet never registered pain; in fact he was in buoyant good spirits, whistling through his fleshy purplish-plum pursed lips. It would not have occurred to me in my naïveté to wonder *Am I a factor in this man's happiness? Is there invariably something sexual in a man's happiness?* Pulled down tight over his head was a grimy knitted navy blue cap with white starburst designs, that looked handmade; the crimson wool scarf looped around his neck, also moderately soiled, flapped in the wind; the khaki sheepskin jacket flapped open, the zipper broken; his hands were bare in the 10°F. cold—he'd lost his gloves. Vernor Matheius was one of those older, driven students perpetually distracted by thought, or by some mysterious urgency that made it impossible for them to get their clothes on right; I suppose I was perceived in this way myself, for I'd long been careless of my "personal appearance"—my "grooming" as it was called—though now, in recent weeks, I'd made a concerted effort to improve. *For how do you make yourself visible, to one who has no awareness of your very existence?*

At the Health Services building Vernor Matheius waved good-bye to me without breaking stride, or breaking off his whistling; blindly I turned in to the building on my fictitious errand; wandered the corridors for five, ten minutes before daring to return to the street; to a pearlescent-gray, windy March day; and when I did, stepping out onto University Avenue, to my astonishment there stood Vernor Matheius, waiting.

His mouth smiled at me, a sly-glistening gap-toothed smile, and said, "Find what you were looking for?"

9

Aged eighteen I'd left home, Strykersville, New York, with no idea of who I was or who I might be; knowing only who I was not, and did not wish to be: all that, until that time, I'd known. At Syracuse, I haphazardly cobbled together a personality out of scraps; like my grandmother's quilts made of mismatched scraps of cloth. You don't inquire into the origin of scraps but only of the shrewd use of which they are made.

From my brother Dietrich (who'd been a Marine immediately out of high school, before returning to farm) I borrowed a way of carrying myself with dignity; from my high school history teacher, a way of questioning others' remarks without being rude (though in fact, I suppose I was sometimes rude); from a girl named Lynda who'd been my closest friend in high school, a way of being "good"—"generous"—without seeming silly; from the Lutheran minister's grown daughter, a way of regarding people with flattering widened sincere-seeming eyes, not the narrow, veiled eyes natural to me; from my father I borrowed a habit of skepticism and doubt, the loser's distrust of anyone who has more money than he has, or even the appearance of more; yet from my father, too, a contradictory impulse, for he had a weakness for card playing and gambling, which attests to reckless optimism. The gambler's philosophy is a simple one. *So little hope of things going right for you, why the hell not bet all you've got?*

At Syracuse there were so many new models for me. At any rate, possibilities.

My most articulate, persuasive professors (who were exclusively male); scattered residents in my freshman dorm, known to me only by name; a number of the Kappa girls who now, when they saw me on campus, stared through me with expressions of undisguised loathing. (The more inventive of the Kappas had spread fanciful rumors of my "congenital leprosy"; my "mixed racial background"; my "disgusting" grooming habits; my "selfishness" is not tutoring them; my "public nervous breakdown" in the presence of Kappa alums. Of these outrages, the last was truly unforgiveable.) My so-called personality had always been a costume I put on fumblingly, and removed with vague, perplexed fingers; it shifted depending upon circumstances, like unfastened cargo in the hold of a ship. Periodically in high school I would make a desperate effort to be "nice"—"normal"—"well-liked"—"popular." When I was once elected to a class office, vice-president of my senior class, I resigned in a panic. I couldn't explain that the sunny-seeming good-girl citizen my classmates had elected to office wasn't me, but an experiment I had not expected to succeed.

The personalities I assembled never lasted long. Like quilts carelessly sewn together, I periodically fell apart. Sometimes the collapse was brief, a siege of exhaustion, nausea and sleeplessness that left me stunned, but purged; at other times, and such times were becoming more frequent, the collapse was more serious, involving a period of manic, nervous behavior followed by a physical breakdown—"flu" I would call it, or that popular undergraduate malady "mononucleosis." I was too weak to get out of bed, too weak and demoralized to read, write or think coherent thoughts; my bowels churned and ached with diarrhea, though I hardly ate; all appetite for food vanished; my body burned with fever and my head with pain. Yet there was a curious solace in such a collapse, a sharp, sour pleasure; for I would be compelled to think *Now you know what you are, now you know.* Stark and simple and beautiful as gleaming white bones picked clean of all flesh. *Now you know.* Yet I lived in dread of the one day I would fall utterly and irrevocably into pieces and would lack the strength, the will, the purpose, the faith to reassemble myself another time.

I never doubted that others, those others I admired, were solid and whole, not made of scraps and pieces like me. I never doubted their natural superiority, only that I could emulate it. Yet there were those like me with whom I felt a surreptitious kinship. One morning in the Ethics class after Vernor Matheius had ceased attending, the professor had been lecturing with a strained, forced energy on "the perennial problem of good and evil"—the "tragedy of man's divisiveness"—and of how such great thinkers as Augustine, Spinoza, Kant, Hegel had dealt with this "problem"; and it came to me—how hollow, how halting the man's voice; how little any of this mattered, without Vernor Matheius to respond. The wintery glare from the tall leaded-glass window beside the professor's podium fell upon the aging man so cruelly it looked as if his skin was about to crumble into bits, and his eyes that were brave and hopeful were about to dissolve into water. I heard his old-man's voice as he must have heard it himself and felt a rush of confused emotion for him, and pity: for the arc of his life was waning, and even had Vernor Matheius remained in our midst it would not have mattered for long.

To win Vernor Matheius's attention, I understood that I would have to make myself visible to him, and "attractive"; I would have to reinvent myself; I shopped for secondhand clothing in the city, choosing things I myself would never have wished to wear, or dared: a lime-green suede jacket in a bygone style, only slightly worn at the cuffs and elbows; a ruffled red long-sleeved silk blouse that looked like an explosion on my narrow torso; a tartan plaid wool skirt several sizes too large for me made of an exquisitely beautiful fabric; a sleek-sexy black linen dress with a V neck and a dropped hemline and an unraveling hem. Out of bins marked $3–$5 I pulled a sweater, a gauzy scarf, a belt made of linked silver ornaments. Each of the items had been many times reduced—the suede jacket, for instance, had been marked down from $95 to $43 to $19—and was certainly a bargain; these were quality clothes of the kind I could never have afforded new; but I could not really afford even these bargains, and had had to borrow money from girls in my residence, even as I suspected I would never be able to repay it—I'd become reckless, shameless. And my hair that had grown out unevenly and fell now to my shoulders in an untidy rippled-curly mass needed attention: trimming, shaping, "styling": I found myself one Saturday morning in a neighborhood beauty salon spending $12 on my hair; staring amazed at the transformed girl in the mirror as the beautician (a heavily made-up, glamorous woman of approximately the age my mother would have been had she lived) said cheerfully, "Some improvement, eh?"

" 'Anellia'——a strange name. Never heard it before."

Frowning, with a skeptic's habitual narrowing of his eyes, Vernor Matheius uttered this name as if doubting it.

I said nothing, and the moment passed.

In the gloomily romantic coffeehouse Vernor Matheius spoke almost exclusively of philosophy. It was his true passion. It might have been his only passion. Such a ferocity of commitment and concentration excited me, for I felt the same way, or nearly; I'd grown to distrust all that was mere emotion, fleeting and ephemeral; the world of sliding, collapsing surfaces; the world of my father's drifting cigarette smoke, vanishing into the ceiling of my grandparents' old farmhouse; the world of clock time. And there was the thrill of a common language. A common religion. Almost, I could think, *As if we were a couple. Lovers.* Vernor was known in this place, and seemed not to mind when his name was spoken familiarly; it struck my ear as risky, and wonderful, that others, strangers to me, could call out "Vernor" so readily, and Vernor Matheius would smile and wave a greeting. Beside a wall of hammered tin squares painted the hue of pencil lead, we sat in a booth with a sticky tabletop; Vernor ordered coffee for us both——very strong, black, bitter-almond coffee of a sort I had never tasted before; swift as a shot to the heart caffeine flew through my veins; my pulse quickened, my very eyeballs began to throb. *As if. Lovers.* Long ago I had sternly instructed myself that sexual yearning is impersonal; though it may seem so, it is not; sexual yearning is the yearning of nature to reproduce itself, blindly.

Vernor asked nothing more about my name, or my background. In a voice that seemed to me, in my state of heightened nerves, both aggressive and seductive, he quizzed me about philosophy: for it was strange to him that "a girl like you" would be drawn to philosophy since "so few girls" were. He spoke of Aristotle, Descartes, Leibniz, Spinoza. Wittgenstein and Cassirer were his special interests. "The universal laws of structure and operation"—that was the only really worthwhile concern of mankind, in Vernor's opinion. When he'd first enrolled in college he had thought he might be a teacher, but soon discovered, to his disgust, how vacuous, how ignorant, how deadly-dull education courses were; he'd dropped out of college and entered a seminary, hoping to learn of God, the pathways to God, and how he might serve mankind in the effort of discovering God, but soon discovered, to his even greater disgust, only a human, confused and contradictory God— " 'Yahweh' like a collective comic nightmare of mankind." And so he returned to college, and enrolled in humanities courses, but soon discovered he couldn't tolerate history—"For what is 'history' except contingency, a mess of accidents." Most of these were bloody; history was mostly war; an appalling record of mankind's cruelty; cruelty compounded by ignorance, unless it was compounded by a malevolent intelligence; mankind no more rational than ants of differing races, creeds, languages ceaselessly battling one another for dominance; for mere anthills; what is politics but rabid self-interest and aggression, even the current civil rights movement—Vernor uttered the words *civil rights movement* with a purely neutral detachment as if it were a foreign phrase—was a distraction from the purity of the philosophical quest: to know what *is*. "Every year, every moment must be equal to every other," Vernor said, frowning as if warning me not to interrupt and argue, for philosophers are trained to argue. "The only truths that can possibly matter, that can *really* matter, are truths that transcend time." How emphatic Vernor Matheius's voice. A voice of seduction, a voice of pleading. A voice of logic, reason, conviction. A voice like a caress, that left me weak, gripping the coffee mug between my fingers. Vernor Matheius's large head, dark-tinctured face; his eyes showing pale crescents above the iris. His warm yeasty bodily odor mixed with the sharper smell of the coffee and rushed along my veins making me begin to perspire inside my showy clothes. I would be late for my cafeteria job. I would not arrive at the cafeteria at all. Though thinking calmly *I can leave. I can stand, turn away. At any time.*

Then somehow we were outside. My eyes blinked against the cold, tears stuck to my lashes. Vernor Matheius was leading me—where? We must have spoken of where. He must have invited me, I must have accepted. Close beside me he walked, nudging me. With what strange familiarity his fingers gripped my green suede jacket at the elbow. We came to Chambers Street. We descended the icy sidewalk. *I am free to turn away, to run. At any time.* Inappropriately, I recalled my Kappa sister Chris; how, the rumor was, she'd been taken upstairs in the fraternity house, drunk; eager and loving, you had to suppose; and what happened upstairs, how many fraternity men had sex with her, no one would know; Chris herself would not know, and would not wish to know; she'd dropped out of school, and was gone. I had no reason to think of Chris. *I am not Chris, I am not a Kappa.* Though if I seemed to be drifting from Vernor, his fingers gripped my elbow just a little firmer. "'Annul-ia'? That's your name?"

There, the stucco building of the indefinable hue of lard. This place I should not have recognized. I was smiling a small, fixed smile; I was certain that I had chosen this; though I did not know what exactly I had chosen; to what I'd agreed when Vernor Matheius had spoken the name "Anellia" in the coffeehouse and stared at me across the sticky tabletop. *Free to leave, to turn away. To run.* As we were climbing the stairway; the stairway I should not have known of, and seemed not to know of; the stairway of my dreams that was a crude wood-plank outdoor stairway with a roof but otherwise open to weather, the steps beginning to rot, swaying slightly beneath us. Vernor Matheius was close behind me, I was just ahead of him; I thought *He is herding me the way a dog herds sheep* and the thought made me laugh. Vernor was joking nervously about his "living quarters"—he was "an underground man aboveground"—there was the surprise of his icy-cold fingers encircling my right leg just below the knee; they were quick, strong, deft fingers; I tried to shake them off as if this was a game; of course it was a game; we behaved as if it was a game, playful and laughing; I thought *He would not hurt me—would he?* There was a garbagey smell, a smell of rotting wood. I opened my mouth to speak yet could not, the words tangled together. I had to leave, I was late for my job in the cafeteria, I had no money, I was desperately poor and would never be able to repay the girls to whom I owed money, a total of $87.50, a sum that might as well have been $10,000. I could not say these things; I could not say that I loved him but was terrified of him; that I had never been with a man or a boy like this; I was terrified of becoming pregnant; "becoming pregnant" was a thought that terrified me though I had no sexual experience; I could not exert any will contrary to Vernor Matheius's will, the playful grip of his fingers at my knee; as in a dream we are unable to exert any will contrary to the inscrutable will of the dream. It might have been (I thought) that whatever was to happen had already happened; in philosophy there was the theoretical possibility of the isomorphic universe, symmetrical in both space and time; a strictly determined universe that could run forward, and backward; to exert will in such a universe was not possible; to be blamed would be unjust. And so now I was climbing the outdoor stairway at 1183 Chambers Street exactly as I'd wished in my dreams; and yet this was not at all the dream I'd wished; I was frightened, and felt sick; I was trembling badly, as if freezing; the bitter black coffee of which I'd had only two or three sips now rose acid and bilious in my throat. *It's the green suede jacket that has brought me here* I was thinking. *It's the smiling-lipsticked girl in the mirror* I was thinking. Biting my lip to keep from laughing, thinking *This is what a pretty girl does, it's time you knew. This is what a "desired" girl does, this is what is done to a "desired" girl.*

Vernor Matheius fumbled with the key trying quickly to open the door to apartment 2D before we were seen, and pushed me inside. For once wordless.

11

The limits of my language are
the limits of my world.
WITTGENSTEIN

And now how lonely.

How alone, and how lonely.

Where once I'd walked into the residence hall cafeteria as soon as it opened at 7:00 A.M., and took a tray, and got my breakfast, and sat alone at a table near a window where I could read and dream in seclusion, now, in love with Vernor Matheius, I felt such acute loneliness, the physical shock and panic of loneliness, I could not bear to be by myself; eagerly and desperately I sought the company of girls whom I scarcely knew, girls I'd previously scorned, superficial chattering good-natured girls with whom I had nothing (or so I imagined) in common. It was like the nightmare of the sorority again where I'd blindly sought "sisters" yet it was not the company of girls I yearned for but the company of Vernor Matheius whom I feared I would never see again. Even with others, safely (if temporarily) with others, I could not concentrate on them but was thinking of course of him; only of him; my fingernails cruelly etched *Vernor Matheius Vernor Matheius* in the soft flesh of the inside of my forearm.

My cafeteria laughter was shrill as coins tossed against the floor, my voice strident. Yet as soon as my "friends" were gone the smile died on my lips, not a smile but a twitch; the manic spark in my eyes was extinguished like a light switched off. Alone, alone. I pushed away into the void like a solitary swimmer pushing out into freezing water; for all swimmers are solitary in such bitter regions of the soul.

Seeing something in my face, what pain what humiliation what despairing hope, one of the older girls waited for me; waited outside the cafeteria for me; hesitantly she inquired, "Is something wrong? You seem so"—tactful, kindly, not meaning to pry—"so sad, somehow." And I was astonished, so exposed. Flaring up like a struck match, "I'm not sad. I'm not sad in the slightest. What an ignorant thing to say. I've been laughing, haven't I?" I said, offended. Unless in fact I burst into tears. The girl, a tall broad-shouldered girl whose name I did not know or out of arrogance did not remember stood in such a way to shield me from the staring, curious eyes of others. My hot tears spilled out onto my cheeks; my nose ran; was this passion, was this romance, *this*—? Incensed as an older sister she asked, practicably, "Is it some guy?" and called me by my name, not "Anellia" but my true, ordinary name, the name by which I was commonly known. Some *guy!* As if she'd reached out to tickle me with rough fingers—some *guy!* The word so slangy, vulgar, commonplace—*guy!* Was Vernor Matheius for all his arrogance, brilliance, power over me in essence merely a *guy?* I had not time to absorb such a revolutionary thought, though such a thought might have saved me; I perceived my benefactor as my enemy, backing away in dislike, stammering, "I—resent such a question. I don't know you and you—you don't know me at all."

Following that exchange I avoided the dining hall. I ate in my room, or skipped meals altogether.

· · ·

How lonely, I wanted to die. To cease to exist. For he had rejected me, repudiated me; sent me away; he had not loved me nor even "made love" to me; my anxiety had been proven causeless, and so contemptible; I was contemptible; he'd sent me away almost as soon as we'd entered his apartment. That was the secret of my hurt over *some guy*.

What memory of Vernor Matheius's apartment I'd seen for such a brief period of time, scarcely minutes . . . Shelves of neatly arranged books; a narrow cot with a thin dark corduroy bedspread pulled up in apparent haste; a flattened pillow in a white, not-very-clean case; curtainless windows, the cracked and stained blinds I'd seen from the outside, from the safety of the ground. *And now I am here, now in apartment 2D with Vernor Matheius, how has such a miracle occurred? And if a "miracle" has occurred, is it a "miracle" after all?* Beneath my feet were bare, badly worn floorboards upon which a cheap, stained pile rug had been laid; the color of the rug was a vague blurred fleshy-gray of the hue of certain kinds of mold; the very floor was uneven, tilted; like the floors of my grandparents' old farmhouse beneath which the earth had shifted in a way to suggest indifference, or scorn; a child's marble, laid experimentally upon such a floor, would roll unhesitatingly until impeded by a wall. At the rear was a shadowy alcove with a single counter; a sink so small as to seem a child's sink; a dwarf refrigerator set upon the floor. The apartment was airless, smelling of cigarette smoke, coffee, grease; the yeasty odor of a man's body; soiled clothes, bedclothes. In such airlessness my nostrils widened in a kind of swoon; a wave of dizziness washed over me; perhaps I was trespassing into forbidden territory, shocked at my own audacity. *This is what a "desired" girl does, this is what is done to a "desired" girl.* Staring smiling at a desk which was the most premeditated and accomplished piece of furniture in the sparely furnished room; it had about it an aura of the sacred, the not-to-be-touched, like an altar, and beside it on the wall was a likeness of Socrates as a sculpted head with blind exophthalmic eyes, and another likeness of a stolid be-wigged man I believed must be Descartes. The desk itself exuded stolid-ity and character; how wholly unlike the cramped, battered, uniform aluminum desks issued by the university; it consisted of a large piece of wood set upon filing cabinets, wonderfully expansive for any desk, measuring perhaps five feet by four and a half feet; its sectors might have been marked off by invisible grids for neat piles of books, journals, and papers were placed at intervals, the highest at the rear and the low-est at the front, spines facing outward for ready identification; there was a clay bowl crammed with pens and pencils; there were much-eroded erasers; there was an Olivetti portable typewriter pushed back to clear a space directly in front of the desk chair, grooves in the desktop mark-ing how the typewriter was pushed back, pulled forward, pushed back and pulled forward again. Rolled into the typewriter was a sheet of pa-per upon which a tight little paragraph of prose had been typed:

> *The claim that philosophy is a battle against "the bewitchment of intel-ligence by language" & this very claim postulated in the syntax & con-tent & contours of Language—*

which I would identify at a later time as an argumentative allusion to the early work of Ludwig Wittgenstein.

Perhaps Vernor Matheius was speaking to me through the pulsebeat in my ears, perhaps he was not; perhaps he was indicating he would help me remove my jacket, perhaps he was not; perhaps he was fumbling with his sheepskin jacket, bulky on his tall, lanky frame like protective armature; perhaps he was not. *He will touch me now. Now it will happen.* Nervously he was tugging down a window shade, and the frayed mate-rial began to tear; he muttered a jokey profanity—"Shit!" And this word, this blunt mechanical brainless expletive in another man's voice: not Vernor Matheius's eloquent voice. As if another, more commonplace and thus more practicable man not Vernor Matheius stood in his place, cursing a frayed window shade. Yet I didn't hear, exactly; I heard but didn't acknowledge; my heart was beating rapidly as I stood rereading the enigmatic paragraph typed on the sheet of stark white paper as if it were a secret, coded message meant solely for me which even its author could not have fully comprehended. It was then that I realized I had been hearing Vernor Matheius's breathing. His breathing like panting. Like a dog's panting. And I smelled the alarm, the fear lifting from his body like heat. "Why'd you come here with me?"—a voice that was raw, harsh; very male; like sandpaper scraping across a splintery wooden surface; a frightened voice; a disdainful voice; not the musical, seductive voice of the lecture hall; not the voice of logic, reason, conviction, irony; not the voice of Vernor Matheius as I'd heard it in my dreams; but a stranger's voice, any-man's voice. I stared at him now, struck dumb; he was frowning, such a frown shifting the glasses on the bridge of his nose, and the lenses of his glasses were opaque with reflected light (as soon as we'd stepped inside the room Vernor had switched on an overhead light and shadows were cast downward on our faces, like appalled skulls we regarded each other out of astonished shadowed eye-sockets); he was saying: "Look, Anellia, you don't want to do this, and I don't, either." We were still in our outer clothes; I had not begun to unbutton the green suede jacket, and Vernor's bulky sheepskin jacket looked more resolutely on his body than it had been outdoors. Yet he touched me, his forefingers gently prodding me toward the door, swiftly he unlocked the door, opened it, murmuring, "—sometime, some other time, Anellia, good-bye—" his voice choked and abruptly then I stood outside the room, in a drafty hall opening onto the stairs, I was blind, blundering down the swaying wooden stairs which only a few minutes before another girl had boldly, tremblingly ascended. Not knowing where I was, or why; not knowing if I was deeply wounded or whether in fact I was relieved, I'd been saved, like one pulled from a rushing river to safety lying spent and exhausted and dazed on the riverbank but safe, saved. *It hasn't happened yet.*

12

He called me Anellia, he'd remembered that name.

Driven from Vernor Matheius's door like a stray dog yet I had not the moral strength to keep away from him. The more he cast me from him with disdain—*You don't want to do this!*—the more I was drawn to him. I could think of no one else. I wished to think of no one else. In a delirium of yearning feeling the angry impress of his fingers against my arm; seeing his blood-darkened face, that look of exasperation and alarm. *Don't, you don't want, Anellia you don't want to do this.*

He was begging me. He was commanding me. He was instructing himself as well as me. And this not out of principle but instinctively.

I began to reason then, with a logician's certainty: it was possible, in the sense that it was not impossible, that Vernor Matheius might love me someday.

Or, allow me to love him.

"Anellia"—a name, a riddlesome sound, that had leapt to my lips as if it were Vernor Matheius who'd named me and not myself.

For each of our lovers invents us anew. Names us anew. The old is erased utterly. Struck dumb.

My own name was so common, ordinary, I'd begun to detect irony in its sound when it was spoken aloud. Since childhood I'd told myself *Differently named, you'd be a different person.*

Yet I worried that, repudiating my baptismal name at the age of nineteen, I was inadvertently repudiating my mother Ida. For Ida had named me.

"Anellia"—strange name. Never heard it before.

Well. You've never met me before.

I did not return to 1183 Chambers Street. More shrewdly I returned to the coffeehouse. In that grungy-romantic interior amid clouds of smoke and black-coffee fumes I wore the green suede jacket with its air of bygone, frenetic glamor; I wore the gauzy scarf that was the color of opalescent pearl; my hair had been shampooed, and was glossily combed; my thin chapped lips were transformed by crimson grease; I was not I but Anellia, drawing glances of interest from strangers. Anellia appeared to be a pretty undergraduate girl with a flattering curiosity about chess—"Oh no, I don't play! Just like to watch good players." It happened that Vernor Matheius was playing chess with a Dutch chemist with whom (I gathered) he often played in the coffeehouse, and so he could ignore me if he wished as I could ignore him. A young man be-friended me; bought me coffee, offered me a cigarette; we murmured together in admiration of certain of the chess players; when he men-tioned Vernor Matheius's name, innocently I inquired, "Who is he?" and my new friend said, "A philosophy Ph.D. student, supposed to be bril-liant, but—" making a vague bemused gesture with his fingers, meant to indicate—what? That Vernor was too brilliant, or only just supposed to be brilliant? That Vernor was in some way eccentric? To be the only dark-skinned individual in most settings in which he found himself, to behave as if this were not a fact visible to all, requires a certain degree of self-definition, which might be mistaken for eccentricity. To my new acquaintance I said, as Anellia might have said, innocently ironic, playful, "Whoever he is, he's beautiful."

Nearly everyone in the coffeehouse was smoking. This was an era of smoking. An era permeated by the haze-dreams of smoking. Blown-up photographs of the heroic, heraldic figures of "French existentialism"— our secular saints—Camus, Sartre, de Beauvoir gazed down upon us from the hammered-tin walls of the coffeehouse through romantically drifting clouds of smoke, cigarettes in their hands, or drooping from their lips. I could not smoke: I hated tobacco: the thought of defiling my lungs, that I knew with my fatalist's certainty would be more vulnerable than the leathery lungs of others, filled me with revulsion. Yet I felt the erotic undertow of smoking. I conceded its cheap movie-screen glamor. There was Vernor Matheius lighting a cigarette distracted by a move of his opponent on the chessboard, I saw the forehead creased in concentration, the squinting eyes, the way in which, negligently, the burning match is shaken out, and tossed toward an ashtray. I saw again my father smoking his endless cigarettes; my doomed, drunken father squinting upward at a light fixture in the ceiling of the old farmhouse, and grinning foolishly; he'd managed to take a snapshot of himself in this strange pose, timing the shutter of the old Brownie Hawkeye camera to click after a count of three; why such a comical pose, for whom was it taken? *Was this evidence of a man I'd never known?* Before I'd left for college I had looked in secret through my grandmother's few mementos, searching for further evidence of my lost father, but I'd found nothing that I had not already seen many times. I would wonder if Vernor Matheius was right: we have no personal identities because we have no personal histories, all that is "personal" must be lost, repudiated. Watching Vernor covertly I saw that his facial bones were sharper, crueller than I recalled.

The schoolboy glasses flashed with malevolent intelligence. I felt again, in a sudden faint swoon, the impress of his fingers on my arm. *I alone of these people have been touched by him. I alone, intimately touched by him.* Naively I prayed for Vernor to win his chess game for *If he wins he will glance up elated and pleased with himself and he'll see me and smile, in that instant Anellia will be invited to join that happiness*; if he lost, I seemed to know that with a sullen smile he'd mutter a few words to his Dutch companion, praise for the other's game, an expletive of disgust for his own, and avoiding all eyes he'd simply walk out. He would take no notice of Anellia at all and if he did, Anellia would be one more reason for his self-disgust, and for his escape. But Vernor and his heavyset opponent were so evenly matched that their game seemed never to be ending; though each had few pieces remaining, their brooding moves required many minutes' concentration, and I was forced to leave the coffeehouse at a quarter to eleven. I would not believe afterward that I'd squandered two and a half hours of my life; desperately, recklessly I'd hung around the coffeehouse like a small thin candle burning wanly, unseen and unknown; if proof of my rational deterioration was required, this was it; yet I felt disappointment only that the game would end, and it might end happily for Vernor Matheius, without me to witness.

"Vernor, good night."

These words I dared whisper, only just loud enough for Vernor Matheius to hear if he wished to hear, or to ignore if he wished to ignore, and leaving the coffeehouse I saw him glance up in my wake frowning, unsmiling, without recognition, yet without an expression of annoyance or rejection either.

I ran back to my residence hall, breathless and elated.

He doesn't hate me. One day, he will love me.

The drama of such sightings. Where panels in the world's opacity slide open unexpectedly, a brilliant blinding sunshine floods us with warmth.

Often in the university library I observed Vernor Matheius at a discreet distance. In so busy a place, the observation of another isn't at all difficult; isn't risky, or not very risky; there were very good reasons for me to prowl about the library's third level which was the domain of philosophy, religion, and theology; before I'd come to know Vernor Matheius, I'd spent hours reading philosophy journals in a cramped little lounge with a single long smudged table and a half-dozen chairs usually occupied by graduate students in philosophy (you could recognize them instantly: many were older, worn, bewhiskered, graying as if they'd been questing truth for a long time, decades and centuries and their faces had grown parched as soil in a time of drought); nothing excited me more than to open the pages of such publications as *Ethics, The Journal of Metaphysics, Philosophical Review,* even *Thomist* intrigued me; though after I'd fallen in love with Vernor Matheius, the periodicals room held less of an enchantment. Of course it was in exciting proximity to Vernor Matheius himself. Of course I knew exactly where Vernor Matheius's carrel was, amid a row of fifteen carrels assigned to advanced graduate students; on this crucial evening I was wearing a pale yellow angora sweater and a pleated tartan plaid skirt that swung at my hips, it was so large for me, and yet (I reasoned) so very classy; what others might call preppy; I believed that I looked attractive; mirrors assured me, my somewhat feverish face had been made into an attractive female face; my hair had not been shampooed for several days perhaps but I'd taken care to comb it in a provocative style as my Kappa sisters had once taught me; my facial expression, too, was subtly calibrated, a thoughtful look neither piously somber nor annoyingly cheerful. As if a comforting voice had assured me *You are worthy of being loved, you are not a clown and a fool and a garbage-digger and shameless offering yourself to this man like a whore not knowing how even to offer herself.* It had been thirteen days since Vernor Matheius had brought me to his apartment, and within five crushing minutes sent me away again. Thirteen days of shame, remorse, mortification, and hope: hope craven as a kicked dog who whimpers with pleasure at the mere presence of his master. Thirteen days of waking in a coffin-sized bed too exhausted and heavy-hearted to push myself out of bed, unless I woke exhilarated and manic, my pulses racing. *He has made me so happy. By existing he has allowed me to exist.* In such a nerved-up state I was inspired to write: the outermost layer of my skin had been peeled away, now the very air hurt me, and wakened me.

One day, fever dreams of this time would be transcribed into the formalist prose pieces of what would be my "first book" unknown and unguessed-at, as a galaxy many light-years distant, in this fevered time.

Making my way along the row of carrels. There, Vernor Matheius's carrel! Yet when Vernor glanced up at me, I seemed not to have expected to see him; in my preppy clothes and pink lip gloss, I didn't smile at him until he smiled at me; a smile leapt instantaneously between us, like a lighted match.

His voice was low, gravelly—"You. 'Anellia.' What the hell are you doing here, this time of night?"

His eyes frankly stared; beautiful lashed eyes of an unnatural size, strained and glaring behind the schoolboy glasses, as if the eyeballs were pushing through the sockets. Obviously he knew (did he?) that I was seeking him out and yet he didn't send me away, he didn't express displeasure; eagerly I thought *He has taken pity on me, my very need of him.* As a master about to kick his dog pauses, seeing in the dog's shimmering eyes a capacity for love, and for hurt, that exceeds the master's wish to give pain. I saw how Vernor took in the pleated tartan skirt that had once been the possession of an American girl whose parents had so loved her, they'd lavished her with expensive clothes; I saw how Vernor took in the angora sweater, which fitted my small chest snug as a child's sweater, which perhaps it had once been. My happy smile *Here I am! let me love you! don't deny me! I will cease to exist!* as in an even voice I told Vernor Matheius that I often worked up here, this was my favorite place in the library, I'd discovered it early in my freshman year.

"Especially the periodicals room. As soon as I first stepped inside, and saw, I think it was the *Journal of Metaphysics*—I knew this was where I belonged."

Vernor laughed. He had no reason to doubt me, yet he was behaving as if he doubted me. Shutting the heavy book he'd been reading, a commentary on Wittgenstein's *Tractatus Logico-Philosophicus,* and shoving it away.

13

"It's late. I better walk you home." Adding, as a point of information, "Your home."

"But it isn't a 'home,' it's just a place I stay."

"Any 'home' is 'just a place I stay.' That's its essence."

We were leaving the library together. A leeching-wet wind shoved against us. Not a sentimental wind. Not a wind of romance. I loved this wind, it made Vernor Matheius feel protective of me. Sidelong he regarded me quizzically, with a kind of interest. Though not touching me.

Propositions came to me, skeins of words. Remarks to make Vernor smile, or laugh. But I couldn't speak. My heart was pounding as rapidly as it pounded sometimes in my sleep.

I had been reading Wittgenstein. There are no philosophical problems, only linguistic misunderstandings. Was this so? If so, why write at such length about it? I could understand Vernor's attraction to such a philosophy. Spartan, rigorous. Surpassingly skeptical. Well, good: philosophers should be skeptical. (No one else is: the mass of mankind is credulous as a gigantic infant, willing to suck any teat.) In the presence of a man like Vernor Matheius it was wisest to say very little. You could see, Vernor could love only a woman who said very little, for speech makes us vulnerable, exposes us. What Vernor liked about silence was that he could break it when he wished. Saying, after a long pause, "You are a strange girl, Anellia. But you know that. Tell me this one thing: what d'you want?"

"—what do I want from—life? Or—"

"No, girl. From me."

There. It was said.

No playfulness between us. No sexual banter. Though there was (I saw, helpless) the swagger of the man's body, the ease of his knifeblade-body, the incline of his head. He began to whistle in his thin tuneless way; you could see it must've been a terrific way of provoking his elders. And maybe rolling his eyes. Big white-orbed Negro eyes. There was the hand-knitted cap pulled low on his forehead, crinkling his skin. A caption beneath this face might read WANTED.

I was taken by surprise. Yet I could not show it. I would examine my obsession with this man as if it was a problem: an intellectual puzzle intriguing to us both. For we were students of philosophy, engaged in a common quest for truth; for paring back myths and subterfuge in the pursuit of truth; and what is philosophy but the ceaseless and indefatigable invention of and "solving" of problems? I understood that Vernor Matheius was asking frankly *What do you want from me that you imagine I can provide you? And what would you presume to provide me, in return?*

By the calendar it was early April. Yet snow remained on the ground like strips of grimy Styrofoam. We walked with our heads ducked against the wind in our common effort; we walked without speaking; Vernor Matheius had posed a question to me which I would not answer glibly; I was in fact stymied by how to answer it at all; his whistling was both companionable and meant to distance him from me; air gusted about us like roiling thoughts. I thought with a smile *If the would-be assailant should see me, he would be forced to re-define me.* And if my Kappa ex-sisters should see me?

Without asking me, without a word of explanation, Vernor Matheius steered me to Allen Street, to a pub called Downy's. Was he really taking me here? Would we be entering this noisy, crowded campus pub together, like a couple? Vernor Matheius a head taller than the diminutive white girl at his side? In the smoky interior, eyes moved upon us; there was an unmistakable shifting of attention, on the part of a number of individuals; a reflexive instinct, and nothing personal. Of course, Vernor Matheius took not the slightest notice. He was accustomed to being *looked-at,* and maybe *stared-at.* He was accustomed to being *visible.*

Vernor Matheius nudged me toward the rear of the pub. Into a small booth in a corner. On the old-wood walls were orange Syracuse pennants; laminated newspaper pages, SYRACUSE WARRIORS TROUNCE CORNELL. I had never been in Downy's before but it was a place much liked by Kappas, and when Vernor went to the bar to get drinks I saw that I was being observed, eyes shifting on me and away, by several Kappas, in the company of their fraternity boyfriends. *Oh my God. Look. And who she's with.* I felt a thrill of defiance, vindication. They had known I was a bad girl, and this was the proof.

Vernor Matheius returned finally with two tall glasses of beer. He'd had to wait at the bar, but you could see the bartenders were busy. And finally he was served. And made his way back to the booth. My first taste of beer, and it seemed to scald my mouth. The bitter dank smell. I thought of my vanished father. The delicious poison he'd been able to extract from alcohol. Vernor Matheius drank, and laughed, his chunky white teeth laughing, not at me but—"This place, know what it makes me think of?" I shook my head, leaning forward to hear. The table beneath my elbows was made of old timber, two crude planks varnished to a dark sheen, covered in carved initials, inked phrases, cigarette burns. "Schopenhauer. The Will. The triumph of the Will." He gestured at the crowd, the smoky haze penetrated by shrill voices and laughter. I said, with an air of contrition, that I didn't know much about Schopenhauer; Vernor Matheius shrugged as if he'd have been surprised, if I had; he was a natural teacher, or preacher; hadn't he said, he'd studied in a seminary; he began to speak of Schopenhauer and his "quarrel" with the philosopher who believed that the individual is but the phenomenon and not the thing-in-itself; though he had to concur with Schopenhauer that in strife, sex, reproduction the individual is the dupe of the species—"The unenlightened individual, that is." When he'd been twenty-four, it was philosophy that had opened his eyes; philosophy that was "an ice pick, a scalpel"; philosophy that was a surgical instrument for analysis, dissection, debridement, and comprehension. I listened fascinated. I had never heard anyone speak so passionately. And to *me*. If I hadn't already been in love with Vernor Matheius I would have fallen in love with him now, within the space of a few minutes; I was lost to him; mesmerized by his voice; his intelligence; the purity of his conviction, and its impersonality. Vernor Matheius's voice amid the drunken clamor of the pub at this, its most crowded hour. How he yearned, he said, for a "life of the mind"; for the clarity of "pure, blazing, fearless thought" to illuminate the murk of history and of time. " 'Better that the world should perish than that I, or any other human being, should believe a lie'—as Bertrand Russell said. Wittgenstein's mentor at first, and then his rival and enemy." When he fell silent, I could not think of a worthy reply; I tried to smile, and didn't succeed; I was overwhelmed by him, like a swimmer who has ventured into a river not knowing how quickly the land falls away, how powerful the undertow. Vernor Matheius saw my perplexity and said it was an irony, wasn't it, he was being trained to teach, yet he hadn't the patience for teaching, at least not undergraduates; probably he wouldn't wind up teaching if he could survive somehow else, there was the example of Wittgenstein who'd been a gardener, for a while; working with your hands is a good antidote for too much thinking; anyway, it wouldn't matter how poor he was; he, Vernor Matheius, was used to being poor; his parents were both dead, long ago; his family was scattered; he himself had no intention of ever marrying, and still less would he sire offspring; he declared he had no interest in perpetuating his precious genes, or the very species Homo sapiens—"They can get along without this fellow's contribution."

But how sad, was my immediate thought.

I said, "Oh, I understand."

He laughed for some reason, I hoped not at me; and I laughed with him. He was a man, I saw, who liked to laugh; yet didn't have much opportunity to laugh; for the professional study of philosophy doesn't inspire laughter, nor any degree of mirth; just as the earthy smell of death is excluded from the philosophical examination of finitude and death, so too laughter is excluded; it was a somber, sobering vocation. I thought *I will help him to laugh*. Inspiration, fueled by the giddiness of the moment. Several awkward swallows of beer. Trying not to gag. Yes, I would inspire laughter in this man; I refused to be one of the women who diminish, not increase, a man's laughter; I refused to be a woman who made *Woman* my life. Quickly I told Vernor what was only true: I agreed with him, I didn't want to marry, didn't want to have babies. (But was this so? Ida had married, Ida had had babies.) Vernor laughed carelessly saying he'd never met a "female" who wasn't maternal—"In her heart, if you could penetrate it. Or another organ."

Hotly I said, "There are exceptions."

"No exception 'proves the rule.' Only disproves it."

I was left behind in all this. Vaguely I smiled lifting my glass. Vernor drained his glass, went to buy another. I sat basking, or dazed, in the aftermath of his words. Had he praised me? Had he made an exception of me?

A couple now. Perceived as such.

It hurt me to recall how, in the Kappa house, I'd overheard my Kappa sisters speak of "niggers." Not meanly, not with malice, but matter-of-factly. One of our house boys was a Negro, that's to say a "nigger." There were categories of girls whom Christian sororities automatically cut: "niggers," "Jews."

A fractional Jew, I could pass.

And there was Vernor Matheius. *I am who I am, none of you can trap me with your language.*

Returning to our booth, Vernor began speaking in a new way. As if, standing at the bar, he'd glanced back in my direction and hadn't liked what he saw. For now he was antagonistic; asking me again what I wanted from him; what I thought I was doing, chasing after him— "Girl, don't wince. 'Chasing after' is it." I felt my face heat; I could not defend myself; I could not say that it was Vernor Matheius who drew me to him, not I who had the volition to be drawn. I could not say *But I fell in love with your voice, your mind, before I even saw you.* For it was preposterous, it would make him laugh in derision. He stared at me, frowning. Saying maybe I was just naive? inexperienced? too trusting? "There are men who'd take advantage of you, you must know. You're an intelligent girl, Anellia." I heard his words, I was thrilled by the sound of *Anellia* in Vernor Matheius's voice. I had no reply to his statement for it was not a statement that could be refuted. I liked it that I was being presented to myself as a problem to be solved; my face was hot with embarrassment and pleasure; it was like being teased by my brothers when they weren't being cruel, exactly; simply to be noticed was a thrill. In noisy Downy's there was happy brainless laughter for which I was grateful, I couldn't be expected to raise my voice against it. I smiled at Vernor Matheius shyly. *Yes but I love you. That is the problem to which all other problems can be reduced.* As if he'd heard my thoughts Vernor frowned again; he removed his glasses and polished the lenses with a tissue; without the glasses his face loomed above me with sudden startling intimacy; the contours in the oily dark skin around the eyes, the somewhat sunken sockets, the lashes long as a child's, the exaggerated flatness of the nose that would have been (I thought this without thinking) disfiguring in a Caucasian face. When Vernor Matheius shoved his glasses back onto his face, adjusting the wire frames behind his ears, he seemed to be glaring at me, seeing me more distinctly.

Without a word he rose. Immediately I followed.

In a haze of not-knowing what would come next I followed Vernor to the door as he shrugged on his sheepskin jacket, pulled his wool cap down on his head. He'd left me to struggle with my own coat. Not out of rudeness (I was certain), he just hadn't noticed. It was time for us to leave, ergo it was time for us to leave. The actual process of making our way through the crowd, to the door and out, was a secondary matter.

Yet, at the door, he remembered me; he paused, to let me pass through the doorway ahead of him; I felt his fingers lightly on my shoulder; again, I had the sense that he was herding me; impatient with me; I didn't think at the time *It's a gesture of possession in this public place. Even if no one is looking. Not that Vernor Matheius wants me sexually or in any other way but he wants to make a public claim, a proprietary gesture.* Behind us I felt the net of eyes and disapproval and I laughed stepping out into the cold; into a damp wind bracing as a slap in the face when you've been a little dazed, giddy. I would have expected Vernor Matheius to say good-bye to me on Allen Street but instead he walked me to my residence hall, several blocks away, an old brick building undistinguished as an old shoe, and no words passed between us; I could think of nothing valuable to say, and nothing I dared say; Vernor Matheius seemed to have run out of words, too; for there are problems that may be too snarled to be solved. At Norwood Hall, outside the lighted front entrance, Vernor Matheius said, "I won't come in. I'll say good night here. I want you to know, Anellia, you're not new to me." He smiled at my look of confusion. I said, stammering slightly, "Not n-new? To you?" He said, backing off, "I saw you a while back. It was you. Scavenging in the garbage behind the Mohawk Bakery." Vernor laughed at my look of distress. How long he'd been waiting to tell me this, I would have to wonder. My face burned with shame, I had no defense.

"Hope you're not scavenging with me, girl."

Vernor walked off. He knew I would stand stricken behind him, staring as he strode away. Other girls and their escorts passed by me, I had no awareness of them. There went Vernor Matheius in his sheepskin jacket taking long strides across the street, away from me without a backward glance to see how I gazed after him.

Yes but I love you, nothing can shame me.

1 4

I'd wanted to be independent. I'd wanted to earn money, at the age of fourteen. So I could say like my brothers that *I worked, I had a job*. If my father telephoned, and if he asked to speak to me, I would tell him about my *work,* my *job*. For work on the farm and in my grandmother's house didn't count, earned me no money or the small respect that comes with earning money. And so I did housework for several Strykersville women, well-to-do by local standards, exhausting day-long jobs arranged for me by a great-aunt of my father's who lived in town and whose relationship to my rural, diminished family was sympathetic, though condescending; one of the women for whom I worked was Mrs. Farley the doctor's wife, an entire Saturday in June just after school ended for the summer; there I was vacuuming, sweeping, scrubbing, mopping, and scouring through the Farleys' six-bedroom Colonial on Myrtle Street; Myrtle Street was Strykersville's most prestigious street; I'd never been inside one of the houses on that street; and now my heart beat in resentment, and yet in admiration and envy. There were classmates of mine who lived in this neighborhood and I'd never thought so clearly of what it might mean in one's soul to live on Myrtle Street *as if one were entitled to Myrtle Street*.

Mrs. Farley's soul had been plumped up living on Myrtle Street, like a hen's breast feathers.

As I worked inside, I could see the Farleys' *lawn boy* working outside. In fact he was no boy but a hump-backed Negro in his fifties with a skin coffee-colored like Joe Louis; he had something of Louis's furtive, watchful manner, carrying his arms high, as if like the boxer he was practiced in the art of self-defense. From the kitchen I could see him; from the upstairs windows I could see him; from the laundry room I could see him; from the rear porch I could see him; he was spading and weeding in Mrs. Farley's flower beds, and not once did he see me; he never glanced toward the house; he worked in the sun fully absorbed in his own consciousness like a man who knows that, if you happen to glance at him, you won't see him. You'll see the *lawn boy*.

Mrs. Farley was a fussy, watchful employer. She'd had problems with other cleaning girls and would have, she seemed to know, a problem with me. She was concerned that I might break one of her pieces of Wedgwood china, or a Dalton "figurine"; grimly she oversaw me as I sat, dirtied and bored, at the dining room table polishing silver: silverware, silver candlestick holders, absurd little cream and sugar bowls, *heirlooms* as Mrs. Farley called them; how she and Mrs. Thayer would have liked each other, in their common passion; still, I didn't hate Mrs. Farley until I heard from her thin-lipped mouth the expression, which was the first time I'd ever heard it—*Negro-lover*. She didn't say *nigger-lover;* this wasn't a term a woman of her pretensions would have said. Instead she said *Negro-lover* in reference to something that had been reported that morning on the radio; the acquittal of white murderers of a black man in Georgia, by an all-white jury; the protests by a scattering of church leaders and politicians in the wake of the acquittal.

Negro-lovers these individuals were, in Mrs. Farley's vocabulary. In Strykersville, there were few Negroes; in our county there was no "civil

unrest"; in nearby Buffalo there'd been "race riots" some years ago, following the end of World War II; but there was no threat of racial strife
in Strykersville, and so Mrs. Farley uttered *Negro-lover* in a bemused
voice, as one might speak of *garbage-lovers, mud-lovers.* I said at once, in
my bright girl-student manner, "Christians are supposed to *love* everybody, aren't they, Mrs. Farley?" The stab of emotion I felt was mixed in
my memory with the stink of bright pink silver polish and the greasy,
disgusting feel of rubber gloves; it was mixed with the startled expression on Mrs. Farley's face as she stared at me, half-smiling as if uncertain
whether I was joking. Her cheeks mottled; her eyes filled with hurt; I
was rubbing savagely at a badly tarnished little spoon; I was thinking
how, as Mrs. Farley watched, I might push the handle into a crack in the
table and bend it, at the same time splintering the beautifully polished
rosewood table; yet I did nothing like this, nor did I say another word;
perhaps my courage had run out abruptly. Mrs. Farley left the room,
and when we next spoke she was curt and polite and cool; if she'd been
trying to like me, thinking to befriend me as a poor farm girl lacking a
mother, she would try no longer. I'd offended her, and just possibly I'd
frightened her. For never again was I hired to clean the Farleys' six-
bedroom Colonial on Myrtle Street for eighty-five cents an hour.

I was glad of this. I told my father's great-aunt so. She said, annoyed
with me, that Mrs. Farley was spreading the word in Strykersville, I
wouldn't be offered housework anywhere—"She says you're sloppy and
careless and arrogant. She says you're too smart for your own good."

It was true: I was too smart for my own good, or for anyone else's.

Negro-lover, nigger-lover. That epithet of the times believed to be unspeak-
ably obscene. Like *cock-sucker* which was an expression of abuse also
used exclusively by men in speaking of, or to, other men; like-minded

men; men who understood one another because they were *men;* and not *cock-suckers* who might resemble men but who were not men. No woman would be called a *cock-sucker* though the practice (I had only the dimmest, repelled notion of what this practice might be) was not limited to men. Would a woman be called a *nigger-lover?* When, in fact, many women loved *Negroes?* It had not escaped my notice that in most interracial couples, the woman is white, the man black. Was I now a *Negro-lover,* was I a *nigger-lover?* When the color of Vernor Matheius's skin was to me of no more significance than the color of a shirt he wore, or the color of his vivid red scarf.

15

Above the gorge of Oneida Creek a mile from the university campus, north and east of Auburn Heights, there was a footbridge made of raw wooden planks. The footbridge was approximately fifty feet across. The gorge was approximately thirty feet below. To look down into the gorge was to feel a wave of dizziness that seemed to rush up from the folds and creases of rock below. The footbridge was maintained by the city and led to a wilderness area at the crescent of which, approached from the other side of the hill by a lane, was a tall water tower. Often that winter, when I had time, I went for walks on that hill, to clear my head; to clear my head of Vernor Matheius; to lose myself in a dream of Vernor Matheius; to replay in compulsive detail each of our conversations and to see again, more vividly in memory than I'd seen in life, every nuance of expression on Vernor Matheius's face. I would wake from a trance and find myself on the bridge, gripping both railings; gazing down at the creek-bed below. Always on the footbridge I thought of Vernor Matheius, and always on the footbridge I thought of Ida. What linked them was a riddle. What linked them was the terrible loss to the world of their deaths: the one a possibility, the other a fact. On cold mornings thin columns of tendril-like mist rose from the creek like mysterious exhalations of breath. To stare at such vaporous columns was to stare into emptiness. *Between one and none there lies an infinity.* So Nietzsche had written tenderly of Schopenhauer. It was the most profound statement of love and of the possibility of loss I had ever encountered.

In April, the frozen creek began finally to unlock. Roiling black water rushed below like a furious artery. The artery was narrow but deep; above the creek, leaning on the railing, I couldn't determine in which direction it flowed. I thought *I should be facing that direction. Facing the future.* If I fell by accident, I should have liked to know in which direction my body would be carried.

16

In the very place of seductive death. A miracle.

One day nearing sunset, a bright balmy April afternoon erratically splotched with rain, I saw, or believed I saw, Vernor Matheius a short distance ahead of me on the dirt path descending to the Oneida Creek footbridge; I was suffused with excitement, and dread; for it was by chance that I was here yet if Vernor Matheius saw me surely he would think I'd been *chasing after* him—wouldn't he? And I was innocent (I believed I was innocent). It had been eight days since we'd been together in Downy's and I had promised myself that I would not pursue the man further; would not *chase after* him like an infatuated schoolgirl; though in fact I was an infatuated schoolgirl, and could not perceive a time when I would be anything other than an infatuated schoolgirl. As, in the throes of nausea or the delirious lassitude of fever we are unable to imagine other states of being. I had vowed never again to humiliate myself and annoy and embarrass Vernor Matheius—telling myself I must wait for him to call me, or approach me; knowing as if it were a death sentence that he would neither call me nor approach me. It was true: I'd returned once or twice to the coffeehouse, relieved to see that Vernor Matheius was not among the chess players; nearly every day I worked in the library and often I found myself on the third floor; but like an early Christian ascetic renouncing all worldly life that gave pleasure I refrained from approaching the graduate students' carrels and did not know whether in fact Vernor Matheius was there in his carrel seventh from the aisle; I may have weakened and passed by the apartment building at 1183 Chambers Street once or twice, but only at such hours when Vernor Matheius couldn't have been there; and I didn't pause to stare openly at the building, still less did I prowl the alley behind it. So it was purely chance that Vernor Matheius and I had come to the gorge at the same time: never had I seen him in the vicinity before, and never had I mentioned to him that I came here. (If I had a life apart from my attentiveness to Vernor Matheius, neither he nor I would have thought it worth mentioning.) I saw him stroll out onto the footbridge; I saw his lips pursed, in a tuneless whistle; he was wearing a rumpled stone-gray sport coat that fitted his shoulders tightly, as if he'd outgrown it, and russet-brown trousers with a crease. He began to slow his pace, as if realizing where he was. High in the air on a wind-rocking footbridge. He shaded his eyes: this view captured his attention. To the north, a small mountain, outcroppings of granite dense and convoluted as if to some mysterious purpose, like folds in the human brain. I saw Vernor Matheius lean against the railing and stare down; lean over the railing and stare down; a thrill of horror touched me—*What if he falls?* I was frightened suddenly and stepped out onto the footbridge. I knew this might be a mistake, he'd think I had been following him, but I couldn't resist; I told myself I would pass behind him, as if unaware of him (for his back was to me, I might not have identified him in ordinary circumstances), and maybe he would notice me, and maybe he would not; in that way, our meeting was left to pure chance. But my heart was beating so hard, the very footbridge must have vibrated! *I will not, I will not speak. Will not reveal myself.* The wind buffeted us on the footbridge as if in mockery. Vernor Matheius, leaning far over the railing, holding his wire-rimmed glasses with both hands as if concerned they might fall off, wasn't going to notice me . . . except my shadow must have brushed against him; and with the instinctive reflex with which one would glance back at someone or something passing close behind him on a swaying footbridge thirty feet above a gorge, Vernor Matheius glanced back at me; I saw his worried face, his creased forehead; I thought naively *He doesn't trust the world!* I lacked the insight to realize *He doesn't trust the white world.* But in the intoxication of the moment neither of us had time for such revelations: our eyes locked, recognition shone in his like a lit match. "Anellia. Again."

My hair was whipping in the wind. I pulled a strand out of my mouth. Vernor Matheius's gaze dropped to my waist, to my hips, legs and ankles and lifted again with masculine ease, lingering on my breasts and face; as if I'd positioned myself on the footbridge, a few feet away, to be so contemplated. Around my waist was the belt of linked silver medallions; I wore a ribbed black cotton-wool top with long sleeves and tight wrists, and a black-and-lavender skirt in a crinkly Indian material that fitted me loosely, like a gown falling to mid-thigh. These were secondhand clothes, costume clothes. "I—I come here sometimes. It's so—" meaning to say *beautiful* but the obvious, over-used word stuck in my throat. Nor could I explain *I wasn't following you, Vernor. Except in my thoughts. How can I be blamed?* He seemed bemused by me. Possibly he didn't hate me. Between us was the memory of the last time we'd spoken, on the sidewalk in front of Norwood Hall. Between us, the humiliating memory of when Vernor Matheius had first seen me.

Scavenging in a trash can!

Yet now Vernor was smiling, smiling at me, if still there was an air of reserve and even reproach in his face. We were talking about what?—ordinary things. My heart that had been pounding absurdly now began to ease. My thoughts of death of only a few minutes before had vanished as if blown by the wind. *Between one and none there lies an infinity.*

It may have occurred to me that in my charmingly funky gypsy-clothes I was *pretty* again. I would be *desired.*

It may have occurred to me that whatever the consequences of such costuming, I would accept them.

Thirty feet above the black-rushing artery deep in rock as if suspended in time.

There was a subtle but vital change in Vernor Matheius, in his manner which was animated, alert, even edgy; in the timbre of his voice, which was higher-pitched than usual; in the way his forehead creased almost too urgently as he spoke. That noon at the university there'd been a civil rights demonstration in front of the chapel that would be denounced in local newspapers as the work of "outside agitators" but given extensive, sympathetic coverage in the *Daily Orange,* the student paper; in the gusty spring day in which a phantom rainbow shimmered in a washed-blue sky there'd been the distraction of amplified voices on the green, disturbing voices where ordinarily there were no voices; these were voices that upset some students and professors; voices that thrilled others; some classes had been canceled so that students could attend but most classes continued; I saw more black faces than I would have believed there were at the university, and individuals who obviously weren't students but organizers. I'd been hurrying from one classroom to another when I heard the speakers, raised voices interrupted by applause, and by some jeers and boos. Of course, I knew of civil rights activism in the South; the arrests and martyrdom of Martin Luther King Jr. and his co-demonstrators during a peaceful march in Birmingham, Alabama; yet if pressed, I could not have said whether the United States government was protecting the rights of the protestors, or the rights of local authorities to arrest them. Two weeks before, there'd been an even more disruptive demonstration on campus, a rowdy gathering of about thirty SANE (STOP ALL NUCLEAR EXPERIMENTATION) pickets of whom all were white, defiantly ill-groomed older students; these pickets, undergraduates had loudly heckled; fraternity men wrested some of their handmade signs from them and broke them into pieces; the SANE demonstrators were denounced as "Communists" or "Communist dupes"; campus police finally routed them off with a threat of arrest. I'd arrived too late; I found a sign in the mud—BAN THE BOMB FOR MANKIND'S SAKE!—and would have carried it away except it was taken from me and torn. The civil rights demonstration had been organized by the Student Non-violent Coordinating Committee and was better attended, and better respected; I looked for Vernor Matheius in the crowd gathered in front of the chapel steps though knowing I wouldn't see him, for such public displays were not compatible with the quieter, more circuitous strategies of philosophy to transform the world. And now on the footbridge above Oneida Creek I sensed how I must not bring up the subject. I must not allude to what had happened, or was happening, back on campus; I wasn't one who knew much about contemporary politics, for I rarely read a newspaper, never saw television; like Vernor Matheius, I was absorbed in the life of the mind; of this indifference, I may have been proud; though that day I'd have liked to carry a picket sign in support of civil rights, for the demonstrators seemed admirable to me, courageous and articulate, and their opponents were embittered and ugly. Vernor wanted to hear nothing about this, I sensed; he was leaning with his back against the railing now, arms outstretched; it was something of a shock to see the man in daylight, in the open air; his youthfulness, his edginess; the faint yellow tinge of his eyeballs; the smudged lenses of his glasses. He was speaking of his work, a new problem in his research; he was hoping to explore the classic problem of "ontological proof" from a purely linguistic perspective. He'd come under the spell of the early Wittgenstein, the lacerating, revolutionary *Tractatus*—"It's almost too banal, to be enthralled by Wittgenstein. Yet, just possibly, there's no one quite like him." I shut my eyes and saw the flattened pillow on Vernor Matheius's bed, I could imagine its scent, the smell of his hair; I could not recall whether in fact I'd seen the pillow and the bed or whether Vernor had so quickly changed his mind about me, and herded me out of his apartment, I'd seen nothing; I'd had to imagine. How strong now the impulse to press myself into Vernor Matheius's arms; to press my face against his throat. *No: you must not. You will disgust him.*

Vernor saw me shivering, and said, "Are you cold, Anellia?" and I admitted, "Yes, I'm cold," for this was true; the sun was obscured by clouds, and about to set; it was spring by the calendar, but high above the gorge the air retained a wintry chill. Vernor Matheius shifted his arm as if to protect me; it was an invitation to move into the crook of his arm; yet I stood paralyzed, uncertain. Oddly he asked, "Is that why you're here?" and I heard myself say, "Yes, that's why." He said, "This seems to me a dangerous place. D'you know, Anellia, this is a dangerous place?" He peered into the gorge below, frowning, yet with satisfaction. I said, weakly, "Yes, it's dangerous. People have jumped." Vernor removed his coat to drape around my shoulders; it was the most intimate gesture that had ever passed between us, and I swallowed hard, I was stricken to the heart. Under the coat Vernor wore one of his white, long-sleeved shirts, rumpled as if he'd been wearing it for days. *This is the Platonic idea of a white shirt. This is not an actual shirt.* He had no woman to launder and iron and cook for him; he wanted no woman to launder and iron and cook for him; I understood this, for in his place I would not have wanted a woman either. Yet how grateful I was, that Vernor Matheius wasn't married: for at the onset, when I'd gazed at him longingly across rows of strangers, I had seemed to see, glinting on his hand, a wedding band; in fact, there was no wedding band; no rings on his fingers; Vernor Matheius didn't even wear a watch, boasting he was no slave to clock-time. He was saying, "I'm not a nature person. I think nature is overrated. Nature is what you turn to when your brain fails. But I like coming here, when I have time. Because it is a dangerous place. I like the footbridge, seeing through the slats. I like the wind making it sway. I've caught god-awful colds out here. I like being alone here knowing there's an instinct in us to push ourselves over a railing like this; an instinct to die to which I'm never going to succumb. I like the mastery of not succumbing and of knowing I won't succumb. I like knowing what I won't do, and what I will do. If I want to do it." I was gripping the lapels of the coat that was much too large for me; I felt overwhelmed by Vernor Matheius's closeness, and the confiding way in which he spoke. He said, "You're right, people have jumped from this bridge. And it's kept quiet. Because dying, especially to no purpose, is contagious. Every year a number of persons will 'commit suicide' as it's called, as if fulfilling a statistical prophecy, though they know nothing of one another or of the prophecy. I like knowing that I, Vernor Matheius, will never be one of these; I don't behave in any way that others can predict; that's not my nature." I could hardly bear loving him so much, it was all I could do to stammer, "No, V-Vernor, that's not in your nature." Had I ever dared call him "Vernor" before? He stared at me, he framed my face in his hands. I was a puzzle to him and he could not determine whether the puzzle was worth it, to solve. At this moment someone stepped onto the footbridge and began to cross; we could feel his footsteps, his weight; oddly, I understood that this intrusion would not evoke a response in Vernor Matheius, or rather it would not evoke a normal response; Vernor Matheius was not one to be affected by the accidental intrusion of a stranger into his privacy. The stranger approached us, and passed close to us; a man in a bulky sweater, who glanced at us only briefly; Vernor paid no heed to him as if he didn't exist; Vernor kissed me, not on the lips which would have been a warm, moist kiss, a kiss of yearning and of promise, but on the forehead, just below my wind-whipping hair where my skin and his lips were taut with cold.

" 'Anellia.' Is that scavenged, too?"

17

I am not a man for any woman to count on, I am not a man who wants to be loved.

As it was not in Vernor Matheius's nature to be predicted, so it was not in Vernor Matheius's nature to be held to any promise. Even the vaguest promise. It was not in his nature to fall into any routine, however casual. Such as: meeting "Anellia" when the library closed and walking with me across the campus which was near-deserted at that hour; in the romance of spring, when even a fine feathery rain was fragrant with renewal. Though sometimes he'd grip my hand, my bare hand, squeezing the fingers so that I winced without his noticing, talking of his work, his ideas; always he was on the edge of a "breakthrough" regarding the ontological problem, Wittgenstein, and language. Yet he would not plan such meetings even a day beforehand. They must be accidental, or seeming so. He might telephone to invite me to meet him at the coffeehouse but if I wasn't in, he would not leave a message; he would not leave even his name. Once or twice a week he dropped in at the coffeehouse to play chess, but there could be no pattern here, either. His chess companions could not depend upon him. Sometimes, sighting me, they would ask, "Is Vernor coming?" and I would tell them with a smile I had no idea. "Only Vernor Matheius knows where Vernor Matheius is, and only Vernor Matheius knows where Vernor Matheius is going." Yet, by chance, if we met, Vernor would seem genuinely happy to see me; perhaps I'd become like the footbridge, not dangerous but a possibility of something undefined; he would ask if I was "free" for a meal, as if, always, I was not "free" for Vernor Matheius; we would enter a darkened Italian restaurant near the hospital, Vernor's hand on my shoulder as if I might need guidance; we might enter Downy's, to sit in a rear, shadowy booth whispering together like any couple; I would reason *If in others' eyes we are a couple, then that is what we are.* Except in the coffeehouse, among Vernor's friends, there were invariably people observing us, curious and hostile eyes; these were the eyes of whites exclusively. *Are they lovers? Those two?* Not that there were no interracial couples in Syracuse at that time. Surely there were. (Though I rarely saw them.) But something in Vernor Matheius's manner was too visible, provoking. And maybe I looked too young.

Most days I did not see Vernor. These were days so defined: as an insomniac night is defined by the absence of sleep, so these days of nullity and edginess were defined by the absence of Vernor Matheius.

Didn't I warn you: don't love me. Don't even try to know me.

Because it can't be done. Knowing me.

Because identity is within. A man's self is within where the rest of you can't measure it.

18

Yet: we were crossing a city street late one evening, gripping hands, in a playful mood, and a crazed car, a carload of drunken kids, not university students but local young-male whites, provoked by the sight of us and yelling "Nigger!"—"Nig-ger!"—"Nig-ger's bitch!"—swerved in our direction; a jeering horn, beer cans flung at us spraying beer like urine. I would remember with a thrill of emotion that Vernor didn't release my hand but gripped it tighter. "Don't look at them. Don't turn around. They don't exist." Vernor spoke coldly, furiously; we walked swiftly along the pavement, and turned a corner; the car was gone; the incident was over; even the flung beer hadn't touched us. I was too shocked to have been frightened, but now I began to tremble. Vernor was trembling, too. But he said nothing further until, shortly afterward, climbing the wooden steps outside his apartment building, his hand still gripping mine, he murmured, "Stay with me for a while." It was not a question nor even a commandment but rather a statement of fact. I said yes, I would. Inside his apartment a single lamp was burning. He said, quietly, "Anellia, take off your clothes."

With that air still of quiet, subdued fury he fumbled to remove his trousers, tugging and yanking impatiently at his white shirt, flinging his clothes toward a chair; I was slow to remove my clothing, my fingers numbed and without sensation, so he turned to me, wordless, thumbs digging into my shoulders; he seemed almost to be lifting me, breathing hotly and impatiently into my face, pushing me toward his bed in a darkened corner of the room; a narrow, hastily made-up bed with a flattened mattress sagging in the center, a flattened pillow of which how many times I'd dreamt swooning in absurd yearning, now inhaling the strong scent of Vernor Matheius's oily hair, the scent of his heated body, the dark crook of his neck, his underarms springy with hair, his flat belly, his crotch, and his feet; his mouth was pressed against mine for the first time, as if to silence me; his mouth larger, fuller, fleshier and more demanding than mine; and his tongue forcing itself into my mouth; quickly, before I could open to receive it; Vernor Matheius did not want me to take him, he wanted me to be taken by him; his tongue an agent of his cold, purposeful fury; for the jeering white boys in the careening car were vanished, and only I remained; I was seized with panic, unable to breathe; I couldn't kiss Vernor Matheius because his mouth mauled mine, and his fingers mauled, kneaded, squeezed, and stroked my body; I was limp and unresisting tasting his enormous tongue, the beery-acidic saliva of his mouth that was so hungry, moaning as if in pain, and I thought, dazed *Now it will happen, at last: he will love me.* I felt his penis swollen and blood-engorged pressed against my belly, it was like a living, groping, demanding thing; I tried to whisper, "Vernor, I l-love you—" as in such erotic fantasies I'd whispered these words, in my fantasies these were magical words, words with the power to transform an urgent, clumsy, graceless act into an act of profound meaning; a prayer with the power to make sacred an act of which crude, callous, and derisory things were said, my brothers saying such things, laughing, secret jokes and signals girls weren't supposed to understand; mustn't allow them to know she understands; but my words were choked, I couldn't draw breath to speak; Vernor didn't hear; Vernor didn't want to hear; this wasn't a time for words, from me. *He wants to fuck you. Nothing more.* Kneeling over me hunched and tremulous, his narrow rib cage heaving with the effort of breath; the bones defined against the tight, sweat-gleaming skin; skin scintillating with tiny beads of sweat like mica I wanted to lick with my tongue; but I could not, I was pinned to the bed by Vernor's weight, a hand pressing my shoulder to the bed so I was barely able to touch him, to reach for him, to slip an arm around his neck. As he'd removed his clothes hurriedly and tossed them aside, he'd removed his glasses, and his eyes were deep-socketed and glistening; without his glasses he was a man I didn't know; the flying skeins of beer like urine had defiled us both, though not touching us; jeering ugly white-man voices *Nig-ger!* in this room with us struggling in the dark so Vernor Matheius grunted what sounded like "*Nig-ger!* who's a *nig-ger?*" He was touching me between the legs, where no man had ever touched me; my skin contracted at his touch, as if with sudden cold; in panic; his fingers were sharp, prodding, impatient where my body had shut up tight; in helpless physical dread I'd shut up tight; to my dismay I'd shut up tight though I wanted to love Vernor Matheius; though wanting to love him, to open myself to him, I could not; I heard him curse; I heard him laugh; his laughter had the sibilant sound of a curse. "*You*—!" As if there was no worse curse. "Jesus Christ, girl—*you*." Vernor Matheius took pity on me, and abandoned me. Damned if he was going to force me. Kneeling above me he held his penis and with quick expedient strokes brought himself wincing to climax; his face contorted like a muscle in spasm, against his will; eyes glazing so he wasn't seeing me, wasn't seeing anything. He collapsed then beside me, nudging my head with his. And still I dared to say, biting my lower lip, "Vernor, I l-love you."

Vernor said nothing. Didn't move. His breath in long erratic shudders. Through my damp eyelashes I contemplated the length of him, this man lying beside me in a rumpled, sweaty bed, his long hard-muscled legs, and my pale legs beside his; I could not say *Forgive me,* I knew he would laugh. The fury in his laughter would be devastating. So we lay for some minutes in silence except for Vernor's breathing which by degrees began to slow, yet still a harsh sibilant sound, the despair of the spirit locked inside the body, the spirit that can be defined only through body, and defiled.

"Go wash up. It's through here."

This was a command, not bullying or unkind but forceful. Vernor was on his feet, and again restless. His naked eyes avoided mine. Avoided even my face, my body. That girl's body glimmering pale and insubstantial before him in the twilight of a room that seemed no longer his, or no longer his exclusively. Wordless, like a rebuffed child I took up my clothes, these scattered forlorn things flung down onto bare floorboards; my costume-clothes, which had worked their magic, until the magic ran out. And how abruptly and rudely it ran out. Stooping, I lifted the belt, ornamental silver medallions that tinkled faintly together like coins of small denominations. For the first time I wondered who'd originally owned this beautiful and utterly impractical belt: my lost twin, a girl with a twenty-three-inch waist. She'd be grown up by now. If she was still alive.

I went into Vernor Matheius's cubbyhole of a bathroom. I groped for a light switch: above the sink, an unshaded forty-watt bulb came on. Out leapt a startled white face in the cabinet mirror; a face I didn't recognize at first; a face both wan and radiant in a kind of triumph. *He did love me. Wanted to love me. We were naked together. Our bodies.* Even if he sent me away forever, such facts couldn't be changed. The bathroom door was made of a cheap warped wood and didn't shut completely. The space contained a sink layered in grime, a toilet and a stall shower with a torn plastic curtain partly mended with adhesive tape. Above the toilet tank was the likeness of a brooding, somber man of young middle age, dark curly hair, a narrow intolerant nose, thin lips. These lips were shut tight with a look of stubborn intensity. I recognized Ludwig Wittgenstein, the "piercing" dark eyes, the military manner; he wore a tweed coat, his shirt unbuttoned at the throat. Clutched in both hands at waist level was a bamboo cane. Wittgenstein had not succumbed to madness, nor to suicide; given the fates of others in his tragic family, this alone was a triumph. I understood why the philosopher was a hero to Vernor Matheius: he'd negated the very premises of his apparent destiny, to re-invent himself as pure, disembodied intellect. It took me another beat or two to realize that Vernor had placed Wittgenstein's likeness above the toilet so that, standing to urinate as he would be doing frequently, he could meditate upon his hero in a posture both submissive and blasphemous.

Beside the sink was a towel rack holding two neatly arranged but not very clean towels. And a washcloth stiffened with use. I was thinking *Vernor Matheius placed those there, not foreseeing how I would observe them.* In my agitated state, this was a consoling thought. Vernor couldn't have foreseen this incident. That I, an intruder, would be in his cubbyhole of a bathroom washing at his sink, taking careful note of the white, chipped-porcelain sink and the soap on the sink rim; the toilet with its ill-fitting tank top and its badly worn plastic seat, the stained bowl within, water quivering as if something had touched it, or the building were vibrating. And there was the pale green plastic shower curtain, a dime-store curtain practically mended with tape, the mending itself meticulously done, so I could imagine Vernor frowning as he applied himself to the task, with the identical precision and stubbornness with which he applied himself to philosophy. Inside was a stall shower so narrow and foreshortened I wondered how Vernor Matheius could fit inside without stooping. (But of course he'd have had to stoop, if he wanted to take a shower.) *None of these could Vernor Matheius have anticipated I would see.*

I washed myself quickly, lathering soap in my hands, not wanting to use Vernor's washcloth or one of the towels. Washing quickly between my legs, and my belly, where his semen was still damp, and sticky; clots of it, transparent and gluey; I felt this in wonder and in dread; how a man's semen leaps from his body, as if it were meant to bridge an abyss; like the clotted seeds of cottonwood trees, meant to be carried through space; I was thrilled at the new intimacy between us, which could not be revoked; though I knew that Vernor might repudiate me as a consequence; and I knew that there was a possibility that I could be impregnated, even if his seed hadn't been shot up into my body. Unlikely, yet I knew it was possible. *We are lovers now.*

Now that Vernor Matheius had made love to me, however incompletely, I felt a new tenderness for my body. Washing, I cupped my hand lightly between my legs; marveled at the prickly, wiry hairs; how distinct the hairs, and how distinct the flesh they shielded; a part of my body I hadn't cared much to consider; not out of shame so much as indifference, impatience; for what have I to do with my genitals, what identification with my sex? Yet I felt now this tenderness for myself; for Vernor Matheius had wanted to make love to me; he had in fact made love to me; we were bound together forever. I dried myself using toilet paper. Dressing then in the cramped space because I knew I must reappear fully clothed to Vernor Matheius. The silver-medallion belt was tricky to fasten, my hands were shaking. Yet I didn't believe that I was upset any longer, or frightened. And when I returned to the other room, there was Vernor seated at his desk as I'd known he would be; at the desk I so admired, twice the size of my own; beneath the noble, ascetic faces of Socrates and Descartes. Vernor, too, was fully dressed; his white long-sleeved shirt buttoned to the throat. Those shirts were cotton, he'd have had to take them to a dry cleaner's to have them laundered and ironed and so it was an indulgence, clearly a necessity. He must have washed himself quickly at his kitchen sink. Washed away the smells of our bodies. Sweat, semen. My desperation. His face looked burnished as if he'd scrubbed it hard. The round lenses of his glasses gleamed. He was himself again, Vernor Matheius.

To protect himself from me he'd lighted a cigarette. He'd pulled the Olivetti typewriter to him as if I were interrupting him in the midst of work; a sheet of paper cranked into the typewriter, a pile of handwritten notes beside it. *There, he's happiest. He won't need you now.* Vernor spoke often of working at night, sleeping for an hour or two and waking and returning to work refreshed, with new ideas; invigorated, excited. The thought of such a method made me tired. I didn't approach him, I understood how he wanted me to keep my distance from him. How badly I would have liked to touch him; slide my arms around his neck; as lovers did, so easily; I would have liked to kiss him, his cheek, his fleshy mouth; I would have liked to bury my warm face in his neck, inhale his fragrance another time, the yeasty-almondy-oily scent of Vernor Matheius's body. But I didn't dare touch him of course. Knowing how he'd have recoiled. Even my shadow brushing against him would lacerate his nerves. So quietly I said, "Good night, Vernor," and went to the door unlocking it, opening it myself; not wanting him to feel obliged to escort me back to my residence hall, nor even stir from where he sat; I didn't want him to feel a tinge of guilt; I didn't want him to feel resentment for that guilt; I didn't want him to feel that I was thinking these things, as if I had a right to think such things; I did not want to provoke him, and endanger our love.

My behavior surprised him—did it? He turned to stare at me as I prepared to leave him. At the door murmuring, softly, shyly so that the man might hear or not hear, as he wished, "Vernor, I love you. Good night."

I fled. I was partway down the outdoor stairs when I heard Vernor call after me in an undertone, protesting, "God damn you, girl, you do not *love me. You do not know me.*"

19

The sleeping man. His face wasn't one of repose but of torment, anguish. His forehead knotted, his mouth twisted into a grimace. The eyeballs moving beneath the shut lids. A quivering of his dark lustrous skin like a rippling in water. *If I could see him as ugly, unattractive. If I could see him as unloved.* I was a child bringing her fingertips to flame, inviting pain; daring pain; disbelieving pain. Trying to imagine my life without Vernor Matheius at its center. My life without loving him.

A hole in the heart through which the bleak cold of the universe might whistle through.

Strange to me, who stared at Vernor Matheius as he slept, on rare occasions when I was privileged to see him sleep, that there were others, Caucasians, a category of individuals to which in theory I belonged, who might gaze at Vernor Matheius in his unfathomable complexity and think merely *Negro.* And dismiss as *Negro.* What madness!

I came to believe that the unexamined life, the life that's led without continuous self-scrutiny, and a doubting of all inherited prejudice, bias, madness. In our civilized lives we are surrounded by madlieving ourselves enlightened.

that year in our windswept northerly city there were cold

driving rains like nails blown against flesh; the rush of happiness in the morning's sunshine would fade by midday when thunderheads gathered like artillery above Lake Ontario and moved south to spill themselves on our heads. Great bruised clouds swollen to bursting. The tumescence of nature. The bursting of nature. My lover's skin smoldered, infuriated. His eyes glancing away. He said *I have no people, no parents, no brothers or sisters; I have no god; I have no home except in the mind. My thoughts are my home.* And I asked *Isn't it lonely there, Vernor?* And he said simply *No. It's lonely here.*

20

"Anellia! Let's examine this. You've told me that you pledged a 'sorority' "—the very word uttered with bemused disdain—"without knowing it discriminated against certain persons? Jews, 'Negroes'?"

It was an examination rough as sandpaper. Vernor Matheius rubbing sandpaper briskly and gloatingly on my bare skin.

I stared at my feet. At the ground. Brittle gravel mixed with mud. I tried to remember: had I known? What had I known? The individual who'd been myself the previous year, before Vernor Matheius, had become a stranger. I could not respect her, only just pity her in her ignorance. Softly I said, like a guilty child, "I would guess—I hadn't known."

"Hadn't known! How is that possible?"

How was it possible? My impetuous, infatuated, unexamined act.

"I—didn't think to know."

"There! You're approaching it, girl. You didn't *think*."

And Vernor laughed heartily, shaking his head. A schoolteacher exasperated and delighted by his star pupil. As if his fingers were running over my body, tickling, if hurting; hurting just a little; and my body eager for this attention, as a puppy eager to be touched. This was Vernor Matheius in a playful mood. Vernor Matheius in his Socratic mood. (For all philosophers yearn to be Socrates, even those who dislike Socrates on principle, and have repudiated his bizarre metaphysics.) He loved it that Anellia who, so smart, such a smart little girl, should also be, frequently, so stupid.

Why had I confessed to him. My sordid Kappa past. My piteous Kappa past. Perhaps I'd wanted to amuse him by describing how I'd been voted out of the chapter almost unanimously—a single vote abstaining. (Whose vote? Never would I learn. Oh, that was unfair: unfair for me to be told such an astonishing fact, but no more.) I'd become *deactivated* from both the chapter and the national sisterhood of Kappa Gamma Pi. Telling Vernor of the experience, I didn't explain that I'd desperately petitioned for release; I'd been instructed how to proceed, sending letters to chapter officers and to the national executive board and to the Dean of Women (a powerful figure in such negotiations) explaining that I wanted to withdraw from the sorority. I could not explain to Vernor that I had never believed it was the fault of my Kappa sisters that I'd been such a failure, and so deeply unhappy, but my own fault; I was a freak in the midst of their stunning, stampeding, blazing female normality; if by magic I might have been transformed into a true Kappa, maybe in my desperation I'd have whispered—"Yes"? Still, they would not have released me for such a trifle as not fitting in. In my ignorance I'd signed documents I hadn't quite understood were legal contracts; I, who'd never signed such documents in my life and had glanced through these with misted-over eyes, scarcely pausing to read a line. To join a national sorority was a bold act binding one to financial obligations; this, I hadn't known. In my letters begging for release I'd explained that I was of *Jewish ancestry* and had *failed to tell the truth* about myself. I'd explained that I could not afford the sorority, and was already in debt for nearly three hundred dollars; under the irrefragable bylaws of the sorority I would have continued to be fined for missing meetings, I would have continued to accumulate interest as a result of this debt, and yet I could not belong to the sorority or even attend the university without working during those hours when meetings were scheduled, and so on *ad infinitum* unless I was granted a legal release, or died.

Are you threatening suicide, I was asked in alarm.

And so they'd expelled me, unanimously. Except for a single mysterious abstaining vote I wished to think had been Dawn, who'd seduced me into the sorority with the hope (and it wasn't an unreasonable hope) that I would help raise the house's grade-point average.

Mrs. Thayer had been released from her contract, too. With rude expediency, immediately after the alumni reception.

I told Vernor Matheius nothing of Agnes Thayer. No longer did I think of Agnes Thayer.

Not truth but the uses to which we put truth. What is done, in the service of desire.

Walking to the Oneida Creek footbridge. It was a day for such a walk: even Vernor Matheius conceded. A strange mood, Vernor's mood. He'd had some good news, reported in the university newspaper; Vernor Matheius was one of four doctoral students awarded a research grant from the National Endowment for the Humanities, to complete his Ph.D. dissertation the following year; when I congratulated him, he frowned and looked away evasively; of course he was pleased, yet he didn't seem to approve of his pleasure; he had to examine the roots of such a small, craven pleasure; taking delight in mere professional, public "success"—something that had to do solely with "career" and not the pursuit of truth. Especially it embarrassed him that in the philosophy department the professors congratulated him and shook his hand as if such a fluke pleased them, too; and this forced him to reconsider his estimation of them. "Oh, Vernor," I said. "Please stop. This is an infinite regress."

He said, quite seriously, "It is. An infinite regress. Next week I'll be thirty years old."

I could not see the connection here. I could not tell him I'd assumed he was older.

This balmy May afternoon in the hills above the university Vernor had reverted to his playful mood. I'd grown to anticipate his shifts of mood: like the sky above Lake Ontario. He believed himself stable, unvarying, a personality like Kant's you could set a watch by, in his temperament if not in his behavior; he believed he was a man devoted sheerly to the intellect, like Wittgenstein. Yet he was volatile, mercurial as the most capricious of the Kappa girls. I was fearful of him. I adored him.

We were walking with Vernor's arm around my shoulders, pulling me against him; an awkward way of walking; we were laughing, for my Kappa story had been intended to amuse; I would not have told any story of my life to Vernor Matheius that wasn't intended to amuse. In my feverish brief collapse after being expelled from the Kappas, one miserable day and a night in the university infirmary, I'd had a waking dream of the clinic in a Buffalo suburb in which (it had been pointed out to me once, years ago by a relative) my mother had gone for chemotherapy after her cancer operation, and this building had been old, regal and forbidding, with a half-dozen columns at the top of a flight of broad stone steps; the roof of the building had been a wet-looking dark blue slate; much of the building had been covered in ivy that needed trimming: the Kappa house: the original. Of such a revelation, and its impact like a rock tossed into my face, I could not have told Vernor Matheius who, in his buoyant Socrates-mood was saying, "So, Anellia, you of all people admit you hadn't thought." I said, "In fact I did think, Vernor, but mistakenly." "How so?" "I'd wanted—sisters. I was lonely away from home"—though I'd been lonely all my life at home, hadn't I?—"and I thought I wanted sisters, I wanted a family to like me." Vernor said, "But you didn't know these girls, did you?" I admitted, "No." Vernor said, "You wanted to be liked, Anellia, by individuals you didn't know? Why?" I said weakly, "I admired them, at a distance. Some of them." Vernor said, "Out of what did this admiration arise?" Like any dupe of Socrates I saw where I was being herded, but could not escape. "Well—they were attractive. They had personalities. They were so very different from me." Vernor said, "You mean they were good-looking? Sexy?" I was embarrassed and didn't answer at once. Saying finally, "Some of them." Vernor said, "But were they intelligent? Did you respect their intelligence?" and I laughed and said, "No," and he said, "Did they value intelligence?" and I said, uncomfortably warm beneath his heavy arm, "I don't suppose they did, no. Except in some way that might be useful to them." Vernor asked, "Useful how?" and I said, my embarrassment deepening, "Sometimes they asked me, some of them, to help them with their academic work; to revise their papers, or write them—sometimes." Vernor chuckled as if he'd suspected this all along; seen what I'd been too blind to see. "You, Anellia, wanted to be 'liked' by individuals you didn't know. Individuals of no special worth or achievement. Racists and bigots. Tell me why."

Oh, why did he pursue this? His voice low, throaty, seductive; cruel and caressing; the voice of my early dream of an unknown man at the periphery of my vision; the voice of the man who was my first love, the first to penetrate my tight drum of a body. The voice I would hear through my life like the murmur of my blood. *Your first love, you'll never outlive. After that first love you will never love another in that way.*

I said nothing. Vernor spoke frankly, "Yet you were the one who lied to them, Anellia. You were the hypocrite posing as someone you were not. 'Anellia'——she-who-is-not."

This wasn't an accusation but a statement. I'd told Vernor my true name one evening. Still he called me "Anellia"——I supposed he couldn't be troubled to learn another name.

We were in the park, no longer on the path. There were voices close by but Vernor seemed not to hear. He framed my face in his hands another time; in this way positioning me, "seeing" me; his strong thumbs bracketing my eyes, pulling the skin taut at the corners. My natural reflex was to shrink away, to free myself; what if he shoved his thumbs in my eyes; what if he gouged out my eyes; I knew of course that Vernor Matheius wasn't about to gouge out my eyes, yet there was the panicky wish to push away from him. At the same time I felt sexually aroused. His lightest touch, his closeness, the intimacy of his gaze. The threat of those strong thumbs. It was like standing beside a tall upright flame: you could not withstand the flame by any act of will. "Why'd you come here with me? What's your intention?" Vernor said. His words were teasing but his expression was intense as if every nerve in his face had tightened. Leading me farther off the trail. Still it was a public place, and in bright sunshine. I stumbled as if intoxicated. A wave of apprehension rose in me, what we might do. I felt the distance between us and this place; the natural world; the world beyond the net of human language; beyond the province of philosophy; for here was the puzzlement of which Wittgenstein spoke; *puzzlement* the inevitable human condition of those who try to think. Vernor Matheius's thumbs tugging at my eyes, the authority in his superior strength. I understood how a predator might run his prey to earth and that prey would go limp in acquiescence, once the jaws had closed about it; once it was clear there could be no escape.

Overhead, a chattering of jays like monkeys in a jungle.

21

The way out. To show the fly the way out of the bottle was the life's hope of Ludwig Wittgenstein but the truth is that human beings don't want a way out of the bottle; we are captivated, enthralled by the interior of the bottle; its glassy sides caress and console us; its glassy sides are the perimeters of our experience and our aspiration; the bottle is our skin, our soul; we're accustomed to the visual distortions of the glass; we would not wish to see clearly, without the barrier of the glass; we could not breathe a fresher air; we could not survive outside the bottle.

Or tell ourselves, in the glassy-echoing language of the bottle, that this is so.

22

As the ancient Jewish people, persecuted by their enemies, interpreted history and the random events of nature moralistically, believing that catastrophes even of weather and geology were consequences of man's evil, so in times of emotional distress we're inclined to ascribe moral significance to whatever happens. We cease believing in chance and cling to a belief in design; we can't accept that we don't deserve what happens to us; we prefer a wrathful, capricious god to no god at all. Like children we try to influence what can't be influenced; we beg to be treated mercifully. We become superstitious. We lose our moorings, we drift into madness.

When I was in love with Vernor Matheius, I did not believe that I could live without Vernor Matheius; with the clarity of thought of a geometrician I believed that to live without Vernor Matheius was to live a life so broken and depleted, it could not have been endured. That season of my life when I became twenty years old and passed out of girlhood forever. That season when it seemed to me (sometimes!) that Vernor Matheius might to some inscrutable degree love me in return; at the very least, there was that possibility. That season when I carried myself in the world like glass so fragile it might shatter at any moment.

That season when I understood that my euphoria, my grief, my fear, my hope were symptoms of madness. Yet I couldn't alter my behavior: I didn't want to alter my behavior; for that would have been to abandon the madness, the hope of being loved by Vernor Matheius; that would have been to abandon the bottle in which the fly was trapped; that would have been to die.

I was convinced that the connection between Vernor Matheius and myself was a force outside my volition as it was outside his; it would consume us both like wildfire. Therefore every glance—every facial expression—every word—every gesture of mine, however casual— had to be controlled. Always I watched myself. Always I judged myself. From childhood I'd known that there is a way of behaving that is good, decent, virtuous, and blameless; yet I had not much cared; for the worst had already happened to me, my mother had died; as a child I could not perceive otherwise than *My mother's death happened to me;* it was difficult to perceive that my mother's death had in fact *happened to her.* So now I reasoned: if I was good, decent, virtuous, and blameless I would be rewarded with Vernor Matheius's love; if not, not. There was no god monitoring such behavior; no more a Jewish god than a god of the Strykersville Lutheran church. But there was no need for a god. I'd become increasingly superstitious: as in the childhood of the race spirits and demons were believed to populate the invisible world, obsessively and absurdly concerned with human affairs, so it seemed to me in my love for Vernor Matheius that invisible forces were on my side, or against me; at all times I had to placate them; I couldn't ignore them or refute them; I couldn't risk defying them; I had to guard against impulsive wishful thoughts; as a young adolescent I'd first realized *If you want a thing to happen, that is the thing that will not happen.* Thinking for instance *Vernor will call me tonight, we will make love in his bed* fatally assured that this would not happen. My thoughts had no power to control my fate yet my thoughts were omniscient. How could this be? And yet it was. To counter these forlorn wish-thoughts all my thoughts had to be strictly monitored. To counter wish-thoughts all my behavior had to be strictly monitored. When I was reading, working, my mind wholly concentrated on mental effort, I was safe; I was relatively safe; my zeal as a student had never been greater because I had never been more driven; I understood too that Vernor Matheius could respect only an intelligent woman, a woman of academic accomplishment approaching his own; this was the root of my motivation, of my high grades. If my lover admired Wittgenstein, I must learn all I could of Wittgenstein. Though not daring to think *He will love me for my intelligence, he will have no choice.*

I was required to be "good." I smiled often, I was gracious, courteous, patient, kind. Even when the effort was exhausting. Even when my heart was breaking. Even when I wanted to die, to extinguish myself completely, to be free of my sick, radiant love for Vernor Matheius, to be free of love.

Is something wrong? is something wrong with your face? one of them was asking. A girl in Norwood Hall who'd seemed to be my friend. I was hurt, I was angry; I stared at her, eyes shining with tears like shards of glass. *What do you mean? what is wrong with my face?* and the girl who'd only meant to be kind said, embarrassed *Your face seems stiff and frozen sometimes, you smile with just one side of your face.*

23

"Anellia, lie down."

So that day he'd urged me. For the first time entering my body as a lover.

Making love clumsily, frantically in the grass; in the spongey earth; we two who'd come together to an impasse where language would fail us. *Nothing but this. This!* Veins stood out in Vernor's neck; a vein at his temple; he breathed quickly as if running; as if struggling; with his strong fingers he gripped my thighs as he pushed himself into me, kneading, squeezing my flesh that would be marbled with bruises for days afterward. I refused to cry out in pain, though I had never felt such pain; I refused to cry *Oh! Vernor I love you* because I knew he expected it of me. He hadn't removed any of his clothing, only opened his trousers, with quick practiced fingers he'd lifted my skirt, pushed aside the crotch of my underwear, guided himself into me. *This, this and this! And done.* Vernor said nothing as he made love to me, and would say nothing when he finished; at the end a soft, drawn-out moan of astonishment; a sound of helplessness and even incredulity. He'd collapsed then on top of me as if we'd fallen together from a height, with no knowledge of how we'd been injured. I was proud that I hadn't resisted; that I hadn't flinched in pain; the pain was a brightly flaring flame into which I thrust myself willingly; I was hammered, pounded, driven into the earth; overhead the sky reeled crazily, I could not have stammered the words for *sky, cloud, pain, love.*

24

We are unknown to ourselves,

we seekers after knowledge.

NIETZSCHE

Now we were lovers, now I would become familiar to him. Now there could be silence between us. The silence that allows us to forget that another is near, or exists.

When Vernor was bored, depressed, restless; when philosophy failed him, and his thoughts backed up like sewage he could taste, then he wanted a girl, he wanted a female body, by chance he wanted Anellia—*C'mon girl: sing for me.* Grinning at me like a death's head. Unshaven. Damp carnivore teeth. And not very white or very even teeth. I tried to object, what gave him the idea that I could sing? Was he mistaking me for someone else? Now glaring at me like a pasha Vernor said *Sing, girl. You can save your life if you sing the right song.* So, barefoot on the floorboards of Vernor's apartment (grimy shades partway drawn, windows shoved upward to dispel the airlessness) I sang what flew into my mind, haphazardly, shut my eyes singing imperfectly recalled song lyrics I'd heard on the radio as a girl, unmediated, shameless female longing for love, and Vernor laughing would clap loudly *Faster, girl! Speed up the beat! Move that skinny little white ass of yours.* I too laughed, for it was funny; out of my mouth burst crazy snatches of song, fragments of my torment in the Kappa house, the simpleminded maddening tunes of the Kingston Trio certain of the girls played repeatedly, and the pop-calypso

> *Hey c'mon Kitch let's go to bed*
> *I gotta small comb to scratch ya head*

which made Vernor burst into louder laughter, hearing such idiocy, such stupid smut, and of course it was black calypso from the Caribbean in a degraded bastardized form, so funny I sang again

> *Hey c'mon Kitch let's go to bed*
> *I gotta small comb to scratch ya head*

as Vernor rose to take hold of me, to pull me to him, with an expression almost of tenderness.

"Girl, you surprise me. Sometimes."

Desire rising in a man's eyes like a swiftly lit flame.

Like a swiftly lit flame, desire rising in a man's eyes.

When he was bored and depressed. When he was (he frankly acknowledged) in one of his shitty moods.

Two kinds of mood: the Inspired and the Shitty. Swinging between them like a monkey on bars.

He would write a treatise on it: *The Epistemology of the Inspired and the Shitty; a Prolegomenon to Any Future Metaphysics.*

On principle Vernor Matheius disapproved of moods. Was there acknowledgement of *mood* in Descartes, Spinoza, Kant? *Mood* as a category of human mental experience didn't exist in serious philosophical inquiry. Succumb to a *mood* and you're no longer a philosopher but something wounded, diminished. Like a violinist who breaks his violin. In such *moods* Vernor Matheius despised himself and in a way remarkable to me (who observed him sympathetically, if mostly in silence) did not seem to know himself.

Bored and depressed! And the spring so rich, rife with smells, even the night air of the city so fresh it made me yearn to walk for hours. But Vernor's thoughts were backed up and he didn't want to see newspaper headlines, pushing away scattered pages of the Syracuse paper left behind on a table in the coffeehouse or in a restaurant where we'd arranged to meet, didn't want to know of the civil rights marches that spring in Alabama, Georgia, Mississippi, the police attack dogs, Ku Klux Klan bombings, arrests of civil rights volunteers; Vernor wished the volunteers well, hoped they would succeed he said but he hadn't time to spare for politics, activism, even the contemplation of such activism. *Time is an hourglass running in only one direction* he said. I did not say *I think they must be very brave, some of them very reckless living in time, in history* for these thoughts hadn't yet crystallized in my mind, the words weren't there.

Love for any one thing is barbaric (so Vernor quoted Nietzsche back to me, but giving the aphorism a personal twist) *yet more contemptible is lust, yet more contemptible than lust the habit of lust, the addiction.* The body's odd compulsion, to grovel in another's flesh. As if redemption, meaning, one's own identity, might be found in another's flesh. That warm eager leap of seed, the promise in it. (Even if thwarted, by Vernor's technique of coming on my belly, not inside me; or tugging a condom on his erect, bobbing penis.) The habit of drinking (yes, Vernor admitted he was drinking more than he wanted to). And smoking (yes, Vernor was certainly smoking more, a foul filthy ridiculous and expensive addiction resulting in overflowing ashtrays and a perpetual bluish haze in the apartment). When his thoughts backed up. When he was in one of his moods. Shouldn't (he knew!) blame Anellia, poor sweet Anellia who loved him when he didn't deserve love, nor even respect; when his work wasn't going well; when he was praised wrongly (by, among others, his dissertation advisor, a professor twenty years Vernor's senior) though his work wasn't going well; and now the Humanities fellowship, which intensified his sense of how his work wasn't going well; yes, his work was adequate, his ideas were moderately original (if it's possible to be moderate in originality), but it wasn't the revolutionary treatise he'd intended to write. When he lost faith in himself, and in philosophy as a discipline to transcend the self; when he fell beneath the spell of *philosophical puzzlement;* beneath the spell of the tragic, lacerating Wittgenstein for whom the posing of unanswerable riddle-questions was a strategy for the postponement of Wittgenstein's suicide (of his four brothers, three had killed themselves) as the nightly storytelling of Scheherazade was a strategy for the postponement of the storyteller's murder; when he lost faith not in philosophy but in the very concept of *faith;* when he despised all who admired him; when he despised me for adoring him; when he despised himself for being adored; for how like any addiction was a man's sexual desire; a man's bluntly physical sexual need; that weakness of imagination he believed he'd conquered years ago in the seminary; yet now it seemed to have returned; how like a sickness that need for Anellia whose true name he declined to recall, the thin palely gleaming body, a Caucasian female body into which he might fall as in a dream without limits. Removing my clothes as if I were a child to be undressed. Studying me with scholarly objectivity adjusting his wire-rimmed glasses. Some of this was joking, playful; yet beneath the playfulness a strange sobriety; like a philosopher in a medieval woodcut gazing upon a skull, in wonderment; brushing away my crossed arms where I tried to hide myself, embarrassed by his scrutiny.

Don't pretend, Anellia. It's too late for that.

Whispering words not meant for me to hear, words of angry endearment or obscenities or curses; the voice was hoarse, cracked; the voice was not Vernor Matheius's voice; it was not the voice I'd originally loved; a voice of helpless, furious desire; a voice of backed-up drains; a voice choked by desire, and by the resentment of desire; but often Vernor would say nothing at all, nor did he seem to trust himself touching me except in a proprietary measuring way, running his thumb against a small vein by my hairline, framing my face in his hands and bringing both his thumbs dangerously close to my eyes. *Such beautiful eyes, Anellia* and this was part of the puzzlement for he'd scarcely been aware of me in the early weeks of our affair, it was as if (but could this be possible?) he'd been blind to me, and therefore ignorant, misled; saying *How can you trust me, who could gouge out your eye in an instant* but of course (of course!) I trusted him, winced but never protested when he squeezed my breasts as if hoping to squeeze liquid from them, squeezed my bruised thighs, my small buttocks smoothly cupped in his hands as he began to make love to me in jagged, pumping spurts, whispering what he wished not to say aloud *Your tight stingy little cunt your skin the color and texture of your skin are repulsive to me don't you know? don't you know? can't you guess? can't you guess? guess? guess?* as he pumped himself into me in accelerating rhythm *How can you love me? how can you be fucked by me? how can you so debase yourself?* Never would I have dared to say *But I love you;* though often in my dreams I said *But I love you:* my lover would cover my mouth with his to suffocate my speech; as his pleasure mounted he would grind his mouth, his teeth, against mine, groaning and cursing; if I began to feel sexual pleasure rising in me, with sudden stealthy swiftness, as a candle flame may be stirred by an invisible breeze, if an overwhelming and obliterating sensation burst between my legs, I dared not scream; he didn't want his neighbors to hear me scream; if he closed his fingers around my throat he didn't want to hear me scream; if he spat into my mouth that seemed to him, in orgasm, ugly and gaping as a fish's mouth, he did not want to hear me scream; he would fill my small mouth with his tongue; he would fill my small gagging mouth with his cock; my dry mouth filled with his immense tongue; my dry mouth filled with his immense cock; he would spill all that had been jealously hoarded of himself into me, that I might choke and drown; yet whimpering almost saying *Oh Jesus!* almost saying my name almost saying *Love, love you* as if such forbidden words were snatched from him as his milky seed was snatched from him in the obliteration of orgasm always so much more powerful than one can anticipate, almost then he would say *I love you Anellia.* In his spidery fingers he would grip my back, my hips and buttocks so that the imprint of his fingers would remain for days, overlaid upon earlier bruises; lying above me, he'd arch his backbone like a bow, he would collapse upon me halfsobbing and delirious from that fall; from that height; he would bury his face in my neck; his groaning mouth, his teeth against my neck; he would press his hot face between my breasts that were chafed, aching; my nipples erect in arousal and fear; exhausted he would lie in my arms, defeated; I would stroke his hair I loved; his nubby tightly curly oily hair that was mine to stroke; I would cradle his heavy, carved-looking head that was mine to cradle; my lover's thoughts came in slow languid waves now; the agitated surf had broken and was now waves; warm shallow waves; gazing slantwise at his face, from slightly above as I held him, I saw his tremulous eyelids; the life in those eyelids; the life of the eye, the vision, the brain inside those eyelids; I understood that it is only in such intimacy that we know another person; it is only in such intimacy that we know ourselves, in proximity to another person; the nakedness of lovers is the nakedness of a mother and her infant; the nakedness of lovers is that first nakedness, or it is nothing; which is why lovers will kill for it, to attain it and repudiate it; at last I would begin to speak, as Vernor's soul subsided and his eyelids stilled, drifting toward sleep; I spoke softly and quietly in the aftermath of lovemaking; I spoke wonderingly to my lover of things I had never seen but only imagined, a bright blue sea rippling in sunshine where on an extraordinary wide, white beach of a kind unknown in my experience, sand fine as confectioners' sugar, I ran splashing in the warm surf and cut my foot on a seashell of remarkable coral-pinkness and my mother who'd been running just behind me lifted me in her arms and kissed me as I cried more in surprise than in pain; though the pain came swiftly, throbbing through my foot; and my mother took me away to wash, and to kiss, the hurt little foot, and made it well; I told him of my mother who'd been only a girl embarking on a voyage, there in the waves I saw her but a hundred yards from shore, alone in a small rowboat, alone with a single oar, how had this happened? why was my mother so far away, and I was screaming for her on shore? my mother whose face was beautiful and loving though I could not see it clearly, a face flimsy (like all faces perhaps) as rice paper to be marred, torn almost by accident; I told Vernor of my father whose body I had not seen, in life (it seemed to me) as in death; a man with a heavy flushed face and his heart heavy inside him; the burden of that enlarged, heavy heart; yet he'd had a handsome face once; a face very different from Vernor's carved-wooden face; a face that seemed boneless, of muscle, gristle, and fat; a face smudged as in a charcoal drawing deliberately ruined; once I'd drawn my father in charcoal, at school; I'd drawn him from memory, brought it home to show the others and they'd been surprised at my skill, showed it to my father and he'd laughed shaking his head *You got me there* an expression I did not comprehend, and later that evening he'd asked to see it again and this time tore it in two; always I would recall my shock, the hurt of it, as my father tore his own face in two; always I would remember his angry laughing; yet if I cried, my tears were insincere for I'd guessed beforehand that I shouldn't have done it; shouldn't have drawn my father's face; it's a transgression to replicate your father's face if you reveal too much. Yet he'd seemed to love me, that day at high school graduation. *Don't let no fuckers out there sell you short.* I told my lover how at night in the country sometimes I would wake suddenly to hear Death outside in the cornstalks in the wind of late autumn; I heard Death entering my grandparents' farmhouse which was too flimsy to keep Death out; I lay awake in my bed too frightened to breathe listening to Death moving across the creaking floorboards downstairs; I prayed that Death would pass me by, and that Death would pass by the others in the house; my three tall brothers, my grandparents and, if he was home, my father; I saw that all who live lie very still in terror of Death at such times; waiting for Death to pass by, or waiting for Death to take another; as in a herd of beasts terrorized by predators there must be the single instinct-wish *Take another! take another and not me!* This was a secret of which adults would not speak; this was a secret known by children, and forgotten by adults; a secret of which the great philosophers would not speak because it is so stark, so simple; a secret lacking revelation.

These things and others I told my lover Vernor Matheius when he lay in my arms, sweaty and spent and at peace; temporarily at peace; Vernor Matheius warm, heavy, and unresisting in my arms; his eyes shut; his face shut; gently I stroked his hair, his head, his shoulders, his arms; this was the great happiness of my life, holding Vernor Matheius in my arms; Vernor Matheius who had once been a disembodied voice in a lecture hall; I thought *Only what we don't deserve justifies our lives.* For I could not believe that I deserved Vernor Matheius. I knew that I did not deserve Vernor Matheius. Sharing in clumsy intimacy in his narrow bed, the mattress flat and sagging in the center like a broken-backed beast of burden; the sheets damp from our bodies and suffused with our sweat, the smell of Vernor's hair, underarms and feet, the smell of his stopped-up semen liquid and milky in the condom drooping from his shrunken penis; Vernor Matheius subdued after sexual triumph which was to him indistinguishable from sexual defeat; we would share this uncomfortable bed, and this hour or hours, but we would not share sleep; we would not share dreams; for where Vernor Matheius drifted in sleep I did not know, could not guess, as I floated on the surface of sleep like froth on water and sank a little, and rose and sank, and sank, my sleeping fingers in the man's hair as I drifted off at last to sleep, knowing where he'd gone I could not follow.

25

And what of my life in those months that was not Vernor Matheius, what of the vast incalculable world not Vernor Matheius, what of a girl whose body I inhabited who was not Anellia but another individual entirely, what connection, what vision seen through her skeptical eyes, had she no future, had she no hope, did no other possibility exist?

Yes. But no.

She would not utter the word *Ne-gro*. You could see her approach and retreat from *Ne-gro*. You could see the fierce ice pick centers of her eyes as she considered, and hurriedly rejected, *Ne-gro*. Saying in her voice of mock-solicitude, "And what is your relationship to, to—to this person of another race?" at last uttered, with an intake of breath, frown lines deepening in her pouchy bulldog face so incongruously peachy-powdered, and her marble-eyes drifting downward in a semblance of feminine modesty, decorum, "—graduate student I believe he is, in philosophy, many years older than you? I have heard troubled reports, I mean I have heard troubling reports, Miss—" pronouncing my name in identically stressed syllables as if in this way she might disclaim her responsibility in making sense of a name so clearly foreign; she spoke with a stoic dignity; her high moral worth of herself prevailed; her title was Dean of Women at the university and it was a title she did not take lightly. Listening, I was stunned into silence; I could think of no reply; long ago I'd muttered *Oh I hate you!* running from my German grandmother and possibly the old woman had heard me, and possibly not; but I could not mutter such a phrase now, I was twenty years old and an honors student at the university. Thinking with a stab of guilt *She knows,*

knows what we have done together, how can she know? I'd been summoned
to the office of the Dean of Women amid one of my crowded weekdays,
between classes and my part-time job (now in the cafeteria); I hadn't
had time to think, even to dread; I'd given up thinking of anything much
beyond Vernor Matheius and my studies, the two inextricably conjoined
for my mind was sharply honed in imitation of Vernor Matheius's flashing mind, my work was written as if to Vernor Matheius's unsparing
judgment, my concentration was monomaniacal and in its way satisfying
as that of a tightrope walker making her way across an abyss; the abyss
was Death; the abyss was my doomed love for Vernor Matheius. And so
I hadn't had time to think, to prepare myself for this unexpected attack.
Sitting dazed and humiliated and by degrees resentful listening to the
Dean of Women lecture me in her drawling insinuating voice; a voice
practiced in scolding, chiding, abrading and humiliating young women;
a voice quavering with its power, and with the unspeakable pleasure of
power. *This is for your own good* such voices assure us. *You are of an age often blind to its own good.* Several times this semester I'd been summoned
to the dean's office and each time had been a painful ordeal. I'd petitioned to be freed from the tyranny of Kappa Gamma Pi but the dean
strongly disapproved of any sorority girl departing any sorority for any
reason, however desperate; evidently there wasn't enough housing at
the university for upperclassmen, and sororities and fraternities were
crucial to the university. Yet this pragmatic fact was never uttered. All
was couched in terms of *commitment, loyalty, contractual agreements; being
true to your pledge.* The prevailing ethic was *You've made your bed, now lie in
it* but the dean wouldn't have spoken so bluntly and honestly. In those
excruciating sessions with the dean I'd had to convince the woman that I
wanted to leave the Kappas for reasons of financial hardship as well as
moral repugnance; it wasn't enough that my Kappa sisters disliked and
ostracized me (and, I knew, complained to the dean wanting to be rid of

me); it wasn't enough that I was wretched in their midst and irrevocably estranged from them; it wasn't enough that I was not Episcopalian as I'd misrepresented myself but had "Jewish blood"; that a non-Christian had lied her way into a Christian sorority; it also had to be demonstrated that I couldn't continue for financial reasons and was already in debt; I'd had to show the Dean of Women financial statements, the most embarrassing a notarized statement from a Syracuse bank; I'd had to defend myself as a pauper. That I was still an honors student despite my difficulties was used against me by the dean; since I'd continued to receive high grades, and reports from my professors were uniformly excellent, how could I claim, as I was, that Kappa Gamma Pi was detrimental to my academic work? *You, a young woman of superior intellectual gifts, don't you feel an obligation to offer aid to your sorority sisters, wouldn't that be a generous, selfless thing to do? Yes?* So the dean tormented me, and revelled in her tormenting; reduced me to exhaustion, and almost to tears; but I'd vowed I would not be provoked into crying; we both knew she hadn't any choice but to approve the petition since my sorority sisters had voted to expel me, I was no longer one of them. And now, a few months later, here I was back in the dean's office again.

It was ironic to be charged with a relationship with a person *of another race* when, in fact, I had not heard from Vernor Matheius in three days. For all I knew, I would not hear from him again. We'd parted awkwardly, Vernor in one of his sudden sunken moods not bothering to rise from bed, lying naked with an arm across his forehead staring at the ceiling; as I emerged from the bathroom, and uncertainly prepared to leave, Vernor said in his grim-jocular voice *Schopenhauer said it: Life is a struggle against sleep and eventually we lose.* That morning I'd violated our unspoken agreement and gone to Vernor's apartment, concerned that I hadn't heard from him in a while; I'd decided I must go, and risk his anger; he'd said he would call me when he wanted to see me and I knew (I think I knew) that he was punishing me; my punishment had something to do with my admiring remarks about the Student Non-violent Coordinating Committee and the demonstration on campus; I hadn't concurred in Vernor's dismissal of politics, activism, history; I'd disappointed him, and he meant to punish me; but I'd dared to go to him anyway, as if in ignorance. And he'd been there, and let me in; and we'd made love eventually, if not entirely satisfactorily; and I'd gone away again and had not heard from him for another three days balanced on the high wire above the abyss and determined not to fall. And the Dean of Women summoned me, I hadn't any choice but to obey. I would soon be twenty years old. Twenty! It seemed to me very old; never could I imagine living another twenty years. The Dean of Women had the power to expel me from the university, or so I was led to believe. A woman in her mid-fifties perhaps with a large sliding bosom and that lavishly powdered peach-tinted face, a face that pretended to know what it didn't know, and pretended not to know what it did know; a face that had never been a mother's face; a face of spite and gloating. "—This adult graduate student, this—person of a, another background—" pursing her lips with a show of concern, and fixing me with her hard marble-eyes, "—have you given serious thought to—paused to consider the wisdom of—is your family aware of such behavior—the responsibility of my office is—is such—" I listened with mounting shame, and with mounting anger; I supposed it was the resident advisor in my dormitory who'd reported me, though I could not imagine why; or how she knew about Vernor Matheius. As I listened to the dean I became increasingly angry; I was frightened of my anger; from Vernor Matheius's tension-filled body I'd absorbed anger; the low hum, the accelerating pulse, the throbbing beat of anger; thinking *She believes white skin is sacred, you've defiled it and her.* I was expected to defend myself but I sat in silence, stubborn and resistant; the dean began to speak more forcibly, in disapproval, "—you seem to have quite a history, Miss——" with grave eyes contemplating the opened folder on her desk, "——your unfortunate experience at Kappa Gamma Pi——your 'troubled peer relations'——'difficulty in cooperating with others'——your 'sociopathic tendencies'——" and at this I spoke, I interrupted her in a voice sharp as Vernor Matheius's, "Excuse me, what did you say——'sociopathic'? Did you actually say——'sociopathic'?" and the dean drew herself up to her full seated height, her bulldog face darkening with blood, "Yes, I'm afraid so, one of our respondents has noted 'sociopathic tendencies'——'inability to adjust'——'continued opposition'——" and I said, "You have no right to be spying on me," I was speaking quickly, angrily, "——I can see a man if I want to; I can love a man if I want to; no one can stop me," and the dean frowned at my sudden crude words, such unfeminine behavior, saying, "That's quite enough. Your behavior will be duly noted on your record," and I said, trembling, "Why is it your business or anyone's business if I am seeing a black man? If I am in love with a——black man?" and at this the dean stared at me as if I'd spoken obscene words, clearly she wasn't accustomed to mutinous young women in her office, "Miss, you've gone too far. You will not speak to me in such a manner. You——" but I'd jumped from my chair and snatched the folder off her desk, saying, "I have a constitutional right to see what's been written about me," and the dean was so taken by surprise she couldn't reply, her powdery face dissolving in shocked awe as I leafed through the folder, transcripts of my grades through three semesters, photocopied forms, high school letters of recommendations and test results, a copy of a document from the New York State Board of Regents in Albany awarding me a state scholarship——*quiet, very mature for her age, highly intelligent*——reports from my university professors——*brilliant but very young, immature——an outstanding student blessed (or accursed) with a skeptical imagination;* and in the stilted backhand of Agnes Thayer which I recognized immediately these condemning words—*willful, troublesome, unattractive girl, rude and sociopathic in tendencies, inability to adjust with others and disrespectful toward her elders. NOT RECOMMEND FOR ANY FUTURE EMPLOYMENT IN ANY FIELD OF ENDEAVVOR.* These phrases passed in a rapid blur before my astonished eyes yet I had time to note the errors *recommend, endeavvor,* and to realize the extent of Mrs. Thayer's emotional upset; by now the dean had heaved herself to her feet, a heavyset panting middle-aged woman, though much larger than I, she appeared frightened of me; a girl of such wild sociopathic tendencies, what might I do next? With as much poise as I could summon, I dropped the folder back onto her desk; I said, "How dare you spy on me? You and Mrs. Thayer—you know what a disturbed woman she was, you know what happened to *her*. If I am in l-love with a—" and now I too faltered, hardly knowing how to speak of Vernor Matheius, for any words assigned to him that dissolved his individuality in a category, a class, were false; worse than false, traitorous. Even to speak of him neutrally, in such a context, was traitorous. I said, stammering, "—if I am in love with any man of any background you have no right to interfere. You have no right to intimidate me. I am twenty years old, an adult! My friend Vernor Matheius is associated with the American Civil Liberties Union and we'll sue you, you and the university both, if you continue in this racist persecution, we know our rights as—American citizens!" and I was out of the office of the Dean of Women and hurrying through her outer office in a blaze of righteousness, retaining a blurred and dream-like image of the dean's stunned face, rushing down the stairs of Erie Hall exhilarated, my blood up thinking *If Vernor could have heard!—he would love me wouldn't he?* Thinking in giddy triumph *Am I sociopathic, am I a pathogen to society? Is that who I am—my essence?*

I was running. I was attracting some attention. I was not crying, my face shone with righteousness. *A pathogen. A pathogen!* It was a term from biology; a helpful term; never had I felt so empowered, so certain of myself. *Vernor Matheius and I: pathogens.* I felt the thrill of the outlaw, the outcast; the object of loathing and taboo; my skin was "white," a camouflage I might wear through life as I wore my costume-clothes; as I wore my "femaleness"; what others perceived as a weakness, I would forge as my strength. How radiant in self-knowledge I was! Crossing a broad, sloping lawn, spongy from recent rain; the afternoon air had turned twilit with thunderclouds obscuring the sun, and glimmered with a peculiar iridescence, like a rainbow; I gloated in my secret *otherness* no one (not even Vernor Matheius) would ever know. There came gusts of sulphurous air. A rolling of thunder. And an unexpected piercingly sweet odor of lilac from a hedge beside the Music School and I was seeing again the ragged lilac bushes that grew behind my grandfather's ramshackle barn, I drew a deep shuddering breath running now in rainwater and mud splashing my legs, my bare white legs, laughing to myself, my face gleaming with tears of laughter, rage, hurt, determination *So I am a nigger-lover, and a pathogen. That is what I am.*

27

Never did I dare tell Vernor Matheius about my adventure in the office of the Dean of Women. I hadn't the courage though continuing to think with childish obstinacy *He would love me, if he knew.* My courage on our behalf.

But was it so? Would Vernor Matheius have loved me, or even admired me, if he'd known? If he'd overheard? Or would he have been mortified, infuriated, disgusted at my appropriation of his name? My boast of *my friend Vernor Matheius* which was the first time, and would be the last time, I spoke his name to another?

But I never told him, he never knew.

Nor did the Dean of Women continue in her harassment of me. So far as I knew. My threat of a lawsuit and my evocation of "civil rights" had been a blind strike in the dark, yet inspired; the exact weapon with which to defend oneself against a college administrator in that era of civil rights reform; of a radically new thinking about race, individuals, civil liberties. The Dean of Women would not have cause to speak with me again that year, nor in my remaining two years at the university; ironically, by what seems in retrospect a remarkable fluke, I would be named valedictorian of the class of 1965 and would deliver an idealistic valedictory speech on the subject of civil rights; afterward, on the commencement platform, I would be warmly congratulated by the chancellor of the university and by a succession of administrators in academic regalia, including of course the Dean of Women; I saw that she was one of very few women in the commencement program, and among so many tall, distinguished-seeming men a figure of female uncertainty, her raddled face too lavishly powdered and her black cap unflatteringly bobby-pinned to her grayish-brown hair. Her mouth pursed as I approached; her small damp eyes fixed upon my face as if in sudden dread of my uttering something sarcastic, rude, damning that would be overheard by her male colleagues. But our meeting, which was also our parting, was amicable. I may have been a little nervous, excited, and still high from giving my speech, and being applauded; I was smiling at everyone, and seeing no one; except there loomed the Dean of Women before me, a black tent of a woman, and there was my hard little hand being shaken by her soft boneless hand, and both hands were cold as if drained of blood; the Dean of Women smiled saying, "Congratulations, my dear. You have lived up to your early promise." I said, "Thank you, Dean. And good-bye."

But this was the future, two years away. A future I could not have fantasized with even my wayward powers of imagination.

28

I am not a man for any woman to count on. Not a man who wants to be loved.

But: love me.

Wanting to surprise my lover, to make him happy. For what makes happy the one we adore makes us happy; what not, not; the universe is a void, an unfathomable inkwell otherwise.

How many times drifting through bookstores seeing books I knew Vernor Matheius would prize and thinking I would steal for him—would I? As I would never have stolen for myself: annotated editions of the works of Leibniz, Hegel, Heidegger; a new commentary on Wittgenstein; a new translation of Plato's dialogues; biographies of Kierkegaard and Jaspers; Ernst Cassirer's essays on the mythic nature of language. Holding one of these precious, expensive books in my hand thinking *How happy it would make Vernor to own this*. Wishing not to think *What a transparent ploy to make the man love me*.

Never stole a single book. Though I'd been labeled an outlaw, a sociopath, yet I never stole for Vernor Matheius, as I would never have stolen for myself; my pride was such, I couldn't stoop so low; nor could I work out how Vernor might respond if he discovered that books had been stolen for him; and he'd known I hadn't the money to buy them. Frequently he'd expressed disdain for any form of dishonesty, above all intellectual dishonesty; he scorned unoriginal thinking in philosophy; he scorned any form of petty crime.

"Petty crimes require petty souls."

Though I couldn't afford it, sometimes on impulse I bought Vernor gifts. Never in my life until then had I experienced that rhapsody of happiness: buying a gift for someone you love. The adrenaline rush *I am the person who can buy this gift. Only I, so privileged.*

These were thrift-shop treasures. I was patient, I could look through bins of cast-off things. I discovered a handsome old fountain pen, black with gold trim, that still functioned; a pair of fake-jade cuff links engraved with miniature sphinxes; a crystal paperweight (only just finely cracked, but still charming) that was also a magnifying glass. For Vernor's thirtieth birthday I gave him a silk vest in an elegant houndstooth check on a gray background gossamer as smoke; when he unwrapped and opened the box he didn't lift the vest out of the tissue paper for a moment, staring down at it, and I worried that such an item of apparel was too personal a gift and might offend him; but Vernor took it up, slipped it on, and frowned at his reflection critically in his single mirror, above his bedroom bureau—"Hmm. Not bad." The silk vest had come from a consignment shop in downtown Syracuse; it had been marked down numerous times, at last priced at $9.95. How beautiful it had seemed to me, the old-fashioned cut, a row of small black wooden buttons; a vest for a gentleman; for Vernor Matheius. He laughed when I told him it was secondhand; its label had been carefully removed. "What it is, no doubt, is a dead man's vest, recycled to *me*." "That's only logical," I said, "since you're alive." Vernor laughed again and asked, not for the first time, why I bought him things—"You don't have any money, Anellia." I ignored this saying proudly, "You look very handsome in your silk vest, Vernor, it suits you perfectly." Vernor said reprovingly, "I don't look 'handsome' and it doesn't suit me 'perfectly' and I surely don't need a vest but thank you, Anellia." Smiling at me, and my heart soared.

"A special occasion. And I have something special to tell you."

Vernor wore the houndstooth silk vest beneath his old gray flannel jacket that fitted him tight across the shoulders when he took me out to dinner for the first time (as it would be the last time) at a good, expensive restaurant in the city, the Brass Rail; he was clean-shaven and his face was sharp planes and angles like carved mahogany; his hair hadn't been trimmed in some time, and rose in a woolly penumbra around his head; one of the earpieces of his glasses had broken and was mended with adhesive tape, which gave him a savage yet scholarly look; he was handsome and swaggering in his best ironic style; he wore the vest, the jacket, a greasy-looking dark necktie and dark trousers with a haphazard crease and his shoes were brown leather, badly worn and water-stained. I wore a black silk dress that seemed to have a life, an identity, an idiom of its own; in the style of the Forties it had a flared skirt, long, tight sleeves and a V neck that drooped to show a portion of my narrow, pale chest and the edges of my pale breasts; the dress had a cloth belt that had begun to curl, to show its underside; the woman who'd owned the dress (of course it was secondhand) had had a waist thinner than my own for the belt had been mutilated as if with an ice pick to make extra holes in it, that it might be buckled tighter, and yet tighter; Vernor thought the dress "erotic"—"smelling of grave mold"; with it I wore a thin tarnished gold chain that had once belonged to my mother; at least, this was what I'd been told as a young girl by my grandmother who hadn't wanted it for herself. Nerves had caused my sensitive skin to break out in random rashes yet my face was radiant, I'd applied layers of makeup including rouge; my eyes shone with the glisten of madness; I thought *This is the happiest day of my life*. Yet could I trust happiness? I could not bear the suspense of what Vernor had to tell me at dinner; immediately he'd made his remark, offhand and casual, I forgot I'd heard it; I looked away, evasive and frightened.

It was a giddy thing, to appear so publicly with Vernor Matheius; the two of us dressed for the evening; his carved-wooden face, my beaming-bright face; his mismatched, rakish clothes and my black silk witchy dress; we walked along the sidewalks, crossed streets, and drew all eyes to us like magnets; I wondered if Vernor was making a declaration about me, about us, at last; we walked hand in hand sometimes, and at other times Vernor seemed almost to forget me; yet there was the glitzy facade of the Brass Rail, where my Kappa sisters' parents took them for dinners, there was Vernor opening the door for me, and the trepidation of stepping inside as if stepping out onto a stage, or into a pit. Vernor had made a reservation; as the maître d' frowned through his book, Vernor winked at me and said I looked the part; what part, I asked nervously; Vernor said, "The part of a young writer celebrating her first sale." And my heart contracted in disappointment for I'd believed he would say something else.

(The special occasion we were celebrating was my having placed a short story in a distinguished literary magazine; one of my flukes of good if improbable luck; I'd written a first draft of this story, back in December, miserable with insomnia in the basement of the Kappa house; because I'd been so desperately unhappy, I had made the story comic; bleakly, savagely comic; it was an excursion into madness even as flames of madness licked at my feet, hands, hair. When I shyly told Vernor this good news, which embarrassed me as winning a lottery would have embarrassed me, Vernor stared at me in frank surprise for a moment then smiled, whistled a congratulatory tune, and told me he "wasn't surprised" at anything I might do. I would wait for him to ask to read the story, but Vernor never asked.)

In the cool, tinted interior of the Brass Rail we were led to our table by the maître d' in his tuxedo; there was in the restaurant a ripple of, not sound, but the immediate absence of sound; a collective indrawn breath. The maître d' with an expression stiff and sombre as a mortician's seated us at the very back of the dining room; a small table near the hallway to the rest rooms; yet it was an attractive table, with a lighted candle on it, and a small vase of carnations; the restaurant was beautiful, if undersea and dim; as soon as we were seated, Vernor reached over to take my hand and lifted it, as he'd never done previously, to kiss my fingertips; a gesture I supposed was meant to be playful, theatrical; yet I was moved by it; I was made uneasy by it; for I was aware of other diners observing us; eyes that, if I glanced around, shifted immediately away. Some time was required before our waiter arrived, and blindly I took from him an enormous menu; there was some fuss about our candle, whose flame had gone out; Vernor insisted it be relighted; a couple at a nearby table stared openly at us; middle-aged, very well dressed and white-skinned (of course); I was beginning to feel the oppression of *white;* the ubiquity of *white;* for everyone in the Brass Rail was *white* except the busboys in white (dazzling white!) uniforms, and these busboys were black. (And how steadfastly they looked away from us. Through the ordeal of our meal, they would not see us at all.)

You! Aren't you ashamed of yourself I heard subterranean murmurs of disapproval, the woman at the table next to ours, our automaton waiter, and I thought *No! No I am not.* Some time was required before our drinks were brought, wine for Vernor, a club soda for me (I was underage), and during this time Vernor gave no sign of noticing how we were being watched; this was the Vernor Matheius of campus pubs and restaurants who never so much as glanced at other people; this was the Vernor Matheius of Oneida Park who'd made love to me a few yards from a public trail; this was the Vernor Matheius of the lecture hall; except this evening he laughed frequently, and sometimes loudly; he seemed very relaxed; I laughed with him, though there was something forced and feverish in his laughter; I thought *Is this a man I know, or a stranger?* Yet how exciting to be in the presence of such a stranger. For much of the meal Vernor interrogated me in his playful-serious Socratic manner; a relentless questioning that was like rough tickling; it made me laugh, and squirm; a rash on the underside of my jaw throbbed; in his eloquent professorial voice Vernor Matheius spoke just distinctly enough to be overheard at other tables; speaking of Heidegger's *Being and Time,* that "untranslatable text" which he was reading in German; in Heidegger it's the weight of language that is as significant as meaning; yet the paradox (Vernor argued, or was this Heidegger?) of language is that there can be no single language, only languages—"The tragic paradox is, each of us speaks and hears a language unlike any other." I said, clumsily, "But people understand one another, usually; at least, they get along," and Vernor said, "But how do you know?—the conviction that you 'understand' and that you 'get along' might be a delusion." He spoke then of Plato's famous allegory of the cave. Though I'd studied it, I seemed not to know Vernor's special interpretation. He was then speaking of his own "cave-origins"—his "ancestry"; Vernor Matheius who'd seemed until this moment to have had no personal history, no "ancestry" at all. Matter-of-factly he told me that his ancestors, those he could trace, had been the luckiest of Africans brought to North America as slaves because they'd been sold up north into Connecticut in the 1780's; and in 1784 slavery was outlawed in Connecticut; there'd been no significant history of slavery in Vernor's background; the name "Matheius" had been chosen by his great-grandfather, from a stranger's gravestone (as family legend had it); which was why, Vernor said, he'd been born with a *free soul* and not a *slave soul*. He addressed me as if I were silently arguing with him and needed to be convinced; he smiled, sipped wine, said belligerently, "Why the hell then should I spend my life being 'Negro' for anyone's sake? I have a higher calling." I was moved that Vernor should confide such things to me; never before had he spoken except vaguely of himself, and never had he asked me about myself; though he was interested in my courses, in what I was studying and writing, he had not been interested in who I was; nor had I been interested in telling him; for *who I am* has never greatly interested me set beside *who I might become*. I asked Vernor where in Africa had his ancestors come from and he said, with a moment's hesitation, "Dahomey—a place I know virtually nothing about, even its location." This seemed unlikely to me; or unnatural; yet I wasn't about to argue with Vernor Matheius. He changed the subject, and we talked now of families; of identities; not specifically but as abstractions, ideas; I realized that since I'd known him, Vernor had never left Syracuse or spoke of visiting his home, nor had anyone visited him; he never received personal mail so far as I knew, or telephone calls; he had a few friendly acquaintances in the Philosophy Department, there were professors and fellow graduate students who invited him occasionally to their homes, but of course Vernor made no effort to reciprocate, and would not have been expected to reciprocate; he'd once told me, his home was in the mind and I saw now that was literally true. His mind was his home, and only one person lived there. "You are free to choose identity by choosing a course of mental action that excludes other courses," Vernor said. Again he reached across the table in his atypical gesture, to take my hand; squeezing my fingers as if I were slow, obstinate; as if I required being coerced into acknowledging. "I will try to believe that," I said; and Vernor said, severely, "But you don't try hard enough, Anellia. Even

Wittgenstein worked at *thinking*. It isn't a pastime like eating, chatting, copulation." I was hurt by this remark for I knew it was calculated to hurt; yet Vernor continued, "In your thinking, Anellia, you disappoint me." I said, "I'm sorry, Vernor." He said, baring his chunky teeth in a smile like pain, "Anellia, there's something I want to tell you." I knew it could not be happy news. Even as I reasoned *Do you believe you merit happy news?—of course not. This is good-bye.* We'd been eating our dinners without seeming to taste them; Vernor had ordered for both of us, the least expensive dinners on the very expensive menu, chicken; still, the cost of the meal would be exorbitant; there seemed an oblique irony in the very fact that Vernor had brought us to the Brass Rail, a place of the kind he'd have ordinarily scorned. I knew I must ask Vernor what he meant, like a character in a Kafka parable who must, so cruelly, participate in his own execution; yet the words stuck in my throat, like the food I was eating, or trying to eat. Vernor said, in his professor's voice, "Better yet, there's something you can tell me." I lifted my eyes to inquire, what? and Vernor said, "What do you want from me, Anellia?"

What did I want from Vernor Matheius!

I pondered this. I may have smiled, slightly. A girl in a black silk dress with a neckline that exposed her pale smooth chest, a white-skinned girl being spoken to, lectured to, earnestly by a sharp-faced black man in a gray jacket, silk vest, greasy dark necktie. I hoped to sound like a girl practiced in sexual wiles, seduction. In the eyes of those diners covertly watching us, a mysterious girl. "Only to be with you, Vernor. If—" He squeezed my fingers harder, as if he felt pity for me, and impatience. As if wielding a piece of chalk, working out a syllogism on a blackboard in Introduction to Logic. "Anellia, there is not the opportunity for that." He might have been making a statement about weather; a self-evident fact; a fact not to be questioned; a fact not to be modified; he chose his words, as usual, as if each word had a price; he was parsimonious with words, and shrewd. Sipping the last of the wine, the dark red liquid he hadn't offered to me to taste. My mouth ached with its unaccustomed smiling; a public display of smiling; a roaring in my ears like the sound of the surf in a dream imperfectly recalled; I could not hear the rest of Vernor's words; Vernor's dark fisted hand enclosed mine as if protectively, lifting so that his knuckles lightly grazed my left breast; the shock of being touched ran through me; I felt my nipples harden, absurd and piteous inside the black silk dress of a dead woman; it was a caress meant to comfort, not to arouse; nor even intimidate; there was nothing sexual in the gesture except in the display of it, and perhaps that display was unconscious; still I felt strangers' eyes upon us, cold and infuriated; I hadn't the strength to confront them, and drew back from Vernor's casual touch. I thought *This is a life: these minute particles of sensation, emotion.* I thought *But can I live this life? Am I strong enough?* Our waiter had departed, and had not approached our table for a long time; he'd prepared the check, and placed it conspicuously near Vernor's elbow; now the maître d' in his tuxedo stood above us imperial and frowning; disapproving; explaining in a tone of perfunctory apology that our table had been reserved for another party at nine; it was now past nine; we would have to leave as quickly as possible; the check could be paid at the front. Vernor lifted his eyes widened in mock solicitude to the maître d', a white man in his fifties with an oblong fattish face, insolent eyes; Vernor seemed about to protest, then said nothing, and with deliberation pushed back his chair and stood, abruptly; in such a way that the maître d' stepped back; not that Vernor had threatened him; a tall knifeblade of a man with very dark, chiseled face and fisted hands. I'd gotten quickly to my feet, wanting only to escape from this terrible place; for the restaurant was air-conditioned, and uncomfortably cool; it was a temperature for men in suits, not for girls in low-cut silk dresses; I'd been shivering through most of the meal. Vernor took my hand and tugged at me, saying to the maître d' in a tone of icy politeness, "Fine. We are leaving, and you needn't worry we'll be back."

And there we are walking through the Brass Rail as diners stare at us wondering was there a confrontation? between the maître d' and that arrogant black man? I try to see us: but there's a blur, a merciful haze; as in a dissolving dream; the gray silk vest, the black silk dress; a face frozen in anger, a face stricken in embarrassment. *Can I live this life, am I strong enough?* I waited outside the Brass Rail as Vernor Matheius settled the bill.

And later. In Vernor's bed in those sheets smelling of our bodies; in Vernor's arms that didn't close about me, but held me loosely rocking as one might comfort a small child; I was trying not to cry for nothing's so banal as crying in a lover's arms, banal and futile; as Vernor said, with unnatural gentleness, "Didn't I warn you, girl, I'm not a man for any woman to count on? Eh?" and, more gently, "I wish I could love you the way you deserve, a girl like you, but I can't, you know I can't, I have never lied or misled you, Anellia, have I?" These earnest words like a pronouncement of death and yet I was pleading, "Vernor, I can l-love enough for us both. Give me a chance!" My absurd makeup had begun to melt on my sallow little face. My hair I'd shampooed that afternoon, brushed to a sheen, now disheveled as if I'd been wakened from sleep. And Vernor saying in that soft resolute voice, "Anellia, maybe you should go away now. Maybe this should end."

I held myself very still, very still, not hearing.

To purify myself utterly, how? To become nothing, bare picked white bones. And then I will be free.

29

On June 12, 1963, three days after our evening at the Brass Rail, a young NAACP field secretary named Medgar Evers entered history; he was shot in the back by a white racist as he was about to enter his home in Jackson, Mississippi. Even Vernor Matheius who avoided the news like a bad smell could not avoid learning of this.

Fuck. Fuckers.

It was a sign of Vernor's debasement, that so common, you could say so clichéd a vulgarity sprang to his lips.

Beginning now to drink in the early afternoon. At midday. Waking late, groggy and still drunk from the night before; dragging himself to work at his desk, or try to work; beer, rot-gut wine, cheap jug wine; refused to leave his apartment, even to wash, put on fresh clothes. He was feverish, he had no appetite. Now the raw sewage was backing up on him. *Stay away* he warned me but I would not. I took advantage of his illness, his weakness; every day, twice daily, I climbed the outside stairs at the rear of Vernor Matheius's building where the door might be locked against me and no amount of pleading could induce Vernor to open it, or the door might be unlocked, might swing open when I pushed against it and an odor of defeat and fury would fill my nostrils so that my instinct was to flee even as, stubbornly, I would not. *Why? Why d'you come here when I don't want you* was Vernor's silent accusation. As I pleaded, in silence taking his hand and lifting it, the sweaty unwashed palm, to my cheek. *I've told you: I can love enough for us both.*

Through that long winter and into the spring there'd been a flu epidemic in upstate New York. Vernor had boasted of being immune to such weakness, but at last he succumbed; joking that he'd been poisoned at the Brass Rail. Within a week he'd lost so much weight I could see his breastbone sharp as the edge of a shovel outlined through his filthy shirt when he lay flat on his back; I saw that his cheekbones had grown sharper, his eyes were sunken and glowed meanly as the candlelit eyes of a deranged Hallowe'en pumpkin. I was frightened for him. I worried he would starve himself to death out of spite like those recluses we'd hear of sometimes in the countryside of my childhood, who hadn't enough to eat during the winter or were too poor or too proud or too stubborn or too deranged to ask neighbors for help. Of the martyred Medgar Evers whose assassin had not yet been named Vernor said *That's what happens when you step into history: history grinds you flat beneath its boot heel.* The remark seemed to give him pleasure.

There were times when he seemed delirious; there were times when he ranted, cursed; once when I let myself in, with a key I'd appropriated from him, I was shocked to see that he'd thrown books and papers onto the floor in disgust, he'd torn down the likenesses of Socrates and Descartes; in the smelly little bathroom, it looked as if he'd urinated onto the likeness of Wittgenstein with his enigmatic bamboo cane. Trying to lower his window shades he'd dislodged them from their rollers and they dangled in strips and shreds I could not repair, and so I removed them; there was broken glass underfoot, there were cigarette butts, ashes; the room stank of beer and cheap jug wine and of smoke and of scorched fabric; there were scattered burn marks in the bed-clothes; I worried that Vernor would set fire to his bed, burn himself and his fellow tenants in the night.

Let me love you. Let my love heal you.

Vernor Matheius heard me perfectly well. He fell into a fit of cough-ing and lay his head on his arms, on the kitchen table.

On his ransacked desktop the portable typewriter had been shoved back against the wall. There were gouge marks in the wallpaper. A sheet of paper looked to have been torn out of the typewriter carriage, and on this paper there were numerous *XXX*'s and a single legible para-graph—

Axiom: if (following LW) the propositional sign is assigned a projective "relation" to the world does it therefore follow that the use of the percep-tible sign of a proposition (spoken or written) is a projection of a possible situation? (See LW, 3.11)

I understood that "LW" was Ludwig Wittgenstein; the rest of the argu-ment, which must have been part of the treatise Vernor was writing for his doctoral dissertation, was lost to me. Nor did I dare to ask Vernor about it since he'd have been furious to know I was looking through his papers. My task was to care for him, and this I did with energy, resolu-tion, and good humor; I would not fall sick myself but would be his nurse, and he would see how I loved him, and did not judge him; for you don't judge the sick, you nurse them back to health; you nurse them back to sanity; you nurse them back to their true selves. I brought food to Vernor's apartment to prepare for him; on his sickest days he hadn't any appetite, food disgusted him and he could tolerate only soup; a thin broth of a soup in which I cooked sliced vegetables; I hummed and smiled as I cooked in his tiny kitchen; it was an old European tale in which a love potion is mixed with a man's food; a maiden who adores him mixes her blood with his food, he eats it and falls in love with her forever; I smiled thinking I would secretly cut my finger on a paring knife and let a drop or two of my blood fall into Vernor's soup; so powerful was my fantasy, I would come to think I'd actually done such a bizarre thing; perhaps in fact I did it; but no crude wishful magic would work on a man like Vernor Matheius. I had to be content with being tolerated in his presence; I had to take pride in what he might eat that I'd prepared; I convinced him to eat a piece of whole-grain toast; I convinced him to drink a half-glass of orange juice; I sat close beside him at the little kitchen table and watched as he ate, close as an anxious mother; Vernor's face was drawn and haggard; he looked like a man suffering from grief; grief indistinguishable from rage; rage indistinguishable from grief; he wore a sweat-soaked undershirt, and sat slump-shouldered, his hard little muscles prominent in his upper arms; his jaws were covered in an ugly black stubble; fascinating to me, every harsh breath he drew; when I held him, to help him stand, or walk, I was disturbed to feel his erratic heartbeat; I was panicked thinking he might be seriously ill; if I suggested taking him to a doctor, or to the emergency room of the hospital a block away, he cursed me; he removed his glasses, drew his forearm roughly across his eyes, and cursed me. *Sick to death, my guts are sick, fuck you leave me alone can't you see I don't want you, your cunt, the color of your skin repulse me.*

I waited to become sick like Vernor. In his bathroom mirror my eyes shone with jaundice; the interior of my mouth was coated with something clammy and sickly sweet; Vernor's sickness eased into me like something clammy and sickly sweet; I did not resist, I entered into his delirium; if he didn't repel me, I lay beside him in his bed gripping his bony hand; it was a big hand, the knuckles prominent, though bony; I curved his fingers around mine so it seemed as if he was gripping my hand; as in the Brass Rail he'd boldly nudged his knuckles against my breast; my breathing quickened, or slowed, with Vernor's breathing; like carved funerary figures we lay together in a suspension that might have looked, from a distance, to a neutral observer, like peace, tranquility; the aftermath of love.

Why why are you doing this?

Because I am strong enough. Because I can love enough for both.

In his soft, soiled underwear Vernor Matheius lay on his couch like a fallen prince amid soiled sheets; he smoked cigarettes I'd had to buy for him, despite my disapproval; he scattered ashes like seed everywhere. When one day in June, a hazy early-summer heat suffusing the apartment, he rose to stagger into the bathroom to shower, not wanting me to help him, I thought *This is the turn, he will be himself again.* (As if I weren't terrified of that self.) Six days and six nights had passed since the onset of Vernor's sickness; seven days and seven nights since the murder of Medgar Evers; and still Evers's murderer went unidentified; for Evers's murderer was ubiquitous in the South, and elsewhere; in that pattern of crazed accelerating cruelty and violence against civil rights activists that would culminate in April 1968 in the assassination of Martin Luther King Jr.; in that future blowing toward us like a dark, ravening wind. *When you step into history, history's boot steps on you.* I did not think at the time *If you fail to step into history, history erases you* for at the time I was thinking only of Vernor Matheius and of his health; while he was in the bathroom showering I began hurriedly to clean the apartment; stripped the soiled bedclothes from the bed with the intention of taking them to a Laundromat; I'd taken a few of Vernor's things to a Laundromat near the hospital a few days before, and brought them back undetected; when Vernor finished his shower, I would add his towels; I would add as many of Vernor's clothes as he would allow. I found a broom in a kitchen closet and swept the littered floor; emptied dustpans of cigarette butts, ashes, crumpled papers and bits of dried food, dirt and hairs into a brimming wastebasket; collected the empty beer cans and wine jugs; trundled the trash downstairs to a Dumpster at the rear of the lot. *As if I live here. I live here now, with Vernor Matheius in apartment 2D.* Now that Vernor seemed to trust me, now I might stay with him through the night; I had the key to his apartment and could come and go as I wished; I wished I would encounter another tenant of the building so that I might have exchanged greetings in a neighborly fashion, another young woman, a young wife, or one of the foreign graduate students. The midday sun blazed overhead; my hair burst into flame; I was made to think of Nietzsche's mad prophet Zarathustra, and of Zarathustra's blazing noontide. *What is man?* cries Zarathustra. *A ball of wild snakes.* Despite the heat of the sun I was energized, excited; I took happiness in such simple physical tasks as hauling trash, sweeping and cleaning floors. I saw the grinning teeth of those who despised me. *Negro-lover! Nigger-lover!* I laughed, and ran back upstairs where the door was opened, as I'd left it.

Vernor was still showering. I listened outside the bathroom door and heard his thin tuneless whistling beneath the sound of the shower and I thought *He is himself again.* I set about restoring order on his desk; that desk I'd so admired, now strewn with papers; except for the Olivetti portable everything had been knocked about; I thought I would rearrange scattered pages (from Vernor's treatise?) into their original neat stacks; but I failed to make sense of them, and gave up. I opened a filing cabinet drawer, curious about what was inside; these cabinets were made of metal painted a pale green, but badly scratched; Vernor had bought them, he'd boasted, for five dollars apiece at a fire-bankruptcy sale of office supplies; the drawer was crammed with manila folders containing typed papers and note cards; some of the folders were meticulously clean, and others were strangely soiled as if they'd been stepped on. *You should not, should not be doing this, this is wrong* a small frightened voice cautioned me but I saw no harm in glancing through the folders; a treasure trove of old, yellowing papers; neatly typed outlines of books of the Bible including such obscure books as *Jeremiah, Hosea, Philippians, Thessalonians* as well as most of the books of the New Testament; in a large and passionate hand not immediately recognizable as Vernor's were written in columns the names of magical-biblical fig-ures—*Moses, Jacob, Joshua, Elisha, Job, Jesus, Mark, Paul, Mary Magdalene*—as if these names belonged to individuals known to Vernor Matheius. In other folders, farther back in the drawer, were more notes and outlines; theology, philosophy, ethics; most of these written in a bold, rapid hand, no more than a dozen lines to a page, as if thoughts had spilled out of Vernor's teeming mind onto the paper, scarcely contained in lan-guage. I smiled to see his college papers: neatly typed, held together with rust-stained paper clips; with such titles as "The 'Problem of Evil' in Milton's *Paradise Lost*," "The Concept of 'Virtue' in Epicureanism," "The Concept of 'Mind' in Bertrand Russell"; if there were red marks on these papers, the marks indicated enthusiasm, praise; Vernor Matheius's grades were uniformly A and A+. I tried to summon up a younger, vulnerable Vernor Matheius, an undergraduate hoping to im-press his professors; how difficult to imagine arrogant Vernor Matheius perceiving himself in a position inferior to anyone. Then staring into another folder I'd carelessly opened, at what appeared to be razored-out pages from magazines and books; an essay on Plato's *Laws* removed from an issue of *The Journal of Philosophical Inquiry,* Fall 1961; a chapter from a study of Spinoza; a chapter from a study of Kant; several dia-grammed pages from an essay on symbolic logic; had Vernor Matheius

removed these from library materials? *But Vernor wouldn't do such a thing.*
Not him. Pushed against the back of the drawer was a folder containing
packets of much-folded letters and creased snapshots; some of these
were in black and white, the rest in bright color; I found myself staring
at brown-skinned strangers, a family; and there was a young, boyish
Vernor Matheius in their midst; sixteen or seventeen, tall and lean and
smiling; and in other snapshots he was perceptibly older, with a thin
moustache, still tall and lean but without expression standing beside a
much shorter, plump, happily smiling young woman with a baby in her
arms and a boy of about two beside her clinging to her skirt; the young
woman, I knew, was Vernor's wife, a good-looking woman in her mid-
twenties with full fleshy lips and a wide pug nose; the little boy was
cocoa-colored, with Vernor's beautiful long-lashed eyes and narrow
face; the snapshot blazed with color, having been taken in a grassy outdoor setting, a wood frame cottage in the background; flowering fruit
trees, dogwood and forsythia; there was a strange, stark, preacherly
look to Vernor in his tight dark suit, long-sleeved white shirt and dark,
tightly knotted tie; the very tie Vernor had worn with his new silk vest
at the Brass Rail; his glasses weren't wire-rimmed and round but black
plastic and oval; he stood slightly apart from his happily smiling little
family and he was staring moodily at the camera and beyond the camera
as if already Vernor Matheius was edging out of the frame, planning his
escape. May 1959. *So he's married, has been married. Has a family, young*
children. He lied.

I meant to replace the snapshots but my hand trembled. Several fell
onto the floor. When I groped for them, my vision blurred. My love for
Vernor Matheius was contracting like an outstretched hand contracting
into a small, hard fist.

There was a sudden swift sound behind me: Vernor's bare feet slapping against the floor. I felt the angry vibrations of his footsteps before I

turned to see him, partly dressed, in trousers and undershirt, rushing at me. He grabbed my arm, shoved me away from the opened filing cabinet; he slammed the drawer shut, and cursed me—"God damn you, Anellia! Get out of here!" His face was contorted in fury, and in chagrin; it was the chagrin I would remember; the lenses of his glasses were faintly clouded with steam from the bathroom; his skin had darkened ferociously with blood. To protect myself, I pushed at Vernor's hand; he pushed back at me, catching the side of my head with his fist; I felt the sharp, hard edge of the filing cabinet cutting into my thigh; blindly I half-crawled away, stumbling to my feet and ran for the door, which opened off the tiny kitchen; Vernor didn't pursue me, but cursed after me as I ran panting and sobbing on the stairs, sick with guilt, and fear of what Vernor might do to me. I ran down the outdoor stairs and heard his voice above me, a furious lowered voice like a wail of grief I pressed my hands over my ears to stifle—*Get out of here don't ever come back God damn you! fuck you! fuck you white bitch!*

30

By space the universe encompasses and swallows me up like an atom; by thought I comprehend the world.

PASCAL

At the foot of the wooden stairs. My thoughts beat like moths against a screen. I sat hunched, hugging my knees; staring out at the rain. Vernor Matheius had driven me away as you'd drive away a dog yet there I sat huddled at the foot of the wooden stairs at 1183 Chambers as night came on.

How long I'd been there, I could not have said. Night now, and steadily raining. A steamy mist rose from the pavement. I was sick with grief and chagrin of my own; I'd run away from Vernor Matheius and wandered in the rain and at last returned, hair dripping in my face, my clothes soaked, I was stunned, I was sick, yet a part of my brain continued to operate as always *What did you expect, wasn't it freedom from him you wanted.* From a distance came the sonorous tolling of the bell tower of the Music School on its drumlin-hill; Chambers Street was on lower ground, in a virtual gulch; the air was heavier here, more viscous and oppressive; the mist rising from the pavement had become fog; my face and throat ached as if I'd been crying, but I didn't remember crying; tears are a child's desperate ploy, and futile. I thought *I will never cry again, no one will ever have the power to hurt me again;* and this would be so. I felt Vernor's hard fingers grabbing my arm, the hard blow of his fist against my head; I saw again the man's look of rage, disgust, yet guilt; something like shame; I'd peered too deeply into his soul for him to forgive me; I'd gone too far; he had loved me or had almost loved me or (I would tell myself) had begun to allow himself to consider that he might, in his way, love me; or that he might have begun to allow himself to consider that he might allow me to love him without irony; and I'd destroyed that, I'd destroyed my own meager hope of happiness, I'd destroyed the purity of my own love for him; I'd destroyed Anellia, who was such a fool. The idolator is always a fool. It was Anellia's wet hair dripping into her face, Anellia's lean arms, lean-muscled legs pressed tight against her shivering body; though the season was summer by the calendar, the air was cold; the rain was cold; Anellia whose soul quavered at the brink of extinction; about to be sucked into the void, which was Nothingness; the bliss of Nothingness; for what was there after all, as Vernor Matheius had once wittily declaimed, except atoms-and-the-void at the start of human time, which was the start of human thinking, and that effort of human futility to which the name Philosophy has been assigned. Yet I saw with a stab of certainty what I would do: I would return to my room and toss my costume-clothes into a heap, my cheaply glamorous secondhand things purchased with such misguided hope; I would cut these things into pieces with a scissors; as once I'd cut my long, bristling hair; to hurt oneself sometimes is a balm; to hurt oneself sometimes is the only way of healing; *debridement* was a term of Vernor Matheius's, and it would be a term of my own; even the silver belt I would tear at until its silver medallions broke apart and clattered to the floor; my heart beat hard with the certainty of all I would do, and would not regret doing; I would step into history, as Vernor had scorned; I would join demonstrators marching and chanting and waving handmade signs; I would join CORE, I would join SANE; I would find a way of bringing my intense inner life, my questing life, into balance with history; I would be fearless, or give that impression; I would be fearless, though frightened; I would march with Negroes and whites and confront the race-hatred of my race; I would expose my heart, as I would expose my body; I would make myself vulnerable, I would expiate my guilt; I would remake myself another time, empowered by loss, grief. No longer Anellia. Waiting to see who I might be, after Anellia.

And there came at last Vernor Matheius's voice above me. And it was a voice of sobriety, and not reproach; a voice still lowered with emotion; a raw voice, a voice of hurt and dismay. "Anellia, is that you?" A pause, a beat. My heart continued to beat calmly with the certainty of what I would do, and what I would not do; what I would not ever do again; and I didn't turn to look up the steep steps at Vernor Matheius. I heard him mutter, "Jesus!" I heard him descend the stairs slowly, like a man just awakened from sleep; he was breathing quickly, audibly. When on the step above me he paused, I had a childish fear he would kick me; and very possibly that thought ran through his head, too; but he said, "Anellia, you shouldn't be here. You'll only be hurt." I might have said *I've already been hurt.* But I said nothing. Vernor stepped down to sit beside me, with a sigh; a sigh like a shudder; stone cold sober the man was, and shaky; I had to ease aside to make room for him, as if it was the most natural thing in the world for us to sit together here in the dark, in the rain; Vernor lit a cigarette and expelled smoke through his nostrils, and after a moment said, thoughtfully, "I don't have a black soul. Because I don't have a black soul, I don't have any soul at all." I said, "Vernor, I thought you didn't believe in 'soul.' I thought you didn't believe in personal identity, history." He said, "I don't. The way a color-blind person doesn't believe in color because he hasn't experienced it." There was bemusement in this remark, and melancholy; a melancholy I'd never heard in Vernor Matheius before. I said, "You have a family, I guess? Young children?" and he said, "No longer," and I said, "What do you mean, 'no longer'?" and he shrugged and said nothing; and my voice quavered with indignation I hadn't known I would feel, since the initial feeling I'd had, seeing the big-boned smiling woman in the snapshot, had been jealousy, "You left your wife and children? Left where? Where are they? How could you do such a thing, Vernor?" and Vernor said quietly, "It's none of your concern who or what I've left behind me or who or what I am. Or what you or anyone else expects of me." And I said nothing, for this was so; this statement of fact could not be contested; I said nothing, but I didn't acquiesce; and Vernor sucked at his cigarette and released clouds of stinging smoke which was the smell of guilt; and it crossed my mind that I would not miss this: the smoke, the stink of cigarettes, my poor father's smoking habit, my father's mysterious dying, the perverse romance of addiction; I would not miss this at all. We watched a car pass in the rain, it must've been a police squad car with a red light on its roof, driving fast along Chambers splashing through puddles; there were rivulets of rainwater rushing down Chambers Street, the steep hill from the university hospital complex. And at last Vernor said in a flat voice, a voice from which all pretension had drained, "My ancestors from Dahomey were tribal people, they were captured and brought to North America as slaves in the 1780's; but they'd been slave traders themselves. They'd captured and sold other black tribes as slaves. This was a secret imparted to me by my mother's grandfather, a minister, when I was twenty-one years old. This was our handed-down secret, handed to me. That my ancestors, his ancestors, had sold other black Africans, other tribes, to white European slavers." I turned now to look at Vernor; I looked at him in astonishment; for this was a man out of whose mouth revelations emerged, and always unexpected. I had believed I could predict him at last, and yet I could not have predicted this; never could I have predicted the sadness in his voice, and the resignation. As if, for him too, something had ended. Yet there came his wry humor, his sidelong grin and squint as if (after all) he and I were allies in this predicament; this problem; as if *Vernor Matheius* were an intellectual puzzle we might contemplate together as colleagues and attempt to solve; like those students of philosophy devoted to logical analysis; enjoined in a singular quest for truth which is the philosopher's life's work. He said bitterly, "But why judge them? My putative ancestors? They were human beings and like all human beings they were cruel, exploitative, xenophobic; they were primitive people in a tribal society in which members of other tribes aren't perceived as fully human; you can kill them, you can sell them into slavery, you can practice genocide like the Germans of the Third Reich, and someone will absolve you—it's 'natural,' it's 'Nature'; it's instinct. So my ancestors sold their brother and sister Africans into slavery and they flourished for a while until it came their turn to be slaves. White men's trading ships sailed from Liverpool to the west coast of Africa and traded textiles, arms, and other cargo for black men and women; the ship sailed across the Atlantic to Jamaica where the black men and women were traded for sugar, which was brought back to England to be sold; for what would the English do without sugar in their tea and pastries; what would the white man's civilization be without sugar in their bloodstream; again the ship sailed from Liverpool to the west coast of Africa and loaded up with black men and women; and so on, and so forth; it was a prosperous business, these were boom times, everyone flourished except those with the bad luck to be branded 'slaves.'" Vernor spoke with the mildest irony; this was a recitation of facts, of history; yet every syllable was damning; every syllable was an outcry of pain. Hesitantly I touched his arm, and said, "Vernor, you aren't your ancestors any more than I am my ancestors," even as my voice faltered, for maybe this wasn't true; and Vernor said practicably, "Then I'm no one. I don't know who the hell I am." I said, "But why should it matter?

Why——now?" For hadn't we faith in pure rationality, pure logic and language pruned of all sentiment, all tribal history; wasn't the dream of philosophy possible, even now? Vernor said, for even at such a moment Vernor Matheius was one to have the final word, "Yes, why should it matter? Yet it does." How strange to be sitting beside this man on these wooden stairs smelling faintly of rot, at such a time; gazing out toward the rain; a couple seated together gazing out into the rain; they live upstairs and have come outside for fresh air, the man smoking and the woman seated close beside him; a harsh, sibilant rain blowing along the pavement beneath streetlights, with a look of antic excitement. Another time we heard the remote sonorous tolling of the Music School bell tower; more chimes than I could count, it must have been midnight. How strange, how uncanny and how wonderful, what elation flooded my small gnarled heart on the eve of my twentieth birthday as I sat beside Vernor Matheius on the stairs at the rear of the shabby stucco building at 1183 Chambers Street, Syracuse, New York on the rain-swept night of June 18, 1963.

If you'd driven by, and noticed that couple, wondering who they were, they were us.

III.

THE WAY OUT

1

To show the fly the way out of the bottle? Break the bottle.

There was the shock of my brother Hendrick's call. One evening at dusk in June 1965. When I was staying in a rented cabin near Burlington, Vermont; living alone for the summer, immersed in my writing. The telephone rang and there was my brother Hendrick!— with news so unexpected, at first I couldn't grasp what he said.

Hendrick's deep gravelly voice and nasal upstate New York accent. Jarring to my ear, for I spoke with him rarely; I spoke with my brothers rarely; you might have thought that I was estranged from them, or that they'd cast me off, and forgotten me. And so my brother Hendrick's voice frightened me as if he were calling me to account for something I'd failed to do, some family obligation I'd failed to meet in my desperate flight from Strykersville one day to be construed as *my career, my destiny.* My voice went small and vulnerable, stammering—"Yes, Hendrick? W-What?" Not absorbing what Hendrick was saying with such urgency as if the distance between us, approximately three hundred miles, were compounded by a distance in time; for Hendrick and I hadn't seen each other since our grandmother's funeral and burial in the Lutheran cemetery eighteen months before; and in my confusion as I

stood in a doorway of the rented and unfamiliar cabin at the edge of a
small lake I struggled to recall Hendrick's adult face for his boy's face
had vanished, I knew, it wouldn't be to that brash careless good-looking
face I must appeal but to a face matured and thickened about the jaws,
Hendrick now thirty years old and though the youngest of my three
elder brothers no longer young; my only brother not yet married, my
only brother not yet a father, yet Hendrick was mysterious and inacces-
sible to me as the others; at the time of my grandmother's funeral his
eyes had drifted onto me, with baffled affection, perhaps not affection
but a subtle resentment in which there dwelt some small measure of admiration, for Hendrick believed it was unfair, God-damned unfair, that
I'd been the one to leave Strykersville on a scholarship to a highly regarded university while he, smart as I, maybe smarter, certainly better
at math, and as deserving, had had to work at demeaning jobs to support himself through school; he worked now at General Electric in
Troy, New York, and the few times we'd met in our new, awkward dis-
guises as adults I'd felt the weight of his brotherly disapproval, his envy
and dislike a hand shoving at me, backing me from him, I'd seen those
mica eyes even as he forced a smile for his younger sister, I'd wanted to
plead with him *Please! please don't hate me, Hendrick, our lives are only luck.*
But I knew that such a remark would only embarrass him, as he
sounded for some reason embarrassed now, and incensed, over the
phone—"Jesus! What a trick. When we'd thought all these years he
was *dead.*"

"Hendrick, what?" I must have heard, but I hadn't heard. I was having
difficulty getting my breath. "Who—is dead?"

"*Was* dead. Turns out, after all, he *isn't.*"

"Who?"

"The old man, who the hell else? Who else was dead, whose body we never saw buried? Who else for Christ's sake I'd be calling you about?"

He meant who else, what else, had the two of us in common, except our father? The burden of his memory?

Otherwise, Hendrick and I were strangers.

Faintly I asked, "Our f-father is—alive?"

"Only just barely. A nurse or someone, a woman, called. This time he's dying for real."

"But he's alive? Our *father?*"

He'd been assumed dead for years. He'd disappeared into the West. I couldn't remember how my brothers and I had referred to the man, forever mysterious in absence, who'd been our father. Through the years of my growing-up. And my brothers, my tall beautiful brothers, so often absent from me, too. We hadn't said *Father,* I was certain. We hadn't said *Daddy, Dad.*

Hendrick said, "Right. He's living in a place called Crescent, Utah. About two hundred miles south of Salt Lake City. He was in a hospital in Salt Lake, now he's been discharged. They let him out to die by his request. I didn't speak with him myself, for all I know he can't talk. Just this woman. Who she is, I don't know. Maybe they're married. Y'know, he's fifty-six? He's dying of some kind of cancer." This was said in the tone of voice in which a minute before Hendrick had muttered the word *trick.*

"Cancer!"

When I'd lifted the ringing phone I'd had no expectation of hearing alarming news. Few people knew where I was, few people had any need to call me. If I'd had to guess who the caller might be I'd have guessed it was a wrong number. *Who? I'm sorry, no. There's no one by that name at this number.*

Hendrick was speaking rapidly now, wanting to end the conversation. Maybe he'd become emotional after all; or maybe the subject was distasteful to him. He would supply me with the telephone number of the woman who'd contacted him, her name and address in Crescent, Utah, and I could call her myself; no further information about my father because Hendrick had no further information, and wished none. I was fumbling with a pencil, trying to write on a scrap of paper, blinking back tears. *Alive! Our father was alive. He'd never died.* It would be one of the profound shocks of my adult life as the news of his sudden and unexplained death had been one of the profound shocks of my adolescence. You could see why Hendrick had said *trick* for there seemed to be an element of trickery in such shocks, and in trickery an element of cruelty.

Behind my brother's hurried voice there came a faint, querulous cry that might have been a child, and a sound of coughing. Was Hendrick living with someone? What was Hendrick's life, unknown to me? Of my three brothers Hendrick was the closest to me in age yet he was seven years older; an immense gulf, in childhood; I had no idea what his life was like now, and could not ask. At my grandmother's funeral Hendrick had stood tall and somber and frowning, apart even from his brothers, with that subtle air of resentment as if the elderly woman's death, like her life, had had very little to do with him; with his own inner, private life; my grandmother had not been a woman of much sentiment or feeling, she'd loved only her son, the man who was our father; in loving her son, she'd exhausted her capacity for emotion; he'd broken her heart, possibly; he'd broken all our hearts; no one else had the power to break my grandmother's heart, and no one else would have wished to have that power. At the funeral my brother Hendrick had watched me covertly; I'd felt uneasy under his gaze, and at the same time defiant; for what right had he to judge me; if I'd seemed to have excelled in a world he had been barred from entering, how was that my fault; I refused to be made to feel guilty by another's envy, as I could not feel pride or superiority for such a reason; I could not form any judgment of myself based upon my family's judgment of me, for they hardly knew me; my brother's unsmiling eyes, my brother's stone-colored eyes like my own, and like our father's. When Hendrick smiled, as sometimes he did, it was a quick teasing flash of a smile and you saw the possibility of warmth in him, and trust.

Before you could respond, the smile vanished.

How badly now I wanted to say, "Oh, Hendrick, why did he do this to us, do you think? Please don't hang up, talk to me."

How badly I wanted to say, "Would you come with me to Utah, Hendrick? To see him? Before it's too late? We could drive out together." How badly I wanted to plead, "You won't let me go alone, will you?"

But I knew what the answer would be. Instead I thanked Hendrick, and hung up the phone.

2

Don't let no fuckers out there sell you short.

The last time I'd seen my father, that sudden rough embrace. The touch of a man who hadn't touched me in years. I would remember it for days, for years.

Four years ago. When he'd come to my high school graduation.

The shock of seeing him there in the audience! For I hadn't known he would be coming, I hadn't known he was in Strykersville. (He'd arrived the previous night, staying at a motel in town.) The prevailing fact of my father during my years of growing up was simple, blunt: when the man was home, he was home; when not, not. *To be in one place for long, he'd have to be dead* my brothers joked of him. But there unexpectedly he was in the high school auditorium. In a white shirt open at the collar, in matching coat and trousers. His hair, what remained of it, slicked back on his head; his nose flattened, bulbous; his jaws unshaven. And I, the girl valedictorian, in a black academic gown of light wool like a nightgown and a pasteboard-cloth black cap, its tassel swinging dangerously near my left eye. At the age of eighteen I more resembled a precocious thirteen-year-old boy; one of those small-boned ferret-faced individuals who ascends to a stage, a podium, confronting an almost palpable wave of resistance in an audience; a polite, subdued, yet perceptible resistance; who is both terrified yet fearless, borne aloft like Icarus by a mere voice, mere words, the very audacity of performance and a passion to utter something not yet said that would not otherwise be said except in this way. And the audience is startled into listening, and startled into applause. And afterward the doubt *Did it really happen? Did they really listen, and applaud? And what does applause mean?* After the ceremony ended, in a haze of smiles and handshakes and congratulations I'd looked around to see him headed for me, my father who was taller, larger, more physically present than any other man in the room; my father with the manner of an upright, just slightly swaying steer; unshaven, flush-faced with drink, and his eyes bloodshot yet gleaming with a combative paternal pride. He'd grabbed me and hugged me, breathing his hot-fumey breath into my face, advising me in a careless loud voice *Don't let no fuckers out there sell you short.*

It's advice I have tried to remember. Even when I've betrayed it.

3

Alone I drove to Crescent, Utah. Twenty-five hundred miles.

It was estimated that my father might live another three or four weeks; I was in terror of flying to him; not of the flight itself (though I'd never flown in an airliner before) but of getting too quickly to my destination.

I would spend days (and nights) on interstate highways in a Volkswagen bought for $535 the previous year, with faulty brakes, a faulty muffler, a noisy motor; a stick shift that operated with some re-sistance; unless I kept most of the windows rolled down at all times, an odor of carbon monoxide wafted from beneath the dashboard. *Except: what you can detect, isn't the poison. Fresh air dispels it!* It was a 1959 Volkswagen with no heat or air-conditioning, of course; what "heat" there was blew in through vents from the motor onto my legs. Yet I loved this, my first car; I was naive enough to love its very smallness and economy; its hunched-beetle shape; unless it was a fetal-shape; origi-nally plum-colored but now weathered and rusted to no single hue. There was a spiderweb crack in the windshield in front of the passen-ger's seat as if a luckless ghost-passenger had been catapulted into the glass, striking headfirst.

In the secondhand Volkswagen I would drive the width of New York State (for I'd been staying in northern Vermont when Hendrick's call came) and I would pass within fifty miles of Strykersville; I would continue west driving along the southern edge of Lake Erie and through Ohio and through Indiana and through Illinois and through northern Missouri and through Kansas and through Colorado and so at last into eastern Utah, on I-70 to the small town of Crescent, Utah, population 1,620. *This, the journey of my life. I will get there on time!* In New York, in Illinois, and in Colorado I'd telephoned the soft-spoken woman known to me only as Hildie Pomeroy, to ask after my father and to learn that he was in "stable condition" and "waiting for you." To save money, often I slept in the car; not at night but mornings or late afternoons in convivial roadside rest areas and parking lots of restaurants; not in the backseat (for a stranger might drift by to stare in at me open-mouthed and vulnerable in sleep as an infant); it was one of the haunting notions of my life, about which I'd tried to write, except not knowing how to seize the notion, the image, the riddle in order to write about it coherently, how we never see ourselves sleeping; we never see ourselves openmouthed, vulnerable as a baby in sleep; in just such a way we never see ourselves, at all; we have no clear idea of ourselves; our mirror reflections reflect only what we wish to see, or can bear to see, or punish ourselves by seeing. *Nor can we trust others to see us either. For they too see what they wish to see, with their imperfect eyes.* In my car, often I remained in the driver's seat when I slept, my hands in a pretense of gripping the wheel so that (though deeply unconscious, head lolling like a stroke victim's against the seatback) I was primed for immediate action, escape. In public rest rooms I managed to wash myself, even my sweaty-sticky windblown hair; I didn't eat often in restaurants, but bought packaged food in stores because it was cheaper, and I filled paper cups with drinking water to take with me; I'd allotted myself a certain amount of money to take me from Vermont to Utah, and begrudged spending money on my-self and not on gas, oil, services for my car. Already on the first day of driving, nearly eight hours, I'd become hypnotized; my eyelids drooped with a wish to sleep, unless it was a wish to dream without the inter-ference of sleep; the Volkswagen was so small that it quavered in the wake of larger vehicles that passed in hissing contempt; even other Volkswagens sailed past me, though their drivers often waved or honked in a gesture of camaraderie. My car shuddered if driven at a speed beyond fifty-five miles an hour and there was such a maelstrom of winds whipping my head, I came to think that the Volkswagen was somehow myself; or, in its woundedness, my father. Amid traffic, I was less susceptible to irrational notions and hypnagogic images; on the open highway, median stripes to the left of my vision, gravel shoulder to my right, open countryside, empty sky, I began to sink into that seduc-tive and treacherous state of mind that precedes sleep; I felt a pang of hurt, that Hendrick had refused to accompany me; I seemed to recall that I'd actually asked him, and he'd said no. He hadn't called me back; I told myself that I hadn't expected him to call back; I had no number for him, and so could not call him; nor did my brothers Dietrich and Fritz call me; I told myself that I hadn't expected them to call; I was not dis-appointed, and I was not hurt. *To them, he's dead. They can't love a dead man as I can.* I fell into the habit of speaking aloud in the car for the noise of the wind and the motor was such I could barely hear myself, this ex-empted me from embarrassment or blame. The soliloquy of the self, plotting what's to come. For what is life, its myriad surprises, except *what's to come.* I seemed to see my father as he'd been at my high school graduation except he was in the old farmhouse, in the kitchen where so often he'd sat, smoking cigarettes and drinking late into the night; he was willing to look at me, and to speak with me, and I could ask him any question I wished; but suddenly I was frightened, and could not speak. For what do you ask your father, if you have but one question? I might have asked, earnestly *Is any future preferable to any past? Do we live only in time?* I tried to recall what Vernor Matheius had said once about time but I could not retain both Vernor Matheius and my father simultaneously; I would not have wished Vernor to have met my father, or even to have seen him; nor would I have wished my father to have met Vernor, or even to have seen him; and so Vernor Matheius faded. Midway through the endless state of Kansas I began to hallucinate flatland even in my sleep; my hallucinations and the landscape were identical; I could not escape the one without being swallowed up into the other; I would sink, I would drown, I would die. Midway through the endless state of Colorado I began to hallucinate mountains far ahead at the horizon; mirage-mountains delicate as watercolor mountains in a Japanese print; yet these mountains weren't mirages, they didn't fade but deepened; they didn't retreat with the horizon, but drew nearer; and suddenly it was evident that the mountains at the horizon were moving toward me; I was moving toward them along the highway; suddenly it was evident that the mountains would enclose me, in time; I would gaze out on all sides and see mountains on all sides; I smiled at the revelation—"The Rocky Mountains! They're *real*."

More jagged the horizon became. The interminable midwestern plains of farmland and dull-grazing cattle had fallen away behind me, now a different and more vigorous-seeming cattle were grazing in a different, harsher landscape; here the landscape was sepia-colored as if bleached by a harsher sun; in the distance, a lunar landscape of hills strewn with boulders, strange rock formations, mountains topped with streaks of white like paint. Here, you are made to realize that a landscape is a living thing; a landscape exerts life; a landscape enters through the eyes, and breathes into you; in the West, I could no longer be the young woman I'd been in the East; in Crescent, Utah, a place unknown to me, a young woman impatiently awaited me who was my-self, yet altered; in Crescent, Utah, I was determined to be this young woman. My father's daughter. The temptation in such landscapes is to believe that beauty exists in a profound and secret relationship to you. The temptation is to believe that you are the first to have fully *seen*. I saw that the high-desert landscape shifted continuously in hue and texture with the rapid, skittish movement of light in the enormous sky; unlike the East, where the sky was diminished by treelines, and sometimes ob-scured completely. My eyes, accustomed to the foreshortened land-scapes and horizons of the East, squinted at so much space in the West; impossible to see such vast space without seeing time; vast reaches of time before human history, human speech, the human effort to name such mute phenomena as *mountains, rivers, canyons, plateaus, glacial troughs*. Such mute phenomena as *rock, sand, salt flats, buttes, mesas, bluffs, badlands.* Crossing the Colorado River, driving into the Grand River Valley and westward into Utah I saw a world of desolation and beauty open up before me, and my heart quickened with hope; I'd forgotten that my mission was to sit at the bedside of a man dying of cancer; I would pay for such forgetfulness, but not immediately. In my little car that vibrated with excitement. Place-names romantic and exotic to my ear as poetry. *Roan Cliffs, San Rafael Valley, Sand River, Dirty Devil River, Green River, Sego Canyon, Diraes Canyon, Death Hollow, Hell's Backbone, Calf Creek Falls, China Meadows, Desolation Canyon, Dead Horse Point, Islands in the Sky.*

And *Crescent,* to which I'd been summoned.

I began to tell myself, fatigued by driving, that I might live in *Crescent.* Hypnotized by the highway, by the steady, numbing pressure of my sandaled foot against the gas pedal and by a continuous sun-glare I began to tell myself a story of how my father had summoned me to

Crescent for a purpose. For the fact of his being in *Crescent* could not be an accident, could it?

"Daddy? This car, I bought with part of the advance a publisher gave me for a book. A book of stories. My first." I tested these astonishing words and my voice began to quaver. For how would the man I'd known as my father whom I'd never called *Daddy, Dad* receive such news? Would he be proud of me? Or indifferent? Would a book of stories, and such elusive "poetic" stories, mean anything to a man, a laborer, who rarely read more than newspapers, so far as I knew; a man born to semi-illiterate farming people who owned no books as if in repudiation of any intellectual or spiritual life beyond the dumb stares of farm animals? (Except: in my grandmother's parlor there was a Holy Bible, as this revered book called itself; unread, except by me, out of curiosity and skeptical wonderment; unread, yet kept in a conspicuous place on a lace-covered tabletop; my German-born grandmother's grudging concession to America, and to Christianity which was synonymous with America. The Holy Bible's simulated leather covers and many of its pages were covered with a powdery, smelly mushroom-colored mold in the humidity of Strykersville summers.)

Now in Utah, that hitherto unimaginable state, on a well-traveled I-70 approaching Crescent, where I hoped to find an inexpensive motel, already I was praying (I, who'd never believed in the God of the Holy Bible, nor even in the God of Spinoza) that my father would live to see this book of mine published, at least. Another six months! He would live to see my name, which included his name, on the dust jacket of the book; he would hold the book in his hand and tell me how beautiful it was, and he loved me.

4

"Yes, Erich wants to see you. But he doesn't want you to see *him*."

How intimate my father's name, on this stranger's lips.

A hunched little woman with a fussily made-up doll's face and a breathy, girlish voice, yet a voice of steely resolve, this woman who'd introduced herself as Hildie Pomeroy, my father's friend. At 3 Railroad Street she'd opened the front door of the clapboard bungalow as if she'd been waiting for me just inside. There was muted surprise in her face, seeing me; for, however my father must have described me, I didn't look like that young woman; and Hildie Pomeroy, who stood no taller than four feet ten inches, and who appeared to have something twisted in her upper spine, wasn't the woman I might have expected, my father's friend and protector. We stared at each other blinking. At the Economy Motel (Singles $6) I'd had a bath for the first time in memory, soaking in a hot tub; I'd washed my hair, combed damp and wavy and shapeless to my shoulders; I'd changed into a fresh but rather wrinkled long-sleeved cotton shirt and cotton slacks, and I smelled of soap, shampoo, toothpaste; I was visibly nervous; surely I didn't resemble the literary-minded intellectual daughter of whom my father might have spoken. And here was Hildie Pomeroy in nurse-white: rayon shirt, rayon pants,

crepe-soled canvas shoes that looked freshly whitened. Brisk and efficient except so unexpectedly made up, like a showgirl: distinctly
rouged cheeks, oily crimson mouth, black mascara beading her eyelashes; and her hair!—savagely dyed black, quite long and unwieldy, but
coiled and crimped about her head with plastic flower-barrettes. The
woman looked like a painted windup doll whose back had been cruelly
broken. Seeing the surprise in my face she said, drawing herself up to
her full height, "You can talk to him, dear, but he won't be able to talk
to you. *I* will do that for him."

"But he—he is—conscious? He isn't—?"

"Your father is sick, dear. He's had three operations in the past year,
for cancer of the throat and esophagus." Hildie spoke in hissed sibilants,
pausing. "He has lost fifty pounds and he—has been disfigured by the
surgery. He's only himself, dear, for a few hours at a time. Most visitors
he won't let in, no more. Only me 'cause I'm his friend and he trusts
me." Hildie flashed defiant eyes at me. "I'm his only friend."

This was a rebuke to me and my brothers; a rebuke I accepted as our
due; I would not protest. "On the phone you said he knows he's—
dying?"

Hildie shook her head sadly. "Oh, he knows, but he don't know. Or
don't want to know. Sick people are like us only just different. Their
minds play the same kinds of tricks on them our minds play, but more
pathetic. A person sick like your father, sometimes he's so weak he can't
move his head, can't open his eyes to see, can't talk even if he wanted
to talk, and gets confused where he is, who's with him, what's happening . . . I had nursing classes," Hildie said, as if I'd challenged her. "In
Salt Lake City I was studying to be a nurse."

"I see. That's so—fortunate. For my father."

I smiled foolishly at my father's friend in white. I didn't know what
to say to her, to placate her anxiety about me.

Hildie snorted with derisive laughter, mirthless and startling. "Oh, yeah! But he'd a whole lot rather be *well*."

Hildie Pomeroy was so much shorter than me, she stood with her neck sharply craned; her head, that seemed disproportionately large for her stunted body, was crooked upward at a painful angle. I felt that simply by standing before her, looming over her, I was discomforting her; my very presence must have been an impediment; the poor woman spoke breathlessly, stroking her hair and fussing with a little gold cross on a chain around her neck. (Her neck, too, had been powdered, but less effectively than her face; you could see a cross-hatching of lines in the powdery surface.) It seemed to me that Hildie Pomeroy had rehearsed some of her remarks; she'd repeated things she'd told me on the phone; her need was to establish absolutely and beyond my questioning her connection with the man who was my father though this connection was a mysterious one, not to be spelled out, neither was it to be doubted by me, an intruder. Hildie fixed me with bright, damp, intensely brown eyes; startlingly beautiful, thick-lashed brown eyes; I could see that a man might fall in love with such eyes.

I must have seemed to Hildie to be in a state of shock; instead of expressing anguish, or grief, I was smiling; my smile felt as if it had been stapled into my face. A remote, ironic voice sounded in my ears *And I've come so far!* Hildie was saying, matter-of-factly, "Your father has told me, dear: you remember him as he *was*. That is his hope. I'll take you to where he's lying, out on the back porch, during the day he likes the back porch, the TV's out there, too, it's a portable TV I can move real easy, and the porch is a comfortable place for him when he wakes up and doesn't know where he is, it's *consoling*. You know, your father did not have an easy life. Even before this, before the operations. When you're bad sick, and go a little out of your head, and your legs and sometimes even your arms don't feel like they belong to you, what you want most is to be *consoled*. So your father wants me to bring you out back to where he is, dear, he's been waiting for you all day. But you'll have to close your eyes. Or I will hide your eyes somehow. So he can see you. Then you can maybe turn around, your back to him, or you can sit, dear, there's a nice chair I brought out for you, and I can help you talk to him, because he can't say words now, not words you would understand but I understand; but only for a few minutes because he gets so exhausted, this time of day he's usually asleep. He sleeps through a hot afternoon and I feed him around dusk, his special foods, then he sleeps. See, dear, I know this is a surprise, the way he is, but it's his wish, and it's for the best." Hildie paused, smiling. "For you, too, dear, it's for the best."

This was a warning. I understood. *A dying man. Death. You don't want to see. You're too young.*

I had in fact been envisioning my father as he'd appeared to me four years before. Middle-aged but still swaggering-young, in the way that men who work with their hands and their bodies out-of-doors seem somehow to remain young; except if you look too closely into their leathery, lined faces. I'd envisioned my father waiting for me here in Crescent, Utah, a little older, more ravaged, but eager to see me, and in a different setting: an airy, high-ceilinged bedroom with a window looking out upon mountains, and a cobalt-blue sky. Crescent, Utah. The West. But Railroad Street was a narrow, poorly paved street that intersected with the town's attenuated Main Street, and the peeling sparrow-colored clapboard bungalow with the grassless front yard was on a block of similar bungalows and trailer homes; the backyard ran into a raised railroad embankment of cinders and weeds. Straggly, diseased-looking cottonwoods surrounded the house. Somewhere close by, a chain saw was being used. *This might be Strykersville. Near the railroad tracks.* And the town of Crescent! So ordinary. Only the name was beautiful as poetry. Looking for a motel, I'd been stunned at how small Crescent was, how diminished its communal life, a scattering of wood frame churches, a downtown of about two blocks, fake-brick facades of a few newer businesses but otherwise everything was old, decades old, older than Strykersville though it must have been settled far later; farther on, the state highway was a jumble of the usual gas stations and drive-in restaurants, sports equipment stores, a derelict A & P, Discount Carpets, a drive-in theater with a broken marquee, beer and liquor stores, taverns. *To have come so far: Strykersville!* Except the small upstate New York town of my girlhood had had a surprisingly good public library, and a YWCA where I could swim, and I could see that Crescent, Utah, was too small for such amenities. A few minutes beyond the town limits was open country, flat and treeless and ungiving; a harsh hot wind blew; even the mountain range, on my Esso map romantically called Roan Cliffs, were dull as eraser smudges in the heat haze.

I told Hildie yes, yes of course I would comply with my father's wishes, and with hers.

"I—I brought him a gift. I mean—both of you."

Holding out to the hunched-over little doll-woman in white a garishly wrapped wicker basket of fruit whose cellophane wrapper crinkled noisily. This absurd gift for a dying man I'd purchased at a food store in Grand Junction, Colorado; I hadn't known what the precise nature of my father's cancer was; I'd been assuming lung cancer. Could the poor man eat fruit? Apples, oranges, mangoes, kiwi, bananas? Was such a gift a cruel, unthinking joke? What had I been thinking? Hildie murmured thank you and took the basket from me briskly, and set it aside. She asked if, before she took me to visit with my father, I would like a glass of water; eagerly I said yes; my throat was parched, I'd been having trouble speaking. Sand and grit seemed to coat my mouth. Hildie led me farther into the house, into a cramped little kitchen with an old-fashioned humming Frigidaire and a gas stove and worn linoleum; the kitchen held an oatmeal-yeasty smell. Through its single window I saw the foreshortened view of the weedy railroad embankment about thirty yards away. What a roaring there must be, when a train came through! My poor father. Like a nurse, though not smiling, Hildie took time to run water from a faucet at the sink until, testing it with a forefinger, she judged it cold enough to drink; she filled a glass for me; I thanked her, taking it from her with shaky fingers, and before drinking pressed it against my warm forehead. It was a hot summer afternoon: in the nineties: a dry, scintillating heat, a sun-glaring-blinding heat, not humid as in upstate New York. *I'm afraid. So afraid. Help me.* Hildie Pomeroy was watching me closely. In that mixture of extreme femininity and steely resolve she reminded me of certain of my school classmates in Strykersville, girls who hadn't gone on to college but had remained behind to be beauticians, dental assistants, nurses, nurse's aides. Almost, observing my pale, strained face, Hildie had an impulse to touch me; to console me; I wanted her to touch me, and to console me; I was terrified of my father's dying; I did not know what I would say to him. "This is kind of you," I said, licking my lips. "This is"—my voice faltered, I hadn't any idea what I was trying to say—"so strange to me. Thank you." Hildie Pomeroy frowned. I saw that my first impression of her had been incomplete. She was a sturdy little troll of a woman, in her rayon-white costume; she might've been as young as thirty, or as old as fifty; she had short, muscled legs and thick ankles, strong shoulders and forearms; a clearly defined, shapely bust that strained at the rayon shirt; her hair so bizarrely dyed, crow-black and lustreless, and her painted doll's face, and those beautiful moist brown eyes! *My father's lover? His wife?* I tried to recall Ida's face and could not. I was too far away from home. Staring at Hildie Pomeroy I could not have said if she was an unnervingly attractive woman, despite her disfigured back, or ghastly; if her painted face, meant to suggest feminine sweetness, and subjugation, and a desire to please, made me want to smile in sympathy, or turn away in contempt.

Hildie saw my indecision. My fear. She touched my wrist, lightly. On her fingers were glittery inexpensive rings; her nails were small talons, painted a lurid bright crimson to match her lips. "You drove such a long distance, dear. By yourself?" She shook her head doubtfully. "It's dangerous. For a woman. How on earth will you get back? On the map, it's so far."

In my fear I seemed to be plucking at, with childish fingers, a consolation of philosophy. Nietzsche's affirmation of eternal occurrence. *We have lived this life, and this hour, many times; we have not yet been defeated; we are strong enough to endure; we must only say Yes.* As Hildie led me to the porch at the back of the house, to be brought into my father's presence.

She'd checked him and, yes, he was awake—"Not awake like you and me, dear, but, for him, awake." He could see me for a few minutes, no more. Gently Hildie took my hand, her warm dry fingers gripping my clammy-damp fingers, and urged me out onto the porch, positioning me where my father could see me but, my back to him, I couldn't see him. "H-Hello, Daddy? Hello. It's—" uttering my name as if my father might not know it; daring to call him "Daddy," as if that had been my name for him when I'd been a child. My knees were shaking, my eyes stared blindly into space. It was dusk; the wooden porch was shaded from what would have been a bright, pitiless sunshine by day, by an immense gnarled vine that might have been grape, or wisteria, but had neither fruit nor blossoms, only a tangle of insect-stippled leaves; and by an inexpensive screen nailed into place between the railing and the roof. The screen was a reproduction of a Japanese watercolor of foliage and butterflies, badly faded, but exquisite in design. Hildie had made up a daytime bed for my father a few yards away, on a sofa with creaking springs. I could sense his presence immediately, though I didn't turn my head so much as a fraction of an inch; I knew that he was staring at me; his vision was weakened from his illness, but he was staring greedily at me. I heard a low straining guttural *Uh-uh-uhhh* which Hildie quickly translated—" 'Hello!' your father says. He's so happy you are here." I said, wiping at my eyes, "Oh, Daddy, I'm so happy to be here, too. I only wish—" Hildie poked me in warning, for what was I going to say; what are the words one utters to a dying man, that require being said aloud? My father squirmed in his bed saying *Uh-uhhh* and breathing harshly, and Hildie translated, "He asks you to shut your eyes and turn to him so he can see your face. But you must shut your eyes tight for if you look at him, you won't like what you see. And he won't like you to see it." I shut my eyelids, which were trembling badly, and Hildie turned me to face the man in the bed; the man I believed was my father; the man who was Death, and yet my father. "Don't be afraid, dear," Hildie said, gently, aiding me by pressing the palms of her hands lightly over my eyes, in such a way that most of my face was exposed. Hildie said to my father, enunciating her words as if my father would have had difficulty hearing otherwise, "Isn't she a brave girl, to drive alone to see you, so many miles! *I* would love her best, too." My father must have been staring at me in wonderment for he was silent; he didn't try to speak again. His breathing had become more labored; you listened with anxious fascination waiting for such breathing to cease. It was a terrible sound to live with intimately and yet I thought *This is the sound of life for Hildie Pomeroy, so long as it continues.*

5

And were they lovers? Never could I ask.

I was shy in the woman's presence as in the presence of any woman intimately and mysteriously connected with my father; knowing secrets about him I would never know. And how proud Hildie was of being his nurse: she sponge-bathed him daily, gently washed what remained of his hair, shaved him, fed him pureed foods, gave him his numerous pills, checked his temperature several times a day, carried away his bodily wastes that accumulated in sacs beneath the sofa. She slept in a room close by his and was wakened every night by my father thrashing about and moaning and she came to him immediately, comforted him, consoled him. "It's his wish to die at home. And this is his home now, he knows"—Hildie uttered this statement with such pride, I felt almost a surge of envy.

Hildie had met my father in the late winter of 1964, in the Rendezvous Café on Main Street where she worked as a cashier. He'd come into the Café for a drink, with a local man whom he knew, a truck driver for a gravel company in town; my father was looking for work as a trucker. This was shortly after his release from the Utah State Facility for Men at Goshen, where he'd served eighteen months of a three-year sentence on a charge of assault in 1961. Hildie passed lightly over this fact to say, with vehemence, "The other man in the fight, where they were working up in Duchesne, *he* was the cause. *He* hit Erich first, with a shovel, and Erich only defended himself. He lost control, he said. You know how a man is. 'It's like an avalanche,' he told me. 'Once it starts you don't know how it's going to end and you can't stop it.' " Hildie spoke to me in a fierce, lowered voice as to a co-conspirator. She was tugging at the thin gold chain around her neck. "The witnesses lied, the bastards! All except one. Swore on the Bible right in court, and lied! So Erich was found guilty when all he'd done was defend himself."

Guilty! Prison! My father had been in prison. The revelation was a shock to me, years after the fact, yet somehow didn't surprise me. There was a melancholy logic to it: my father had wanted us to think he'd died. Better dead, than a criminal. He'd wanted to spare us shame; he'd guessed that, for his family, grief might be more tolerable than shame.

I wiped at my eyes. It was unfair! He hadn't given us a choice. He hadn't given me a choice.

Hildie was squinting at me suspiciously. "You knew this, didn't you? Your family?"

I told Hildie yes, we'd known. Something.

"And not one of you came to see him at Goshen? That's so?"

I told Hildie yes, that was so.

"An innocent man! Your father."

Hildie was disgusted with us, shaking her head. *She* would have visited her beloved Erich under any circumstances. That went without question.

I was staring at my hands that looked blameless. They were slender, restless hands; attractive hands, I suppose; I wore no jewelry, unlike Hildie and her glittery rings, and only a loose-fitting inexpensive Bulova watch on my left wrist. The short, evenly filed nails I'd managed finally to get clean, at the motel, before coming to see my father. It has never been my nature to defend myself against another's moral indignation; in the presence of individuals who assume moral superiority, I lapse into silence; think what you wish to think, what you need to think, is my acquiescence. For though my brothers and I hadn't known that my father was in prison in Utah, it's quite possible that we wouldn't have come to see him in any case. It's possible that, in our deepest hearts, we'd preferred to think he was dead; he'd read our hearts correctly. This was utterly possible. I could not debate Hildie Pomeroy, a stranger who would claim to know my father better than I knew him.

Hildie said, aggressively, "He's a man of pride, your father. Anybody insults him, he gets what he deserves, see?"

I told Hildie yes, this was so.

"In the fight he was hurt bad in the throat, he said. That started the cancer. He'd have these coughing fits in the prison but they never gave a damn, said it was just from smoking. Finally they paroled him. The bastards!"

I pressed my fingertips against my eyes. I had no reply, no words. We were in the Rendezvous Café, in a booth near the cashier's glass-topped counter. Hildie had had several glasses of beer and spoke loudly, others in the Café could overhear. Very likely they were listening: they were curious about me, a stranger. It was as if the more vehemently Hildie spoke, the greater the possibility my father wouldn't die.

"An innocent man, treated like shit. I told Erich he could sue. *We* could sue. There's an uncle of mine in Salt Lake City, he knows one of these 'contingency' lawyers—"

I would have liked to ask Hildie Pomeroy how she knew with such certainty that my father was "innocent"; and what exactly did "innocent" mean to her? How does a woman know what she so fiercely wishes to believe? *Truth is wish; we wish to believe; what we believe, we invent as truth. And where love intervenes, truth is lost.* I was thinking of Vernor Matheius whom I'd loved, or had imagined I'd loved, more than life itself; more, certainly, than my own life; I was thinking of the man's duplicity, dishonesty, betrayal. I knew that I could believe the very worst of anyone I loved, no matter how much I loved him; for all things are possible. I could have believed that my father was a violent man, even a murderer; it wouldn't have changed my fundamental feeling for him. But this is unnatural, isn't it? In a woman at least. A passionate "feminine" woman like Hildie Pomeroy. As a woman you're supposed to deny ugly facts, you're supposed to be faithful, loyal. Hildie, breathing deeply, incensed, didn't seem to guess how I felt, how my heart beat in revulsion for her self-righteousness; gently, she touched my wrist as if to console me. "But I'm taking care of him now. He knows he can trust me. I own that house, that's mine. It was my parents' house for fifty years and now it's *mine.*"

Hildie had invited me to the Rendezvous Café where she worked five nights of the week. The owner was an old friend of hers, and knew about my father; everyone who knew Hildie in the Café seemed sympathetic with her situation, asking after the man they called Erich; to a few of these people Hildie introduced me as Erich's daughter—"She's come to visit him, for now. She's a good girl." Hildie had apologized for not offering me supper at home; most nights, she ate at the Café; she'd gotten out of the habit of making meals for herself, only for my father. She'd been working at the Rendezvous Café as a waitress, then as cashier, for twenty-two years; she'd lived in Salt Lake City for a while after high school—"But that didn't work out."

A small painful drama in those elegiac words. *It didn't work out.*

Twenty-two years at the Rendezvous Café! Amid the single row of fake-leather booths against a wall, the dozen tables and the sticky linoleum floor and the walls of mirror panels alternating with advertisements for beer and cigarettes; a radio permanently tuned to a local station except when the TV was on, blaring news and sports and weather and advertisements. The grease-filmed front window of the Café was covered partly in aluminum foil to keep out the sun, and a dully throbbing air-conditioning unit jutted out of a rear wall; a smell of beer, cigarette smoke, fried foods prevailed. Outside, pink neon tubing RENDEZVOU CAFE. In this place, Hildie Pomeroy was at home: a hunchedback little doll-woman painted and powdered and her dyed-black hair coiled around her head and affixed with showy rhinestone barrettes; wearing, for the evening, a frilly sunflower-splotched dress that outlined her shapely bosom. How like a crayon drawing Hildie looked, executed with a flourish. Seated, her head high, she might have been a normal-sized woman; so long as you faced her, you couldn't see her poor deformed spine.

When I asked Hildie whether my father had a doctor in Crescent, she shrugged her shoulders irritably. Drinking beer, and muttering what sounded like "Bastard!" Awkwardly I said, "It's very kind of you to take care of him. It can't be easy—"

Hildie flared up as if I'd insulted her. " 'Kind'! What d'you mean, 'kind'? Erich is my *dear friend*."

"Oh, I know. I—"

"Look, before he got so bad, we were planning to *marry*." Hildie spoke with an air of incredulity, as if the thwarting of such plans was difficult to comprehend. "It happened so goddam *fast*. After the last operation he just was—was—never himself again."

Hildie drained a beer glass, and her bright damp eyes seemed to wink at me over the rim. Marry? But why not? I had no right to doubt her word.

A customer had come to the cashier's counter to pay and to buy a pack of cigarettes. Hildie quickly heaved her trim little body out of the booth, teetered on high heels to perch on a stool at the cash register. Basking in the attention of male customers, Hildie fairly quivered with pleasure. It was as if a camera were turned on her. "H'lo, Petey! How's things?" Casual banter, long-running jokes, flirtations. In the Rendez-vous Café, Hildie Pomeroy was a fixture, a "character"; over the years she'd been in love with Rod, with Garry, with Ernest, with Tuck; possibly with Pete, complaining jocularly about something, and picking his discolored front teeth with a toothpick. Hildie nodded vehemently, sympathetically. You listened, you nodded, you smiled and you laughed, it was what you did with your life, for, otherwise, what?

Before I returned to my motel that evening the manager of the Café, whose name was Rod, a burly man in his fifties with an oily pitted skin and watery eyes, shirt partly unbuttoned to show a swath of graying chest hair, that male-sexy manner that has nothing to do with a man's age or his actual interest in any woman, leaned over me in the booth, dropping his voice so that Hildie at the cash register wouldn't hear, "It's real good for you to be with Hildie right now, the poor gal's gonna be hard hit."

6

Three times I would be brought into my father's presence, and three times cautioned not to turn to look at him.

Three times I would be brought into the presence of Death, and three times I would escape.

And the white-garbed woman in attendance upon Death assuring me, plucking at my wrist with talon fingers, "The way he is now isn't *him*. It's what has happened to him. Oh God!"

She never wept in my presence except quick hot startled tears of rage. The tears of one whom life has cheated, how many times!

Strange that, during the seven days I was in Crescent, Utah, and Hildie Pomeroy and I were so much together, she never spoke my name. Even on the telephone, she hadn't called me by name. Often it was *dear,* as in the Café she called customers *dear, hon* in an airy flirty voice. Often she called me nothing at all. I'd told her my name more than once but she chose not to hear it. For I was a stranger to her, an intruder; a girl with pale worried eyes whose natural response to distress was silence, not chatter; the books I'd brought with me to read and underline, while waiting for what Hildie called the right time to see my father, were books that, when she leafed through them, made her face crinkle in playful derision. "*This* is never gonna be made into a movie, eh?" Or: "How come nobody talks in these books you read? Just *thinking?*" Hildie laughed at me, as if to make a joke of me. Or stared at me, in assessment.

I was evidence of the dying man's former life. I was his daughter, I could claim his heart. I'd been named by another woman, long ago. How could Hildie trust me?

Coming to me breathless and urgent where I was sitting on the front steps of the bungalow staring at the beautiful blank pitiless sky—"He's awake, dear! Oh, he's *good*. His eyes so clear! He wants to see you!" And I dropped the heavy book I was reading and stood, shivering with anticipation. Now Hildie looked at me greedily with her bright, brimming eyes as if I were a gift to be brought to her lover, proof of her devotion.

"Don't be afraid, dear! *C'mon*."

Hildie Pomeroy suddenly roused to action, brisk and efficient as any nurse in dazzling rayon-white and soundless crepe-soled white shoes, twining her fingers through mine just tightly enough to indicate who was boss. "Remember, dear: keep your head turned. Respect your father's wishes!" Leading me through the shadowy house and to the rear porch where the invalid lay still as Death, and as I stepped across the threshold and into his space my head was turned from what I most yearned to see, in reversal of the fated Eurydice, or Lot's wife. In her breathy girlish voice Hildie cried, "Here we are, Erich! Here she is."

This second time I was better prepared of course. For the harsh wheezing breath that threatened with each inhalation to cease, and the sweet-rancid odor as of wet, rotted leaves, and the anguished *Uh-uhhh-*

uh like water rushing over pebbles in a shallow stream. I was aware in my confusion that Hildie had sprinkled a flowery cologne around the porch to counteract the odor.

"Daddy? Good m-morning!" A voice cheerful as any TV weather girl's. My smile desperate and girlish though no one saw.

There came then a faint whimpering groan, a squeaking of springs. Hildie translated excitedly, "He says isn't it a nice day? It *is!*" Strong fingers gripping my shoulders from the back, Hildie sat me in a wicker chair a few feet from the sofa upon which my father lay, and she would remain standing behind me, one hand on my shoulder and the other gripping my father's hand. Hildie was our mediator: we could not communicate without her. Happily she chattered to us, translating. I tried to hear my father's *Uh-uhhh* as not guttural sounds but individual words; it was painful to think that speech could become so twisted and tortured, yet remain speech of a kind; at times, almost I thought I could understand what he was saying, but the meaning eluded me as in a dream that fades rapidly when you wake. I was staring at a cobwebbed corner of the porch ceiling. I was staring at the Japanese screen, and seeing nothing. That hideous sound! The guttural cry of Laocoön in the grip of the sea serpents.

I was in awe of my father's courage. I could not imagine myself so courageous, or so strong. To whom would I struggle so to speak, in such anguish!

"Dear? He says tell him about your life?"

Hildie had leaned over, to murmur seductively in my ear.

"My l-life?"

"Where you live? Back home?"

But I don't live back home. I don't have a home.

My life was transparent to me as water in a glass and of no more interest. I was impatient with my life, it was to me nothing more than a vehicle like the battered little Volkswagen rusted to no-color through whose windows I observed the West. How to speak of what's invisible? "I—I'm—" I was sitting up very straight staring now into the backyard of Hildie's house; at the weedy railroad embankment; I believed I could hear in the distance the rumbling of a train approaching; I was stricken with shyness; foundering about like a big fish tossed gasping onto the ground. "—I'm so happy to be here. I've m-missed you, Daddy. We all did. Hendrick, and Dietrich, and Fritz, and—" How strange to call this stranger *Daddy;* how perverse, to call Death *Daddy;* my very voice eager and yearning as a young child's; a child who will utter anything, in order to be loved. I didn't know if what I said was true, probably it wasn't true; for how could you miss a man who had always eluded you; yet it had the plausibility of truth. Inspired by Hildie's commandment to speak, I was able to speak; the train rushed by, a short freight train; I stared at the passing boxcars, seeing SANTA FE SAN DIEGO PHOENIX SALT LAKE CITY BOISE, names I would not have seen on freight cars passing through Strykersville. I waited until the thunderous train passed, grateful for the noise. Deafening! Yet I seemed to understand that Hildie and even my father scarcely heard it.

As, in the West, surrounded by mountains, red-rock canyons and lunar deserts, the inhabitants took their world for granted as one might take for granted any painted backdrop to a play. In a store in Crescent I'd seen a brattish boy of about ten wearing a T-shirt inscribed THE STARS ARE THERE TO SHOW US HOW FAR OUR WISHES CAN GO.

I heard my anxious chattery voice speaking of my brothers, of what I knew of their lives; what I didn't know, I invented; I said they were *happy;* I said they were *working hard;* I said they were *doing very well;* I spoke of my grandparents, who were my father's parents; what quarrels and disappointments and heartbreak between them and my father, I didn't know; I spoke of these old, deceased individuals with a tenderness

I hadn't felt for either of them in life; nor would they have wished for tenderness from me, the last-born, the girl, the *little one* who simply by being born had caused my mother's death and expelled my grieving father into the world, to his doom. I spoke not of my grandparents' bitterness in old age or of their grief at their son disappearing from their lives, a grief that was hardened in time to a dull, smoldering resignation you might interpret as Christian acceptance. (The minister of the Strykersville Lutheran church had so interpreted it.) I spoke of their *peaceful deaths* and of their burial in the church cemetery near my mother; I was conscious of Hildie's sharp nails in my shoulder, and of my father's wheezing breath; this was dangerous territory, I knew, and yet I continued, though I didn't say what I so yearned to say *Why did you leave us! We needed you.* Wiping at my eyes, for I'd begun without knowing. My father seemed to be thrashing in his bedclothes, in distress, making his choked straining sounds *Uhhhh-uh Uhhh* and instinctively I began to turn my head but Hildie stopped me, pinioning my head, scolding sharply, "No! You *don't.* You promised, you would *not.*" How quick and strong, how vigilant Hildie was. That sturdy stunted little body, deft as a girl guard intervening a basketball pass, she'd caught me, caught my head, holding me still. I smelled perfume, and felt the hissing heat of the woman's breath.

Afterward I would think that, in the presence of Death, living beneath a roof with Death, how many days, weeks, months, Hildie Pomeroy had become a little crazy. I didn't blame her, for I was becoming a little crazy myself. Certainly I didn't judge her.

In fact, I was grateful she'd stopped me from seeing whatever it was I was forbidden to see.

7

My seven days in Utah! Driving for hours out into the desert, into red-rock country. Since I could see my father for only short spells, and not every day. He couldn't bear the strain of most visits, Hildie told me. Sometimes he fell asleep while she was feeding him. While she was bathing him. No TV show could keep him conscious for more than a few minutes any longer. "It's a mercy, I suppose," Hildie said grimly, confronted with this truth she'd only now begun to acknowledge, "how a person just slows, *stops.*"

Powerful drugs dulled the pain of terminal cancer, though not totally. You had to pay a price for being awake and conscious and at some point the price just wasn't worth it. *Because Ida went before him when they were both young. All his life he's had that pull.* To keep from going crazy, unless this was another form of craziness, I drove out into the high desert south of Crescent along a narrow, radiantly glittering highway into the San Rafael Valley. Temple Mountain was the highest peak, to the west. Here there was no human habitation and except for the road, no sign of humanity. I felt such relief! Such freedom. Even in the quavering little car (I'd been warned might overheat). If I remained in Crescent, I would be forced to think of things I didn't want to think about, and which exhausted me; if I didn't think of my father, whose physical predicament seemed to me a nightmare, I thought of my mother who'd died so long ago, you would suppose I'd put that loss behind me forever. But in the open country, these thoughts faded. The vast silent distances of the West. Where individual deaths can't matter. The deaths of entire species can't matter. The only reality is Time: the natural drama of the earth is Time. In civilization, this simple fact is obscured. In the West, you can't escape it. All things are shifting, sinking, eroding. In my life, a single day (a single hour! when I'd been sick with love for Vernor Matheius) had counted for something profound. In the West, a single day was nothing. A year, a lifetime—nothing. The wink of an eye. Nor was there anything to say of the blunt terrifying beauty of the red-rock formations past which I drove, and so I would say nothing about them. My father's death could cast no shadow here. All was erased here as in an overexposure of light.

Could turn off the highway. Drive into the scrubland. If no one sees. No witnesses. Drive and drive in the glaring sunshine until the car runs out of gas. Or breaks down. What better way to make an end to grief. Hildie would have no idea, no one would know. A mercy!

Yet: if my father's dying and my own dying mattered so little, why shouldn't I at least look at the man, before it was too late? The most painful of ironies, that I'd driven so far and wasn't allowed to see my father's face. *But I will see him! I will.* Like a mutinous child I plotted how it might happen, innocently. Next time Hildie brought me out onto the porch I would sit obediently with my back to my father but suddenly I'd become faint; I'd slump forward in the wicker chair, maybe fall out of it onto the floor; Hildie would try to lift me and in the confusion I'd glance back over my shoulder at my father; or, Hildie might hurry away to get cold water to sprinkle onto my face, and while she was gone I would glance at him. *But he'll see me then, he'll know.*

No: I couldn't do such a thing. I could not turn my head as Eurydice and Lot's wife had turned their heads, with such tragic results. If my father's wish was that his daughter not look upon his disfigurement, how could I disobey?

Disfigured by the surgery Hildie had said. There was a horror in such a statement. The jarring word *disfigured.* For Hildie it was an unusual word, uttered with clinical detachment.

Another day, not long before my father's dying, I was very restless, I drove out to the Green River campground a few miles from Crescent. Here I hiked along a bizarrely striated rock terrain stained to the hue of dried blood; terrain that lifted slantwise from the earth like a humped, hunched shoulder; I followed a deep, narrow gorge; out of the shadowed depths of the gorge a chill, rank, sulphurous odor arose; what horror it would be, to slip and fall into this narrow gorge; though I tried repeatedly, I couldn't see to the bottom. There was some mystery here I felt compelled to explore though I wasn't wearing hiking boots and hadn't remembered to bring along a bottle of water. I'd been warned by Hildie's friends in the Rendezvous Café not to go into the canyons alone, but I didn't intend to stay long.

By space the universe encompasses me like an atom; by thought . . .

I couldn't remember the rest of Pascal's words.

Pascal's boast! For all of philosophy is boastfulness, at bottom. The proclamation of atoms. The stammering of thinking reeds.

And how indifferent it was to such wisdom, the world. The world entering through the eyes, and through feet, fingers, touch. This dry brilliant air. The vast sky overhead. *I will remain here in the West. Now he's called me here. It must be for a reason.* I wondered if my father had loved the West. Or had he only just fled here out of despair with his life in the East. America was atoms in the void; atoms moving in a continuous stream; touching, and ricocheting; rebounding into space. For much of his life my father had been a laborer. Working with his hands outdoors. I wanted to think such a life had been his choice. As my life, a life of the mind, was my choice. But now his poor body was wearing out, like an old piece of farming equipment. The junked tractor in my grandfather's hay barn, covered in dust.

But only fifty-six. Too young!

In the flatter, less treacherous terrain in which I was now walking, shading my eyes against the glaring sun, vegetation was sepia-colored, bleached like bone; here was sagebrush, a dusty gray-green; the predominant color of the rocky earth was a dull rust-red like the blood-veined interior of the eyelid. I'd begun to feel winded, as if I were hiking up a mountainside. My head ached and swirled but I couldn't turn back just yet: there was such silence here, and such promise; a powerful spirit had taken possession of this space, and I was both fearful and eager to enter. Faint voices called to me comfortingly, unless they were jeering. *Now he's summoned you here. Must be for a reason!* In this landscape objects had a surreal significance as in a Dalí painting. Distances and proportions were confused. I saw a shimmering blue flame on a hillside and when I drew closer, it became a broken jug. I saw a sculpture of pale twisted shapes and when I drew closer, it became the bones of a jackrabbit. I saw a white pony grazing in sagebrush near a dry creek and when I drew closer, it became something manmade like plywood or Styrofoam. I saw the boy in the T-shirt reading THE STARS ARE THERE TO SHOW US HOW FAR OUR WISHES CAN GO and when I drew closer, it was a confusion of sunlight on rock. Beneath a rock formation was a gorgeous burst of crimson, like peonies, that, when I drew closer, became something cheaply plastic. Human heads and hands that were rocks or debris, rags weirdly puffed up with sand like scarecrows. My vision narrowed as if I were wearing blinders. A pulse beat at my temple. When I saw the rags, I stood for a long time staring; I didn't dare come closer, for fear of seeing something ugly; the previous night at the Café, a man who'd come over to sit with Hildie and me had told us of discovering a corpse on his ranch years ago, the mutilated body of a young Ouray Indian girl. *There's dead folks all out there. The place to dump 'em. The ones nobody reports missing.*

In waves of heat on a bluff there emerged the profile of a female shape like Hildie Pomeroy's; hunched and tense like a bow drawn tight; a deformed human body, yet unmistakably human; when I came nearer, I saw that it was a rock formation at least twenty feet in length. Yet, in my wavering vision, it had seemed the size of a woman. I saw that rock, like sand, and water, was comprised of ripples and waves; I saw that vibratory currents were the fundamental structure of nature; as in sexual passion we're caught up in such currents that beat impersonally through us, using us; using us, and discarding us like husks. Spinoza said we yearn to persist in our being. Yet more powerfully, we yearn to persist in our species' being. Feeling again the excitement of the casual drifting eyes of the man who'd slipped into the booth the night before with Hildie and me. His name was Eli? Unless I'd heard wrong, his name was actually Leo. I'd been so tired, my eyelids heavy, not thinking clearly, and not hearing clearly, for the noise in the Café was loud, laughter and raised voices and TV sports and I'd waited hours for Hildie to announce that it was the *right time* to see my father, except it had not been the *right time* all that day, he wasn't ever fully conscious and when conscious he'd been hallucinating. In the Café, I'd drunk two glasses of beer. I'd eaten barbecued meat and french fries and washed my sticky fingers in the women's room that smelled of backed-up drains. Hildie had asked point-blank if I'd ever been in love and I said yes I had; had I been hurt, Hildie asked, watching my face closely as if to determine if I told the truth, and I said yes, with lowered eyes, yes I'd been hurt. Hildie touched my wrist with her crimson fingernails—"Well, hon, don't let it happen again. The bastards!"

And later there came Eli, or Leo. His drifting assessing eyes. A rancher, Hildie called him. He'd asked me if I would like a ride back to the Economy Motel since he was going in that direction and I thanked him and explained I had my own car. A few minutes after I'd shut and locked my door in the Economy Motel there came a knock at the door and I opened it, though leaving the chain latch on, and it was Eli, or Leo, asking could he come inside, and I told him no; no, that isn't a good idea; asking then could he see me the next night, and politely I told him no; asking when could he see me, he'd like to see me, and quickly I told him no, no I can't, I'm here in Crescent because of my father, my father is dying please understand. After a pause the voice came, embarrassed—"Sure, I understand. I'm sorry."

In Crescent, I could become pregnant. Return to the East and have my father's child. That would balance the injustice, wouldn't it.

The interior of my eyelids throbbed. I hadn't realized my eyes were closed. I was breathing through my mouth like a spent boxer. I wondered if in the sun a blood vessel might swell and burst? An aneurysm? Waves of unreality moved upon me like cartoon clouds. My forehead and the nape of my neck were clammy with sweat. *Perplexing unreality:* there was a grandiloquent German term for this sensation that Vernor Matheius had once read aloud to me out of Heidegger's cobwebby prose, we'd laughed together at the word. *Perplexing unreality!* It's all around us, Vernor said, bulging his eyes in a mimicry of paranoia, terror. Vernor had astonished his adoring professors by abandoning his Ph.D. dissertation and quitting philosophy altogether and enrolling in law school at the University of Chicago; we'd lost contact; I wouldn't hear from Vernor for twenty years; by which time he would have become a nationally prominent figure associated with the Children's Defense Fund in Washington, D.C. *Perplexing unreality!* I laughed aloud in this silent stony place, wiping moisture from my eyes. I saw my own bones bleached white in the sun, a shimmering spectacle in the distance like a work of art. I saw my hat, my broken sunglasses, my long-sleeved shirt and shorts puffed with sand. I told myself *Turn back now. Don't hurry, and don't panic. You're not lost.*

Eventually I found my way back to the striated rock terrain that looked like a humped shoulder. And there was the deep, narrow gorge which I followed back to the campground parking lot. There were two other vehicles parked near my car, both with Utah license plates. As I crossed to the Volkswagen I was panting and swaying and soaked in sweat but I hadn't panicked, and I hadn't gotten lost. Still the strange visual distortions prevailed. I seemed to be staring through a tunnel; I saw near a trash can a tall column of shining light beckoning to me as if with an outstretched hand and when I drew closer, it turned into a four-inch shard of broken mirror.

8

Two days later, Hildie Pomeroy led me into the presence of my father for the last time.

"He's been asking for you, dear. But he isn't sure you're really here. He thinks you've been a dream, I guess! It's like his mind is breaking up into *bits.*"

Hildie hadn't slept much of the night. She'd made up her sallow face hastily and there were flecks of crimson lipstick on her teeth. Her dyed hair looked like a wig, disheveled and needing to be washed. She'd been crying so much, she couldn't apply mascara; her reddened eyes were raw and lashless. The white rayon shirt and pants weren't fresh and an odor of cologne and distress rose from her antic little hunched body. She told me that my father was so weak now he drifted in and out of consciousness; he hadn't eaten for two days and didn't always know where he was, and cursed at phantom enemies. When I'd approached her house at about eight o'clock that morning I could hear her on the telephone talking shrilly; when I knocked hesitantly on the screen door she shouted at me—"Come *in!* It's time."

Hildie seized my hand; her fingers now were icy-cold, twined tightly through mine. Terrified by what rushed at us with dark beating wings but her terror had turned to bright, scattered energy. "Hurry hurry hurry *hurry*." As we stepped out onto the porch, Hildie made certain that I'd turned my head; she led me to the chair, forced me down and fairly pinioned my head in her arms. "Now, promise not to turn your head. Promise!" I murmured yes, I promised. "Good girl! Erich, your good girl is here, see her?" I swallowed hard and said, "Daddy? Good morning."The sickish odor of Death was stronger even in the fresh dry air of morning. My father's strangled *Uhhhh-uh* was weaker than usual and wholly incomprehensible. Yet Hildie quickly translated, "Oh, he's happy to see you, dear. He thought you'd gone away." Shockingly, Hildie laughed. She stood behind me leaning against me, gripping both my shoulders with her strong talon fingers. "He has his insurance papers. His will. *I* wasn't ever welcome to see them. *I'm* not in the family, I guess!" Hildie was panting, laughing quietly. She whispered in my ear, "C'mon, *talk*. Why you're here, girl. Tell your daddy of—anything. And *talk loud*." So I began to speak. I spoke of how wonderful it had been, when my father telephoned home; when the phone rang after eleven o'clock, we'd know it would be him; it was like Christmas; it was so exciting; he was working in Alaska, and in Canada, and in the Pacific Northwest; I seemed to recall how my father had spoken to me at such times—"It was so special to hear from you, Daddy. You can't know." Hildie began to relax her grip as I spoke. I'd showered quickly and carelessly that morning in my motel room and my hair was still wet, sticking to my neck; I would discover afterward that I hadn't rinsed the shampoo fully out, and snarls of soap remained; nor had I taken time to dry myself adequately, my underwear clung damp and uncomfortable to my body; I too was panting, as if I'd been running in a desperate race to get here. My father responded only vaguely to what I was saying; yet I believed he was listening; I told him about Hendrick telephoning me in Vermont; I told him of driving to Utah—"Me! Driving so far alone."

Among my circle of friends and acquaintances I was known for my independence and what they called my *not-thereness,* meaning presumably my inaccessibility, yet to hear me speak to Daddy you would have thought I was eleven years old. I heard myself describe my car with the deprecatory affection with which people commonly speak of family curiosities, eccentricities. I heard myself say how I'd come to buy the car, with the advance from a publisher for my first book of stories; though I didn't say, for I didn't yet know that this would be so, that I would dedicate this book so precious to me *to the loving memory of my parents Ida and Erich.*

It seemed to me a childish boast put to a dying man. My first car, my first book. But Hildie said quickly, like a woman plucking at hope, "Oh, a book? Like in a library? A real book not like"—possibly she meant to say *paperback*—"Mickey Spillane? Tell your father about your *book,* dear."

"My—book? It's—" A long pause. Every pulse in my head was pounding. I didn't know if I felt shame, or merely embarrassment; or a confused pride; or if something of Hildie's hope had caught at me. "—stories. Set in Strykersville. I mean—not the actual place, Daddy, I call it by another name, but—" But what did I mean? My father continued to breathe hoarsely but he didn't attempt a reply; perhaps he was too exhausted; the effort of breathing was all his failing body could manage. I said, "Daddy, I wanted to make something beautiful," and now tears were stinging my eyes, for was this true? could it be true? what was *beauty* set beside the harsher requirements of *truth?* "I wanted to make something that would last a while, I hope s-someday you can see it, Daddy—I mean—" Oh, what did I mean? Saying such things to a dying man? I halfway thought Hildie would reach over and slap me. "My writing isn't my l-life exactly, Daddy, but I—I can't—I couldn't—live without it like—dreaming? Breathing?" My words rose into queries, like balloons.

There I was sitting in my father's presence stammering words I could scarcely comprehend. I was sitting in a wicker chair with a sagging seat, my clothes damp and itchy; sitting straight as if someone were yanking at the hair at the top of my head; since the age of eighteen I'd become one whose posture is ramrod straight out of a terror of fatally slouching, slumping like a jellyfish, no spine at all; as, those terrible times, I'd glimpsed Vernor Matheius slumped at his desk, rubbing his eyes with hurtful thumbs inside the lenses of his smudged glasses; I was sitting straight and tall and staring beyond a tangle of vines and leaves like a curtain growing on Hildie's porch, staring in the direction of the railroad embankment thinking *No train will rescue us today.* Hildie had stopped translating my father's strangulated sounds even before he'd stopped making them; maybe she no longer understood what they meant, or dared pretend she understood; or maybe she'd become distraught. (Though Hildie had told me many times that no goddam doctors were going to be involved in my father's final hours, I seemed to know that Hildie had been on the phone that morning with a doctor's office, or with a medical clinic.) When I ran out of words, Hildie whispered, "Keep talking! You can't stop now." I thought *I will tell Daddy I love him; I will tell Daddy that my writing is about love, because it's about truth.* I was preparing to say these difficult words even as I had a premonition that I must not say *Daddy I love you* for at that instant my father would die.

We were hearing—what?—a ringing telephone. A phone in the house. Hildie dug her nails into my shoulders and warned me not to turn my head while she was gone. "Remember! You *promised.*"

I did not turn my head so much as a fraction of an inch after Hildie hurried to answer the phone; but I'd brought with me that morning, in a shirt pocket, the piece of mirror I'd found in the parking lot; covertly I slipped this out of the pocket and raised it slowly to eye level, in s-position that, even if my father were watching me closely, which I believed he was not, he wouldn't have been suspicious; as I continued to speak, hardly knowing what I said, and aware that my father wasn't listening any longer, I moved the mirror stealthily to the left and saw a sight that I couldn't at first interpret, my vision was blurred and blotched as if I were staring through water. *A skeletal figure propped against a filthy pillow. A bald head that looked enlarged or in some way misshapen, and a ravaged face crosshatched with deep lines and veins; the skin was both ashen and reddened, as if it had been boiled; the gaping mouth disappeared into the upper jaw and the lower jaw was hardly more than a flap of lacerated toothless gum; there were welts or burns on the right side of the face and throat, and the throat looked as if it were melting into the shoulder. The eyes! I would not have recognized my father's face except for the eyes. They were deeply recessed and shadowed, with drooping lids; they were enormous staring sightless eyes; yet, as in a dream of horror, as I stared into the little mirror close beside my face, the eyes seemed to shift to mine; the face angrily creased, like a glove being crumpled in a hand; the skeletal body shuddered, and there came a groaning, near-inaudible Uhhhh-uhh of reproach.*

A terrible faintness rose in me. My eyes rolled in my head, the sliver of mirror fell from my fingers to the porch floor and shattered into pieces.

9

He didn't see! Couldn't have seen me.

I am to blame. I am the cause of his dying.

No: he couldn't have seen. Not those eyes.

He saw, he'd never forgive.

He saw nothing and there is nothing to forgive.

He saw, and he'd forgive. A dying man forgives.

Even in the confusion of my father's dying, on my hands and knees struggling not to faint I had cunning enough to sweep the mirror-slivers into my hand, and hide them in my shirt pocket.

1 0

After my father died I was sick for some time. But I recovered.

Though Hildie Pomeroy would become my enemy, yet I exercised the first fully adult act of my adult life: arranging to ship my father's body home to Strykersville, to be buried in the Lutheran cemetery beside my mother.

Poor Hildie: she'd planned for my father to be buried in Crescent; she was desperate for my father to be buried in Crescent; I understood her wish to bring flowers to his grave for the remainder of her life; I understood her wish to powder her face dead-white and paint her lips a brooding maroon and wear frilly black clothes of mourning; I understood her wish to pass through her life in Crescent like a ghost, arousing respect, awe, sympathy, and even envy. *That's Hildie Pomeroy whose lover died. Not a day passes she doesn't weep for him.* I understood, but I couldn't acquiesce for my father had had contrary wishes.

Hildie was livid with rage and cursed me for betraying her. She and my father had been planning to marry, before Erich got sick! Everybody in Crescent knew, and could testify! God damn, it was unfair.

Hildie said bitterly, "You! Why'd I let you in my house! I knew I shouldn't call any of you! Should've told him nobody answered! You got no right to come into my Erich's life so late in his life. Erich loved *me*."

Yet there was my father's painstakingly hand-printed will, dated just a few days before his death. *If there is insurance money to cover such expenses I wish to be buried in the cemetary of the Luthren church at Strykesville NY & I ask my daugther to fulfill this. Insurance $ is hers. I do not wish to be a burden to survivers. My earthly possessions possesions I wish to divide betwen my daugther & my friend Hildegard Pomeroy with grattitude.* There would be money remaining after burial expenses: my father had a life insurance policy for $7,000; though the last several premiums hadn't been paid, the insurance company agreed to pay out $5,800, which was more than enough.

I was my father's beneficiary! The news was stunning to me.

Yes, it was unfair. Hildie was right. I told her I didn't want what I didn't deserve. I told her that after the burial expenses, I'd make sure that Hildie received the rest of the money. Hildie wept and cursed. She didn't want my goddamned charity, she said. I protested it wasn't charity—"You brought him into your house, you took care of him until the end, you loved him. And he loved you." Hildie stared at me with wild glistening eyes. Since the morning of my father's death, she no longer painted her face; no longer applied mascara to her eyelashes; she'd become a swallow-skinned middle-aged woman with girlish features and a stunted yet perversely shapely female body, and that exotic black hair. What she said now so shocked me, I felt as if I'd been slapped: " 'Loved me'! Know what?—you're shitting me. Think I'm stupid?" I shook my head no, no, I didn't think she was stupid; of course she wasn't stupid; she was a kind, generous, noble person; a courageous person; a good person; I told her that my father had loved her very much, hadn't he named her in his will? Hildie snorted in derision, "Oh, sure! That.

'Earthly possessions' when all he had was junk. The money he leaves to you. Bullshit."

Still, when I sent Hildie Pomeroy a check for $3,200 a few weeks later, Hildie cashed the check.

I sold the Volkswagen for $285. I flew back east to Buffalo. It was my first plane flight, a thrilling experience; in a delirium of exhaustion, sorrow, relief; but the relief was predominant. My father's body was shipped air freight on a separate flight. The funeral at the Lutheran church was small, attended by fewer than thirty people; most of these were relatives and neighbors whom I hadn't seen since leaving Strykersville, and who seemed scarcely to recognize me. *Ida's girl? That's her?* Of my brothers, only Fritz took the time to come. For the joint grave I would replace my mother's marker with a small but, I thought, beautiful granite marker engraved with both my parents' names, birth- and death-dates. I would not be joining them in that rocky soil, but my family was now complete.

If things work out between us, someday I'll take you there.